One

Nina Kaye is a contemporary romance author who writes warm, witty and uplifting reads with a deeper edge. She lives in Edinburgh with her husband and much adored side-kick, James. In addition to writing, Nina enjoys swimming, gin and karaoke (preferably all enjoyed together in a sunny, seaside destination). Nina has previously published *The Gin Lover's Guide to Dating* and has also been a contender for the RNA Joan Hessayson Award.

Also by Nina Kaye

Take A Moment
One Night in Edinburgh

NINA KAYE

One Night in Edinburgh

CANELO

First published in the United Kingdom in 2022 by

Canelo
Unit 9, 5th Floor
Cargo Works, 1–2 Hatfields
London, SE1 9PG
United Kingdom

A CIP catalogue record for this book is available from the British Library.

Print ISBN 978 1 80032 543 2
Ebook ISBN 978 1 80032 542 5

Look for more great books at www.canelo.co

Printed and bound in Great Britain by Clays Ltd, Elcograf S.p.A.

1

MIX
Paper from
responsible sources
FSC® C018072
www.fsc.org

For James

Prologue

'*I'm done.*' I bound through the door of the empty sixth year common room and leap on to Connor's lap. 'No more school exams – ever!'

He plucks out his earphones and pecks me on the lips, causing my grin to widen further.

'Congratulations. We're free… at last.' He lets out a satisfied sigh 'This is going to be a summer to remember.'

'It so is.' I casually drape my arm around his shoulders. 'Let's go out tonight. The others were talking about getting drinks in at Charlie's – his parents are out for dinner, so we'll have the place to ourselves – and then heading on to Subway. You in?'

Connor frowns as he contemplates this. 'West End or Cowgate? And are the "cool crowd" headed there?'

'West End. And no, they're heading to George Street from what I've heard.'

'Then I'm in. But only because I know you love it there.'

'Awesome. It's gonna be such a great night.' This time it's me who kisses him. 'Hey, wait a minute… you love cheesy music as much as I do, so why—'

'Steph, *shhh…*' Connor puts a finger to my lips to silence me and jerks his head in the direction of a fellow

I

schoolmate reading through some pre-exam notes. 'Don't go sharing my deepest, darkest secrets about. It's not cool to be into cheesy music if you're a guy.'

'Shit, sorry.' I lower my voice to a whisper. 'Didn't see Becca there. She's a right gossip. Don't think she's paying any attention though.'

'Here's hoping. So, that's us then. You're off to uni in four months, and I'm set to enter the world of work full time.' He puffs out his chest proudly.

'I still wish you were coming with me.' I put on a petted lip. 'Won't be the same without you.'

'You'll make friends quickly; it's not like you're moving away or anything. We can hang out when I'm not on shift, and when I'm working you can study. You'll have to do some of that at uni, you know. It's not all parties and nights out.'

'I know. But I'll miss *this*, you know?'

Connor chuckles. 'You hate this place. You've been counting down the days till we can leave.'

'Yeah, but it's the schoolyard politics I hate – the stuck-upness and the judging and the bitching. Not this. I love being able to hang with you at break and lunchtimes, and being able to walk home together, and...' I tail off awkwardly.

'And what, Stephy?' Connor fixes me with his piercing blue eyes. 'Come on. Out with it.'

I shift awkwardly in his lap, adjusting my school blazer while self-consciously twiddling a lock of my deep red box-dyed hair. 'I still don't get why you're not going to uni. Or college even. You'll get the grades – not for one of the top unis, but good enough to get a degree and a decent job at the end of it.'

'Uni isn't the be-all and end-all.' He shrugs. 'I don't fancy it; it's that simple. Never been the academic type. I'm more of a practical guy.'

'Yeah, but going full time in your weekend supermarket job is… well, it's not moving on, is it?'

'It is for me. They're going to put me through their management training programme. That's moving on, just not in the same way as you.'

'I guess.'

'And, as I'll be earning and you'll be a poor student, I'll be able to treat you.'

'Now that's a plus for sure.' I give him a cheeky wink, but then my face turns serious again. 'I'm concerned for you is all, Connor. I want you get the most from life, and… I don't want us to grow apart.'

'So that's what this is all about.' He slips me off his lap and on to the seat next to him so our eyes are level. 'Stephy, you and me are forever, you know that.'

'I know… but—'

'*Hey*… no "buts"… we made a pact. We're soulmates. There's *nothing* that can come between us.'

I drink in his floppy brown hair and the sincere expression on his face, and my heart melts like a Mr Whippy on a warm summer's day. Connor is my world. He's also the hottest guy I've ever met in my life. I can never understand why the self-styled *biatches* in my year have never given him a second look. But then I *really* wouldn't want them to, so it's actually a good thing.

'You're right.' I beam at him. 'Nothing. We're forever.'

We simultaneously lean in for a kiss, sealing our commitment to each other, and what starts as an innocent smooch quickly turns into a full-on snog.

'Get a room, weirdos,' Becca sneers at us as she flounces out of the common room, causing us to pull apart suddenly and dissolve into giggles.

'And that's why we can't wait to get out of here,' says Connor. 'Now… as we're all good, you've got to hear this. I reckon it's going to be the song of the summer.'

He flicks through the songs on his iPod, then hands me one earphone and stuffs the other in his own ear. A catchy, upbeat pop-slash-R&B track fills my ear and within seconds I'm bobbing to the rhythm on the spot.

'I can't *wait* to dance to this tonight.'

Chapter 1

Nine years later

'Steph, are you ready to go?'

'Give me five minutes, Anna.' I run the curser down the rows on the spreadsheet, stopping when I find the details of the person I'm looking for. 'I want to make one final call.'

Anna leans against the doorframe with a chuckling sigh. 'Think you're the only person I've ever met who's happy to work Hogmanay and isn't desperate to get away as early as possible.'

'The kids we look out for don't stop needing us just because it's New Year.' I shrug, picking up the receiver from my desk phone.

'Sure. But the spring fundraiser isn't till April. We've plenty of time to source the items for the auction.'

'That may be the case, but people are at their most generous this side of the holidays. Once the mammoth hangovers and the January blues kick in, that spirit dissolves faster than their Alka-Seltzer. Plus, I don't want to miss the chance to sweep up some unwanted Christmas gifts.'

'Fine. You win. Make your call.'

I give my friend and colleague a grateful thumbs up, then punch in the number and wait for a response.

'Mrs Carmichael? Season's greetings to you. It's Steph from Edinburgh Youth Kickstart.'

'Steph, how are you, my darling?' Mrs Carmichael's overenthusiastic, plummy voice sounds like it's laced with a rather expensive brandy. 'Season's greetings to you, too. Are you working today? Goodness, you are a dedicated young lady.'

'It's hardly a chore.' I smile into the receiver. 'Nothing quite like knowing that fewer youngsters will end up on the streets in the coming year.'

'Absolutely. Now, what are you after? I feel in the mood for a good deed today.'

I raise my eyebrows at Anna to punctuate my earlier point, aware that she can hear every word Mrs Carmichael is practically bellowing down the phone at me.

'I'm on the hunt for items to auction at our spring fundraiser. Preferably high-value goods that are brand new. It helps entice people to come along, and also means we can set the starting bids quite high.'

'*Right*... let me think... you are in luck, Steph. I have a couple of items I bought in the Boxing Day sales that I have changed my mind about: a television, quite top of the range, and one of those enormously heavy mixers for baking. Watched a lot of cooking shows in the run-up to Christmas, so thought I would try my hand at some bread making. But I have just discovered the most *darling* little artisan bread shop nearby and my housekeeper, Angelika, would be extremely put out if I baked my own cakes, so I don't need the mixer after all. Would save me a trip back to the store if you can take those two off my hands.'

'Those would be perfect. Thank you so much, Mrs Carmichael.'

'Of course, Steph. Anything I can do. Actually... I also received one of those vibrating things as a gift... what do you call them...?'

There's a snort of laughter from the doorway, and I hold up my hand to warn to Anna to be quiet. I know exactly what's just entered her mind.

'An electric toothbrush?' I grimace as I suggest this, sincerely hoping my lewd-minded friend is not correct.

'No... a massager thing that fits onto my armchair like an extra layer. I have *such* terrible pain in my back, so my son bought me it for Christmas. Quite state of the art he said, but I can't get the hang of it. I can package it up as new for you.'

'OK, fantastic. As long as you're sure. I wouldn't want to take something from you that might help you feel better.'

'Not at all. Think I shall stick to traditional massage. There is a wonderful masseuse five minutes away who gives me exactly the pummelling I need.'

This time Anna's face is the embodiment of a crying-with-laughter emoji, while I have to fight hard to stifle a giggle.

'That's brilliant, Mrs Carmichael. Thank you again. When's convenient for me to come and collect the items?'

'You can swing by anytime this afternoon if that suits?'

Anna waves her hands forcefully signalling for me to decline.

'Sure,' I reply. 'I'll be there in half an hour.'

I end the call with further expressions of gratitude and turn to Anna. 'What?'

'Why did you agree to go over there? That old crow just wants some company, and you fell for it. You'll be held to ransom with mince pies and shortbread, and I doubt you'll get out without having to sing Christmas carols by the piano.'

'That's fine. I don't mind giving her some company. She's a very generous donor, and she's probably spent most of Christmas on her own. Why shouldn't she get something in return?'

'You're too bloody nice, you are.' Anna shakes her head at me reprovingly. 'She's that blinking rich, she could probably keep twenty of our kids off the streets for life. And live out her days in a life of luxury. If she *really* wants to help, why doesn't she do that?'

This comment makes me smile. Anna and I have been best friends almost since the minute we started volunteering for Edinburgh Youth Kickstart on the same day several years ago – and later being lucky enough to each secure a permanent job with the charity. We're aligned in many ways, except for her tolerance levels and lack of tact, which might just be the things I love most about her. Oh, and she's a bit of a man-eater, whereas I'm still with the guy I got together with in high school.

'I know how you feel, and I get it.' I pat her on the arm as I join her in the doorway, and we leave the office together. 'But that's not how life works. Mrs Carmichael's still making a generous contribution, whether you think it's big enough or not.'

'Hmm…' Anna purses her lips in protest at my statement, but she doesn't say anything.

'Well, have a good one,' I say to her as we stand opposite each other on the pavement of Great Junction Street, our breath billowing in front of us. 'Maybe I'll bump into you at the street party.'

'Let's message and meet up if the networks don't get jammed.'

'Sure, but if I don't end up seeing you, have a great night.'

'You too. Say hi to Connor from me.'

We part, and I quickly head to my car to drive to Mrs Carmichael's house, shivering as I go. It's a lovely clear, calm day, which means perfect conditions for the fireworks later, but it's going to be damn cold, too. As I walk, I pull my phone out of my handbag and see a WhatsApp message from Connor.

Will you be back soon? Need to talk to you about something.

There are no kisses at the end of his message, which in itself doesn't bother me. He sometimes forgets. But the bluntness of the message sends a ripple of unease through me. Connor is easy-going. So much so, he's almost horizontal: a trait that has bothered my family no end since we got together in high school, but which I love about him. He's the complete opposite of my highly strung, high-performing parents. He doesn't hurry me on anything, and he *never* says we need to talk. What can he suddenly need to discuss so urgently? Either something's happened, or something's about to happen. And it doesn't sound like it's good news.

Chapter 2

Anna's pretty much spot on about my visit to Mrs Carmichael. After almost two hours, I finally manage to escape, brandishing the goodies she's donated. But not before she's force-fed me a sugar shock-inducing 'snack' of shortbread and mince pies, washed down with three cups of her most recent local purchase: 'top quality, ethically sourced and one hundred per cent arabica' coffee from El Salvador. Apart from feeling completely wired, I consider it a win; especially as I caught her poised with a bottle, ready to 'garnish' my drink with her extortionate brandy. So thankfully I'm still able to drive.

Only as I pull into my parking space in the underground garage of my apartment block in Newhaven do I remember Connor's text. I had completely forgotten to reply because I was so focused on getting to Mrs Carmichael's house. Pulling my phone from my bag, relief washes over me as I see that he hasn't followed up with any further calls or messages. It can't be that urgent then.

My focus shifts to the notifications that are showing on my screen: a bunch of new chat messages in my family's WhatsApp group. I quickly scroll through them, seeing that they're about our plans for the New Year's Day dinner together the next day. My dad is asking what kinds of drinks we'd like as he's nipping to the supermarket. These requests have been met with humorous retorts

(Jägerbombs, vodka shots…) from my brother, Mikey. Meanwhile, my sister, Kayleigh, has warbled on in about eight messages informing Mum about the dessert she's preparing, and exactly how it will need to be stored when she arrives.

I pay the exchange little attention until my eyes zone in on Connor's name, and I let out a gasp of annoyance as I read the words on the screen.

> **Mum:**
> Steph, is Connor joining us? I know you said he was a maybe, but it would be nice if he would commit either way.

> **Kayleigh:**
> Does Connor commit to anything?? LOL.

> **Dad:**
> Sweetheart, if Connor is coming, please ask him to park his car on the street, not in the driveway. We'll need to keep the drive free in case I need to pop out for any last-minute supplies.

Yeah, right. I'm sure that's why Connor is to park his car on the street. Nothing to do with the fact that it's a ten-year-old Vauxhall Astra that doesn't match the tone of the estate. Smarting with irritation at my family's unjustified jibes at Connor, I quickly tap out a response.

My mum's reply is almost immediate.

I shake my head, seething at the way Connor is treated like a second-class citizen by my family: all because they think he's not good enough for me. The only one who's even slightly accepting of him is Mikey, but that's more because he's protective of me rather than that he particularly likes Connor. The fact that Connor never went to university and works as an assistant manager in a supermarket, means that he is labelled as lazy and worthless in my family's eyes. Their measure of a person is by what they do and what they've achieved in life (in particular, how much money they make). Connor doesn't fit the mould.

It frustrates the hell out of me because none of that stuff really matters. What's important is who the person is on the inside. If they made a bit more effort to accept and welcome Connor, maybe he'd be more willing to commit to joining their social gatherings. Then they'd get to know the amazing man I've loved with all my heart almost since the first day I laid eyes on him.

I fire back another message to suggest a nice vegetarian quiche instead, then get out of the car and carefully bundle the boxes into the lift one at a time. Minutes later, I arrive in the hallway of our two-bedroom apartment, huffing and puffing.

Connor emerges from the living room to meet me.

'What's all this?'

'Hi to you, too.' I step forward to greet him with a kiss. But, unless I'm imagining it, he dodges this, picks up the box with the mixer in it instead, and carries it into the spare room.

'Just as well no one was planning to stay over here tonight,' he says. 'They wouldn't be able to find the bed.'

'It's not that bad.' I follow him into the room carrying the television and wince as I register the piles of items strewn across the bed and stacked on the floor, almost to windowsill height. 'OK, maybe it is, but it's only till my work's storage unit opens up again in a few days. Then I can shift it all along there.'

'Did you get my text?' Connor asks, and I note for the first time that he's looking a bit shifty.

'I did, yes. Sorry I didn't reply. Mrs Carmichael was trying to ply me with booze. I had to keep a hawk's eye on her. What's up?'

I return to the hallway to hang up my coat before he has a chance to answer. He follows, staying silent. Curious as to his behaviour, I turn to him to ask what's going on, and nearly trip over a suitcase and a rucksack that I hadn't noticed were there before.

'What the… what's this stuff doing here?'

Connor's face reddens.

'Oh, my goodness, Connor. Have you booked us a night away as a surprise? I wondered why you wanted it to be just you and me at the street party tonight. You were plotting this all along, weren't you?'

Connor's shiftiness reaches a whole new level.

'You're such a sweetheart. Oh, no...' I put a hand to my mouth in realisation. 'I haven't ruined your plans, have I? If I'd known I needed to be back by a certain time—'

'Steph, stop. Please.'

Taken aback by his uncharacteristically stressed tone, I do as he asks and look at him properly for the first time since I walked through the door. *Shit.* Something *is* wrong.

'Connor, what's going on? Has something happened to one of our family? Is that what the bags are for?'

'No... Steph... uh, hell... I don't know how to do this.'

'You don't know how to do what? What's going on, Connor?' I'm asking because I'm genuinely confused, but my subconscious is already starting to catch up: a slightly sick feeling gurgles in my stomach.

Connor looks more pained than I've ever seen him; than I ever could imagine he could feel. He's not one to let anything get to him.

'Steph. The luggage... it's mine. I'm... leaving.'

'You're leaving? Leaving... *me*?'

'Yes—' His face is now etched with something resembling guilt and terror – probably in fear of my response.

'But why? We're good. We've... always been good, you and me.' The sick feeling in my stomach is joined by a disorientating swirling in my head. 'Haven't we?'

'Yeah, we've always been good, Steph, but that's the thing... is "good" really enough? We don't even have anything to compare "good" to.'

'What does that even mean, Connor? I just said "good". I probably meant "great". We're great. And what's with needing a comparison all of a sudden?'

Connor takes a deep breath, a clear attempt to summon some courage, while his eyes go to the floor. 'We're not "great", Steph. Far from it. We live like a middle-aged couple who have been married for twenty years.'

'What? No, we don't.' I stare at him in disbelief, my eyes stinging in the face of what's being thrown at me. 'But we have been together a long time. We're past the jumping into bed at every opportunity stage, but we've got something solid.'

'What if I don't want "good" and "solid"?'

This statement winds me like a punch to the gut. 'What do you mean, Connor? Is it that you don't want *me* any more?'

His eyes lift and reluctantly meet mine, and I almost can't bear to face the pity that's so evidently there.

'I don't want to put it like that, Steph. It's not what you deserve, but yeah, I want something else.'

Realisation floods through me as it dawns on me exactly what's going on here. 'You've met someone else. Who is she?'

'Let's not do this, Steph. This is about you and me. Things have just run their course.'

'That's not it. You forget I know you, Connor, almost better than you know yourself. What's really going on?'

'Steph, please…' Connor's face is contorted with all the unbearable feelings that inevitably go with a charged situation like this.

'No, Connor. That's not good enough. I know you're not the world's greatest talker when it comes to the serious stuff, but it's time to suck it up and give it to me straight. I deserve that at least after all this time.'

'You're right… OK, so the thing is… shit, Steph, I'm so sorry… his name is Rob.'

'*A guy?*' I blanch as the full weight of his words washes over me.

This isn't something I could coax him back from. That might work if it was a fling with another woman, because the hot and steamy bit would only last so long. But him being gay? That's not negotiable in any way.

'I'm sorry, Steph. I can't pretend any more.'

'But… are you sure? This seems to have come out of nowhere. How long have you… known?'

Connor rubs the back of his neck, his deep discomfort at having this conversation painfully obvious. 'I've been confused for a long time. Convinced myself it was just admiration of other blokes, but when Rob joined my work, it was like I finally woke up to it all. I'm sure: one hundred per cent.'

'Wait… you've talked about Rob to me. He joined months ago. Have you—'

'I've done nothing behind your back, Steph. I have too much respect for you for that. But Rob has told me he has feelings for me as well, and I know I can't hold off with him any longer.'

A huge lump of emotion forms in my throat, tears pricking at my eyes, as I process all this. I want to be angry at him. I want to kick him in the balls for hiding this, and wasting my time – for all these years. But I can't. He's being honest about who he is, and it must have taken real courage to admit that to himself, never mind to me. Whichever way I look at it, Connor's been my best friend as well as my partner, and I can't bear that to end too.

'Connor, I don't know what to say other than I don't want this.' Big fat tears spill down my cheeks and I stand there hopelessly – all too aware that the one person who normally comforts me, is the one who's breaking my heart. 'But I know that's pointless. All that's going through my mind is… why right now? It's Hogmanay. We had a lovely night planned. You wanted it to be just you and me…'

He steps forward, his instinct to protect me as strong as mine is in wanting him to make everything OK. Then he obviously thinks better of it, and just hangs there, like my mirror image.

'I know.' He gives a long, anguished sigh. 'I wanted us to have one last amazing night out together: a memory we could hopefully look back on in years to come and laugh about. Because, Steph… I can't bear the thought of losing you from my life altogether.'

'At least we're together on that.' I laugh weakly, wiping the relentless stream of tears from my cheeks.

'No question. We're still soulmates… just not in the way we thought.'

I take a shaky breath and scrutinise Connor's face. 'So, why didn't you let us have that one last amazing memory then?'

'Because it felt wrong.' He hangs his head. 'I'd made my decision. It would have felt like I was deceiving you. And also, perhaps it's only symbolic, but I thought it best for us to see in the new year in the way that we'd live it.'

'Which means you're off to spend Hogmanay with this Rob, and I'm going to spend it alone.' I let out a disgusting, snorty sob. 'That bodes well for the year ahead, doesn't it?'

'Please don't talk like that, Steph. I know you're hurting, but I'm certain that once you've had time to think about this, you'll see that this is the right thing for both of us. I've never fitted in with your family, and we've been lukewarm in a romantic sense for so long. You deserve someone who's going to set you alight – not literally, obviously.'

'Good to know.' I give him a teary smile. 'Because I'm not sure our friendship has much future if you're secretly hoping someone's going to off me.'

Connor makes a *that's-really-not-what-I-meant* face, and a kind of manic urge to laugh overwhelms me. Unable to compose myself, a shock-induced hysteria consumes every part of my body, and I end up laughing uncontrollably until I'm doubled over in pain; a concerned-looking Connor standing over me helplessly.

'Go, Connor.' I wave him away. 'Go get your man.' A fresh wave of hysteria overcomes me as I say this.

'Are you sure? I don't think I should leave you like this.'

'Like what? I'm laughing, aren't I?'

'In a weird, freaky kind of way, yes. Maybe I should stay the night after all? I can sleep in the…' He trails off as he takes in the stockroom that was our second bedroom.

'Seriously, *go*.' I straighten up and open the door. 'We can talk again soon. I'll be fine.'

'You're positive?'

'Completely. I'll sort myself out, and then go join Anna and the others at the street party.'

I actually don't know if I'll be fine. My strange behaviour certainly doesn't suggest so, but right now I just need Connor to leave and for this unbearable interaction to end.

'OK, then.' He looks relieved to hear this as he picks up his stuff and walks through the open door. 'I'll be in touch.'

'Bye, Connor. Happy New Year to you when it comes.'

'And to you.' He smiles gingerly and somewhat sadly, then disappears down the hallway to the lift.

Closing the door behind him, I turn and lean against it, trying desperately to control the tsunami of emotions that are engulfing me. But it's all too much. Everything I've known since I was a teenager has gone up in smoke. Connor and I were meant to be for ever: that's what we promised each other. I have no idea how to be on my own; how to date; how to be with other men. The idea of it all scares the living daylights out of me.

Defeated and devastated, I slide down the back of the door till my backside hits the floor, and I lose myself in huge, heartbroken sobs.

Chapter 3

A few hours later, I take the bus into town in a state of numbness and battle my way through the lively Hogmanay crowds towards the street party entrance on Hanover Street — which is where I've arranged to meet Anna and her friends. Though the temperature has plummeted further, it's still dry and clear. I can feel the frosty nip of the air on my face, but I've got so many layers on, the rest of me is nice and toasty.

As I walk, my mind automatically turns things over: how did I never so much as suspect that Connor was gay; who's going to get the apartment; can I afford the rent by myself if he offers it to me? It's a string of questions that feel so utterly surreal. However, having sobbed my heart out and nearly thrown up in the sink, I've landed in a surprisingly calm place, which I assume is the slightly delayed numbing impact of shock. My mind, clearly unable to deal with the emotional side of things, is focusing on the facts and the practicalities instead.

'Steph, over here,' a voice calls out, and I spot Anna on the other side of the road.

'Hi.' I wave at her, then cross the road easily due to the city centre traffic having been temporarily diverted for the event. 'You're on your own?'

Anna reaches me, and instead of answering my question, pulls me into a big bear hug, which causes me to well up all over again – more from her sympathetic embrace than anything else.

'How you doing?' Her concerned eyes search mine. 'Was worried about you when you called earlier. I said to the others we'd catch up with them later. Thought we could have some time to ourselves first.'

While Anna allowing me the quiet and private opportunity to get things off my chest is a thoughtful gesture, I'm not sure it's what I need. But I don't want to seem ungrateful, and Anna's naturally going to be concerned about me, so it's best I play along.

'I'm all right, I think.' I take a tissue from my jacket pocket and dab at my damp, undoubtedly red-rimmed and still puffy eyes, trying not to smudge my eye makeup in the process. 'It has knocked me on my arse though. I wasn't expecting it at all.'

'I'll say.' Anna hugs me again and slips her arm through mine as we continue to wander towards the street party entrance. 'So, he's really gay?'

'Seems so. Didn't pick up on that at all. I feel *so* stupid.'

'You have nothing to feel stupid about, Steph. A friend of my parents was married for nearly thirty years before she announced she was leaving her husband for a woman. She'd hid it all that time, and obviously felt she had to – which was a real shame for her. But it was like a bomb going off for the husband.'

'Maybe not the best choice of language for a public event?' I suggest as we approach the entry point to the street party, which is flanked by multiple security staff and uniformed police.

'Good point...' She eyes up one of them to our left, a good-looking, stocky man talking into his earpiece. 'I find that so sexy, don't you? It's like he's from MI5 or something.'

'You watch too much crime drama.' I nudge her with a smile as we wait to have our tickets checked, then enter the festive buzz of the street party.

'Think I'm just finding any male with a pulse attractive right now. It's been a while... if you know what I mean!'

'Maybe I should have dropped off Mrs Carmichael's "vibrating thing" at your place? Could have given you a loan.'

'Ha, yeah, maybe,' she smirks. 'Anyway, sorry... back to you. Are you all right or are you putting on a brave face?'

'Honestly... I don't know.' I shake my head absently. 'I felt absolutely devastated when he left, but right now I'm just numb.'

'That's a perfectly natural reaction.'

'All I can think about is our apartment, what's going to happen next, and how I have no idea how to date or be with another guy, you know, like... sex. Apart from a teenage fumble in the woods that I'm not sure even counts, I've only ever done that with Connor.'

'Well, I can help you with that.' Anna looks at me with a wicked glint in her eye.

'Whatever you have in mind, tone it down massively.'

'How did you know I was thinking in numbers? I have twenty-seven notches on my bed post, which – by the calculation you've just given me – means you have at least another twenty-five men to sleep with.'

I laugh loudly. 'That's like the most inappropriate math problem ever. Imagine that had been on our high-school exam papers. Anyway, no thanks. The idea of adding even one notch is terrifying enough, never mind a couple of rugby teams. I don't even know how people our age "do sex" because my experience originates from the noughties.'

'You'll be fine. You just need to give it a go. Tearing-each-other's-clothes-off sex is like—'

'Please don't say, "like riding a bike".'

Anna shrugs and grins. 'No. That sounds dull. I was going to say it's like finding your favourite gin. Nothing to do with the maturity of the product. It's all about personal taste.'

'Nice metaphor. Well, the most important point is that I'm nowhere near ready for anything like that. I've got a lot of healing to do.'

'Fair enough.'

We wander along in silence, in contrast to the jubilant party atmosphere around us, and I know Anna's trying to be respectful: allowing me space to deal with things my way, in the turmoil of my own mind. After two fresh replays of Connor's exit, annotated with what I could or should have said, despite the fact it wouldn't have made a blind bit of difference, I decide that my own mind is the last place I want to spend the New Year. I also remember Connor's words about starting the year as we aim to go on.

'Anna?'

'Yes, Steph?'

'Can we not talk about Connor or my breakup any more? Maybe for the whole night?'

'Sure. If that's what works for you.'

'It is. Thanks.'

She catches my eye meaningfully. 'You know you can bring it up at any point though. Even while we're in adjoining toilet cubicles, or during the countdown to the bells… I'm here for you. Anything you need.'

'I appreciate that.' I squeeze her arm gently.

'So, if you don't want to talk about that, what do you want to do?'

I make a show of considering this. 'I want to lose myself in the midst of this magical night, get a bit drunk and party hard.'

'That's my girl.' Anna high-fives me. 'Mulled wine to start?'

'Let's do it.'

We up our pace, pushing our way through the boisterous crowd towards the Christmas market that skirts the Royal Scottish Academy and fills the whole of East Princes Street Gardens. As we cross Princess Street, I look in the direction of the West End, and the sight before me lifts my spirits: thousands of noisy, excited revellers already making the most of the biggest night of the year. This scene is perfectly framed by bright, colourful festive lights with Edinburgh Castle perched majestically on Castle Hill in the background: the understated showpiece of the evening.

On entering the Christmas market, my senses are heightened further as a waft of grilled bratwurst, crepes, mulled wine, freshly made churros and hot chocolate teases my nose and tastebuds.

'I literally want to devour everything in sight,' I say. 'With all that's gone on today, I've barely eaten a thing.'

'Better get something to line your stomach then. Keep some room for the booze though, yeah?' Anna gives me a little wink.

We take a quick tour round the wooden stalls and I eventually decide on fried potatoes topped with melted

Swiss raclette. Once I've got my food, I find a spot at a standing table while Anna gets us a couple of *kirschweins* from the authentic German *glühwein* stall. She returns soon after with two steaming mugs and a ginger snap wedged between her teeth.

'I love the free biscuits they give there.' She plonks the mugs down on the table and demolishes the ginger snap, before lifting her own drink again. 'Cheers.'

'*Prost.*' I opt for the German expression to match the experience, clonking my mug against Anna's, some of the wine slopping over the sides as I do.

'Let's do a selfie for my Insta.'

Normally I'd protest such a request, being a bit camera- and social-media-shy; however, the atmosphere seems to dull my sense of insecurity. We strike a pose and Anna completes her post; then we sip away at our hot drinks – the alcohol adding an extra comforting heat – while I enjoy my food. It's another companionable silence, which unfortunately my over-reflective mind takes as permission to switch into high-gear again.

To distract myself, I look around at the nearby stalls and watch the people enjoying their evening. As I do this, I unintentionally make eye contact with a man standing at another table, two along from ours. He's tall and athletic-looking, with kind eyes and a sort of lop-sided grin. He's wearing a cute woollen beanie hat and a puffer jacket to rival the Michelin man, which I expect is bulked up by him also wearing several layers underneath it. He holds my gaze until awkwardness overwhelms me, and I look away.

'You OK?' Anna asks.

'Yeah, why?' I try not to show that I'm flustered.

'Your face has turned bright red, and you look out of sorts. If this is too much for you, we can head back to yours and have a quiet one. It's no problem at all.'

'That's the last thing I want.' I grimace at the thought of letting my mind roam free for the rest of the evening. 'I just caught some bloke's eye by mistake when I was people watching, that's all.'

'Ooh… where?' Anna turns in the direction I'm facing.

'Don't look,' I hiss, but I'm too late.

'Ding ding, he's a bit of a hottie, isn't he? Love the beanie.'

'Stop it. He already caught me looking when I wasn't really *looking* at him. Don't want to give him a big head.'

In my discomfort, I involuntarily glance at the man to see if he's clocked Anna, and accidentally make eye contact all over again.

'*Shit*. What is wrong with me?'

'Nothing.' Anna chuckles. 'He's super cute.'

We continue eating and drinking, and sharing crap chat until unexpectedly, the man with the beanie appears at our table.

'Hi, ladies. How's your evening?'

He has a sexy west Scotland accent, which immediately has Anna fawning all over him with her ninja flirting skills.

'It's great, thanks,' she purrs, her false eyelashes flapping at the rate of a hummingbird's wings. 'Even better now you've joined us. I like your hat.'

'Want to try it on?' He grins at her, and she reaches up and plucks it from his head, revealing a tumble of brown man curls.

Anna pulls on the beanie, then gets her phone out and takes another selfie. 'What do you think?'

'Suits you,' says the man, who then turns his attention to me. 'And how about you? Good night?'

I shrug. 'Tasty food. Mulled wine. Good atmosphere. What's not to like?'

I'm caught in a strange dimension between thinking this man is super-hot and kind of wanting him to leave because I'm heartbroken and only just holding it together.

He smiles at me. 'A perfect summary. Although you missed the excellent company. Is it just the two of you?'

'For now.'

'Does that mean there are two bruiser boyfriends due any minute with bratwursts, beer and a penchant for beating up blokes who chat to their women?' he jokes.

'No...' I narrow my eyes at him, trying to work out where I'm at.

'Is that "no, there are no boyfriends", or "no, our boyfriends have evolved past that kind of caveman behaviour, you weirdo"?'

'Oh, sorry,' I laugh. 'The former is probably more accurate.'

'Probably?'

'We're both single,' Anna interjects, then makes a pained face, mouthing 'sorry' to me as I visibly recoil.

I hadn't reached the stage of facing my new relationship 'status' yet and this realisation hits me like a train. I'm single, for the first time in more than a decade.

'Right, brill.' The man, completely unaware of my inner turmoil, looks pleased by this confirmation. 'I'm Jamie.'

'Anna.' She holds out a hand for him to kiss, which he does.

'I'm Steph.' I give him a weak wave, even though he's standing about three feet away from me.

'Well, Anna and Steph, it's great to meet you. Strange that two women as beautiful as you aren't attached, but all the better for me.' He gives us a sly nod.

'Oh yeah?' says Anna. 'And what makes you think—' She comes to a halt on seeing my face, which from the way I'm feeling, must be somewhere between grey and green. 'Um… actually, Jamie, we need to head on. Sorry, mate.'

Without warning, Anna bundles me off around the corner, leaving a bewildered Jamie standing alone with our abandoned *kirschweins*. She practically strongarms me into the ladies' toilets, which are housed in a large portacabin that creaks and shakes as we enter it. Then she turns me towards her and scrutinises my face.

'You OK, hon? You looked like you were going to throw up, so I thought it best to bring you here.'

'I genuinely thought I was.' I grab the edge of the sink to steady myself. 'Although, I can't think of anything worse than spewing my load in here.' I screw up my nose as the smell of stale urine floats around my nostrils. 'And I probably will if we stay much longer.'

'Balls. Let's get you out of here then.' Anna manhandles me back out of the portacabin, causing me to trip on the steps as we exit, and then more or less drags me across to the other side of the walkway. 'That better?'

'Sort of. But I'm starting to feel a bit like a carthorse with vertigo,' I laugh weakly.

'Sorry.' Anna makes a cringey face. 'I'm worried about you, that's all.'

'I get that. When that guy started fishing to find out if we were single and you…' I trail off, unable to complete my sentence.

'I know.' She rubs my arm protectively. 'I'm sorry. I should have been more tactful. Unfortunately, on a night like this, when everyone's high on the excitement and boozed up, they're going to be more forward than they might usually be – which is unfortunate given your current predicament.'

'It wasn't your fault – or even his. He didn't know.'

'No, of course not. But if we went back to yours—'

'We're not going back to mine.' My tone is firm. 'I'd rather spend the whole night on the brink of chundering, than sit in my apartment watching all this on TV, kicking myself for not being part of it, and simultaneously mourning the loss of the boyfriend who never truly was.'

'OK, fine.' She holds up her hands in defeat. 'But maybe we should give men a wide berth for the night. How about that?'

'Works for me.' I smile at my friend, who suddenly looks thoughtful. 'What's going on in that head of yours, Anna?'

'Nothing really…' She's clearly weighing up whether to share what's on her mind. 'I was thinking… it's a shame that Connor didn't drop this bombshell a couple of weeks earlier.'

'What? So I could have a miserable Christmas as well as Hogmanay?'

'No. Definitely not! I just meant that you would've been a bit further along by now. Because that Jamie guy was *h-o-t*. And he was totally into you.'

I assume a sceptical expression. 'No, he wasn't. You were the one flirting with him.'

'Exactly. I was the one flirting, yet his attention was on you.'

'I'm not sure I got that.'

29

'No, obviously you didn't, because your chat was terrible. I am going to have to give you a lesson in flirting.'

'*Hang on*. I may not know how to be with other men, but I can flirt. I wasn't trying.'

'Sure.' Anna grins at me. 'Well, we'll not put that to the test tonight. But for the record, you shouldn't need to *try* to flirt. It should come naturally.'

'Whatever.' I stick my tongue out at her. 'Now can we go and get some more drinks, and maybe some chocolate fondue? I can still smell those toilets from here.'

Chapter 4

We get another drink in and explore the street party, tracking our way through the crowds to the top of The Mound, then back down and along the length of Princes Street until we're almost opposite the castle. It's a great way to check out all the entertainment on offer, and the mood is so buoyant and full of hope and joviality I can't help but be swept up in it. This is a huge relief, as spending the night battling my rising nausea was not a prospect I was relishing.

'Do you want to give your friends a shout, and see where they are?' I ask Anna, as we pass a group of inebriated blokes attempting to build something resembling a human pyramid. They're being talked down by a policeman who's warning them exactly how badly that's going to end.

'Nah, I'll give them a shout later,' says Anna. 'Want to be sure you're managing all right before I bring anyone else into the mix, and who knows what'll come out their mouths.'

'OK, sure.'

'Plus, I'm quite enjoying it being just you and me.'

'Me too.' I wrinkle my nose and smile at her, pleased to hear this. 'Feel like we don't catch up enough outside of work. I'll have all the time in the world for it now though.'

I ignore the unpleasant swirl in my gut that accompanies this comment.

'Suits me.' She looks at her watch. 'It's coming up for ten p.m. Shall we go and find a good place to see out the bells?'

'Sure. We could find a spot to get the best view of the fireworks… or we could go somewhere to have a bit of a dance – maybe at one of the music stages?'

'Ooh, yes, if you're not bothered about watching the fireworks, how about we go back up the hill to The Ceilidh Stage on The Mound?'

'Perfect. Let's do that. Maybe they'll play *Auld Lang Syne* after the bells. I always love that, and we'll still see some of the fireworks from there, too.'

We do a U-turn, and retrace our steps, getting in on the general banter and dodging the merry revellers attempting to proposition us as we go. Judging by how many blokes try to chat us up in a cheeky affectionate way, not a sleazy way, you'd think the whole city's drinks had been spiked with some kind of love drug.

As we approach The Ceilidh Stage, the familiar, jaunty music drifts across the evening air towards us. It's something I love about being Scottish. The sense of identity and pride that comes with our national traditions – pipe bands, men in kilts, singing *Loch Lomond* at the end of a wedding, and *Auld Lang Syne*, of course. Gets me every time.

The music grows louder the closer we get, until we're swallowed by the mass of punters cheering and dancing. Before we know it, we're caught in the middle of a make-shift Strip the Willow, being twirled round and round, back and forth along a line of clapping, foot stamping party-goers. It's such an exhilarating feeling. Anna and I laugh and hoot until we're spat out the other end of the dance line, breathless and giggling.

We fully immerse ourselves in the fun, dancing at every opportunity, while intermittently joining the queue for a bar or the ladies. Having such a great time, we almost miss the fact that it's time to recharge our glasses for the bells at midnight, but thankfully we make it to the front of the bar queue with five minutes to spare. Then, brandishing our proseccos, we make our way to a less busy spot to toast the New Year when it comes.

'*Ten… nine… eight… seven…*' The crowd excitedly chant together, counting down the final moments of the current year.

'*Three… two… one… Happy New Year!*' Anna and I celebrate together by throwing ourselves into a squeezy, jumpy hug, as the boom and crash of the fireworks erupts around us, lighting up the sky above Edinburgh Castle.

As we look up and take in the impressively choreographed sight of incredible colours and patterns, we almost miss that the very experience I was seeking is happening right now. The ceilidh band have launched into a moving rendition of *Auld Lang Syne*, and people are forming sporadic lines in front of the stage.

I take Anna's left hand as a woman around our age takes her right one, and we are pulled into a line of around ten people. I'm so lost in the moment, belting out the words, I don't think twice when someone takes my free hand, joining us with another line of singing bodies. It's only when I glance at the person beside me with a friendly smile that I do a double take. It's Jamie from the Christmas Market.

He looks back at me, grinning in recognition and I offer him a faltering smile in return; this time fully appreciating how good-looking he is – and wondering what the hell he thinks of me after our sudden departure earlier.

'Hi, again,' he calls over the music. 'I hope I didn't offend you earlier.'

'It wasn't anything you did, I promise,' I call back. 'Sorry for abandoning you like that.'

'That's OK. Not the first time a woman has dissed me, though it is possibly the first double whammy I've experienced. I'll try not to let it dent my ego.'

I chuckle by way of a reply, and we resume singing and swinging our arms rhythmically. At the point when we cross them over for the second verse, Anna glances across and clocks Jamie. She raises her eyebrows, and I confirm non-verbally that it's fine and just a coincidence. Then we lose ourselves in the moment again, laughing and singing as the song becomes significantly more upbeat and comes to its climax. There's no room for the customary running forwards and backwards at the song's conclusion. So we settle for jumping up and down on the spot, singing as loudly as we can, the fireworks adding their own off-time percussion in the background. And while all going down, I keep catching Jamie stealing glances in my direction, and find myself doing the same.

As the song comes to end, I can't help feeling a little disappointed that I'll have to release Jamie's hand. Then, on realising what I'm thinking, I find myself battling a flurry of emotions in response: a deep sadness that I'm not having this experience with Connor; guilt and a touch of shame that I'm drawn to another guy so soon after our breakup; followed by indignance – I shouldn't feel bad about that, because *Connor* was the one that left me.

'Eh... OK if I have my hand back?' Jamie asks.

I look down and realise that while I've been wrestling with my feelings, the song has ended, and I'm still clinging on to him.

'Oh, sorry.' I feel my cheeks immediately flame.

'Not at all. I only want it back so I can open my next drink.' He locks eyes with me, causing my flush to deepen; then he pulls a can of lager from his rucksack.

It suddenly dawns on me that jumping around like idiots doesn't mix particularly well with fizzy liquid, but before I can warn Jamie, he opens the can and it explodes, spraying him, myself, and a couple of other unfortunate bystanders with a hoppy shower. A small cheer goes up as others notice what's happened, making us laugh.

'Sorry about that.' He looks a bit sheepish. 'Wits aren't the same after a few.'

'It is New Year,' I console him, wiping the droplets from my coat. 'If there's any time of the year you can get away with that, it's tonight.'

He reaches forward with his lightly gloved hand to mop some foam from my hair, and as it unintentionally brushes my ear, a strange sensation runs through my body. It's a bit like a mild electric shock, but more pleasant than that, causing me to jerk in surprise. As I do, Anna's immediately on it.

'Want me to get rid?' she asks urgently in my ear.

'Actually… no.' I look at Jamie, keeping my voice low as well. 'It might be the alcohol and the party spirit talking, but why shouldn't I have some fun tonight? If Connor's already off restarting his life, then surely I'm allowed to chat to another bloke.'

'Of course, you are. You can do a bloody lot more than that too if you want!' She highlights this statement with a sly wink.

'Not sure I'm quite in that space, but the point is, I can do what I want.'

'Exactly that. Good for you, hon.' Anna gives me a waist-level high five and starts chatting away to the bloke next to her, while I return my attention to Jamie.

'Can I buy you a drink?' I ask him. 'As an apology? And because your drink's a write off?'

He grins at me. 'You've already apologised, but sure, that would be great.'

I signal to Anna where we're going and offer her a drink, but she simply waves me off, already in full-flirt mode with a couple of cute Spanish guys. Jamie and I make our way to the bar and join the queue, which is about ten-deep, and all of a sudden, I don't know what to say to him; as if the effects of the alcohol have worn off in an instant. He smiles at me, and I smile back shyly, willing him to start up a conversation.

'So, Steph, where are you from?' he eventually asks, to my relief.

'I live in the north of the city. Newhaven, right on the water, but I grew up in an area called Colinton. You?'

'I'm from South Lanarkshire originally.'

'That explains the accent then. I knew it was west coast but couldn't quite place it. And now?'

Something unreadable passes across his face. 'And now... I'm currently Edinburgh-based... at The Shore area in Leith, not far from you.'

His hesitation makes me frown. 'That doesn't sound very permanent.'

'It's complicated.'

There's an awkward silence between us, and I begin to wonder if this drink was such a good idea. He's obviously not an open book, and with my unanticipated stage fright we're not exactly hitting it off. I also realise I haven't noticed him with anyone else on either of the occasions I've bumped into him.

'Are you here alone?' I ask.

'Sort of. My mate's the accordionist in the band.' He points to the stage.

'That's fab.' I'm deeply impressed and slightly relieved by this revelation. 'The band are fantastic.'

'Sure are.' Jamie nods. 'It was a last-minute arrangement. The guy who should've been playing the accordion came down with the flu. Bet he's regretting not paying for a flu jab.'

'Totally. He's missed the chance to be on the telly.'

'Great exposure for my buddy though. He lives up north, so normally only catches gigs there. It was pure luck that he'd decided not to take a gig and come here with me this year, so he was available to step in. There aren't many accordionists available at the last minute on Hogmanay.'

'I bet. Lucky for him... not so much for you.' I feel a wave of empathy for Jamie having found himself celebrating New Year alone, as I very nearly did myself.

'Shit happens.' Jamie shrugs, non-plussed by it all. 'I'll catch up with him when he's done. By the way, Happy New Year to you.' He catches me off guard by leaning forward and kissing me on the cheek.

His close-cut beard tickles my face while his musky eau de toilette teases my nostrils, sending a rush of feeling through me that I recognise as desire; a feeling I haven't felt since Connor and I were early in our relationship, but I can still remember what it was like. As quickly as it washes over me, it's replaced by a further wave of nausea.

'You OK?' Jamie's peering at me in a perplexed manner.

'Oh… yes… sorry. I'm fine.'

'You look a bit like you did earlier at the Christmas Market. You're not about to do another bolt on me, are you?'

'No. Definitely not.' I plant what I hope is a convincing smile on my face.

'Well, that's a relief. Not sure my self-esteem can take a second blanking from the same beautiful woman.'

'You're quite the charmer, aren't you?' I give him a playful nudge, and then feel a tug that I recognise as my conscience telling me to be up front.

Scrutinising Jamie's face to try to get a proper measure of him, I decide that honesty is the way forward. I'll likely never see him again after tonight anyway, so what does it matter what I tell him?

'Can I share something with you?'

'You can tell me anything.' He touches my arm reassuringly. 'Think of me as your New Year confidante.'

'OK…' I take a deep breath to make sure I deliver this with some composure. 'Until this afternoon, I had been in a relationship since I was sixteen. I'm a lot older than that now as you can probably tell—'

'And thank goodness for that, otherwise I'd be a bad, bad man luring you to the bar with me.'

I giggle. 'Indeed you would. Anyway… my high-school sweetheart whom I thought I was going to spend the rest of my life with, broke up with me this afternoon.'

Jamie looks mildly taken aback. 'Well, he's an idiot. Is he blind?'

'No. He's… gay, as it turns out. He's left me for a bloke.'

'*Sh-i-i-t.*' He exhales heavily at this revelation, his eyes immediately filling with sympathy, which feels a little demeaning, but the Prosecco at least takes the edge off. 'That's rough, Steph. No wonder you had a whitey when I made that comment about you both being single.'

'A what?'

'A whitey. Normally used to describe an unpleasant reaction to cannabis: you go pale and throw up. It seems to fit your reaction nicely.'

'Right.' I raise a questioning eyebrow.

'I don't smoke it myself.' He shakes his head to accentuate this point. 'I used to volunteer at the youth club where I grew up. They have a programme to try and keep the teenagers away from drugs – or get them off them, as it was for some. Those kids used to talk about people "whitey-ing" all the time.'

'Seems fairly accurate. That's cool that you did that volunteer work.'

'It wasn't a big deal. I went to the same youth club when I was young. It kept me on the straight and narrow, so I wanted to give back, if you know what I mean.'

'I do.' A pulse of excitement darts through me as I realise Jamie is a kindred spirit who cares about giving and helping others too. 'My day job is at a charity that supports young adults with difficult home circumstances – people who find themselves being turfed out for whatever reason, and who are too old to get support from the system. Our aim is to help them set up on their own, and give them a chance at a future.'

'Sounds like a job with a real sense of purpose.'

'I love it. I work on the fundraising side of things these days, seeking out regular donors, setting up charity events, that kind of thing.'

We finally reach the front of the queue and make our order; then, drinks in hand, we return to the spot where we were standing before. I look around for Anna, but she's nowhere to be seen. This doesn't concern me at all. She's the adventurous type: likes making new friends, but also very protective. I know she will be back to check on me, if she hasn't already got eyes on me from afar.

'Cheers.' Jamie lifts his plastic pint glass.

'Cheers.' I tap it with my own drink.

'To new beginnings?' His kind eyes probe mine with what feels like more than an attempt to find the positive in my crappy circumstances.

'That sounds very appropriate.' My stomach gives a little flutter, as he holds my gaze for way longer than would be deemed appropriate – and I can't help wondering exactly where this night might be heading.

At one a.m., the band wraps things up and the street party comes to a close. Jamie and I haven't moved from our spot, but there's still no sign of Anna. I'm about to get my phone out to call her – knowing full well the networks will probably be jammed – when she appears out of nowhere, looking slightly dishevelled.

'Do I even *want* to know what you've been up to?' I survey her with a mock-appraising look.

'Probably not. But let me tell you, it involved a tree and a very hunky Spanish man.'

'Nice mental image, thanks for that.'

'Calm down.' She chuckles. 'It was just a snog. A very raunchy snog, I must add.'

She gives us a sneaky wink, and Jamie laughs loudly while I shake my head in despair.

'So, where to now?' she asks.

Jamie and I look at each other uncertainly. We've been getting on brilliantly since I explained my situation. The banter has been in full flow, with plenty of turbo-charged looks and super-sexy flirtations (by my standards it was high-level flirting anyway). Now, an unspoken question lies between us: do we want to take it any further? He knows I'm very recently damaged goods, so to speak, and he's got a good friend he hasn't seen all night. On the other hand, I don't know whether I'm coming or going. I'm basically fumbling around in the dark as far as my raw emotions and my experience with new blokes go.

'Um... my mate will be ready shortly,' says Jamie.

'He's the accordionist in the ceilidh band,' I supplement for Anna's benefit.

'Ooh, I've never been with an accordionist. Is he single?'

'Engaged,' says Jamie. 'Sorry to disappoint. We're heading to The Shore to meet some of his friends.'

'Perfect,' says Anna. 'We'll join you.'

I flinch at her boldness, and look to Jamie for his reaction.

'Great stuff.' He grins at the two of us. 'As long as that's OK with you, Steph? I completely understand if you'd rather call it a night.'

He puts a reassuring hand on my back to let me know it's fine whatever I decide, and that single touch is all it takes to make up my mind. All I can focus on is that hand, his lips, the question of what kind of body is under that puffer jacket... Maybe I should ease back on the drink for the rest of the night. I've gone from completely broken to full-on lust in less than twelve hours. That can't be good – or healthy. But taking that out the equation, I know two things: in terms of hotness, he's off-the-scale, and second,

I don't want this night to end yet, so we may as well join them. It's more or less on my way home in any case.

'Let's go,' I announce. 'You got transport booked?'

'My mate arranged a taxi earlier.' Jamie flashes me a sexy smile that indicates he's more than pleased with my decision and I don't know if it's just me, but the outside temperature seems to rise by several degrees in an instant.

'Jamie, mate, how was your night?' A man whom I recognise as the accordionist from the band bounds up to us, slicing right through the growing sexual tension between us.

'Neil, buddy, you were awesome up there tonight.' Jamie shares a handshake-cum-hug-cum-slap-on-the-back with his friend.

'Thanks, pal,' says Neil in his distinctive north of Scotland accent. 'I enjoyed it. They're a brilliant band.'

'Neil, this is Steph and Anna.' Jamie gestures towards us. 'Steph's been kind enough to keep me company for the last hour. They're going to come to the pub with us. I assume that's all right.'

'More the merrier.' Neil spreads his arms out in a welcoming gesture. 'Steph, Anna, lovely to meet you. Shall we get our taxi then?'

Chapter 5

Twenty minutes later, we reach the rather charming urban area that is historic Leith, a.k.a The Shore, and bundle out of the taxi and into a pub: a traditional but also quirky establishment overlooking Leith Docks. The windows are clouded with condensation from the sheer number of people packed inside it, and there's volume to match, both from the bass-driven music and the excited, chattering voices of the merry punters. I can tell immediately that it's going to be good fun.

'What can I get you?' Jamie shouts over the noise. 'It's my round, remember?'

I scan the bar for inspiration. 'I actually fancy a beer.'

'Coming right up.' He turns to head back to the bar, then stops and faces me once again. 'Can I say something?'

'Of course.'

He takes my hand and leans in towards me, so he doesn't have to shout. 'You're a great laugh... and seriously beautiful. I'm glad you decided to join us.'

A delicious shiver runs up my spine in response and all I can manage is a faint: 'Me too.'

The second he's gone, Anna pounces on me. '*Wowsers*. He's not just into you. He's *into* you.'

'Is that not the same thing?' I slink my arm around her waist.

'It's so not the same thing. Honestly, it's a shame you've only just split from Connor, because he's giving me all the feels.'

'Meaning?'

'I think he's top-quality boyfriend material.'

I put on a sceptical face. 'You have almost nothing to base that comment on.'

'My spidey-senses are tingling.' She waggles her eyebrows at me. 'That's enough.'

'That's probably more a sign that you've drunk too much.'

'Whatever, "Ms Amateur". I know shit. Hashtag just saying.'

'Now I know you've had too much to drink,' I scoff. 'You only speak like that when you're two Proseccos short of announcing your undying love for every bloke in whatever bar you're in. Anyway, whatever this is, it's only for tonight. To dull the pain and give me a much-needed confidence boost.'

'You sure?'

'Deadly.'

'Fine.' She gives a resigned shrug. 'Your call, I guess. But you may regret that decision.'

Jamie returns with two cans of beer and hands one to me, while Anna makes a beeline for Neil and his friends, probably to scope out if any of them are single.

'Thought we could take them to a table outside, so we don't have to shout to hear each other,' Jamie suggests.

'Sure. The hypothermia hasn't yet had a chance to take hold, so why not.'

'That's the spirt.' He nudges me playfully.

I take a slug of my drink as we head back outside. 'Mmm… that's lovely. Kind of light and citrusy, but with something else.'

'That'll be the lime and mango,' says Jamie. 'It's my favourite beer. Much prefer this stuff over the heavier beers these days. Artisan all the way for me – does that make me sound like an arse?'

'Only a little. It is really good, so I'll let you off.'

We make our way around the side of the building to an outdoor seating area of picnic-style tables right at the edge of the docks. Some other people have done the same, but it's still a lot quieter than inside.

There's another silence between us. This doesn't seem to faze Jamie, but I'm not quite so at ease. My beer can is suddenly of huge interest to me. I inspect it as if it's a fascinating piece of art; it's actually very nicely designed, kind of hip and funky, with abstract images of colourful flying animals. Then my eyes focus on the name of the beer.

'Serve Minus Pigs? What kind of a name is that for a beer?'

Jamie looks at the can thoughtfully. 'Would you want pigs in your beer?'

'No.'

'Then I'd say it's quite aptly named.'

'There are a lot of things I wouldn't want in my beer.' I smirk. 'Cigarette ash, the bar tender's spit, a date-rape drug…'

'True.' Jamie acknowledges this with a bob of his head. 'But also, not pigs. Right?'

'Right… I guess.' I screw up my nose in bafflement.

'You're cute when you do that.'

'When I do what?'

'Scrunch up your nose like that. It's an endearing char-acteristic that's unique to you.' His smiling eyes – which I've now registered as being an attractive moss green – lock on mine and I feel my cheeks burn.

'Stop it, you're embarrassing me.'

'Why does that embarrass you?' he asks.

'I don't know. It just does.'

'I'm going to guess it's because you're not used to someone finding you attractive.'

The weight of this comment slams down on me heavily, and I realise it must be true. All the fondness between Connor and I that I mistook for a lifelong romantic connection must have been totally platonic from his side. Perhaps he didn't properly realise that – until Rob came along. It means that I don't know what it's like to be truly desired by another man – not one I've been with anyway.

'Ah shit, I've done it again, haven't I?' Jamie's words break through my consciousness as he gets up from his seat and comes round to sit next to me. 'Steph, I'm sorry, that was thoughtless.'

I look at him blankly, my mind a jumble of unwel-come thoughts, then shake my head gently to bring myself around. 'No, it's fine. You didn't mean any harm. It was an observation, and a damn accurate one at that.'

'You're right, I didn't mean anything by it, but I could try harder not to send you into a whitey at every turn. You must feel like you're on a very long and head-wrecking rollercoaster.'

'Another scarily accurate description.' I grimace. 'But… it seems I've just reached the highest point, and I have a choice: I can scream in terror the whole way back down… or I can take in the view and enjoy the ride.'

My breath catches in my throat as I say this, and before I even realise what I'm doing, I lean in and kiss him. I feel Jamie stiffen at first, unsure whether to go with it, but then his animal instincts take over: he shifts closer to me, his hands on the small of my back, pulling me even closer into him.

'Just don't throw up in my mouth, yeah?' he murmurs.

On hearing this, I can't help myself, I burst into loud raucous laughter that, for the time being, has completely killed the moment.

After a pretty steamy make-out session – one that leaves me in no position to be judging Anna for her earlier impulsive rendezvous – Jamie and I head back inside to join the others. My head spins from the exhilaration of the experience, making me feel like I'm a teenager again. Unfortunately, all good things come to an end and after what seems like no time at all, last orders are called, we've finished our drinks, and we're back out in the cold.

'So...' Jamie stands opposite me, looking slightly bashful, the light from the main entrance of the bar giving his bearded face a warm glow. 'That was a fun night.'

'It was.' I bite my lip. 'Guess I'd better get a taxi.'

'Or I could walk you home?'

I get a fizzy, flip-floppy feeling as he says this. The idea of getting to spend a bit longer with him is super appealing.

'I'm happy to walk,' I say. 'But don't you live somewhere around here? It would be almost an hour round trip for you.'

'Only if I take the return journey.' Jamie's eyes twinkle suggestively as my stomach just about leaps out of my throat.

He's suggesting we spend the night together – what's left of it anyway. My instincts go into overdrive at this thought, competing impulses colliding like feuding stags. The thought of Jamie's muscular arms wrapped around me almost sends me into orbit, but at the same time, I'm filled with leaden terror at the idea. What if I don't live up to his expectations? I'm not experienced in the way he probably is. And did I shave my legs earlier? I can't even remember.

While I'm preoccupied with these worries, guilt begins to nag at my consciousness. Connor may have left, but it's still *our* apartment. How will he feel about me bringing someone home? It might really hurt him. Then I realise how ridiculous that sounds. Connor's probably in someone else's bed right now, so why should I feel bad about taking someone back? Other than I haven't changed the sheets.

I'll change the sheets.

'Let's walk,' I say finally. 'Then we'll see whether you're on a one-way ticket or not.'

'Nice.' Jamie looks delighted by my response. 'The pressure's on.'

'How so?'

'To prove to you in the next half hour that I'm not a womanising, bed-hopping tyrant.'

I blanch. I hadn't thought of that. With inexperience comes naivety – and I've just discovered I'm completely vulnerable on that front. I'll have to savvy myself up fast.

Before we all say our goodbyes, Anna pulls me aside.

'I got the lowdown on Jamie from his mate, Neil. Seems you could do a lot worse. Apparently, he's an entrepreneur who Neil's had pegged as a future billionaire since he met him at uni.'

I frown. 'You know I don't care about money or status, Anna.'

'I know. But still thought you might like to know.' She gives me a little wink. 'Anyway, I'm heading to the guys' hotel – we're going to make use of the twenty-four-hour residents' bar until the breakfast buffet opens. Did I overhear that Jamie's walking you home?'

'He is.'

'OK, make sure you use protection.'

'What… what do you mean?' I splutter.

'Oh, come on.' Anna bats me gently with her handbag. 'Don't tell me it hasn't crossed your mind. I can see the lust puffing out of your brain. I don't blame you; he's so hot. Just make sure it's on your terms – and use protection.'

My face is on fire. I'm unable to refute any of what she's saying, but I feel horribly awkward being given 'the talk' like this.

'Anna, do you think…?' I trail off, struggling to verbalise the question swirling in my head.

'Do I think what? What is it, hon?' She pulls me further away from the group.

I purse my lips in consternation. 'Do you think… he's using me… you know, for a one-night stand?'

She watches Jamie for a moment, as if she's sizing him up. 'No, I don't think so. He seems like a straight-up guy, and he's really into you. I think the question here is more: are you using him?'

'No. Definitely not.' I shake my head to punctuate this remark. 'I like him and I'm enjoying his company.'

'And does that mean you want a relationship with him?'

'*What?* No. I mean, I don't know. I haven't thought beyond tonight. I'm not ready for that. My relationship with Connor may be over, but it isn't even cold yet.'

'Well, there you go.' She gives the top of my arm a reassuring rub. 'Even if neither of you have intentions beyond this night, it still doesn't mean you're using each other. All you're doing is sharing a moment in life. If it comes to something later, great. If not, you'll remember him as the gorgeous stranger who got you through the New Year when your ex broke your heart.'

'You know, I like that.' I smile at her. 'Thanks, Anna. And thanks for being there for me.'

'I'm always here for you,' says Anna. 'Whenever you need me. Now go have some fun, and don't think about tomorrow.'

'You're right, I'm going to enjoy this for what it is, and not give it a second thought once it's over.'

It's nearly one p.m. on New Year's Day when we finally stir. After another couple of hours of Jamie and I 'getting to know each other' when we got back to my apartment, we had reluctantly succumbed to our exhaustion around eight a.m., wrapped in each other's arms.

When I first waken, bleary-eyed, with a mouth like sandpaper and a head like a clanging bell, it takes me a moment to orient myself – and to remember that it's not Connor lying next to me. When I do, I frantically wait for the regret to set in, but it doesn't come. This in itself is immensely puzzling. Though to be fair, it would be hard to regret lying in bed next to a man this incredible – wouldn't it? I mean, look at him.

My only real shame is that I forgot to change the bed covers. Though these ones hadn't actually seen any action since they'd been put on (or for some time before that for that matter), so perhaps that's not such a big deal. Jamie certainly didn't seem to bother.

'Morning,' he croaks at me in a voice that suggests he's a little worse for wear. 'How's the head?'

'Pounding. Yours?'

'Same.'

'Shall I make us some coffee?'

'That would be amazing.' He pulls me in for a kiss, before releasing me so I can go get our drinks.

I potter around in the kitchen, making us fresh coffee and some toast to help with our hangovers. It's a good opportunity to have another check in with myself, and I find I'm remarkably calm and content. Is it that I'm still numb about things? If so, this is one hell of an anaesthetic – it's almost as if my feelings of loss have been frozen.

Several minutes later, Jamie emerges from the bedroom, wearing only his jeans and sporting the ultimate sexy just-out-of-bed look. I get to appreciate his six pack for the first time in the sober light of day, and it's no less impressive than it was when I had my hands all over it hours before. As these thoughts whirl through my mind, I feel myself face start to blush, so I turn my back to him and prepare the toast, not wanting him to spot this.

'Here, you can start with that.' I hand him a plate of buttered toast once I'm confident I've got my faculties back under control. 'There's jam and marmalade in the fridge if you want either. Wasn't sure what you'd like.'

'Magic. You're a star.' He takes the plate to the dining table and plonks himself down on one of the seats, while watching me fuss with the cafetiere. 'Instant would have done, but I like this place. Think I'll come back.'

Even though I know he's probably joking, I feel a swell of buzzy excitement inside me. I pad across with the coffees and sit down on the seat next to him.

'How are you feeling today? About everything?' Jamie asks me.

I do another quick self-check. 'I'm... OK. Way better than I expected. I could put it down to the fact that you're here and distracting me, but I think it's more than that. I'm sad about things, of course I am, but I'm not devastated in the way I expected to be. Either I'm still in denial, or I'm—'

'Not as heartbroken as you think you are?'

'Yes.' I narrow my eyes at him curiously. 'How did you know?'

Jamie shrugs. 'I can sense it. Could it be that your relationship – given you've discovered your ex is gay – was more platonic than you realised?'

I nod slowly, mulling this over. 'I think it's possible. Obviously, I now know it was platonic from Connor's side, but I thought I was still madly in love with him. He did the dumping, I was on the receiving end, and that felt awful yesterday. But maybe that was more because it was so unexpected and deep down it had become platonic for me too, without me even realising it. Does that make any sense?'

'It does. I can imagine the physical part of your relationship might have been lacking a bit, and maybe you didn't realise because you didn't have anything to compare it to—'

'And now I do.' I grin at Jamie and plant a kiss on his lips. 'Is this really happening? Have I just wasted more than a decade on... a good friendship?'

'I wouldn't say wasted.' He reaches across and strokes my hand reassuringly. 'I'm sure there were a lot of real feelings there at some point.'

'I guess. It's so weird though, to think that this may actually be a good thing — provided we do stay friends. Connor's a massively important part of my life. All that aside though, it's like I've been sleepwalking through my love life and I've finally woken up.'

'It certainly works in my favour — if I can be selfish for a second.'

'How's that?'

'Because it means that maybe it's not too soon for you to consider dating someone else.'

I raise my eyes to the ceiling in mock contemplation. 'Well… I do have a lot of lost time to make up for.'

'Then I would be more than happy to help you with that. Starting right now…'

Jamie abandons his toast and scoops me up in one smooth movement, then carries me back to the bedroom. I'm giggling furiously as he lays me down on the bed, and does a gracious bow before diving in next to me, and kissing me tenderly. We quickly become lost in each other — so much so that we almost miss the apartment buzzer sounding.

'Who's that?' Jamie's head shoots up.

'Probably just the postie.'

'On New Year's Day?' He gives me a meaningful look.

'Crap.' I freeze, and we share a panicked look as the buzzer sounds again.

I leap out of bed and lift the handset in the hallway.

'Hello?'

'It's Connor.' His voice comes crackling through the earpiece. 'Can I come up?'

'Oh, erm… yes, of course.'

I buzz him in and slam the handset back in its cradle.

'It's Connor.' I rush back into the bedroom in a panic. 'Shit. Shit. Shit.'

'I don't suppose he'll be happy to see you've moved on already?' tries Jamie.

'I don't know. Maybe. But I don't know why he's here. What if he's come to tell me he's made a huge mistake? He'd be crushed. And even if he hasn't, he's not going to be best pleased to find someone he's never met in his bed, is he?'

'You're right. I'll go.' Jamie jumps up and pulls on his clothes at lightning speed. 'I can slip out before he reaches this floor.'

'I'm so sorry, Jamie. This was so not part of the plan.'

'The plan?' He throws me a quizzical look while pulling on his socks.

'You know what I mean.' I'm almost dancing on the spot with anxiety.

'Don't worry at all. I'll take the stairs. He'll never know I was here.'

He kisses me hard on the mouth, and slips out of the apartment, shoes and jacket in hand, while I rush to the kitchen to clear away the second mug and plate.

Chapter 6

Ten seconds later, there's a knock at the door. I open it to a miserable-looking Connor.

'Hi. Why did you buzz? Forget your key?' I gesture for him to come in and he follows me through to the kitchen.

'I didn't think it would be fair for me to swan in here after what I did to you yesterday,' he says.

I take in his forlorn expression, and all I want to do is hug him and tell him everything's going to be OK. Resisting that urge, I opt instead for some words of comfort.

'It's still your place, too, Connor.'

'Yes, but I also wondered if… you know… you might have someone here.'

I feel my face turn scarlet and have to turn away to hide my blushes for the second time today.

'Tea?' To keep my cover, I fill the kettle, and get out a couple of mugs before he even answers.

He eyes the used cafetiere. 'I'd love a coffee if it's not too much trouble?'

'Not at all. Take a seat and I'll sort that, then we can chat.'

Once I have our drinks ready, I join Connor at the dining table, while desperately trying to keep my mind off the delicious kisses I was sharing with Jamie only half an hour before – in the very same spot.

'Happy New Year to you, by the way,' I say.

'Oh, yes, sorry. Happy New Year.' He flashes me an anaemic smile.

'Connor, for someone who's freed himself of the burden of having to live a lie, you seem pretty down. Rob didn't reject you after all that, did he?'

'No.' He stares into his coffee miserably. 'It's me. I'm the one who's not dealing with things well. My head's a mess and I totally regret what I've done.'

It dawns on me that Connor may indeed be about to tell me he's made a huge mistake. The problem is, I'm not sure how I feel about that. If he's not gay, and this was just some kind of blokey infatuation, then he might want to pick things up with us again. But I don't know that I do. It may only have been a matter of hours since he up-ended our lives, but I feel like so much has happened since then. I've woken up and seen things for what they really are. His sexuality isn't the only issue. Even if he's straight, or possibly bi, it's become clear that we've been nothing more than great friends for a long time.

'Connor...' I take a moment to gather my thoughts through my hangover. 'It's understandable that you're confused. It would be odd to have a defining moment like you did yesterday and then everything fall perfectly into place. This isn't Hollywood. Real life is messy and complicated.'

'I know that, Steph.' His tone is almost resentful. 'I'm not deluded. But with Rob... it wasn't what I had been imagining at all.'

'Maybe that was your mistake, building it up like that. Maybe you had unrealistic expectations? You remember our first time together? That wasn't exactly smooth going either.'

'That was different.'

'In what way?'

'I was so nervous, I almost couldn't do it.' He chuckles weakly at the memory.

'And this time?'

'It didn't even get that far. He was... the way he... I just didn't feel *anything*.'

'Right...'

'And all I could think of was you.'

'Oh.' I take a contemplative sip of my coffee. 'So, are you saying... that you want to get back together?'

A pained look flashes across Connor's face. 'Uh... Steph, that's not what I'm saying. I meant that all I could think of was how much I'd hurt you. While I regret how I left yesterday, and treating you so badly after such a long time together, I'm *definitely* gay.'

'Oh, thank goodness for that,' I bluster, before I even realise what I've said.

Connor's face is a picture. 'You're relieved?'

'Bugger, that came out wrong.' I cringe, trying to hide behind my mug. 'Sorry, Connor. Now I'm the one making an arse of things. Yesterday when you left, I was heartbroken. Devastated, even. And then I wasn't. I thought I was numb from the shock, but I've realised overnight that things hadn't been quite right for some time.'

I intentionally leave out that it was Jamie who helped me to reach this conclusion.

'We'd become a habit, you and me,' I continue. 'A comfortable one. But not necessarily a habit that was going to make for a great life together as a couple in a romantic sense. You've done the right thing, and in the process, you've set me free as well.'

'Right.' Connor's face lightens at this, and then turns serious again. 'I couldn't bear the thought that I'd broken you, Steph. I might not be in love with you in the way that I thought, but I do love you more than anyone I know. If that makes any sense?'

'It makes perfect sense.' I put a reassuring hand on his forearm. 'I feel exactly the same.'

'So, we're good? We can stay friends?'

'Not friends, Connor. Besties.'

His face finally breaks into a genuine and relieved smile, and we share a heartfelt hug that's brimming with all the best of us as a twosome: unconditional (platonic, I now realise) love, loyalty and trust. As we half-squeeze each other to death, I'm overwhelmed by a wave of emotion, my eyes wet with tears that are a mix of happiness, relief, and a touch of melancholy – because even though I know it's the right thing, we're breaking up and things will be different between us. It's still a loss of sorts and a change that I'll need to get used to, but it's the best possible ending we could have to our romantic relationship. Had it gone any other way, it could have involved hurt, resentment and a broken bond of trust that could never be repaired.

'Thanks for being so understanding, Steph.' Connor pulls away from me and I see his eyes are red and glistening.

I shrug easily, reaching across to wipe a tear from his cheek as it spills over. 'What can I say? There's something about realising that I won't ever be able to satisfy your needs that really takes the edge off. If it had been another woman, I can't guarantee the claws wouldn't have come out – regardless of whether I realised it was the right thing or not.'

'That would have been understandable.' He takes my hand in his. 'No one wants to feel they're not good enough. Can't imagine you with claws though. You're more fluffy-baby bunny than General Woundwort from *Watership Down.*'

'True. But I like to think I can kick some backside if I need to.'

'Is that not what Anna's for?'

'Yes. She has many talents: ninja flirter, minder of vulnerable broken-hearted ladies, spin doctor...' I think back to her antics the evening before and the great outcome they produced, and grin involuntarily.

'What's that look for?' Connor eyes me suspiciously.

'What look?' I immediately neutralise my expression.

'You're basking in a nice memory. You think I can't tell? I know all your facial expressions, Steph Ashworth.'

Shi-i-i-t. He's totally busted me. I can't share this though – can I? Problem is, I'm also completely incapable of lying.

'Come on, out with it,' he prompts me.

'Connor, it's not... there's no... *argh*... I can't tell you this.'

'Because it involves a bloke and you don't want to hurt me?'

'Yes.'

'You do remember I'm gay, right?' he laughs. 'And that I abandoned you on Hogmanay for a bloke myself?'

'Yes...' I wince, still unable to bring myself to say the words.

'Look, if we're going to be "besties" as you put it, surely we can tell each other anything.'

'But it's weird,' I wail.

'It'll only be weird for a few minutes. Look, I haven't shared the extent of my disastrous liaison with Rob... I wasn't going to because it's mortifying. But if it makes

59

you more comfortable, I'm willing to take the hit. How about I share mine and then you can share yours?'

My curiosity now piqued, I'm willing to feel some pain to hear what Connor's got to share.

'OK, fine. Go.'

Connor momentarily disappears into his own memory of last night, and emerges back in the room, half-grossed out, half-laughing, but it's a mortified laugh.

'When I left here, I messaged Rob to say I was on my way,' he says. 'He sounded so pleased, and said he'd be waiting for me.'

'And?'

'And he was. He greeted me at the door wearing a gold G-string and nothing else.'

'Oh my gosh.' My hands fly to my mouth in humiliation on Connor's behalf.

'I was horrified. I tried to pretend everything was fine as he served me Champagne and assumed the role of sexy waiter for the evening. But I'm telling you, all the feelings I had for him literally extinguished the moment I clapped eyes on him in that doorway.'

'That's a complete nightmare.' I start to giggle uncontrollably – more a shock reaction than finding it funny – at the idea of poor Connor, taking his first tentative steps as a gay man, and being faced with that. 'I wouldn't have blamed you if you'd run headlong for the closet and locked yourself in for good after that experience. Sorry, I know I shouldn't laugh…'

'It's fine. Laugh away. If I don't laugh about it myself, I might end up doing exactly as you say.' Connor looks at me with wide, traumatised eyes. 'The worst thing about it was that he insisted on feeding me all these aphrodisiac foods and he assumed this sort of hungry wolf expression that he so couldn't pull off.'

'*Oh no*,' I hoot, tears now rolling down my cheeks. 'This is too much. What did you do?'

'The only thing I could think of. I told him I could feel a migraine coming on, and I made my excuses.'

'So where did you spend last night then?'

'At a crappy hotel off Leith Walk. They gave me a late check out, at least.' He shrugs pathetically, which only sets me off even more.

'Oh Connor. That's the worst.' I attempt to compose myself. 'You hear stories of people doing weird shit on dates – I know some women who've had some horrific experiences through dating apps – but I've never known anyone who's faced anything like that. I'm so sorry that happened to you.'

'Me too. I'm considering resigning from my job, because I can't bear to face him after that.'

'He's the one that should be feeling that way, not you. What was he thinking, behaving like that with someone who's only recently come out? Or anyone really?'

'I don't know.' Connor shakes his head in complete bafflement. 'Had no clue he had that side to him at all. He's so quiet at work – almost shy. That's what attracted me to him.'

'Well, maybe you could go on a dating app or something, and find some better matches. There'll be good guys out there who'll treat you with far more respect.'

'Maybe. Think for now I'll concentrate on figuring myself out; then I can decide how to approach the world of dating. Don't want to unwittingly walk into another clanger like that.'

'Wise words.' I pat his shoulder sympathetically.

Connor takes what appears to be a therapeutic glug of coffee. 'OK, so I've shared. Now you go.'

I smile at him. 'You know, this isn't nearly as weird as I thought it would be. It's just you and me, enjoying spending time together as we always do – but without the physical stuff.'

'To be fair, there hasn't been much of that for quite a while.'

'True. All right, it's basically the same, apart from the fact we're talking about our love lives – with other people.'

I clear my throat, still a little uncomfortable about sharing my own story, but now it's because my night went stupendously well compared to Connor's.

'So, I went to the street party as planned, and met up with Anna. We got talking to this cute guy at the Christmas market, which initially didn't go so well...'

I fill Connor in on the whole story, including my recurring 'whitey' moments and Jamie ending up sleeping in our bed and legging it out the door seconds before Connor arrived.

'That's brilliant.' He gives me a very genuine congratulatory high five. 'Funny the way things work out. I end our relationship to be with someone else, and you're the one who gets the big score. I kind of like that. Makes me feel a whole lot better about how I handled things.'

'Good, I'm glad.'

'When are you seeing him again then?'

'I'm... eh... oh, shit.' I blanch as the realisation hits me. 'We were in such a panic trying to avoid you seeing him that we didn't swap numbers. I've no idea how to reach him.'

Chapter 7

At around six p.m., I pull into the frost-covered driveway of my childhood home in Colinton, and open the boot of the car to get my overnight bag. Still feeling rough from the Hogmanay shenanigans, this family dinner is the last thing I want to be doing this evening, but it's a tradition of my parents'; neither my brother nor sister or I have been brave enough to rebel as yet.

Having worked some stuff out with Connor earlier, we've agreed that we'll keep living together, but he'll take the spare room, once it's emptied of the items for the auction in a few days. In the meantime, he's going to stay with his mum, and spend some time with her once he's told her his news. He was hopeful that it wouldn't be too difficult a conversation as his mum's very liberal and laidback – and in her words, Connor, her only child, is her single reason for living. We have also agreed that I'll let my family know we've split up, but that I won't disclose the reason why, not until Connor's told the most important people in his life, and he's feeling more comfortable about things.

I'm stalling for time, unnecessarily rummaging through the stuff in the boot, when the front door to the house is hauled open and my dad emerges.

'Sweetheart, what are you doing? You've been out here for more than five minutes.'

'Not that anyone's counting.' I grimace at him, as he reaches me and hauls my luggage out of my hand, insistent as always that he delivers it to my room like he's a hotel concierge. 'Happy New Year, Dad.'

'Of course. Happy New Year to you, too.' He gives me a quick kiss on the cheek. 'You're in the single room tonight.'

'No change there then. You know, I may be the youngest, but surely that doesn't mean I should always be relegated to the smallest room and given the last say on everything. What if Connor was with me? We couldn't have slept in a single bed together.'

'He's not coming then?' My dad ignores my protestation, and instead adopts an irritating tone of we-thought-as-much.

Instead of pleading Connor's case as I normally do, I keep quiet because I'm not yet ready to break the news of our expired relationship. Dad seems to notice this uncharacteristic silence, and gives me a curious look. To avoid his scrutiny, I pretend I'm interested in the evening ahead.

'What kind of roast did Mum land on in the end?' I tramp along behind him into the house, which is bursting with all the wonderful smells of a banquet-style dinner. 'I'm hoping for lamb.'

'Your mother's outdone herself this year with a duo. We're having a leg of lamb and roast duck!'

'Ooh, that sounds good. Have Kayleigh and Mikey arrived yet?'

I'm sincerely hoping so, mainly so that I can get a bit of banter going with my brother, but also so that I'm not under the microscope with my parents. I'm more lukewarm about my sister, who's a wannabe socialite, and extremely snotty and annoying. The extent of her 'banter' is boasting about how many new followers she's acquired on Instagram, and bleating on about the latest mishaps of some celebrity or another that the rest of us have never heard of. Real world-changing stuff.

'They're both here,' says my dad. 'They arrived earlier this afternoon. Kayleigh's been busy helping your mum in the kitchen.'

This is a pointed comment to highlight the fact that I've arrived later than expected; his assumption being that I'm trying to dodge helping with the dinner preparations. However, the truth is that I spent a good portion of the afternoon nursing my hangover, constantly checking my phone – despite the fact I never even gave Jamie my details – and scouring all the social media platforms I can think of to try and track him down. I even hoped he might turn up at my place again to check on things, but that was perhaps a little over-optimistic. For all Jamie knows, Connor came crawling back to beg my forgiveness, we leapt into each other's arms, and Jamie's been relegated to nothing more than blip in our perfect relationship record, never to be mentioned again.

'Good for her,' I reply to my dad. 'I'll go say hello to them then.'

I leave him at the stairs as he heads up to my room, which happens to be the bedroom I had as a child. It's been redecorated since and converted into an office, so my night will be spent on a fold-down chair bed that digs into the base of my spine in a way that no sleep-related furniture ever should. Wandering into the spacious living room, I find my brother camped out in front of the TV, peeling a huge mountain of carrots with a tub in his lap for the peelings and the finished carrots in another on the sofa to his right.

'Hey Mikey,' I greet him. 'Happy New Year. Nice little set up you've got going on there.'

'All right, wee sis?' He looks up at me with a toothy grin. 'Happy New Year. Mum wasn't too happy about this, but I told her it was either that or I puked all over the kitchen counter.'

'Nice. How did that go down?'

'Told her my hangover's so bad, my head's spinning every time I stand up. Total BS obviously, but it means I get to watch *Home Alone* instead of listening to those two cheep on about utter shite.'

'Well played.' I can't help feeling in awe of my brother's uncanny ability to get out of literally any situation that doesn't suit him.

'Score, eh? I wondered if you were going to pull a sickie. Big one last night, was it?'

'Something like that.' I flop down on the armchair opposite him. 'Is Shelley here as well?'

'Nah, she went to her own parents' place for a few days. Bit soon for bringing her in on the family traditions, don't you think?'

'Why? Because you don't want to scare her off?'

'Nope. Because I don't want to scare *me* off.'

'Mikey, you're such a loser. You're thirty-four. When are you going to grow up and stop playing Peter Pan?'

'When I meet someone who can handle me.' He gives me a theatrical wink.

'I don't even want to know what you mean by that.' I gag a little, and he chuckles, pleased to have grossed me out.

'Connor not here?'

'No.'

'Something up?'

I quickly weigh up the options of how this could go. Either I tell Mikey first and face the pain sooner than I wanted, but I might at least have an ally in him when I tell the others; or I could stretch it out till the last possible second, and drop the news just as I'm heading out tomorrow. While the latter is probably the most attractive option to avoid the inevitable twenty questions, and the let's-assassinate-Connor's-personality-and-in-the-process-take-down-Steph's-poor-life-choices routine, I decide that having Mikey on side will help me fare better in the long run.

'Steph?' Mikey prompts me. 'There's something up, isn't there?'

'Eh... yeah. Connor and I have broken up.'

'Aww, sis, I'm sorry. What happened?' He pats the couch on the opposite side from the bowl of carrots, and I cross the room to sit next to him.

'We've just grown in different directions.' *Really* different directions.

'Are you OK?' Mikey asks.

'I am actually. Think we were on course for it for a while, but I still didn't see it coming.'

'So, he ended things?'

'Yes.'

'Want me to punch his lights out?'

'Thanks, but no,' I chuckle.

Mikey looks thoughtful, and I'm sure I know what's going through his mind. He's considering whether to give me the speech I expect to hear several different versions of, as my other family members receive the news. Mikey's will undoubtedly be the most palatable.

'Say it, Mikey. I know what you're thinking, so get it over with.'

'I don't want to upset you, Steph.'

'I know you don't, but you've never rated Connor, I know that.'

'It's not that he's a bad guy. He's just... not right for my wee sister.' Mikey reaches up and ruffles my hair.

'Will anyone ever be "right for your wee sister" though?' I duck out of the way to avoid looking like an unkempt sheep.

'Yeah. The bloke who'll step up and give you the future you deserve.'

'Which is?'

'A house... keeping you financially comfortable... worshipping you... coming to the pub with me to escape from family stuff like this.'

'I don't need someone to keep me financially comfortable. I'm not money obsessed, nor am I a 1950s housewife. And Connor would have come to the pub with you if you'd ever talked to him.'

'I did talk to him.' Mikey's tone becomes defensive.

'I mean properly. Like blokey banter.'

'Listen, it's not my fault we don't have anything in common.'

'By that you mean he doesn't like football – and beer. Not all guys do, Mikey.' I give him my best schoolteacher look.

'True. And that's fair enough, but the thing is, Steph, us guys don't talk about our feelings and fluffy shit. So those things – football and beer – they're what creates a proper friendship, you know?'

I raise a scrutinising eyebrow at him. 'I've changed my mind. You're no Peter Pan, you're more caveman.'

'Think you're funny, eh?' He prods me in the ribs affectionately. 'Seriously though, I'm sorry things didn't work out, but I think it's for the best.'

'That makes two of us. Connor's still one of my closest friends though, so go easy on the jokes.'

'Noted. Do Mum and Dad know yet? And Kayleigh?'

'Not yet, so don't say a word. I'll tell them when I'm ready.'

'Scout's honour.' Mikey puts two fingers to his head to pledge this.

'Thanks, Mikey. Guess I'd better go say hi to Mum and Kayleigh.'

I leave him to his carrot peeling and wander through to the kitchen where Mum and Kayleigh are in the throes of dinner preparation. Watching them from the doorway, tattling away to each other over the noise of the food processer in loud, squawky voices, I can see why Mikey has given them a wide berth. I'm even tempted to retreat myself.

As I enter the room, my mum clocks me and switches the processor off. Kayleigh, with her back to me, doesn't anticipate this, and her voice carries like a foghorn as silence falls across the room.

'...and it's so damn typical of her to defend his rudeness— Oh, hi, Steph, you're here... We were just talking about, um, this, um, woman in my yoga class. You don't know her,' she finishes hastily.

This is, of course, a lie. She may not have mentioned any names, but Kayleigh's hesitation and concocted decoy gave her away in an instant. She was quite obviously talking about me and Connor. I don't call her out on it though because I can't be bothered with her petty nonsense, but mainly because I never win in this situation.

When it comes to taking Connor apart, my Mum, Dad and Kayleigh are always poised and ready to pounce, and I'm really not in the mood for guerrilla warfare today.

'Sounds fascinating.' I opt for an air of sarcasm instead.

'You finally decided to make an appearance then,' says my mum.

'Yes. Here I am.'

'And Connor?'

'Not here.'

'Good thing I didn't make that quiche in the end,' she huffs. 'Would have been a waste of my time.'

'Sure, whatever.' I sigh. 'Anything I can do to help?'

'It's all pretty much done. If you'd wanted to help you would have turned up earlier. Interesting how you put so much effort into helping the strays and deadbeats of this world, Steph, but you don't have time for your own family.'

I roll my eyes at her overly dramatic response. 'Those "strays and deadbeats" you talk of are decent people in genuine need of a helping hand. You have a bloody island in your kitchen—'

'That's enough, Steph.' My dad enters the kitchen and cuts me off. 'Your mother has worked all day to put a lovely meal on the table for you. You could show a little gratitude.'

'Thanks, Mum,' I mutter, and quickly leave the room before any more New Year fireworks go off.

After what turns out to be a very tasty meal with some not totally unpleasant conversation – other than Kayleigh prattling on about some VIP opening event she's managed to stalk her way into – we load the dishwasher, and I plant myself at the kitchen sink to do the remaining washing up. This has been my plan all along – to help with the clearing up; I welcome the bit of headspace it gives me from my high-maintenance family.

Elbows deep in bubbly hot water, listening to Sia, my mind runs through the experiences of the last couple of days: in particular, the issue of Jamie's sudden departure and the fact that I have no way of contacting him. All my online searches came back with nothing, which is hardly surprising, given I don't know his surname. It's especially annoying because he doesn't know what happened with Connor after he left, so he'd be unlikely to try and contact me. Or am I wrong in assuming that? I don't know enough about him to tell whether he's the type to stand back and gallantly allow a bruised relationship to mend, or go after what he wants, regardless of the circumstances. His friend did suggest that Jamie was the go-getter type. The question is, whether that's just in business, or if it extends to his love life?

As I'm pondering all this, the upbeat music pumping through my earphones unexpectedly fades, and a message alert signals in my ears. A bolt of unmerited excitement whizzes through me as my irrational mind asks: 'Is it him?'. I pull off my rubber gloves and snatch my phone from my hoodie pocket, only to be disappointed to see Anna's name illuminated on the screen. Not that I don't love hearing from my best friend. It's just that all the romantic movies I've ever watched seem to have accu-mulated in my mind, resulting in some ridiculous illusion that, after all these years of not knowing what true love really is, it came and found me on Hogmanay.

> Hey hon. How's the head today? Hope you're doing OK, and that sexy Jamie was able to distract you from your woes. Give me the goss! Xx

I chuckle at the end of her message. She'll be dying to know what happened. I decide not to keep her waiting, and send a reply. This is as much in the hope that she'll be able to help me track down Jamie, as it is to give her the juice she wants, and also to find out how her own early-morning liaison went.

> Hiya. A bit delicate today – hangover not heartbreak. Everything fine between me and Connor. He even knows about Jamie, and he was cool with it. I've realised that what we had wasn't the real thing, and I want the real thing, so he's done me a favour. Jamie was unbelievable, but no contact details for him. Any thoughts? How was your hook up? ;) xx

I've just put my rubber gloves back on and resumed listening to my music when my phone signals a response from Anna. Despite the effort it will take to get my phone back out again, I can't control the overriding impulse to read her reply straight away.

> What the actual fudge?? Need to know more. Meet for a walk on the cycle path tomorrow? 2 p.m.? Usual place? Xx

I let her know I'll see her there, stuff my phone back in my pocket, and then resume my task as my dad enters the kitchen.

'I'm going to make the coffee, Steph. Are you nearly done?'

'I will be shortly.'

I finish up clearing in the kitchen, then join the rest of my family in the lounge. Dad brings through a tray of cups and saucers, a cafetiere and a plate of homemade short-bread, and we all dig in. I've decided that now's the time to break the news. It means that I won't have to endure too many of their self-satisfied looks and insensitive comments before I head off to bed.

'Who fancies a game of Pictionary?' asks my mum.

Kayleigh and Mikey groan simultaneously.

'Actually, can it wait a minute?' I ask, as all eyes land on me. 'I've got something to tell you.'

Chapter 8

'What is it, Steph?' My mum's enquiring eyes fix on me like a drone to a target.

Feeling the full force of my family's searching looks, I recoil slightly. On the brink of losing my nerve, my mind frantically seeks some other update I can share with them that could be passed off as 'news'; when Mikey reaches over and gives my hand a little squeeze.

'You've got this.' He offers me a reassuring smile, and it's what I need to find the courage to continue.

'Connor and I have... um... we've broken up.'

There's a stunned silence, followed by an exchange of looks as if to check with each other how serious I am.

'I see,' says my mum. 'And if I may ask, how did this happen?'

'He ended things.'

'*He* ended things with *you*?' My dad looks incredulous.

'Yes.'

'What a silly little blighter.'

'He's not, Dad.' I sigh at his predictability and his tone softens.

'And how are you feeling about this?'

'I'm OK. It came out of nowhere, but the more I get used to the idea, the more I realise it was the right thing. We've...' I think back to my earlier conversation with Mikey '...grown in different directions.'

There's another exchange of looks, followed by a mood lift that seems to light up the room. They're clearly trying to be discreet, but I can see how delighted they are. I can well imagine if I weren't here, and I'd delivered the message by phone, they'd be cracking open the bubbly by now.

'Well, all things come to an end eventually.' My mum goes for an air of diplomacy, which I assume is an attempt to wrap up the conversation and move on, but Kayleigh has other ideas.

'What reason did he give?'

She's a pain in the arse my sister, but very perceptive when it comes to uncovering dirt. I waver in my response, unable to offer anything: I can't lie, but I also can't break Connor's trust on this one. I see Mikey watching me with narrowed eyes. He didn't ask me that question so now he must be wondering the same thing as Kayleigh, but has the brotherly instinct to protect his youngest sister at all costs.

'Don't think there's any need to pick over the carcass of Steph's relationship, Kayleigh. You might think that's OK because of all the crap reality TV you watch, but it's not.'

'I was only asking,' she retorts.

'Well, don't. Think our wee sis has been through enough. Give her some breathing space.'

'*Whatever*.' Kayleigh flicks her hair back in annoyance and rolls her eyes in Mum and Dad's direction.

To my surprise, both my parents say nothing more on the subject, making me think they might possess a shred of humanity after all. I excuse myself to the bathroom in the hope that when I return, they'll have moved on to Pictionary or at least another topic of conversation.

Unfortunately, that's not the case, and as I'm about to re-enter the room, I hear them talking amongst themselves in hushed tones.

'It's more than good news,' says my mum. 'It's blinking marvellous. Finally, our Steph can move on with her life.'

'Totally,' says Kayleigh. 'It's like she's been stuck in some post-high school delusion for the last ten years.'

'Don't be such a drama queen, Kayleigh,' says Mikey. 'He wasn't right for her, but it's not like her whole life has been on hold.'

'Has it not?' says my mum. 'She's settled for a job that's beneath her and she's living in Leith.'

'Newhaven, actually,' Mikey corrects her. 'And there's nothing wrong with Leith. It's an up-and-coming area that's really popular with young folk.'

'Well, anyway, it's good riddance as far as I'm concerned. That boy never made any effort to fit into this family.'

'It's certainly a positive step forward for our Steph,' agrees my dad. 'We could see if any of our friends and acquaintances could help with some suitable introductions when she's ready.'

'Good thinking, Dad,' says Kayleigh. 'Otherwise you know what she's like. Who knows what she might drag in off the street this time?'

'Yeah, and she'll be *so* pleased to know you lot are setting up her next relationship for her,' scoffs Mikey.

I feel myself start to shake with anger. How *dare* they. It's one thing to disapprove of my partner and choices in life, but to talk as if I'm some loser who needs them to fix me? That's too far. The only saving grace I've heard is Mikey looking out for me and challenging them on their ridiculous views.

I'm about to storm into the room and (attempt to) lose my shit, when I have a moment of clarity, and realise that this will only fuel their arguments that I'm incapable in every aspect of my life. I'm not going to give them that satisfaction. Nor am I going to slope off to bed as I originally planned, and let them think I'm heartbroken.

Taking a few deep, calming breaths, I push open the door to the living room and sit back in my original spot on the sofa.

'So...' I look around my family. 'Are we playing Pictionary or not?'

At two p.m. the next day, I'm standing by the light-house at Newhaven pier, gazing out across the calm water of the Forth Estuary, waiting for Anna to appear. It's another crisp afternoon, but not as cold as the previous days – perfect for a long walk and a catch up together.

I scroll absently through my phone as I wait, my mind on other things – most notably my family and how much they wind me up. After a fractured night's sleep, I managed to retain my sense of grace this morning: refusing to react to any of the usual inflammatory language and derogatory statements that are casually thrown around regarding my life. Despite the fact that Connor is no longer infringing on my family's cosy little world, they continued to put a huge amount of effort into scoring points against him. This, I can only assume to be part of a campaign to make sure that, if Connor sees what a mistake he's made, I'm under no illusion as to their feelings about him. In some ways, it was quite amusing; little do they know that the chances of Connor having a reverse revelation and announcing that he's straight after all, are about as likely as Kayleigh giving up Instagram for Lent.

Looking up from my phone, I give Anna a little wave as I spot her approaching through the car park.

'Hiya. It's a shame there are no cafes open today,' I say as she reaches me. 'I could do with a coffee to heat me up.'

'I brought a Thermos, two mini hot water bottles and a blanket.' She pulls a rucksack from her back and opens it to show me.

'Oh, you're good.'

'I know. Shall we sit by the water's edge?'

'Perfect.'

We walk along the path until we find a nice spot on the breakwater, then Anna spreads the fleecy blanket out on the stones. Sitting down on it, we pour our coffees while each cradling a hot water bottle in our laps.

'*Ahh...* this is what it's all about.' I breathe in the salty air and stare across to the blue horizon of the Fife coast. 'The day after a crappy hangover is like being born again.'

'Sure is. How did you get on at Fort Arrogance?'

This is Anna's not-so-affectionate nickname for my parents' house. While she's never been there herself, she's heard enough stories to have conjured this up in her head.

'Oh, you know, the usual character assassinations and belittling of my life choices. All the good and nurturing stuff that helps to grow my self-esteem.'

Anna lets out a theatrical grumble. 'They need a lesson in real world problems. And how are you really doing after the whirlwind of Hogmanay? You said in your message that everything's OK?' She gives me an uncertain look.

'It is, honestly. I know it sounds cheesy, but it's like it all happened so that I could finally see things for what they were. Connor and I... we're just great pals. It certainly explains why there's been such a lack of physical intimacy between us for so long. I can't remember the last time we had a proper snog, never mind any mind-blowing bedroom gymnastics. Thought that was normal for couples who had been together so long.'

'Oh yeah. And Jamie was the super-sexy eternal being brought down to Earth to help you reach this alternate conclusion?'

'Hilarious...' My expression is deadpan, then my eyes widen. 'Do you think he was?'

We both let out a snorty laugh at my ridiculous comment.

'I think he was something sacred all right, but more along the lines of sex-god than angel of enlightenment.' Anna sips at her coffee. 'Plus, you may do good stuff to help people, but I've seen your naughty side, and the jury's out on whether you'd get into heaven.'

'Thanks for that.'

'Don't want to give you any false hope. Anyway, you were saying...' She prompts me.

I tell her the whole story, filling her in on the bits and pieces she missed during our night out together, then giving her the full rundown of our late-night walk back to my apartment, and all the events that followed. Right up until Connor left the next day and went to his mum's. The only thing I hold back on are the juicy details, which are, of course, what she wants to hear most.

'*Oh, come on*, give me something here, Steph. Was he... you know...?'

'You realise that having only really been with one man before him, I'm unable to answer that question. But I can say for certain that he had a cracking six pack, and nice muscular arms. He definitely works out.'

'Fine. I'll settle for that, I suppose. I'm glad you're coping OK after what's happened, and also that you and Connor will stay close friends.'

'Me too.' I sink the last of my drink thoughtfully. 'Though I do wonder if I'd be quite as OK if Jamie hadn't popped up in my life. And I'd definitely be a huge mess if Connor had wanted a clean break. At the moment, the romantic part of our relationship ending feels a bit like coming to the end of your mobile contract: you know – you've had a good run with your old phone, but when you're offered a shiny new upgrade, you're like "yes, please".'

Anna chuckles at this straightlaced comparison. 'Makes sense. Shall we get walking to keep ourselves warm?'

We get up and pack the stuff away, then make our way along the pier to the main road and continue tracing the water's edge until we join Trinity Path just off Lower Granton Road, which was previously an old railway line. Anna tells me about the rest of her night, which turned out to be fun, but without any further romantic liaisons.

'I thought the guy you were talking to was single,' I say. 'What was his name again?'

'Nish. He was, and he was really cute, but he wasn't giving off the signals unfortunately. Didn't even waver when I switched to turbo-flirt mode.'

'*Gosh*, there aren't many men who are immune to that.'

'I think there was someone else on the scene. He had this look in his eye every time someone mentioned a woman called Denise. Apparently, she was meant to be joining them, but she never showed.'

'Aww... poor Nish.'

'That's what I thought. Though I could have offered him a decent distraction for a few hours...' Anna shrugs.

'Not everyone sees a pull in quite the transactional way you do,' I nudge her affectionately. 'Plus, he probably wouldn't have wanted Denise to hear of anything through one of the others. Probably scupper his chances altogether.'

'True.'

We walk along the path which, after a gentle upward gradient, levels off and becomes a very pleasant stroll. It's flanked by trees and vegetation: a haven of tranquillity, and a precious way of escaping the traffic and getting closer to nature in one of the most densely populated areas of Edinburgh. Whenever I walk here, it makes me feel like I've left the city altogether – that is, until I'm nearly flattened from time to time by a kamikaze cyclist who doesn't acknowledge the signage requesting them to be respectful of other path users.

'What about Jamie then?' Anna asks. 'You said you guys never swapped details.'

I chew my lip, pondering this question. 'I don't know. I'm assuming he's probably unsure what to do, with Connor having unexpectedly reappeared like that. Maybe he thinks we got back together.'

'And you're sure he wanted to take things further?'

'He certainly hinted at it. No… it wasn't even that subtle. He said that he was pleased that I was OK about my breakup, because it might mean I'd be ready to date again soon after.'

Anna grimaces. 'He may have said it, but do you think he *meant* it?'

I blink at her, confused. 'What do you mean?'

'What I mean is that men say stuff. Sometimes they mean it, and sometimes they don't. Or in the moment, they *do* mean it – or at least they *think* they do – but then once they're out of the situation, they back off.'

'But why? That makes no sense at all.'

'That's the billion-pound question, Steph.' Anna throws out her arms to exaggerate this point. 'If us women could work out what goes on in the heads of men, our love lives would be a hell of a lot easier. And they have the cheek to call women complicated!'

'You mean… he might have… played me?'

Anna bobs her head in a non-committal way. 'It's possible, but I'd say unlikely. He did seem like a genuinely good guy. Maybe he got swept up in the moment, and then, when he had to leg it from your apartment yesterday, he decided it wasn't a situation he wanted to get involved in.'

'Huh.' A slightly sick feeling washes over me as I take this all in.

'Or—' She clocks my despondency and pulls me into a sideways hug. 'Maybe he's biding his time, and he's going to find a way to contact you once you've had a bit of breathing space.'

'I like that version better.'

As I say this, I don't feel any real sense of possibility, because now that the exhilaration of my night with Jamie has worn off, I'm starting to wonder how that particular outcome could even come about.

'Ooh…' Anna's face lights up. 'Maybe he's doing a stakeout outside your apartment with binoculars and night-vision goggles and all – watching your every move to decide on the right time to re-establish contact.'

I frown at this image. 'Think you've been watching too much *Homeland* on Netflix, and now you've turned him into a stalker. Back it up a bit.'

'Was only trying to make you feel better.'

'You don't need to do that. I suppose I'm getting a taste of what everyone else has been through in the last decade in terms of their love lives, while I've been shored up in my protective Connor bubble. I watched the agonising and second-guessing from the sidelines, and I was always glad I wasn't part of it. Now, I'm the one at a severe disadvantage. You're wise to the games, and I'm the virgin dater limping along at the back with no clue what I'm doing.'

'Hey… you'll be fine.' Anna stops at the mouth of the long, cavernous old train tunnel we're about to enter, and hugs me properly. 'You've got me. I'll teach you everything I know. OK?'

'OK.'

'That wasn't a very convincing "OK".'

'No.'

'Because you like Jamie.'

I exhale heavily. 'There was something real between us. I felt it, Anna.'

She plants her hands on my shoulders and looks me straight in the eye. 'Well, here's hoping he gets in touch then, because right now, only he can make contact. But if he doesn't—'

'Let's not go there.' I pull away – unwilling to entertain whatever's about to come next – and enter the tunnel, which is as cold and empty as my heart currently feels.

'I'm just trying to help you be realistic.' Anna follows me.

'I know. But don't, not yet. Right now, I need to believe that he meant everything he said, and he's going to be in touch very soon.'

Chapter 9

One week later, I'm back at work and Anna and I are at full throttle organising the spring fundraiser. Mrs Carmichael's donations have also made their way from my spare room to the storage facility near our office.

There's been no word from Jamie, nor have I been able to find any trace of him online – despite spending an inordinate amount of time trying to track him down. This even included trying to track down Jamie's friend, Neil, but my social media and Google searches were fruitless (it turns out just typing 'Neil accordionist Scottish Highlands' doesn't produce the goods in the way I thought it might) and when I contacted the agent of the band from Hogmanay to ask for his contact details, my request was met with what I can only describe as suspicion. I found myself pleading with the woman at the end of the phone, and immediately regretted it as I received a lecture about data protection regulations being there for a reason.

It's a crushing disappointment, and I know I shouldn't take it so hard. Yet I can't shake the feeling that there was something special between Jamie and I – and that there's something holding him back from getting in touch. Anna, of course, thinks I should get over it and move on.

'You need to get on a dating app.' She prods me in the ribs as we walk along Great Junction Street towards Tesco to buy our lunch. 'I can set you up with a profile and help you figure it all out.'

'Hmm...' is all I can manage in response to that.

'Not interested, eh... What if Jamie's on one of these dating apps and you're missing the opportunity to find him?'

My mood immediately lifts. 'I never thought of that. Do you think he is?'

'I don't know, but at least it got you to join the conversation.'

'It's a possibility though, right? How many are there? I should get on them.'

'What?' Anna scoffs. '*All* the dating apps?'

'Yes.'

'It would be impossible to manage that many accounts. Why don't you start with one?'

'OK, sure.' My mind goes into overdrive at this new possibility. 'And if he's not on that one, I can close it down and set up another one.'

Anna stops me suddenly, resulting in us nearly tripping up the pedestrians behind us. She takes my hands in hers.

'Steph, I love you, but you're going to drive me bonkers with this one. Remember the "stalker image" I created of Jamie with his night-vision goggles? The one you didn't like on our New Year's Day walk?'

'Yes...?'

'Here's another one: "Crazed woman joins every dating app possible to hunt down one-night stand after he doesn't call her". How does that sound?'

'This is different,' I whine.

'How is it different?'

'He hasn't *not* called me. He doesn't have my number.'

'No. But he didn't ask for your number either, did he?' She gives me a pointed look.

I feel myself brimming with frustration. 'He was running out the door carrying his shoes. It was hardly going to be the first thing on his mind.'

'Sure, but he could have asked for it sooner if he was that interested. He also knows where you live, but he hasn't turned up at your place – as you said yourself.'

We start walking again, and carefully cross the busy road at the bottom of Leith Walk.

'I've thought about that,' I say, as we reach the other side. 'I was being totally unrealistic expecting that he might come by my place. I can't see him doing that when he doesn't know the situation with Connor. Plus, would he even have remembered which apartment I live in?'

'OK. That point, I concede,' says Anna. 'I still think you need to forget about him and move on though. If he turns up, great, but if not, you'll have had the chance to see what else is out there. Join a dating app, *please*?'

I mull this over. 'I'll agree – on one condition.'

'Name it.'

'You come out with me for drinks tomorrow night.'

'That's an easy condition to meet.' Anna looks delighted. 'Hell, yeah. I love a Friday night out.'

'Great. We're going to have a night out at The Shore.'

'The Shore? We never hang out there.'

'I know.' I do my best to keep my expression neutral. 'Wouldn't it be fun to give it a try?'

As we approach the entrance to Tesco on Duke Street, I dig in my purse for some change, and give it to the homeless man begging outside.

'Cheers, darlin',' he calls up to me. 'You're always so good to me.'

'No problem,' I smile kindly at him. 'I'll bring you a sandwich on my way out.'

'Buy him a good one and I'll pay half,' says Anna. 'Anyway, so, The Shore tomorrow night. It's a bit different, but I guess it could be fun. It was certainly a good laugh on Hogmanay... wait a second...'

I pretend to be immersed in choosing my sandwich, as Anna eyeballs me suspiciously. Her stare is so hard I can feel it on the side of my head.

'You want to go out at The Shore to try to find Jamie!' Her tone is accusatory.

'*What?* No, I don't.' I feel my face turn beetroot.

'Yes, you do. Steph, you're the worst liar in the world. So don't even try to convince me that's not what you're up to.'

I turn and face her defiantly. 'So, what if it is? He said he was living in Leith, and it's not that big a place, so what's the harm in seeing if we bump into him while we're out and about?'

Anna plucks a cheese-and-ham sandwich from the refrigerated shelf and sighs with exasperation. 'No harm in that, I guess. Provided we only do it once.'

'But... what if he goes out on Saturday instead of Friday?'

'Then your paths are not destined to cross. Steph, he could go out or not go out on any weekend or on any blinking night of the week. That strategy is doomed to failure. I'll entertain your crazy plan for one night, if you promise me you'll join a dating app and go on a minimum of three dates.'

'OK, deal.' I cross my fingers that our night out will come up trumps and I won't have to go on any dates at all – other than with gorgeous Jamie, of course.

By the time Friday night rolls in, and we're on the bus to The Shore after a bite to eat at my apartment, I'm fizzing with nervous anticipation. The idea that we might walk into one of the bars and see Jamie sitting there is so exciting, but also hugely nerve-wracking. What would I even say to him? '*Hey there, remember me?*' It's not like he'd have forgotten in such a short time. '*We forgot to swap digits.*' Maybe a bit forward to start the conversation that way. '*Do you come here often?*' Yuck. Super cheesy.

I decide I'm overthinking things. The conversation flowed between us before. There's no reason why that wouldn't happen again. The main thing is that I track him down, and then I can take things from there.

We start at the same bar we were in on Hogmanay, but there's no sign of him. I even try asking the barman if he knows Jamie, but my question is met with a curious look – especially when I'm unable to give any other details about him, such as his surname.

'The barman treated me as if I'm some kind of bunny boiler there,' I say to Anna as I plonk our G&Ts down on the table.

'You didn't ask him if he knew Jamie, did you?'

'I did. What's the harm in that?'

'I'm not even going to answer that question.' She picks up her glass, clinks it against mine, and takes a refreshing sip while shaking her head at me.

'If this were a Hollywood romance, my searching for the man of my dreams would be considered romantic.'

'Nice try. This is nothing like a Hollywood movie. I'm already on the verge of disowning you over this, and I dread to think what you'll be like once you've got a few of those down your neck.' She nods towards my drink.

'You wouldn't do that.' I stick my tongue out at her.

'Nah, probably not, unfortunately. You're lucky you're cute enough to pull this whole thing off.'

'Aww, thanks. Shame the barman didn't agree.'

'I do draw the line at spending the whole night on this though.' She gives me a pointed look. 'You're going to have to give me some decent chat as well.'

'Obviously.'

'It's not that obvious. You're wired like a ship's radar, following every movement around us in case it's him. Will you chill a bit, please?'

'Sorry.' I wince at Anna's description of me. 'What do you want to talk about?'

'How are things with your family? Has there been any improvement in their attitude now Connor's off the scene, romantically speaking?'

'Not really. I've been doing my best to avoid them. I'm concerned that this "victory" as they see it, is a reason to stay on my case. They're already dropping hints that I now have an opportunity to approach things differently.'

'They mean your job, right?'

'Yup. Job, career, general life choices. Obviously, I'm not going to give in to that sort of pressure, but it did get me thinking. I've decided to speak to Lizzie about getting out in the field again, working directly with the people we support.' Lizzie is our manager and a way better role model than any of my family. 'I miss that side of things, and I don't want to make more money, I want to make a difference – to people's lives. And when I do, my family will see how wrong they are.'

'Good for you.' Anna doesn't look overly convinced by the chances of that happening anytime soon with my family, but we clink glasses in solidarity anyway. 'On a different note, how about we sign you up to one of the dating apps?'

'What, *now*? I'm not sure if that's a good idea… what if Jamie—'

'Steph, you agreed to do it.' She throws me a condescending look. 'Come on, it'll be fun. We can have a giggle creating a profile for you: you look freaking hot tonight, so we can get some good photos of you to add to it.'

No. *Please, no.* This is the last thing I want to be doing right now.

'I don't know, Anna. Surely it's better to do it when I'm not drinking?'

'That's your first drink, and you're making excuses.' She pulls out her phone and starts snapping photos of me.

'Oh… wait, no… please. I hate getting my photo taken.'

'Ooh, hold that pout.' Anna holds the phone closer and takes more photos. 'Good one. You're quite photogenic, you know. Don't know why you have such an issue with it.'

'Anna, *stop*…' I duck out of the way, but she keeps clicking away. 'Oh, for goodness' sake… at least let me see the pics then, so I can vet them.'

'Thatta girl.' She hops off her seat and comes round to sit next to me. 'They're all pretty good… apart from those ones… that's more Hulk than sulk, and ooh… not pretty at all.'

'Delete them – *now*. I don't want them "accidentally" making their way onto your Insta.'

Anna jabs at the screen. 'They're gone. Now, let's choose which app to sign you up to and create your profile.'

She looks at a few options while I scan the bar once more.

'Maybe we should head somewhere else?' I suggest. 'There are quite a few pubs and bars in this area, and he could be in any of them.'

'Or he could be sitting at home watching the footie with a takeaway pizza.' Anna throws me a withering look.

'Humour me, please.'

'Fine. We'll do one drink in each place, but I'm not done here yet.'

I eye her glass, willing her to speed up. She's clearly on to me, because it's the longest I've ever seen her take over a drink. If I want her to play ball though, I'm going to have to sit on myself and meet her halfway, so I reluctantly engage myself in the online dating conversation.

We decide on the app I'll sign up to, and then chat through some ideas for my profile. Despite the fact that I don't even want to entertain this whole online dating thing, it's actually a bit of a laugh.

When Anna finally finishes her drink and we move on to the next bar, I'm disappointed to find no Jamie in there either.

'Damn it,' I huff, slumping down in a seat with a (not Instagrammable) pouty face.

Anna gives me a sympathetic pat on the arm and heads to the bar.

This isn't working. What I really want to do is walk into each bar to see if he's there, and if not, move on to the next one. However, it's not fair to drag Anna around like a reluctant King Charles spaniel, so I need to suck it up.

'How does this sound?' Anna returns with our drinks, looking enthused. "*I'm not a flirt, but I'll flirt with the idea of meeting someone who's up for a good time. I have an eye for candy, so don't get in touch unless you're delicious.'"*

'Sounds like a cringy contestant from *Take Me Out*.' I raise a questioning eyebrow. 'What's it for?'

'It's for your profile. It's fresh, fun and quirky.'

'Am *I* fresh, fun and quirky?'

'You're definitely fun. When you're not relentlessly obsessing over your Hogmanay one-night stand.'

'Ha, ha. Very funny.' I assume a faux resentful expression. 'I guess whatever we put on there, it needs to reflect the real me.'

Anna laughs out loud. 'You have *so* never done online dating. Everyone exaggerates or makes themselves sound more appealing. You only have to look at the doctored photos to know that. There are even people who post pictures of someone else on their profiles. That one blows my mind.'

'You're really selling this to me here.' I wrinkle my nose in distaste.

'It's fine. Promise. But I need to give you some tips on safe online dating, especially as this is all new to you. There are loads of decent guys on there. Anyway, back to your profile. What are your thoughts?'

'How about something like… *"I'm all give and little take, but I won't give a taker my time… love the water, love gin (with tonic, not water)… selfies are not part of my world, and I want to keep it that way."'*

'Love it. It says so much about who you are. Give me it again, and I'll type it in.'

I repeat what I said as best I can remember, while she taps away at her phone. Then she adds my photos, and shows me her handiwork.

'Wow, that's quite cool.' I take the phone from her and inspect my new profile. 'So, what happens next?'

'Wait for the action.' Anna's eyes twinkle mischievously. 'Seriously, if one guy showing you interest on Hogmanay helped you to deal with your breakup, this will do wonders for your confidence. With that photo, you'll be getting propositioned from all angles. Dick pics galore.'

I nearly spit out my drink. 'Are you kidding me? I don't want people sending me pictures of... *that*.'

'Par for the course, I'm afraid. Delete and block the senders, then forget about them.'

'Oh, Anna, what have you gotten me into?' I feel my head start to spin.

We finish our round and head on to the next bar, then the next and the next, all with no sign of Jamie. By midnight, I've accepted defeat. Anna was right: it was a stupid idea – less long shot and more needle in a giant field of multi-storey haystacks.

'Last round?' Anna asks tentatively as we stand at the bar waiting to be served.

'Yeah. That's enough of this nonsense.' My face is glum.

'Sorry, hon. It would have taken some luck for this to have worked out. Same again?'

'No, I'm G&T'd out. Think I'll have a beer.' My eyes seek out the beer fridge, and as I scope out the options, a flash of inspiration hits me as sharply as Voldemort's killing curse. '*That's it.*'

'What's it?' Anna looks rightfully puzzled.

'I know how to find Jamie.'

Chapter 10

'Steph, hon, I've been thinking, this plan of yours...
you've officially lost the plot.' Anna shakes her head at
me while sawing through a plump pork sausage.

I rest my cutlery on my plate with a frown. 'I have *not*.
I'm seeing things very clearly, I'll have you know.'

It's the next morning, and Anna, Connor and I are out
having Saturday brunch in a cosy little cafe overlooking
Newhaven harbour. In some ways, it's no different to
usual: the three of us have hung out a lot over the years,
with Anna occasionally bringing along her squeeze of the
moment on the rare occasions they've made it past the
six-week mark with her. However, this is a new dynamic,
where we all discuss my love life together, and it's more
than a bit weird. I have warned Anna to keep off the
subject, but it seems she can't help herself.

'Anyway,' I continue, 'you can't judge what you've
never known.'

Anna scoffs. 'And what's that?'

'A real connection with someone.'

'You think you're a better judge?' She nods her head
towards Connor.

'*Anna*. That's so out of order.' I fix her with a disapproving stare.

'No offence, Connor,' says Anna. 'But I need to make
my point.'

'None taken,' he says through a mouthful of French toast. 'I get it. Though in Steph's defence, I *was* confused and in denial for a long time.'

'Fair enough, but surely you can see that Steph's plan is totally bonkers.'

Connor considers his words carefully. 'I think it's highly creative… but unfortunately unlikely to work.'

'Hey,' I complain. 'Why are you taking her side?'

'I'm not. But I am thinking about the logistical side of things. I know my way around stock production because of my job, and I can also imagine how expensive the design side of things would be.'

'Hmmph,' I glower at him for failing to support my master plan.

Connor smiles at me affectionately. 'Stephy, in some ways it's genius. Having been made to watch many, *many* romcoms with you over the years, I can appreciate the romantic element to it, and it's an idea that definitely belongs in a movie. It's just… unrealistic.'

'Well, we won't know for sure till I check it out, will we?' I pull out my phone and google the details I'm looking for. 'I'm going to call them, right now.'

Anna facepalms, while Connor winces. Ignoring them, I get up from my seat, and step outside into the icy gust. The scenic view in front of me is tainted by a threatening dark sky and ominous-looking, choppy water. Quite a contrast to the beautiful days we had around New Year. I tap on the contact number on the web page and put the phone to my ear. A gruff male voice answers after three rings.

'Links Brewery, how can I help?'

'Oh, hi. I have… an enquiry.'

'Sure, love. What can I do for you?'

'I was wondering how much it would cost to do a "milk carton" style campaign with your company.'

There's a short silence. 'Sorry, love, I'm not sure I understand. What are you looking for?'

'A person. I'm trying to track someone down, and I'd like to do an appeal using your beer cans. You know, sort of like the milk carton appeals they used to do in America?'

'Would you not be better contacting the police?' The man sounds perplexed. 'I'm sure there's a whole department dedicated to missing persons.'

'No, no. It's not someone who's missing,' I clarify. 'It's someone I want to track down.'

'And you think putting their face on our beer cans would help you find them?'

'Yes, but I only want to do it with one specific beer: the one called Serve Minus Pigs. And it's not their photo I want to put on the cans, it's a message. I'm trying to find a guy I met at Hogmanay.'

There's another silence, then a stifled snigger comes through the receiver. 'Ahem… right… you do realise that would cost thousands, and it would be weeks before we'd have the stock out there with the new cans. Your boy will likely have found himself another woman by then.'

I feel myself flush with embarrassment as disappointment floods through me, alongside a flicker of irritation at the way this man is speaking to me.

'I see. Well, I guess I'll have to come up with some other plan then.'

'Sorry, love. Best of luck with your search.'

I try to ignore the hooting laughter and delighted shout of: 'Hey, Malky, you'll never guess what that was about—' which pierces my ear before the line goes dead. Stepping back inside, Anna and Connor look at me expectantly as I sit back down again, and resume eating my breakfast.

'Well?' Anna prods me with her elbow.

'It's not possible.'

'Because?'

'Financial and logistical issues – *apparently*.'

'It would cost thousands, Steph,' says Connor.

'That's what the guy on the phone said – before he laughed his arse off at me.'

Anna cringes, catching Connor's eye and he puts his arm around me.

'Stephy, if it's meant to be, you'll bump into Jamie again. He might even turn up on your dating app.'

'Oh, Connor, I love you, but you're normally the last person to spin me that fate bullshit.' I put down my fork. 'I've not completely lost it. I swiped through a gazillion online dating profiles last night before I went to sleep, and there was no sign of him. Nor was there anyone on there that I was remotely attracted to. Then I woke up this morning to a bunch of creepy-slash-pervy messages, so I deleted the app.'

'You know that doesn't actually delete your account,' says Anna.

'Whatever. The point is: no one's going to match up to Jamie, so I have to find him. There must be another way… something similar to the idea I had, but without the insane price tag and the… oh…wait… *I've got it.* I'm going to print out my own sticky labels and ask all the pubs to add them to that specific beer in their stock.'

Anna does another facepalm.

'You do realise they might not be up for doing that?' says Connor.

'Yeah, maybe, but I won't know till I try, will I?' I feel the adrenaline coursing through my body with this sudden boost. 'I'll even stick on all the labels myself if it means they'll let me do it. Come on, eat up you guys, we're off to PC World.'

By five p.m., I've designed and printed my own labels (which included setting up a new email address so that I don't have to give out my personal one), and I'm on the bus back to The Shore where I will execute my plan – this time by myself, so that no one can talk me out of it, or hold me up. The rain has come on, but it's light and drizzly, so the only thing that will suffer from the experience is my hair. I've got the labels tucked carefully in my handbag, which is reasonably waterproof.

Having decided to start with the places that are furthest away, I hop off the bus just before it turns on to Leith Walk, and hurry along to the pubs and bars on Constitution Street – this being as far as I'd expect anyone who lives at The Shore to go if they were visiting their 'local'.

Approaching the first pub, I'm momentarily thrown by how busy it is. It may be Saturday, but it's only late afternoon and the middle of January. Pushing open the door, it's immediately apparent what the attraction is: there's a football match on. The noise of the fans and commentators is blaring out of a couple of large screen TVs, with all eyes in the pub glued to them. I fight my way through to the bar, and try to catch the barman's attention, but he's as engrossed in the match as the punters.

'Excuse me,' I call across to him, but I'm either not loud enough or he's oblivious. I try again. 'Excuse me.'

The man briefly glances across at me, then reluctantly makes his way over, eyes still on the screen. 'What can I get you?'

'I'm looking for a favour.' I try and fail again to get his full attention.

'I serve drinks, not favours.'

'Very funny.'

'Sorry. What is it you want?'

'I'm hoping you'll help me with something. Do you sell the beer, Serve Minus Pigs, here?'

'We do.' He automatically reaches for the fridge for a can, eyes never leaving the screen. 'That'll be five pounds sixty.'

'No, I don't want one,' I clarify. 'Technically, I want access to all of them.'

'You want to buy *all* of our beers?' The man looks at me properly for the first time.

'No. I'm trying to get a message to someone, and I was hoping you'd be kind enough to add these labels to all your cans of Serve Minus Pigs – including those in your stock room.' I hold up a plastic pocket containing the printed labels.

The barman takes it from me and reads aloud. "*Jamie, what a Hogmanay, Connor is still gay, if you felt what I felt, please don't leave my heart to melt. Contact: steph@operationfindjamie.headquarters.*" He looks up at me in complete and utter amazement. 'Is this for real?'

'Absolutely.' I give him a bright smile, while heat creeps up my neck under his scrutiny. 'Look, I know what you're thinking. I've heard it all already from my friends. Will you stick them on the cans?'

'Eh… sure. Don't think the boss will mind, as long as they don't cover up the information on the can that has to be displayed by law.'

'They won't. I purposely used address labels so they'd take up as little room as possible. So, you'll do it?'

'Who am I to stand in the way of true love.' He chuckles. 'I'll get right on it.'

I take the folder back, and hand him several sheets of labels, noticing that his eyes keep creeping back to the TV. Watching him for a few seconds, it strikes me that I can't trust this guy to deliver. He'll set the stickers down somewhere, then forget about them, and they'll end up in the bin.

'Umm… any chance I can do it myself?' I ask. 'If you get the cans, I can put them on right here.'

The barman doesn't have to be asked twice. He empties the fridge, and brings through a couple of boxes from the storeroom, then returns his attention to the game. Pleased that my plan is now well and truly in action, I make myself comfortable on a bar stool, and work my way through the haul.

By 8:45 p.m., I've made my way around all the pubs and bars in the vicinity, and I'm starving. But I'm quite pleased with the result – most places agreed, as long as I did the work myself, and only a couple refused my request (the miserable sods – have they no sense of romance?!), so my chances of finding Jamie have significantly improved. I just have to hope that he doesn't habitually stick to one local, and if he does, that it's not one of the pubs where the owners wouldn't play ball. I'm also getting used to people having a laugh at my expense – but who cares? As long as my plan works.

Sheltering at the bus stop, shivering slightly from the cold, I'm about to board a bus back home, when I look along the road, and spot the bright lights of a local super-market in the near distance. Crap. I didn't even think of shops. What if Jamie normally buys his beer to drink at home? I stride back in the direction I've come from, pulling my hood up as I walk. The rain is still quite light, but it's now coming down almost horizontally from the gusty wind that has picked up even more.

Spotting a specialist off-licence on the way, I drop in there as well. They do sell that particular beer, so I'm relieved to have caught that one. Then after ticking that off (thanks to a friendly young woman who was taken by the romance of it all), I head a few doors along to check out the supermarket. To my relief, they don't sell Serve Minus Pigs. Much as the small businesses have been quite amenable, I'm not sure I would have had as much luck when dealing with one of the big brands.

Before I leave the supermarket, I quickly check online that I haven't missed any other places in the area that might sell artisan beer. Then, finally happy that I've covered all bases as far as I can, I head back outside, dropping a couple of quid in the paper cup of a homeless man who's sitting there as I go. He looks up at me and mumbles a polite thank you. I can't help feeling sad for him, and a bit guilty that I get to go home to a nice warm apartment, when he's sitting outside in the freezing cold getting soaked.

Once I'm on the bus though, this temporary dip in mood has passed, and a feeling of nervous excitement is building in my stomach. I've got my message for Jamie out there! Now all I need to do is wait for a response.

Chapter 11

I arrive back at my apartment to hear Connor and Anna laughing and joking in the next room. This doesn't surprise me. Having helped with the label design and production that afternoon (while continuing her monologue that I've lost the plot), Anna had announced there was no way she was leaving until she saw how this 'comedy gold turned out'.

On entering the kitchen-living room, I can immediately smell that they've had a takeaway.

'Where's the pizza?' I plead in place of a greeting. 'I'm famished. Please tell me you left me some.'

'We didn't just leave you some,' says Connor. 'I got you one of your own: a nine incher with pepperoni and olives. It's in the fridge.'

'Connor McCrae, you are the best ex-boyfriend-slash-gay-best-friend I could ever have.' I lean over and kiss the top of his head before heading straight for the fridge.

'You're welcome.' He grins across at me. 'So how did it go? You're back late.'

'Yeah, we were wondering if we should call you,' says Anna.

'It went fine,' I reply.

I'm deliberately making them wait, because I know they're dying to know everything, and I'm not handing them a laugh at my expense that easily. I catch them sharing a look and shake my head. Couple of vultures, the two of them, picking over the desperate moments of my attempt to get into the dating game – with the right guy.

Switching on the oven, I load my pizza on to a tray and stick it in to reheat. Then I pour myself a glass of white wine from the open bottle in the fridge and plonk myself down on the sofa beside Anna.

'So?' She gives me a pointed look and whirls her finger in an impatient gesture of 'come on, spill'.

I sip my wine and lean back with a relaxed sigh. 'There's not much to tell. I went round all the bars in the vicinity of The Shore and also an off-licence on Bernard Street that stocked the beer. They mostly agreed to the labels, but I had to stick them on myself, which is why I'm so late.'

'And?'

'And what?'

'Oh, come on, you know what I'm looking for.' She pounds the sofa in frustration. 'How did they react? Did they take the piss? Give me something... I knew I should have followed you. Connor, why wouldn't you let me do that?'

'You were going to follow me?' I eyeball her, before Connor can respond.

'Uh, *yeah*. Who wouldn't want to be a fly-on-the-wall it in that situation? Apart from boring, super loyal Connor here.' She sticks a resentful tongue out at him, and he responds by throwing a cushion at her.

'OK, you two. Break it up.' I chuckle. 'Connor, thank you for keeping her on the leash. I appreciate it. Video footage of my venture on Instagram would not have been a happy outcome.'

'It could have supported your cause,' Anna huffs. 'We could have turned it into a proper search campaign. #find-Jamie. That would have got you the result you're looking for.'

'Not such a bad idea…' I muse. 'Though I still wouldn't want compromising videos of me splashed all over social – there is a line, you know.'

'Interesting where you draw it though.'

'OK, fine. You want the dirt that badly? Here it is…' I give the pair of them a full run down of my experience, complete with every sarcastic and/or incredulous comment, starting with the barman watching the football in the first bar I visited. I only pause briefly to get my pizza out of the oven and throw the first slice down my throat hungrily, while trying desperately not to burn my mouth.

'Now that's why I stayed here all day,' Anna declares, as I complete my blow-by-blow account. 'Steph, you're a legend! I've honestly never met anyone who's gone as loopy over a bloke before – and I've seen some pretty desperate men and women. Though you do it with style, I have to give you that.'

'I'm going to take that as a compliment,' I say. 'So, what have you two been up to since I left?'

'Well, Anna persuaded me to go on a dating site,' says Connor. 'I'm now the proud owner of username Conacrae23.' This announcement is accompanied by a slight grimace.

'Anna, you *didn't*.' I survey her with disapproval. 'Seriously, you need to learn to stay out of other peoples' lives.'

'What?' Anna shrugs defensively. 'He had a bad experience, so he needs to get back out there before he loses his nerve altogether. You know, climb back on the horse and all that.'

'He's not a bloody jockey.' I pause to take another bite of pizza. 'He's a gay man who's only just come out, and he needs time to work through things. It's not as straightforward as it is for you hopping from one bloke to the next like—'

'Ladies, please,' Connor interjects. 'I love that you're fighting over me, but please stop before you give me a migraine.'

Anna and I immediately fall silent.

'Thank you.' He acknowledges us individually with two nods of his head. 'Now if I may, I'd like to give my own view on this. Steph, you are correct, this is all new to me and I know I'm not ready...'

I throw an *I-told-you-so* look at Anna.

'But then Anna made a very solid point,' he continues. 'The best way to become ready is to spectate from the sidelines, so that's what I'm going to do.'

My expression remains blank from this non-revelation. 'What does that even mean, Connor?'

'It means I've "hired" Anna to manage my new online dating account for me. She's already created my profile, and she's going to manage all my interactions for me.'

'When he says "hired", he's not paying me, just to clarify,' Anna chips in. 'I'm more than happy to do it.'

'I bet you are.' I absently down the last of my wine as my troubled mind processes this. 'Connor, you do realise that Anna's a loose cannon when it comes to this kind of stuff. Do you really want her going rogue with your dating life?'

'Hey, I object to that.' Anna purses her lips in fake indignation.

'It's true though, isn't it?' I smirk, giving her a little wink.

'No. Connor and I have agreed some ground rules – and I've also agreed to stick to them.'

'You'd better have them written in blood,' I say to Connor, shaking my head and heading to the fridge for a refill. 'Because if there's a loophole, she'll find it.'

'It's fine, Steph,' Connor calls across to me. 'All Anna's going to do is help me get a feel for what's what online. You know, who to avoid, who to keep chatting with. She's going to manage the account for me for a couple of weeks to begin with, then once she's got a few potentials lined up, she's going to consult with me on each interaction before she responds.'

'Huh. I guess that doesn't sound so bad, as long as that's how it plays out. And she keeps it clean.'

'Who do you take me for?' Anna complains.

I'm about to respond when my phone buzzes on the floor beside the couch. We all stop and look at each other, then Anna leans over and grabs it.

'It looks like a response to your appeal.' She hands it to me with wide eyes as I rush across and quickly read the email.

'*Oh, my goodness.* The sender says he got my message and can I call him. He's given me a number. What if it's him?' After nearly two weeks of trying to track Jamie down, I'm suddenly a bag of nerves at the thought that I might be about to speak to him.

'Then you'll have succeeded with your goal,' says Connor. 'What are you waiting for? Call him.'

'OK, OK.' I tap on the number in the email, put the phone to my ear and walk back into the kitchen, trying hard to keep myself calm.

'Hello?' a male voice answers.

'Hi, is that Jamie?'

'Yes, it's me. Hi, Steph.'

On hearing this, I feel like the breath has been kicked out of me, and for a moment I can't speak. My heart is hammering in my chest. I glance across at Connor and Anna who look completely gobsmacked by this turn of events.

'I got your message on the beer can,' Jamie prompts me.

'Right, of course. Wow. I can't believe how quickly that worked. I... um... so do you want to meet up?'

'Definitely.'

'OK, great. When would work for you?'

I'm now practically dancing on the spot, elated. But I am also feeling some level of awkwardness at how this communication has come about. He's not as chatty as I remember either.

'Half an hour?' he suggests.

'Half an hour's fine. Whereabouts? Same pub we met in before?'

'Eh... how about we meet on Commercial Quay?'

'OK... sure.' I'm puzzled by this request.

'There are plenty of places for an alfresco quickie round there.'

As he says this, I hear a surge of raucous laughter in the background.

'What the hell...' I cut the call and stare at my phone in disbelief, filling in my friends on what just happened. Seconds later, another email comes through from the same email address. I open it, hoping that this time it really is Jamie.

Aww go on! I'll rock your world. Guarantee you'll forget all about Jamie after ten minutes with me.

'Eww. It's him again.'

'Ignore him,' says Anna. 'He's clearly not getting any.'

'I can't believe a guy would do that. What a cheek. And completely gross.'

'At least he didn't follow up with a dick pic.'

'Oh, stop it, Anna, please.' This comment makes me feel a bit nauseated.

I'm fuming, but also desperately disappointed that my hopes were raised and then dashed like that. Tears prick at my eyes and I blink them away so that neither Connor nor Anna can see how much this has upset me.

'It was always going to be a risk putting yourself out there like that.' Connor puts his arm around me, giving me a squeeze.

'I know, but I never imagined that people would be so cruel.'

'I don't think it's personal, hon,' says Anna. 'They're out drinking and they spot this message and to them it's all a big laugh. It's how people are. They don't think of the consequences.'

'I suppose.'

My phone signals the arrival of another email. I pick it up and read out loud.

> Hey, I saw your message on the beer can. Is Connor single? He's probably more my type ;)

'What have I done?' I wail. 'Connor, Anna, please tell me this isn't going to continue.'

Connor and Anna share a concerned look.

'I'm not sure either of us can give you that reassurance,' says Anna.

'Maybe you could delete the email account if it gets too much?' suggests Connor.

'What?' I stare at him, almost unable to process what I'm hearing. 'Connor, I'm not doing that when I've just put out an appeal for Jamie to get in touch. All my hard work gone to waste – and I'd definitely never hear from him.'

'In that case, you'd better get used to idiots like that using you as a source of entertainment – and don't assume that any of them are Jamie until you've vetted the person on the other end.'

Chapter 12

Six weeks later

By the end of February, the evenings are getting lighter and snowdrops are lining the cycle paths, signalling the first indications of spring. I'm also feeling more fulfilled from doing some additional hours as a key worker again after my conversation with Lizzie. It's given me a lift knowing that I'm making more of a direct difference to people's lives once more. But unfortunately, that's where the positives in my life end. Not only have I not heard a peep from Jamie in that time, I've also had to put up with an inordinate number of 'hilarious' self-styled comedians from Leith's pub-going population responding to my beer-can appeal. As much as they clearly think they're the next Kevin Bridges, they're about as funny as a cervical smear test.

'That another one?' Connor asks from his stretched-out position on the opposite sofa from me as my phone buzzes on the floor and I emit a frustrated groan.

We're indulging in a Saturday afternoon box-set marathon together.

'Will they *ever* stop?' I pause the programme we're watching and look at him defeatedly. 'It's been six weeks.'

'They're certainly reducing in volume. Must be four or five days since the last one. That's got to be a good sign.

Hopefully means the stock of beers you added the labels to is nearly finished.'

'I suppose.'

I pick up my phone intending to delete the email without even reading it, but as with every other time, there's still a tiny part of me that wonders if it might be Jamie, so I have to read it. Navigating to my email account, I sigh with chronic disappointment as I see the words on the screen.

'Here's a new one.' I read the message out loud to Connor. '"Are you looking for a particular Jamie? Cause if you're not fussy, I reckon I could fit the bill. I shower every day and I'm house trained. That what you're after?"'

Connor smirks with amusement. 'That's actually quite a good one. Better than the cheesy chat-up lines and obscene photos.'

'Don't remind me.' I gag a little as he says this. 'I thought the only place I'd come across that particular occupational hazard was on a dating app. It's so much more of an intrusion when they land directly in my inbox.'

'Aww, Stephy, sorry this hasn't worked out for you.'

'You did warn me. Feel free to gloat.'

'Not at all.' He flicks his hand in a gesture of batting away my comment. 'I only said the approach with the brewery was a non-starter. Your DIY plan could have worked, and if it had, that would have been amazing.'

'But it didn't.' I pout my lower lip and give Connor the full force of my puppy-dog eyes. 'Why do you have to be gay, Connor? No, scratch that – why did you have to tell me you were gay? This is all your fault.'

'What? Would you have preferred things to stay as they were? A lifetime of no sex and never knowing what true love is?'

'Well, I'm hardly on the path to either, am I?'

'You've had a handful of first dates and you're even got a second date lined up. I consider that progress. You're doing way better than me.' He gets up from the sofa and wanders across to the kitchen. 'Want a cup of tea?'

'Yes, please. You know you're not going to get to a second date if you don't have a first one.' I tut at him. 'I was concerned when I found out Anna had taken the reins on your love life, but now I'm starting to think she's going too easy on you.'

'Listen, if you'd had the Hogmanay experience I had, instead of your fairy-tale night with Jamie, you'd understand. I'm fine with her managing the messaging for now. That way she can filter out the weirdos early on.'

'Fair enough. But surely you need to get involved in the chat sometime, otherwise all these lovely blokes will be falling for Anna's version of you instead of, well, the real you.'

'I will.' He takes the milk out the fridge. 'Anyway, back to you and your second date with… what's his name again?'

'Sean.'

'Show me his photo to remind me?'

Getting up to join Connor in the kitchen, I open up Sean's profile on my dating app and pass him the phone. He assumes an appraising expression as he scrutinises the picture.

'He's quite hot. Man, it's so good to finally be able to say things like that out loud.' Connor glances up and grins at me, and I return his smile with an approving nod. 'Provided he doesn't have a penchant for playing naked butler on the first date, I'd go out with him.'

'He doesn't. I can't imagine him *ever* playing naked butler. He's quite... tame.'

'Give him a chance.' He hands the phone back to me and resumes making the tea. 'You women can be really intimidating. I may not have dated many of you, but I've hung out with enough of your friends over the years to know that. Anna especially is terrifying. She'd eat most men for breakfast, lunch and dinner.'

'Probably explains why she's terminally single.' I chuckle. 'OK, I'll give him a chance, but if he doesn't give me a proper belly laugh soon, I'm going to have to call it a day. There's only so much painful small talk I can endure.'

Connor slops some milk in our mugs and turns to face me. 'Fine – but offer something up. Don't expect him to put in all the work. That's not fair.'

'I'm not. I'm just disappointed that the chat with him doesn't flow the way it did with Jamie.'

'That's your problem right there. If you make Jamie the benchmark for every guy you go out with, they're all going to be a miss. Sean isn't Jamie... so find out who Sean *is*.'

'All right, all right. I'll try to keep Jamie out of my mind when I'm on the date.'

'Not just for the date.' Connor holds my gaze to show he's serious. 'For good. He's in the past, Steph. That's where he needs to stay.'

'Sure.' I frown, aware that what Connor's asking is an impossible task.

My phone buzzes again in my hand and Connor and I share a helpless look. Reluctantly tilting the screen upwards to meet my eyeline, I see that it's not another wannabe fake-suitor-slash-comedian but a notification from my family WhatsApp group.

> **Kayleigh:**
> Steph, I've got a blind date lined up for you! This guy's a right looker, super successful and well connected. Are you free tomorrow night?

Irritation swells in me. What the hell does Kayleigh think she's doing? She's the last person I'd trust with my love life. And why does she have to broadcast this on the family group? She could have messaged me privately.

A buzz of my phone and another message pops up before I can respond – then another.

> **Mum:**
> He sounds wonderful, Kayleigh. How kind of you to do this for your sister.

> **Dad:**
> Yes, that's thoughtful of you, sweetheart.

That's why she didn't message me privately. She wanted to garner support from the ranks, the sneaky cow.

'Oh, bugger off, the lot of you,' I grumble at my phone.

'Everything OK?' Connor peers over my shoulder and reads what's on the screen.

'Can you believe her? She's such a piece of work.'

'She's never been my flavour of soft drink, but I guess she means well.'

'She does not.' My voice rises half an octave through my indignation. 'This is her trying to control the situation: she wants me to end up with someone they'll all approve of. This is her attempt at a coup.'

'Would it be so awful to go and see what the guy is like?'

'I can imagine exactly what he's like: rich, impeccably dressed and with teeth that are so white they glow in the dark.'

'Well, that sounds… awful.' Connor's tone drips with sarcasm.

'It's not my type at all.' I return to the sofa with my tea and toss my phone on to the cushion in frustration.

'Funny you say that…' Connor does the same but without the phone-throwing tantrum. 'Because that description sounds remarkably similar to how you described Jamie to me. Didn't you mention that his friend predicts he'll be a billionaire one day? And I definitely heard you talking about his perfect teeth.'

'That was different.'

'How?'

'Jamie was lovely. He taught football to kids to keep them out of drugs. He was… the exception, you know? And he was an entrepreneur. I guarantee you this bloke will have some high-flying top-level management role, an ego the size of Calton Hill, and banter that revolves around how much richer and more successful he is than everyone else.'

'That's not judgemental at all.' Connor raises an eyebrow at me. 'You're not that person, Stephy.'

'Seems I am when it comes to my sister.' I trace a pattern on the sofa cushion with my finger, feeling ever so slightly ashamed. 'Look, I've lived with her all my life:

she's all of that and more. It's reasonable to expect that her crowd will be too.'

'If you think so. I'm just not sure you should attach that label to all of them without knowing what they're like.'

'You mean you think I should go on the date.'

'It's your choice.'

'It is.' I nod. 'And there's no way I'm going; if I do, this thing will snowball. I'll never get my family to stay out of my business. That's so not happening. I need to meet someone who shares my moral compass, even if it means my family hates them.'

'Like they hate me?' Connor sips at his tea reflectively.

I wince as I realise what I've said. 'They don't hate you, Connor. They just don't understand you. I'd take that as a compliment.'

'Is Sean starting to seem like not so bad an option now?'

'Maybe…' I make a pained expression, grab my phone and start typing a semi-polite thanks but no thanks to Kayleigh.

At the same time, another message pops up in my family WhatsApp group.

> **Mikey:**
> Kayleigh, you're about as qualified to find Steph a bloke as I am teaching women how to use tampons. Steph, I know loads of top blokes. No pressure, but I reckon they'd be more your thing. I'll message you some photos from their Facebook profiles.

'Oh man,' I groan, casting my phone aside as Connor laughs loudly. 'I need to find myself a boyfriend – fast. Even if it's a fake one to keep the wolves at bay.'

As the evening rolls in, I find myself distracted and twitchy. It's partly cabin fever from having not left the apartment all day, combined with a lingering lack of enthusiasm over my interactions with Sean. I know Connor's right: that I should give the guy a chance, but surely if there was going to be any chemistry between us, I'd at least have seen a glimmer of it by now. And I know I shouldn't be comparing him to Jamie, but it's almost impossible not to.

Sighing, I pick up my phone and start tapping out a response to Sean's most recent message about possible places to meet for a drink on our second date (it feels like we've been discussing this for way too long), when an email alert flashes up on my screen. Frowning at it for interrupting my flow – especially because it's clearly another joker using my beer-can appeal as the source of their Saturday night entertainment – I swipe it away and finish my message to Sean.

'Want to go out for a drink?' I ask Connor, who's barely moved from his position on the sofa since this afternoon. And who, unlike me, looks remarkably relaxed and content.

'Hmm?' is all I get as a reply.

'I'm bored. I feel like the whole world is out having fun and I'm just sitting here in my own stink.'

This time Connor sits up and looks at me. 'What's up, Stephy? It's not like you to get all FOMO.'

'I don't know. I'm restless. Will you come for a drink with me? Please?'

'OK, sure, if it will make you feel better. But you owe me. I was well comfy there.'

'Thanks Connor. It will.' I leap off the sofa, giving him a grateful peck on the forehead as I do, and head for my bedroom to get ready.

After changing into suitable Saturday night attire and putting on some makeup, I'm zipping my lip stain into the inside pocket of my handbag when my phone buzzes on the bed. Picking it up, I see an email notification that appears to be a forwarded message. Curious, I open it and see that it's a forwarded version of the email I received earlier when I was messaging Sean. The one I haven't read yet. All it contains is a short message.

Sorry, forgot to say, it's Jamie!

'Ha, not so clever, are you.' I scoff at the screen. 'If you're going to prank me, at least remember to include all the necessary information.'

Feeling like I have the upper hand for the first time, I scroll down to the original message, hoping to triumph further over this idiot. Scanning the text, I automatically roll my eyes at the predictability of the opening line – '*Hi Steph, I got your message…*' – and I'm about to shove my phone in my bag, when something catches my eye. It's subtle: just a turn of phrase in a random sentence that might otherwise have had no specific meaning. But it triggers something in me, transporting me back to that night at New Year. I catch my breath, realising it could mean something or nothing at all. I've been here before.

I quickly draft a response:

How do I know you're really Jamie? I've had dozens of emails that go exactly like this. I'm not taking any more crap, so either prove it or stay out of my inbox.

The moment I hit send, I instantly regret my choice of words. If it is Jamie then they don't exactly show me in a great light. But as it's most likely not him, and having been the butt of people's jokes for weeks now, who can blame me?

As with all the other messages I've received, the response is swift, which triggers a feeling of disappointment as I picture a gaggle of friends sitting round a pub table, snickering and eagerly anticipating my response. Despite this, I still read it.

> I'm sorry you've had to deal with that nonsense. Would anyone but the real Jamie know that you live at Western Harbour? Or that your friend is a top-class flirt called Anna? They certainly wouldn't know that we enjoyed hot buttered toast together on New Year's morning – and that's not some seedy innuendo, as you well know.

A feeling of shock and disbelief washes over me as I read the words over and over, almost not trusting what I'm reading. Then a shivery tingle runs through my spine and my heart starts to pound in my chest as realisation dawns. This time it's him. *It's really him.*

Chapter 13

'Jamie... oh my goodness. I didn't think that I'd see you again.' I'm still stupefied that, after replying to Jamie's email with my phone number, I'm now taking to him. *The* Jamie. Not some arsehole who gets his kicks out of pretending to be him.

'Me neither,' he replies. 'Until I saw that beer can. Very creative approach, I must say.'

I cringe as I imagine him reading the cheesy poem I wrote. At the time, when I was desperate to find him, it seemed perfect; now, knowing he's read it, I feel insecure and a bit daft.

'I've experienced a level of piss-taking I never knew possible for that,' I mutter.

'Is that right?' He chuckles. 'Well, as they say... what doesn't kill you—'

'Makes you die a little more inside every day.' My face contorts into a grimace. 'A painful way to go, I assure you. Think I'd prefer a quick death to this.'

'Aww, Steph. I really am sorry for what you've been through.'

'It's OK. Wasn't your fault. I'm kind of kidding anyway. Exaggerating at the very least. Although... you knew where I lived but you never got in touch...' I leave this statement hanging as more of a question.

Jamie goes silent again. I can hear his breathing at the other end of the line then he lets out a short sigh.

'I didn't know what the situation was,' he says eventually. 'When I legged it out of your apartment, I was back at The Shore before I realised we hadn't swapped numbers. It was too late. You were at home with your ex, who I figured, by his unexpected return, had realised he'd made a mistake. For all I knew, the two of you were back together. I didn't want to risk turning up at your apartment not knowing how you – or he – would react.'

'But I told you I thought it was for the best. You helped me reach that very conclusion.'

Jamie sighs again. 'I know. And that was wrong. It was Hogmanay. We were drinking, got carried away. I was all too aware that once your ex came home, you could forget me in an instant.'

'That's what I said to Anna!' I'm jubilant as it dawns on me that I was right all along; I had predicted this. 'That's why I did the stupid beer can thing.'

'It wasn't stupid at all. It was genius. I… um… was going to ask if you wanted to come and meet me for a drink at The Shore, but—'

'Absolutely. I can be there in half an hour.'

'Great, I thought you might be busy. It is Saturday night after all.' He sounds surprised but also pleased at my sudden availability.

Shit. Connor. In the excitement of Jamie finally making contact, I've forgotten that I just cajoled Connor into coming out with me, and he's in the next room getting ready. I also feel an additional but less significant sense of guilt over Sean, whom I'll definitely not be seeing on that second date now. But who am I kidding? He's not

Jamie. He could never come close. I can make my excuses in a delicate way.

'I'm not doing anything I can't easily rearrange,' I say. 'See you in the same pub as New Year?'

'Can't wait.'

Ending the call, I knock on Connor's bedroom door and dance around impatiently as I wait for him to answer.

'What's up?' He pulls it open and a waft of eau de toilette hits me square in the nostrils, accentuating my feeling of discomfort over what I'm about to do.

'I just spoke to Jamie.'

'Huh?' He's understandably confused.

'He emailed me. I thought it was another prankster, but it was him.'

'Oh wow. That's incredible. And a bit… unbelievable. You're sure it was him? You did vet him properly?'

'Yes, silly.' I chuckle at Connor's overprotectiveness. 'So… um…' I focus my attention on wiping away a mark on the doorframe.

'You want to go meet him now.'

'Yes. I'm so sorry.'

'After you made me get out of my comfy spot?' Connor fixes me with an appraising look.

'I'll make it up to you, I promise.'

'I'm kidding.' He nudges me affectionately. 'You know I didn't really want to go out anyway. Go and see Jamie.'

'Oh thanks, Connor. You're the best.' I pull him into a big squeezy hug, then grab my things and rush out of the apartment to meet Jamie, my body coursing with adrenaline as I imagine ten different versions of how our eyes will meet for the first time after so long.

Twenty minutes later, I'm standing at the bar waiting for Jamie to walk through the door. My stomach is in my throat: part excitement and part fear that he either won't show – or he won't find me attractive any more. I'm so jittery, I feel like a pneumatic drill. I even consider ordering a shot of tequila to take the edge off, but decide that being caught downing it as he arrives probably wouldn't look the best.

I force myself to remain facing the bar each time the door opens. This is almost unbearable, because I've already counted seven people walking through it, most of whom – judging by the smell – have been smokers coming and going.

When the door opens and closes for the eighth time, I sense someone behind me.

'Steph?'

Biting my lip to keep my composure, I turn, and my smile instantly dissolves. The man standing in front of me isn't Jamie. Not even close. I feel the nervous excitement that had built up inside me drop like a stone as I take in the fifty-odd-year-old man standing in front of me. He's short and plump with facial hair that would pass for a novel species of wildcat.

'Oh, you are kidding me,' I wail, forgetting myself. 'I've been *catfished*?'

Then I remember the email and the phone call.

'No!' I point my finger at him accusingly. 'There's no way you'd know all that stuff, there's no way you'd know where I live or Anna's flirting habits or our morning after breakfast. Right? *Right?*'

The man caresses his beard self-consciously and looks quite intimidated by my outburst. This ignites a spark of regret in me. But I'm so wound up, I appear to have forgotten my standards, as well as my manners.

'Come on. Seriously. What's going on?' I demand of him. 'And what is with that beard?'

'I… uh…' His eyes dart all over the place in avoidance of my accusatory stare. 'I'm just the… um… Jamie – the guy I assume you're here to meet – asked me to come in here and tell you he's outside at your table from New Year.'

Having completed his task, the man shuffles off in the direction of the toilets – and the realisation hits. Jamie's really here, and I've just yelled at and insulted a total stranger who was nothing more than a messenger.

I hesitate, unsure what to do. The part of me that's waited nearly two months for this moment wants to forget that unfortunate interaction and dash straight outside into Jamie's arms; while the real me – who's thankfully now made a reappearance – is appalled by my behaviour, and feels an urgency to go and fix the situation. Of course, nice Steph wins, because that's who I am.

'Excuse me? Sir?' I rush after the man, who looks terrified as he discovers I'm following him and dashes into the toilets.

I wait impatiently outside dance around outside the door for him to do his business, until it dawns on me that he's probably hiding out in there. Sighing with frustration, I tentatively open the door a crack, my nostrils immediately engulfed by the stale smell of urine that seems to lurk in every male pub toilet. Not that I've been in many – and only when I've been bursting and the queue for the ladies is longer than my bladder's ability to hold out.

'Eh… sir? I'm sorry to do this, and I hope I'm not interrupting…' I cringe, sincerely hoping he wasn't going in there for a number two and I'm now hounding a man sitting with his trousers round his ankles. 'I wanted to apologise for the mix up and for how I reacted. You see, I've been trying to contact Jamie for some time, and I did it in a way that made me a bit vulnerable and… well… I've had to deal with a lot of jokers and chancers, so I jumped to the wrong conclusion and assumed you were another one of them.'

I stop talking and listen, but the man doesn't reply. The toilets are completely silent.

'Anyway…' I decide to continue because I know he can hear me. 'I'm so sorry… I was just frustrated and—'

'Steph?'

I freeze. Now *that* voice I do recognise. Turning slowly, I lock eyes with a grinning Jamie. He's wearing the same puffer jacket as when I last saw him, and is holding two cans of Serve Minus Pigs. It's almost as if I've been transported back to New Year, except for the excruciating situation I find myself in.

Had this been the reunion I'd imagined, I'd be so overcome with excitement and teenage hormones, it would have taken an enormous effort to resist the urge to run and leap into his arms – like Martine McCutcheon did to Hugh Grant at the end of *Love Actually*. However, having been caught peering through the doorway of the men's loos, that urge unsurprisingly escapes me.

'Jamie. Uh… hi,' is all I manage.

He takes in my scarlet face and my awkward stance, and I can tell it's taking everything he's got not to laugh.

'One question… no, two actually,' he says. 'Why haven't you come outside? And… why are you harassing some poor unsuspecting gentleman when he's at his most vulnerable?'

I shift slightly on the spot. 'I was… that guy… oh, man, this is really not the reunion I'd hoped for.'

'Yeah, sorry about that. But when you didn't come outside, I naturally wondered what was going on.'

'Naturally.' I silently berate myself for not doing a better job of resisting my impulses and my need to be a decent human being.

'So, are you coming outside, or shall I leave you to… do whatever this is you're doing?' The corners of his mouth twitch with amusement.

'Funny.' I throw him a sarcastic look and rub my forehead with embarrassment. 'Look, please could you do me a favour?'

'Sure. What do you need?' He raises a curious eyebrow.

'Would you go in there and tell that poor man that I'm terribly sorry for my behaviour, that I've had a difficult time, and that I think his beard is… artistic.'

'Artistic?'

'Yes. Or feel free to supplement with another positive and appropriate adjective.'

'What did you do to my poor messenger?' Jamie's obviously having to try hard to swallow the mirth that's now bubbling to the surface.

'I'll tell you after. See you outside.'

I walk past him, face blazing, grabbing a can of beer from his hand as I go. Once outside, I take a seat at the same table we sat at before, and slug at my drink. It's half-finished when Jamie joins me on the other side of the table, his face giving nothing away.

'How is he?' I wince as I ask this.

'Think he'll survive. Though he's definitely going to lose the beard, or take it a lot shorter at a minimum.'

'Oh no. I'm an awful person.'

'No, you're not. To be fair, I think you've done him a favour. It did resemble some pretty grotesque taxidermy I once saw in an old castle up north.'

'Still...'

'Forget it.' He gives me a meaningful look. 'It was a misunderstanding. He's fine. Just found you a little... intimidating.'

'I really didn't mean it. I'm not a nasty person. I thought he was—'

'Steph.' Jamie reaches across and clutches my hand reassuringly, sending a wonderful warm tingle up my arm. 'I know that's not you, even with the short amount of time we've spent together. Honestly, don't give it another thought. I bought him a pint, so he's quite happy.'

'You did? Thank you. I can give you the money for it.' I reach for my bag.

'Absolutely not. It was my fault. I was trying to be smart, replicating our night together at New Year, making it seem like the weeks hadn't passed. I never thought to factor in what you told me about having had a rough time with the locals.'

I flush and look at the ground as he says this.

'Hey.' He gently takes my hand in his. 'Please don't be embarrassed; I thought it was sweet. And here we are – reunited – so surely it can't be a regret for you.'

'No, it's not.'

Looking up, I meet his gaze and take him in properly for the first time: his thick brown man curls, those gorgeous moss-green eyes, and his sort of lopsided grin. My heart skips as I register that he's here. He's right in front of me. After weeks of hoping and then losing hope, we can start again.

Maintaining eye contact, I get up and walk round to his side of the table and plonk myself down beside him. He quickly gathers me into his arms and pulls me into the most incredible kiss I've ever experienced. My body responds hungrily, this time tingling all over – from the top of my head to the tip of my toes. This is why I held out so long when Anna thought I'd lost the plot, and she and Connor kept on at me to date other guys. They hadn't experienced this.

We eventually pull apart breathlessly and just stare at each other, smiling, as if unable to believe this to be real; like even one blink would mean the other would disappear, and we'll discover it wasn't real. Well, that's certainly what I'm thinking anyway.

'I hope I didn't get in the way of anything tonight?' Jamie asks, once we've emerged from our semi-trance. 'It sounds like you had plans.'

'Oh… no. I was just going for a drink with Connor. He didn't want to go out anyway.'

'I was wondering if you might be on a date. And was hoping you weren't.'

I don't know why, but I redden slightly at this comment.

'You're seeing someone else.' Jamie looks gutted all of a sudden.

'No, I'm not. I was in the middle of planning a second date though when you got in touch.'

'Right. Good guy?'

'He seems nice enough. Anna and Connor talked me into signing up to a dating app.' I pluck my phone from my handbag and show it to Jamie. 'They said it was time to move on.'

'I used to be on that one.' Jamie takes the phone from my hand. 'Nice profile photo – and bio. Lucky for me that I saw your message, otherwise I might have lost you to...' He taps on my matches '...Sean.'

'Nah, don't think so. On our first date the conversation only seemed to flow after a few drinks.'

'That's a tell-tale sign it won't last the distance.'

'Yeah, I think you're right. He'll be fine. I do hope he meets the right woman for him though, because everyone deserves to have love in their life.'

'Look at you.' Jamie reaches up and strokes my cheek affectionately. 'You're a proper angel – seriously beautiful, inside and out.'

'Do angels call out middle-aged men for having uncouth facial hair?' I wrinkle my nose awkwardly.

'Only on a bad day.' Jamie grins at me, then picks up his can of beer and holds it out towards me. 'To new beginnings?'

'Hey... that's the exact toast we made at New Year.' I reach across the table and grab my own can, but hold back, waiting for his response.

'I know. And I'm hoping that if I play this evening out exactly as I did then, I'll be allowed to walk you home again.'

'Ah... I see what's going on here. We know where that's going to lead.' I sip at my beer coyly.

'Exactly.' Jamie winks at me and threads his fingers through mine.

'Only this time my ex will be sleeping in the room next door.'

'I can live with that. We'll just have to be quiet. He's definitely gay then?'

'Yes. Definitely. It's written right here on the… *oh…*' I turn my beer can three-sixty degrees, then check Jamie's. 'There's no label on these. It's new stock, which means if you hadn't seen it today, you might never have seen it at all.' The realisation sends an unpleasant chill down my spine.

'Don't think about that.' He rubs my fingers gently as if unconsciously trying to warm them up. 'Think about how it all worked out and how we can stay in bed all day tomorrow, making up for lost time. And also how I won't have to bolt from your apartment with no shoes on, dying for a pee.'

'You were? I didn't know that.'

'Neither did I until the cold hit the soles of my feet and I heard the lapping of the waves on the breakwater.'

I giggle as Jamie pulls me into him again, and we spend the next couple of hours snogging like teenagers – in between me recounting the tales of my beer-can campaign.

Chapter 14

By the time Jamie and I reach my apartment block —
having taken the scenic route by the water as we did at
New Year — we've had a few more beers, and we're more
than reacquainted. The journey takes twice as long due to
being literally unable to keep our hands off each other.

I'm expecting us to wander off the breakwater path
and straight through the main door to my building, when
Jamie unexpectedly stops, looking uncertain.

'What's up?' I cock my head like a springer spaniel.
'This isn't part of the whole re-creating New Year thing,
is it? I know we had the "will we, won't we" shenanigans
going on that night, but I think we've established hours
ago that you're coming home with me tonight.'

'I know.'

'Then what's the problem?'

He doesn't answer immediately — just looks shifty and
uncomfortable — and stares out across the estuary of the
River Forth to the twinkling lights of Fife.

'Are you sure your ex will be OK with this?' he asks
eventually.

'Yes. Connor and I have talked about this.' I laugh,
finding this little show quite endearing.

Jamie continues to stand there, looking unsure, which
causes me to sober up instantly.

'Jamie, is there something else going on? Because I'm sensing that Connor isn't the sum total of whatever's going on here. Are you having second thoughts about us?'

He looks at me and seems to come round from his indecision.

'No. Definitely not. I'm… I like you a lot, Steph, more than you realise. Forget I said anything.' His eyes lock on mine leaving me in no doubt that he's being sincere.

'You're not… nervous then… are you? About… you know…'

'Uh… no, it's not that… I want to get this right is all. Maybe I'm concerned about us rushing things and messing it up.'

I take in his face, etched with concern, and all I feel is a rush of empathy and strength of feeling for him. 'Oh, you're so adorable. But it's fine. Not like we haven't already shared a bed, is it?'

'I guess not. I'm obviously overthinking this. Let's go inside.'

He follows me into the building, and we take the lift to the fifth floor, where I unlock my apartment door and we creep inside, careful not to wake Connor. Unfortunately, Connor's bedroom light is on and he emerges fully clothed the second we close the door behind us.

'Stephy, I've been waiting up for you. How was… oh, hello…' He gives me a look of 'the big reunion clearly went well', which I return with a sly grin.

'Connor, this is Jamie.'

A broad smile spreads across Connor's face. 'So this is *the* Jamie. The guy you haven't stopped jabbering on about for the last eight weeks?'

'OK, I think that's a bit of an exaggeration.' My face starts to flame.

'Jamie, good to meet you.' Connor reaches out to shake Jamie's hand. 'And I'm not exaggerating at all. She's been a nightmare.'

'Is that right?' Jamie looks highly amused and quite pleased by this.

'Totally. I'm just glad that crazy plan of hers finally paid off.' Connor clocks the daggers I'm sending him. 'Anyway, great to meet you. Maybe see you in the morning.'

He retreats into his bedroom, but not without a final glance at me that says, 'I want to know *everything* tomorrow'. I respond with an almost invisible nod, then usher Jamie into my room before Connor can re-emerge and do any more damage.

'So, that was Connor. Still think he's in love with me?' I cheekily ask Jamie.

'No, I do not. He was… more than OK with this, it seems.' Jamie approaches me and unzips my coat, then discards it on the floor. 'Which is good news for me, I guess.'

'Told you. And about what you said before… we can take things at any speed you're comfortable with.'

'Thanks… I appreciate that. I really want to do this right, Steph. You're not the only one who's spent the last couple of months feeling you've lost out on something great.'

'You did?' I look up at him with wide eyes.

'Of course! I was there that night at New Year, too. It was incredible. I even came round this way a couple of times in the hope I'd bump into you, but no such luck.'

On hearing this, I'm even more consumed with lust than before. I feel an animalistic urge to be close to Jamie, to feel every part of his amazing body against mine. He slips off his own jacket and before we know it, we're pulling each other's clothes off, unable to wait a second longer to be properly reunited.

Next morning, I wake before Jamie and go through to the living room, where Connor's also up, dressed and eating breakfast at the dining table.

'Good night, last night?' He raises an eyebrow at me.

'Oh no, you didn't hear us, did you?' I feel myself blush.

'No, you're fine. I slept like a baby. Was referring to your moment of triumph in finally finding your man. Tell me everything.'

I fill Connor in on my evening with Jamie while I make myself a cup of tea.

'Poor Sean.' He muses. 'No way he's getting that second date now.'

'I know.' I cringe. 'I sent him a message to say I didn't think us going out again was a good idea after all and he didn't reply. He must hate me.'

'I'm sure he doesn't. It's probably just wounded pride. He's probably hitting the app again already.'

'All right, Connor.' I take a seat next to him at the table with my tea. 'I don't want the guy to be heartbroken, but I also don't want to be *that* forgettable.'

'Sorry. You're right.' He bites into a slice of toast before continuing. 'So, what's the deal with Jamie now you guys have hooked up?'

'I… um… I don't know actually. But I'm going to try and arrange another date with him before he leaves today.'

'That is – if he does leave here today.' Connor flashes his eyebrows at me, an impish grin on his face. 'I'm off to my mum's once I've eaten this. Helping her build some flat-pack furniture she ordered, then we're having dinner later, so you'll have the place to yourself.'

'Aww, I love your mum's food.' I feel a pang of envy. 'Tell her I said hi.'

'I will. You should come with me to see her sometime. She'd love to cook for you. Think she misses you.'

'That would be great. Maybe I could bring Jamie to meet her. How cool would that be? Introducing my new bloke to my ex's mum.'

A fleeting look crosses Connor's face.

'What was that?' I narrow my eyes at him.

'What was what?'

'That look. You reacted to what I said.'

'No, I didn't.'

'Yes, you did. Tell me, Connor.'

He screws up his face in discomfort. 'OK, but don't go off on one.' Connor lowers his voice. 'It was the assumption you made there, Stephy. About Jamie coming to meet my mum. Don't you think it's a bit soon to be thinking that way? I mean, you've only just reconnected with the guy, and, while I'm sure the sex is good—'

'Connor.'

'Oh, come on, you've been sleeping with a closet gay man for nearly a decade. It must be bloody explosive.'

'It is pretty damn good,' I admit with a shrug of agreement.

'There you go. Which means you're blinded by lust. You need to remember that you don't know Jamie. You've only spent a few hours in his company – and you must have spent at least some of that time sleeping.'

'True. Though we didn't sleep much,' I add with a twinkle in my eye.

'I can imagine.' Connor looks like he doesn't want to hear the details. 'He did disappear for weeks without getting in contact, Stephy, just remember that. He did know where you lived.'

'I already explained why. I know you're not going to trust him straight away, Connor – you need to check people out. But I feel like I can. I sense he's a good guy. It's like we're aligned somehow.'

'I see. And your destiny is written in the stars?' He throws me a sarcastic look.

'Oh, bugger off. You want it on a logical level. Fine. He's successful and financially solid from the sounds of things, which means my family would love him.'

'That's not even remotely on the list of criteria I want him to meet. That's your own insecurity coming through. I want you to be able to say he's loyal, dependable, and he'll take care of you, like you will him. None of which you can confirm until you know him a lot better.'

'You're so frustrating, Connor.' I sip at my tea distractedly. 'Can you not at least give him points for getting back in touch and being an amiable guy?'

He smiles at me as he clears away his breakfast dishes. 'All I'm saying, is be careful and don't invest too much in this too soon. You haven't had the dating experience that most other people have had by your age – neither have I. You are sweet and innocent, and that makes you a bit vulnerable.'

'You mean I'm naive.'

'That's not what I said.'

'But it's what you mean.' I eyeball him accusingly.

'No. I do admit I'm probably a bit overprotective though.'

'A bit?'

'What are you two bickering about?'

We're immediately silenced, looking like pair of toddlers who've raided the biscuit tin as Jamie enters the room, wearing only his jeans. He shakes out his T-shirt and pulls it over his toned body, and I have to stifle a giggle as I notice both Connor and I are momentarily mesmerised by this.

'Oh… eh… nothing, really.' I force my face back to a neutral expression. 'Apartment stuff. You know how it is.'

'I do.' Jamie raises an inquisitive eyebrow, which tells me he doesn't believe me for a second. 'You sounded like an old married couple from the other room. You sure you've split up?'

I glance at Connor, unsure what his reaction will be to Jamie's sense of humour, but he seems fine with it.

'Sometimes I wonder myself,' Connor quips. 'Anyway, I'm headed out, so I'll leave you two in peace. Have a good one.'

'You too,' I call after him as he leaves the room.

Moments later, the apartment door opens and closes, signalling his departure.

'So… we have the place to ourselves…' Jamie approaches me and slips his arms around my waist.

'We do indeed.' I reach up on my tiptoes and plant a smacking kiss on his lips. 'How ever shall we make the most of it?'

'I have an idea.' Jamie's eyes glint mischievously. 'How about we devour some coffee and hot buttered toast?'

I look at him and laugh. 'That wasn't what I was expecting at all.'

'Oh, yeah? And where was that lewd mind of yours headed?'

'Let's just say I was expecting you to talk about devouring something else.'

'Well, as you asked so nicely…' He suddenly scoops me up and carries me back to the bedroom, where we enjoy a delicious pre-breakfast workout.

Chapter 15

'I still can't believe that bonkers plan of yours paid off.' Anna surveys me over the top her computer screen while sipping at her takeaway coffee.

It's Monday morning and I'm back at work – although there's not much working going on, because it's Anna's first opportunity to interrogate me face to face about the weekend's events. There's no way she's letting that pass.

'I never doubted for a moment that my plan would work.' I assume a casual expression and fiddle with the stationery on my desk.

'Well, that's a massive pile of BS if I've ever heard one.' She gives me an appraising look.

'OK, my confidence did waver after a while, I'll admit.'

'It did more than waver. You gave up hope. Don't pretend otherwise.'

'All right, I did, but it came good. Jamie's back in my life, and I'm super smitten.' I punctuate this statement by waltzing round in my desk chair with a broad grin.

'You've certainly got that smug I've-been-laid-by-the-world's–hottest-man glow about you.'

'*Anna.*' I throw her a stern look and glance towards the office door.

'What?' She holds up her hands in a questioning gesture. 'No one's gonna walk in. Lizzie's stopping by the venue for the fundraiser on her way in this morning to make sure all the operational elements are coming together. How are the prize donations doing, by the way?'

'Great actually. We now have more than thirty high-value items, and Lizzie left me a note to say Mrs Carmichael has another one for us. I've said I'll pop over soon as I get a chance.'

'Ha, I bet she bought something else just so she could lure you over for tea and biscuits.'

'So what if she has.' I shrug. 'It's all harmless. *Oh* – get this – that new boutique hotel up by the Playhouse has donated a two-night stay in one of their suites – with dinner and a wine-tasting package on both nights, as well as an afternoon in the kitchen with their pastry chef. How good is that?'

'Oh wow, that's amazeballs. Bet you wish you were allowed to bet on that. You and lover boy could have a right bonk fest there.'

'I was about to tell you off for being crass again, but you've given me an idea.'

'Which is?'

'For Jamie and I to go on a mini-break together.' My eyes glaze over dreamily. 'Somewhere secluded, out of the city… a roaring fireplace and a bar. My apartment is fine and all, but Connor does live there, too.'

'Why don't you just go to Jamie's place? Have you seen it yet?'

'Slow down,' I tut at her. 'We've only just got back in touch.'

'Says the woman who already wants to go on a mini-break with him. I bet you're even thinking about asking him to be your plus one at the fundraiser.' She eyes me suspiciously and my cheeks redden, giving me away. 'I *knew* it. You're such a saddo.'

'I'm not a saddo. When you know, you know, Anna.'

'Whatever. I recommend you see his pad before thinking any further ahead. What if he lives like a minger and has smut all over his walls?'

I frown at this statement. 'I highly doubt that will be the case. He clearly takes care of himself. You've met him. You saw.'

'You never know.' Anna puts her reusable takeaway cup down on her desk and wanders round to mine. 'Some of the guys I've dated have been well turned out, but their places have been utter shitholes. So…when are you seeing him next?'

I avoid her laser stare. This is the question I've been dreading. Anna's like a sniffer dog on speed, and I don't want her going off down the wrong trail with this one.

'I… eh… I don't know. I'm waiting for him to get in touch.'

'What? Why?' she asks. 'You should text him. That's not being too keen, as long as you keep it light and flirty.'

Oh, please don't go down this route, Anna.

'He'll be in touch.' I smile sweetly at her. 'I know it. Just have to be patient.'

'No, you don't. If he's a good guy he'll be pleased to hear from you whether it's five minutes or five hours since you last saw him. Text him now. It'll be a good test of his character.'

I hesitate, unsure how to manage Anna's persistence. Unfortunately, she reads me like an attention-seeking post on social media.

'You don't have his number.'

'Not exactly.' I wince, suddenly interested in what's on the computer screen in front of me.

'Why the bleep not?'

'Because he called me from a landline on Saturday night before we met up and he hasn't given me his mobile number yet.'

'Who uses landlines anymore? And why wouldn't he give you his mobile number? Tell me exactly how it went down.'

'It's fine, Anna. Don't make a big deal out of it. He asked for my number as he was leaving yesterday, and I wrote it down on a scrap of paper. I expected him to punch it into his phone and then call mine, so I had his number too, but he didn't.'

'And why didn't you ask for it?'

'I didn't want to come over too keen.' I resume fiddling with my stationery. 'You taught me that. I was following your advice. Plus, when I gave him my number, he said he'd be keeping it very safe. It was sweet actually. Then he kissed me *really* passionately and left.'

Anna purses her lips as if she's wrestling with herself to hold something back. She returns to her desk and sits down.

'What's going on, Anna? What are you thinking?'

'I'm thinking – sorry Steph – there's something a bit off about that. He took your mobile number then used diversion tactics to take your focus off the fact he didn't give you his. It doesn't smack of someone totally genuine, and it's making me wonder what he's got to hide.'

'Nah, you're wrong.' I firmly reject this. 'You're over-dramatising things again – looking for a story that's simply not there. Maybe you should cut your Netflix binge-watching down a bit. These shows are messing with your sense of reality.'

She throws back her head and laughs loudly. 'That's rich coming from you, little Miss I'm-living-and-breathing-my-very-own-Hollywood-romcom.'

'Shut it.' I chuck a screwed-up piece of paper over the computer monitor at her, and she ducks out of the way still chuckling to herself. 'He'll be in touch. But if I don't hear from him in the next day or so, I'll call the landline number he called me from.'

'Sure, whatever. I guess all I'm saying is be careful, Steph. I don't want you to get hurt. Maybe the next lesson I need to teach you is not to fall too hard too fast.'

Here we go again.

'You and Connor are as bad as each other,' I say.

'Or we're good friends wanting to look out for you. At least consider that a possibility before you write us off.'

I'm about to respond that there's a difference between looking out for me and being way too overprotective when our boss, Lizzie, unexpectedly breezes into the office looking distracted.

'Morning,' I call across to her.

She looks across at me without really seeing me, then snaps her fingers in a moment of clarity. 'Ah, Steph, yes. Can I have a word?'

'Of course.' I follow her into her office and close the door behind me. 'How are things going with the venue for the spring fundraiser? Do you need me to do anything?'

'Everything is great.' She leafs through some papers on her desk, clearly looking for something. 'I wanted to ask you something. The extra frontline work you're doing with our young people. Is it working for you? Giving you the sense of fulfilment you're seeking, I mean.'

'I think so. Why do you ask?'

'Well, I was wondering if you'd like to join me at my appointments this morning? I'm meeting with the MSP for Edinburgh North and Leith to discuss the youth crisis support available in the area, and then I've got my monthly update with our accountants.'

'Sounds interesting.' I purse my lips thoughtfully. 'Any particular reason for wanting me to come along?'

Lizzie stops what she's doing and meets my eye.

'I want to help you understand that you can feel connected to the cause in other ways: for example, through convincing a politician to fight for more emergency resources, or finding accounting opportunities to cut costs so we can divert more money to the frontline.'

'OK, sure.' I shrug. 'If you think that will help.'

Lizzie emits a peep of satisfaction as she snatches up the document she was looking for and finally looks at me. 'It will help. How do I know? Because I was exactly in your shoes once, before I set up Edinburgh Youth Kickstart. Now grab your stuff and let's go.'

I hurry back to my desk for my coat and handbag, noticing that Lizzie's already on her way back out the door.

'What was that about?' Anna asks as I pack up my things.

'Seems I'm on an impromptu development day today. Shadowing the boss.'

'Great stuff. Enjoy. Sounds way better than what's on my to-do list.' She holds up her notepad and waggles it unenthusiastically. 'Oh, and think about what I said before about Jamie. I'm just looking out for you.'

I have absolutely no intention of entertaining any of the claptrap Anna was spouting earlier, but now is not the time to voice that. Instead, I give her a little salute and follow Lizzie out of the office.

By the end of the day, I'm mentally and emotionally exhausted. After an intense, but very interesting, morning with Lizzie, I had to endure an afternoon of Anna grilling me about Jamie again. And despite making every effort to ignore her emerging conspiracy theories about him, she's well and truly got in my head. She may have my best interests at heart as she claims, but all I have from our conversation is a growing anxiety over the fact I haven't yet heard from him. On a rational level, I'm confident Jamie will be in touch, because he said he would. What reason do I really have not to trust him? But the thing about rational thought is that it tends to disappear at the most inopportune moments, allowing your mind to bend in directions you'd never normally allow it to go.

At one point earlier, I even caved and called Jamie's landline number, only to discover – when a ballsy teenager answered and gave me a load of arrogant backchat – that it was, in fact, a payphone. That didn't help at all. With Anna's words echoing in my head, it led me to wonder why Jamie would call me from a payphone, and if I would ever hear from him again.

What is wrong with me? What does it matter how Jamie called me? The point is, he called. I've never once felt insecure over a guy. Not that there have been many. Before Connor, I had a couple of boyfriends, but those 'relationships' – apart from the teenage fumble in the woods I previously told Anna about – mainly consisted of claiming a patch of school corridor to hang out in, making awkward small talk, and a quick three-second snog when the bell rang. None of them lasted more than a few weeks and I did the dumping both times. I never had to worry about Connor either. He never so much as looked at the other girls in my year. Of course, I realise now there was probably a reason for that.

So, this feeling of insecurity is new for me, and I don't like it one bit. It's like a bug has crawled into my brain and hit 'turbo niggle mode'. When will he be in touch? *When?* I need some reassurance, and I certainly can't deal with another indefinite wait.

I'm working myself into such a lather on the bottom deck of the number ten bus I'm taking home – almost convincing myself that Jamie has in fact disappeared from my life once again – that I almost miss the message on my phone. Only when the follow-up alert comes through do I feel the buzz from my coat pocket and frantically snatch it out, praying it's not a message from Anna, Connor or any of my family.

Illuminating the screen, I see that it's a text message from a number I don't recognise, which is a good sign. I hungrily gobble up the words.

> Hi, beautiful. Hope you had a good Monday. How are you fixed for Saturday? Wondered if you fancied a walk and a bag of chips together? Jamie. X

I'm so elated that he's finally made contact, nothing else registers other than I'm going to see him again. Then, as I eagerly type out a response, a couple of things dawn on me. Firstly, there's no flirty banter; nothing that invites me to start a conversation with him. Secondly, Saturday is a *long* way away. This stops me in my tracks.

The timing I guess I'll have to put up with. Though I don't have much experience, I'm guessing that's a reasonable interval, given we're both probably working during the days in between, and we've only had two 'dates' so far (if you even count New Year). It's still very early days. The lack of invitation for an interaction flummoxes me though. He's straight to the point: a perfectly functional text in that it achieves what it sets out to do, but it's so different to Jamie's natural banter. Where's his humour and chat?

I attempt to shoehorn some light-hearted flirting into my response in a blatant fishing expedition – trying to get him to bite and give me something to get excited about – but all the responses I try out ('my Monday's better now you've been in touch', 'I'll happily share a bag of anything with you') seem a bit forced-slash-desperate-slash-cheesy. Which isn't a surprise – the guy asked me a direct question. The only way to respond is to answer it.

After agonising over this for the rest of my short journey home, including the walk from the bus stop back to my apartment – of which I have no memory by the time I unlock the door – I eventually hit send on a pretty basic response.

> Hi, Jamie. Great to hear from you. My Monday was long! Hope yours wasn't as slow as mine. A walk and a bag of chips on Saturday would be lovely. What time and where? xx

As I'm slipping off my coat and boots, my phone alerts me to his reply, which is quick, at least.

Brill. 2 p.m. outside Custom House at The
Shore. See you then. X

I stare at the message, perplexed. It doesn't even ask me
to confirm this as an acceptable time and location. I can't
help feeling a little deflated by the whole exchange, but
if I can access my rational brain, I trust it will show me
this is a perfectly acceptable interaction. We've arranged
another date, I'm seeing Jamie again in a few days and he
called me beautiful. What more do I need? Maybe he's
not into messaging back and forth. Some people aren't,
and that's fine. I'm sure Connor will agree with that; he's
a rationally minded person.

'That does sound a bit strange.' Connor looks
thoughtful as he spears the sorry-looking, over-boiled
piece of broccoli on his plate.

'I was hoping you were going to tell me I'm
overthinking it.' I push my almost untouched plate aside
and rest my elbows on the table, propping up my face with
my hands glumly.

'It's always a possibility, but I've seen this guy. He's
a charmer – and sociable from the looks of things. The
first impression I got of him doesn't match the message
exchange you've described.'

'So, what do you think could be going on?'

'Honestly? I've no idea.' He adds salt to the broccoli in
a bid to make it taste more appealing. 'The only person
who knows what's going on in Jamie's head is Jamie. It's
odd, but I wouldn't freak out about it.'

'I suppose.' I tap the table with my index finger,
thinking this over. 'Anna thinks he's hiding something
because he didn't give me his number when he left
yesterday. But I have it now, so she was wrong about that.'

'Well, there you go. Let things play out and I'm sure it will all be fine.'

'You're right. I'll do that.'

I pull my plate back towards me and push my own portion of soggy broccoli around it absently. 'You don't think a walk and a bag of chips is a bit "teen movie", do you?'

Connor pauses on a forkful of mushroom stroganoff and sets it down on his plate.

'You obviously do.' His eyes show the slightest hint of amusement.

'I'm not saying that exactly… but was it unreasonable of me to think a meal out might have been on the cards? It will be the third time we've spent time together.'

'Is there a rule book on this stuff?'

'No.'

'That's a relief. Because if there was, I'd be asking for a copy.'

'Don't make fun of me, Connor.' I glare at him in a sisterly kind of way.

'I'm not, but now I do think you're overthinking things.' He puts a reassuring hand on my forearm. 'What does it matter what kind of date he suggested? The important thing is that he asked you out again. Your last two "hook ups" – sorry to be blunt, but that's what they've been essentially – have resulted in the two of you getting drunk and falling into bed together. Maybe he's trying to create a different experience.'

It's like an LED lamp has been switched on in my brain.

'Connor, you're a genius. That's exactly what it is. Jamie said he wanted to get this right. He nearly didn't come back here the other night for that exact reason. Oh, I feel so much better now. Thank you, Connor.'

'You're welcome.' He grins at me, while continuing to shovel food into his mouth. 'I'm here every evening.'

'Actually, you are.' I eye him as I finally resume eating my dinner. 'You need to get out more.'

'I do get out. Was at my mum's yesterday.'

'I mean socially. And don't say your mum is part of your social life. Family stuff doesn't count.'

Connor stops eating and meets my gaze. 'Stephy, you do realise that *you've* been my social life for the last ten years. I don't have many friends who live nearby any more – most of my old school pals have moved on.'

He digs back into his food as a pool of guilt forms in the pit of my stomach. With all this focus on finding Jamie and creating the perfect romance, I've failed to realise that if Jamie and I start to see a lot more of each other, I'll be depriving Connor of his best friend.

'Um… Connor?'

'Yes?' He avoids looking up in way that suggests he knows exactly where I'm headed.

'I'm wondering… you know… as I could be around less, if I start to see more of Jamie… whether you're ready yet to consider chatting with some of the online matches Anna's primed for you?'

I'm expecting to get a Connor-style brush off that will immediately put me back in my box; instead, he takes a deep, contemplative glug from his glass of water.

'You know, I think I might finally be.'

'Really?' I'm delighted to hear this.

'Yeah. I was chatting with my mum about stuff yesterday and she was so supportive and… almost excited at the thought of me having a boyfriend I could bring home to meet her. The way she talked, as if it was the most normal thing in the world, it made me wonder why I'm letting one bad experience hold me back.'

'It *is* normal Connor. It's normal to want to find love – if there's such a thing as normal, that is. I don't like that word, or labels in general.'

'Me neither. But, you know, it's not that simple. Things I wouldn't normally bat an eyelid at – like holding my other half's hand walking down the street, or sharing a kiss in public – are now things I'll be acutely aware of, because of the way some people are. The threat of homophobia is real, and if I'm honest, it scares me a little.'

I take Connor's hand and he looks at me with a slightly troubled expression, which makes my heart ache for him – and for every person who has had to deal with the injustice of our judgemental world.

'Then dip your toe in gently. Maybe we could have some double dates?'

'That's a bit of a passion killer for you and Jamie, is it not?' He smirks. 'Surely you don't want to buddy up *Celebs Go Dating*-style while I pick off one awful match after the next?'

'I don't mean like that. I mean when you've found someone you like. It might help you feel more at ease, and if anyone even so much as looks in your direction, I'll rip their heads off.'

'Is that not more Anna's style?'

'Not when it comes to my best friend.' I puff myself up in my chair to prove my badass-ness.

'Eh… OK then. And obviously you know Jamie will be fine with this, because you've got him all figured out.'

'Ha, ha, very funny.' I stick my tongue out at him. 'Consider it an arrangement in principle. I'll get him to rubber stamp it this weekend.'

'Or you could wait a teeny-weeny bit longer.' Connor illustrates this by holding up his thumb and forefinger poised millimetres apart. 'Maybe until you know his surname? Or what he does for a living? Or any sort of detail about his life, to be honest.'

'Fine, we'll just leave it then…' I roll my eyes as I pick up my cutlery and finally start eating my dinner, my mind continuing to pore over things.

Connor is my closest friend in the world, and I love him with all my heart, but sometimes he can be a right buzzkill. It's clear that Jamie and I are going places. Connor needs to catch the hell up.

Chapter 16

After an excruciatingly long week, Saturday finally arrives along with the beginning of March and poses the dilemma of how to kit myself out for this date.

After a ridiculous amount of deliberation and chopping and changing, something I'm not in the habit of and can only put down to pre-date nerves, my room resembles a migraine-inducing, giant patchwork quilt. I eventually decide on ankle high black jeggings, my favourite sporty jumper (not really that sporty – just fast fashion's version of it) and the barely worn Nikes I bought in the autumn sales after eyeing up Anna's ones for four months prior to that.

'What do you think?' I burst into the living room where Connor's putting away the shopping he's just brought home.

He reaches up and shoves the box of cereal he's holding into one of the top kitchen cupboards then turns and gives an appreciative whistle. 'Very sexy.'

'It's not too casual?'

'I think casual is the way to go with this date.'

'OK, cool. That's where my head was at. I've got a little extra make-up on though, and I've done my hair differently.' I spin on the spot to let Connor see the flirty curls I've tonged into the ends of my hair. 'It doesn't make me look twelve, does it?'

'No, you're fine.' Connor abandons his bags and wanders across to me, chuckling. 'Not nervous at all are you?'

'Is it that obvious?' I fiddle with my hair anxiously.

'A little. But only because I've witnessed you tearing through this place like a tornado this morning. That's why I went shopping. I could tell you needed the space to go through... whatever this process is.'

I glance across at the living room, essentially an extension of the chaos I've created in my bedroom, and laugh awkwardly as I see it properly for the first time.

'Sorry, Connor. I'll get this tidied up before I go.'

'Don't worry about it. I can probably find a corner of a sofa to sit on.'

'No way. It would be really rude of me to walk out and leave you in this mess. I don't need to leave for another ten minutes, so I'll dump it in my room.'

'Honestly, it's not a problem.' Connor shrugs easily. 'But if you insist, let me help you.'

He follows me to the main living area and we gather up my stuff: hanging bags over our shoulders, draping clothing across forearms and grabbing smaller items such as make-up and jewellery. Much as I've had the common sense not to overdress for the occasion, it apparently didn't stop me considering everything from an ankle-long floaty skirt to a leopard print bodysuit, which I'm surprised I even own. What the hell was I thinking? After years of being calm and balanced, I'm borderline here. Is this what happens when you meet the man of your dreams?

We carry my stuff back to my bedroom and Connor gasps in surprise at the sight of it.

'It's like a clothes bomb went off in here, Stephy.'

'Yeah.' I wince and look around for somewhere to put the stuff we're holding, but I can't spot a single free space of furniture or floor. 'Just chuck it on top of the other stuff on the bed and I'll sort it out later.'

'There's a bed in here?' He gives me a cheeky side-glance.

'Oh, you're hilarious. Here, give it to me.'

I ditch the stuff that I'm carrying on to the bed and then take the rest from Connor and do the same with it. Surveying the mess that used to be my bedroom, I let out a little peep of 'I'm dreading having to deal with this later'. It now looks less like a giant patchwork quilt and more like a ball pit – if ball pits were filled with textiles instead of colourful plastic balls.

'Right then...' We leave my room and I deliberately close the door behind me in the hope that will make the chaos disappear. 'I'd better go. Wish me luck.'

I offer Connor a faltering smile that betrays a combination of unquenchable excitement and jangling nerves.

'You don't need luck.' Connor pulls me into a bolstering hug and plants a kiss on the top of my head. 'He's not blind or stupid. I might not fancy you like that, but if I were straight, you'd never have the chance to be with anyone else, because I'd never let you go.'

'Aww, thanks, Connor.' I hug him back. 'Then maybe all I need to do is not scare the life out of any more bearded strangers like I did last time. And hopefully Jamie is well on the path to falling in love with me.'

Twenty minutes later, I hop off the bus at Custom House at The Shore, right next to where the Water of Leith joins the Albert Dock Basin. The whole area is busy with weekend visitors – the fact that it's a peaceful, sunny day and the first to reach a temperature of double figures

155

this year makes it more of a draw than usual. The Leith Market is set up in the cobbled car park of Dock Place and I'm pleased to see the market traders doing a roaring trade. Many times, I've passed on the bus in the pouring rain and whistling winds and felt so sorry for them. A beautiful day must make all the difference to their spirits – and sales.

With so much foot traffic and the pavement obstructed by people waiting at the bus stop, I climb the regal stone steps of Custom House to avoid causing any additional blockages to the flow of pedestrians. It also happens to be a helpful vantage point from which to spot Jamie approaching. I'm right on time, so he should be here any second. Just as I'm checking my phone to make sure he hasn't sent a message saying he's late, a familiar and unwelcome voice crashes through my consciousness.

'*Steph*. Hey, Steph. *OMG*. I can't believe I've bumped into you.'

I look up in mild horror to see my sister climbing the steps towards me.

'Kayleigh? What are you doing here?' I glance around me self-consciously, now willing Jamie to be late. 'You normally turn your nose up at any mention of Leith.'

'I'm here for the market.' She announces this with a flick of her long dark hair, then gives me one of her superficial hugs. 'It's vegan week – first Saturday of every month apparently. I just *had* to get in on that.'

'But you're not vegan.'

'No, but it'll look great on my Insta. All these quaint little stalls with their artisanal produce. It's perfect.'

'You're such a fake.' I shake my head at her disdainfully.

'Hey, I'm not. I don't have to be vegan to support the vegan movement. It's going to save the planet, you know.'

156

I suck air between my teeth as this comment jars with me. Funny how Connor being vegetarian was such an issue and an inconvenience, but when it's for the right audience Kayleigh suddenly sees veganism as a tool for self-promotion. I'm about to respond to that effect, but then stop myself and try to rise above it.

'A better way to support it would be to actually become vegan,' I say instead.

'Well, yeah. But if I do that, I'll have to stop wearing silk... and wool... and leather shoes.' She looks at me through terrified eyes, as if she's found out there's a price on her head and she's fleeing the country.

'Tragic.' I roll my eyes. 'You know, you could just do the dietary thing, and it would still help the planet. You don't need to become an ethical vegan.'

'*Hmm...*' She considers this new information as if it's a priceless gem. 'That is a good idea. I could Insta my journey to veganism: the wins and the struggles. My followers would love that...'

I tune out as she witters on about this prospective project, my mind on other things. As I perform another anxious scan of the vicinity, there's still no sign of Jamie, but now I can't decide whether that's a good thing or not. Him being late means I can hopefully still get rid of Kayleigh before he arrives, but it also means he's... well, late – which at worst, could mean he's not going to show. I check my phone. It's 2:08 p.m. He's not overly late, but the absence of any message to explain is causing an uncomfortable churning in my gut.

'So, anyway...' I interrupt Kayleigh's diatribe, having not heard any of the last sixty seconds. 'You should get on and get your selfies done.'

'They're not selfies, Steph.' Kayleigh pouts. 'They're a cultural culinary exploration. I just happen to be in a lot of them, because my followers need to see me. Sort of like a branding thing.'

'Sure, whatever.' I continue to look around apprehensively.

'Hey, what's up with you?' Kayleigh picks up on my behaviour. 'You seem uneasy.'

Damn it. Her and her bloody juice radar.

'Me? Oh, I'm fine. Waiting for, um, a friend, but they're late.'

Kayleigh narrows her eyes and looks me up and down. I swear I even see her take a sniff at me, but perhaps that's my overactive brain playing tricks. I do my best to look natural.

'Who are you meeting?' she asks.

'Eh… Anna.' I look away guiltily as I say this.

'Right… why don't I believe you?'

'Hey, Steph.' A grinning Jamie appears on the steps out of nowhere. 'Sorry I'm late.'

Bollocks. This was the last thing I wanted.

Seeing Kayleigh standing there, he leans in and plants a kiss on my cheek instead of the more intimate embrace I had hoped would kick off this date. Then he stands back politely, waiting to be introduced. Kayleigh looks delighted that she's managed to inadvertently gatecrash what is very obviously a date. She cocks her head expectantly, and with the two of them silently and patiently watching me, I have no choice but to do introductions.

'Jamie, this is Kayleigh. Kayleigh, Jamie.'

They smile at each other politely and say hello. I hope that leaving it at that will make things awkward, and that Kayleigh will do the right thing and head off on her merry way. Unfortunately, that's not even close to Kayleigh's style.

'Jamie, I'm Steph's sister. I know we don't look alike. Sometimes I wonder if one of us is adopted.' She emits her signature tinkling laugh: totally false and which grates on me like a blister in a pair of cheap shoes.

'Nice to meet you.' Jamie continues to smile politely at her. 'I can actually see a bit of a resemblance.'

This comment, though well intentioned, earns Jamie a filthy look from both of us. He immediately picks up on this.

'It's only very slight. So… Kayleigh, what are you up to on this fine day?'

'She's going to the market.' I fill in for her to prevent Kayleigh from giving an unnecessarily long response or revealing a window into her poisoned soul. I don't want anything scaring Jamie off at this early stage.

'That's right,' she simply confirms.

Relieved that she's picked up on my steer, I'm hoping that will be it and she'll trot off to entertain her online followers, but it quickly becomes clear there's a reason why she's not talking about herself for once.

'You look kind of familiar, Jamie…' She makes a show of trying to work out where she knows him from. 'I'm wondering if we move in the same circles.'

This is an out and out lie. It's Kayleigh's way of getting someone to share information about themselves without her having to do anything as grubby as ask for it.

'I'm from the west of Scotland, so it's probably unlikely,' says Jamie.

'Ooh, I know people from there. Which part?'

'South Lanarkshire.'

'And you live here in Edinburgh now?'

'Currently, yes.'

Kayleigh flashes me a look, which says, 'did you know he might not be sticking around'? This makes me fume inside, but I make sure it doesn't show in my expression.

'Wait a minute...' She makes another show of searching her memory. 'You're in investments, right? I'm sure I've seen you out with Rod and his crowd.'

'Wrong,' says Jamie, and it dawns on me that he's wise to what Kayleigh's up to.

If she wants some juice, she's going to have to lower herself enough to come out and ask. She's clearly met her match and floundering – but her need to get the goss on Jamie is overriding her usual boundaries.

'I see... so what do you do, Jamie?'

I simultaneously want to give my sister a slap *and* also hear the answer, given that I don't even know this myself.

'I'm an entrepreneur,' says Jamie. 'In the business of start-ups.'

'Anything I might have heard of?'

'Unlikely.' He shakes his head.

'Have you had much success?'

'Kayleigh.' I finally jump in, unable to stomach any more of this. 'Jamie and I... we need to go. We're... having lunch.'

'How lovely.' She smiles sweetly at me. 'Anywhere nice? I hear there's a fabulous new seafood restaurant that's opened up at Newhaven harbour.'

Like I'd tell you. You'd probably turn up.

'Nowhere you'd be interested in,' I reply.

To my relief, Kayleigh's realised she's not going to get anything else out of this encounter, so she's lost interest.

'Right, yes, I must go, too.' She gives what I think is meant to be an alluring shake of her raven-coloured hair. 'Great to meet you, Jamie. I'm sure I'll see you again soon.'

Not if I can help it.

'Good to meet you, too, Kayleigh.' He flashes her one of his dazzling smiles and I swear I see her go slightly weak, before she flounces back down the steps and disappears into the crowd at the market.

'Sorry about that.' I offer Jamie a cringing apology. 'I'm sure you weren't banking on meeting Cruella de Vil today. It wasn't part of my plan.'

'It's fine.' He chuckles. 'She wasn't that bad. Based on your colourful illustrations of your family, I was expecting much worse.'

'That was her on her best behaviour.'

'Ah.'

'Can you even imagine how she would have reacted if I'd shared that our lunch arrangement is a bag of chips on a bench?'

'Now that I would have liked to see.' Jamie grins and greets me properly with a lingering kiss on the lips that leaves me wanting a lot more. 'Shall we head off?'

Chapter 17

An hour and a half later, we've walked around the docks, along to Granton and up to Trinity, returning via the network of pathways on the former railway line. Before we set off, Jamie and I had agreed to eat after our walk to feel like we've earned it – a harmonious decision that has made me feel very encouraged about our future relationship potential.

We've talked about everything from our childhood experiences and first pets to our political alliances and worldviews, and we seem very much on the same track. Unlike my family, Jamie totally gets my need to make a difference in the world. We've also had a minimum of three snog stops, having repeatedly been overcome by the chemistry between us, like there's some magnetic field sucking us together. All this leads me to think this is going very well indeed. So much so, that I've already started to daydream about our wedding: not consciously, my mind just wanders every now and then, and that's where it seems to end up.

We're walking hand in hand, tracing the Water of Leith along the final stretch before we arrive back at The Shore. The swans glide regally in the glistening water, while the ducks dabble and shake their tails, eyeing us in the hope that we'll throw them some food. They're used to humans here, quite tame and inquisitive.

'I wish we had something to feed them,' I say. 'I'm sure they're fed all the time, but I always think they look so hungry.'

'Maybe we can come back with some seeds and oats for them another day, to make sure they're being looked after. How about that?'

'That would be great.'

I gaze at Jamie, delighted by what I've just heard, while he continues to watch the ducks, unaware of my eyes on him. It wasn't quite an invite for another date, but it was good enough for me.

Eventually, we walk on and rejoin the road at Sandport Place, crossing the bridge onto the cobbled road that runs parallel to the water.

'Ready for some food?' Jamie asks me.

'*So* ready,' I reply. 'My stomach's growling at me as if I'm intentionally starving it.'

'You didn't have any lunch before you came out?'

'No.'

'I'm sorry, you should have said. We could have eaten first.'

'It's fine.' I wave away his concerns. 'Means I'll enjoy my chips even more.'

We continue walking and take a right along Bernard Street, which is home to the best chip shop in the area. As we step inside and join the small queue, the smell of fresh deep-fried food wafts around us, causing my stomach to go into full protest with a very loud gurgle-cum-roar. It sounds disturbingly similar to the noises those evil little buggers in the film *Gremlins* make when they're melting into a pile of putrid slimy stuff. Clutching at my midriff self-consciously, as if that will somehow cease the rather unfortunate and elongated gastro-orchestra, I try to ignore the fact that everyone within three feet of me has heard it.

'Hungry, love?' The elderly gentlemen ahead of us in the queue turns and asks with a chuckle. 'Skip ahead if you want. You clearly need a feed more than me.'

'I'm OK, thanks.' I shrink down with mortification as he continues to chortle to himself.

Jamie looks down at me and smiles. 'I think it's cute. Suits you.'

'My stomach sounding like a dying goblin is cute?' I look up at him incredulously.

'Everything about you is cute.'

I feel myself turn scarlet at this, and I look away bashfully.

'You won't be saying that when you hear me snoring,' I joke, in an attempt to divert the attention.

'I already have.' He nudges me affectionately. 'It's adorable.'

Well, that shut me up.

I spend the rest of the wait for our chips smarting with embarrassment and wondering what I sound and look like when I snore, imagining the worst. I'm thinking wildebeest: big snorty noises, my mouth hanging open, and a lot of drool. Horrified at this mental image, I decide I must ask Connor about it when I get home.

Jamie insists on paying for the chips and even offers an upgrade to a fish supper, which I politely decline, because a portion of chips alone always fills me up. Then, armed with our food and a couple of cans of juice, we retrace our steps along Bernard Street and wander in the direction of Albert Dock, where we make ourselves comfortable on a bench overlooking the water and the imposing Victoria Swing Bridge.

'These are delicious,' I announce with great enthusiasm. 'The small crunchy ones are the best.'

'I agree.' Jamie nods vigorously. 'Sometimes I wish they'd sell those just themselves. Reckon they'd do a roaring trade.'

'Oh, me too. I've thought that about chip shops in general so many times.'

'Ah, we're so in sync.' He slips his arm around me with a satisfied grin, while I dare a glance at him. As I catch his eye, I'm certain he's feeling everything that I'm feeling.

There's obviously no need to worry about his stark style of text messaging. If that's his way, then that's his way. Although maybe I'll casually mention it at some point.

Turning my attention back to my chips, I focus on the feeling of bliss coming from eating tasty food in the early spring sunshine, while sitting next to the hottest and most incredible man I've ever clapped eyes on. However, my zen only lasts until I feel my phone buzz in my pocket a minute or so later. Tempted to ignore it, I continue eating until it buzzes again, and curiosity takes over. Wiping my greasy fingers on a napkin, I pull my phone out of my pocket, illuminate the screen and gasp in horror as my eyes dance across the message preview in front of me.

'*Oh, you little—*'

'Everything OK?' Jamie asks.

'Um... yeah... sorry. It's fine.'

It's so clearly not fine, but I need to know the extent of the damage before I share any further. Unlocking my phone, I go into my family WhatsApp group to read the message in full.

I'm incensed at Kayleigh's audacity, feeling myself start to tremble inside. How *dare* she. I fully expected she'd go and run her mouth off the moment she had the opportunity, but to make those comments about Jamie without knowing anything about him is completely out of order. As I'm silently fuming over this, another message pops into the group, then another and another.

I feel myself reddening again, but this time it's due to white hot anger.

'Oh, *piss off*, the lot of you,' I hiss at my phone, before I even realise what I'm doing.

'Hey…' Jamie glances at me, but thankfully remains respectful of my privacy and doesn't try to look at the messages. 'You're not fine.'

'No, I'm not.'

'Want to talk about it?'

'Not really. You can probably guess what or who it is though, from our earlier run in.'

'With your sister?'

I nod.

'I thought as much.' He gives me a sympathetic squeeze. 'Let me guess, she's gone and blabbed about me to your family.'

'Spot on.' I throw him an exasperated look.

I intentionally don't mention that Kayleigh's already sowing doubt about Jamie in the minds of my family – and generally being a stuck-up cow. He doesn't need to hear any of that. It does make me wonder though – how I'll ever be able to bring a bloke into my family without them being judged and made to feel uncomfortable. Luckily, Jamie probably *is* closer to the first of Kayleigh's two categories, based on what his friend said at New Year about him going placcs.

That's it. That'll shut them up.

I quickly tap out a response and hit send.

> **Steph:**
> Kayleigh, you're so out of order! That was my news to tell, when I decided to share it. I don't know Jamie that well yet, because it's still early days, but to get you to shut the hell up, his friend said he's got him pegged as a future billionaire, so he must be successful at what he does.

I'm about to stuff my phone back in my pocket furiously, when Kayleigh replies.

> **Kayleigh:**
> Awesome! Definitely like the idea of having a billionaire in the family. Pass me his info and I'll do an online search to get the juice on him.

'I *so* will not.' I snort at her cheek.

'You "so will not" what?'

Jamie's question snaps me out of my funk. I've been so busy working myself up into a stink that I almost forgot he was there, and that's hard to do. It's a measure of how much my family – especially Kayleigh – press my hot buttons.

'Sorry, it's nothing. Kayleigh winds me up something awful.'

'I know this is rich coming from me. I've only met her for a few minutes, and you've had to deal with her for a lifetime, but you shouldn't let her get to you like that.'

'I know.' I absently stuff a chip in my mouth and chew and swallow it quickly, so I can continue. 'Easier said than done. We've never seen eye to eye. She's a self-obsessed drama queen who'd sell anyone out if it would get her ahead. And I'm...' I trail off, unsure that I want to define myself in front of Jamie.

He smiles at my reluctance. 'I'll go. Beautiful, kind-hearted and caring.'

'You make me sound like Mother Theresa. I'm definitely no Mother Theresa.'

'Well, obviously. I mean, for a start, she'd have never used the language that just came out your mouth.'

I giggle at this. 'That's only because she didn't have a sister like Kayleigh.'

'How do you know?'

'Well, if she did and she didn't lose the rag over her, she was a better woman than me.'

'I think the fact that she was Mother Theresa makes her a better woman than you. Sorry.' Jamie grins at me mischievously.

'*Hoi.*' I give him a playful push. 'I thought you were trying to make me feel better.'

'I am. But I'm also an honest guy.'

I laugh loudly and take a drink from my can of juice.

'Seriously, though,' Jamie continues. 'You're all of those things I described. You work for a charity and you care about that cause – so much that you're doing extra hours there. You were so upset that you'd hurt a total stranger's feelings that you followed him to the men's to apologise. And you're worried about the wellbeing of the ducks on the Water of Leith. I may not know you well, but I can see the kind of person you are. So that, as well as your stunning good looks, is what draws me to you… oh, and you're a good laugh too, which always helps.'

With his arm still around me, Jamie pulls me in for a delicious salt–and–vinegary kiss that allows me to temporarily forget my woes. When we pull apart, he looks at me inquisitively.

'You said you're an Edinburgh girl…?'

'Born and bred,' I confirm, slightly puzzled at him asking me this.

'Yet you had salt and vinegar on your chips, not salt and sauce. Is that a result of your family's influence? Is salt and sauce beneath them?'

'No.' I shake my head. 'They like to think chip shops are beneath them.'

Jamie laughs. 'I should have anticipated that one. I can't imagine your sister in a chippy.'

'Not unless it's a chippy that's "Instagrammable".'

'You're not a fan of social media by the sounds of things?'

'No, I'm not a fan of my sister.' I look at him, deadpan.

He laughs again. 'I'm loving this east coast humour of yours.'

'Is that what it is?'

'I don't know, maybe. It's certainly different to what I'm used to. Anna's got a bit of it, from what I remember, too. So, back to social media: I'm interested in your relationship with it.'

'Oh, don't worry, I'd pick you any day, and I never cheat,' I quip.

'Very good. I had that coming.' He closes and latches his polystyrene tray, having finished his chips well ahead of me.

I puff my cheeks out in contemplation, giving Jamie's question some proper thought. 'I'm a bit middle of the road, I'd say. I'm not that into it – not in the way that Kayleigh and Anna are – but I am on Facebook and Instagram. I only really keep up with other people's feeds, wish folk happy birthday, have the odd "to and fro" with people I know. Don't post much myself. What about you?'

'I'm not on any platforms. Came off them a while back, but you probably already know that, because apparently you searched high and low for me.' He playfully steals a chip from my tray.

'That's true, I did.' I chuckle and bat him away. 'But I didn't think I wasn't finding you because you weren't on social. I thought it was because I didn't know your surname. There are a lot of Jamies in Edinburgh, some of whom – rather unhelpfully – don't put photos of themselves on their profiles.'

'I see.'

'So, what is your surname then, Jamie? And I'm not asking so that I can stalk you online, I promise.'

My last comment causes Kayleigh's message on the WhatsApp group to suddenly spring back into my mind. It distracts me and makes me fume all over again. Jamie immediately picks up on this change of mood.

'You're thinking about Kayleigh again, aren't you?'

'Yes, how did you know?'

He reaches up and tweaks my nose. 'Because your nose is scrunched up and you have the same look on your face you had when you were reading her message. Do I need to up my game further to help you put her out of your mind altogether?'

'Were you already doing that?' I frown. 'I didn't notice.'

'You weren't meant to. You're a hard one to get off topic once you've got a bee in your bonnet, you know.'

'Funny you should say that, Connor said something very similar the other day.'

'Clearly a wise man.'

Jamie takes my empty chip tray from me and pops it in a nearby bin along with his own.

'So, what's next?' he asks, as I get to my feet.

'Not had enough of me for one day?' I flutter my eyelashes at him comically.

'Definitely not. How about we go back to yours and watch a movie or something? I noticed you have a TV in your room.'

'OK, sure. I have Netflix too, so we'll have plenty of films to choose from.'

I'm so delighted he doesn't want our date to end here, it takes me a minute to twig that we're following the same pattern as our two previous encounters – only this time without the booze. Maybe that's OK though, given we've spent quality time getting to know each other this afternoon. We've eaten, we've exercised. What else could we do other than hit the pub?

We could go to his place instead of mine, my brain offers.

'What's on your mind?' Jamie asks, as we head in the direction of my apartment. 'I can almost see it ticking over.'

'Oh, I… um… was just wondering if perhaps we should go to yours instead. You know, mix things up a bit? I'd love to see your place.'

I glance at him in time to see a look of uncertainty flash across his face, but it's gone before I can follow up on it.

'Nah, my place isn't as cosy and inviting as yours,' he says. 'Plus, I don't have Netflix. We'd be relying on there being something to watch on Freeview.'

'I don't mind that. I'm sure we we'd find something half decent.'

'Not sure about you, but I'd rather not spend the afternoon watching a kid's film or something my gran used to nod off in front of. Come on, let's just go to yours and we'll do mine another time.'

'All right then.'

I study his face, searching for any trace of the expression that was there before, but he simply grins back at me, causing me to cast aside any concerns. His reasoning makes perfect sense. I'll see his place eventually and get to know more about his current limbo situation – whatever that's all about.

We walk all the way to my apartment, which while I enjoy our walks together, leaves me feeling a bit weary. Jamie's energy levels appear to be limitless.

Unlocking my front door, we step inside and take off our jackets.

'You can head into my bedroom and start looking for a film if you like,' I say to him. 'I'll get us a cup of tea?'

'Perfect,' says Jamie. 'It's like you read my mind.'

I'm hanging up our jackets on one of the pegs in the hallway when there's a loud gasp.

'*Wow.* This is a bit different to last time I was here.'

Confused, I turn and follow Jamie's line of sight, then clamp my hand across my mouth in horror. I forgot that I left my room looking like it had suffered a nuclear explosion.

Chapter 18

'I was *so* mortified.' My face flushes in illustration of my point.

'I bet you were.' Connor chews thoughtfully on the piece of toast he's eating.

It's the next morning and I'm still reeling from bringing Jamie back to a room that looked like a rubbish tip.

'Thank you for saving the day.' I glance over at him gratefully. 'If you hadn't realised what was going on and kindly offered us the living room to hang out in, I'm not sure what I would have done. Were you really going out to meet someone or did you just make that up and sneak back into your room?'

'I went for a walk… but I might have been socialising as I did that.' He looks shifty all of a sudden.

'What does that mean?' I scrutinise Connor's face. 'Oh… were you chatting to your online matches?'

'I was.' Now it's Connor's turn to get all embarrassed. 'Just the one bloke: Lukas. On Anna's recommendation, after she vetted him to a level that would impress GCHQ. I walked along to the end of the breakwater, where the grassy bit is, and sat on a bench messaging him for about an hour. He seems cool, and he's also just come out, so we're in similar places.'

'Connor, that's wonderful. I'm so pleased for you. Are you going to meet up with him then?'

'I think so. Can we change the subject?' His face is growing redder by the moment.

'Of course.' I reach across and ruffle his hair affectionately. 'I'm pleased for you. Just you take your time with this, and I'll be ready to hear more if things progress. Anyway, I'd better go get ready. I'm heading out for Dad's birthday lunch.'

Having started off well, my morning is hijacked by Anna calling to get the gossip on my date with Jamie yesterday. I chat to her on speakerphone as I'm getting ready and soon regret this when the conversation descends into another analysis of Jamie's character and motivations towards me – all because I still don't know his surname or what he does for a living.

Anna even has me starting to wonder why I don't know these things about him, until I realise, the only reason he didn't answer my question about his surname on our date was because I got all distracted over Kayleigh's behaviour. And anyway, Jamie's and my conversations haven't really been like that. They're almost as though we've skipped a stage because we get on so well. Yesterday we were connecting at a deeper level – properly getting to know each other. That's so much more important than knowing what someone does for a living.

What's worse is when I challenged Anna on her proclamations that Jamie is 'either married with kids, living a double life or on the sex offender's register', Connor, who was part of the conversation on speakerphone, joined in and backed her up. Not to the extent that he entertained her ridiculous conspiracy theories, but he did say it sounded like Jamie was withholding information about his current circumstances. When Connor suggested I find out what's going on before taking things any further with Jamie, I decided I'd had enough and called time on the conversation.

On arriving at the restaurant in the New Town where we're having my dad's birthday lunch, I've decided that Anna and Connor aren't just wrong: they're so far off the mark, they're pissing on their own shoes (as my brother would so eloquently say). I'm also late for the lunch, which means I'm going to get it in the neck – *again*.

Pushing open the door to Malkin's, one of Edinburgh's handful of Michelin-star restaurants, I'm immediately greeted by a smiling man around my age, wearing a smart suit.

'Good afternoon, madam. Are you with the Ashworth party?'

'Yes, that's correct.' I smile back at him.

'Excellent. May I take your coat for you?'

'Oh, sure.' I slip it off and hand it to him.

'Thank you. Maria will see you to your table.' He gestures to a young woman who has materialised by his side. 'Have a wonderful afternoon.'

I trail through the fully occupied restaurant behind Maria to a table where the rest of my family are already seated. They glance up as I join them, and I'm sure I spot a look being exchanged between my mum and Kayleigh.

'Nice of you to join us.' Kayleigh wastes no time in taking a swipe at me.

'I'm only…' I glance at my phone to check the time '…oops… twenty minutes late. How did that happen?'

I know exactly how that happened: Anna and her nonsense about Jamie.

'Sorry, Dad.' I give him an apologetic hug.

'We all make mistakes.' My dad pats me on the back lightly. 'I'm glad you're here.'

Taking my seat beside Mikey, I smile gingerly at him and he gives me a 'shit happens' shrug. I then concentrate on the menu to avoid the death stares being fired at me by my mum and sister. A waiter appears at my left shoulder and pours Champagne in my empty flute, which I have to admit is very welcome indeed. I'm going to need a lot more of that if I'm going to make it through this afternoon without lamping my sister one for being such a suck and a shit-stirrer. My mum has a right to feel put out. She made all the arrangements for today and I turned up late, but Kayleigh's just point scoring. It's her favourite sport.

We make it through our amuse-bouches and our starters uneventfully. Dad enjoys reminiscing about other birthdays and family occasions over the years, which keeps Kayleigh and Mum's gossiping to a minimum. Mikey shares some entertaining work-related stories, which always give us a laugh. Had he not ended up with a career in Sales, he would have done very well as a stand-up comedian.

The food is also superb. Having ordered a starter of Orkney scallop with Iberico ham confetti and sugar snap pea foam, and a main course of Highland wagyu beef served with pommes dauphine and a spiced whisky jus, I'm in culinary heaven. Accompanied by the top-notch Australian Shiraz my dad has chosen, it takes me to a happy place I'm not sure I've experienced in the company of my own family for a very long time. Probably not since I was too young to understand what a bunch of pretentious, judgemental snobs they are – Mikey excluded, of course.

Obviously, I still love them – they are my family after all and the only one I have – but 'love' doesn't translate to 'like' a lot of the time. Especially not with Kayleigh, who has obviously decided she's not getting enough airtime at this event.

'So, Steph...' She shoots me a devilish sneer over her pan-seared halibut with parsnip puree. 'How's the lovely Jamie?'

I throw her a withering look by way of a response.

'Oh, *come on*. Tell us a bit about him.'

'Yeah, Steph, tell us. Is he a hottie?' Mikey puts on a girly tone as a way of mocking Kayleigh and I snort into my napkin to avoid guffawing loudly.

'Shut. Up. Mikey.' Kayleigh's tone is acid.

'Will you all stop it.' My mum looks around anxiously to check no one's noticed our table descending into battle of the brats. 'Honestly, you're adults, but you don't seem to know how to behave in a sophisticated environment. I thought I brought you up better than this.'

'Not me. I'm Wetherspoons' Curry Club through and through,' quips Mikey, and I share a high five with him to the disgust of both my mum and sister.

'Well, today, Michael, can I ask you to spruce up your manners a bit for the sake of your father and I?' My mum eyes him disapprovingly, shaking her head, and Mikey seems to instantly regress twenty-odd years.

'Sorry, Mum and Dad.'

I mouth the word 'traitor' across at him and he gives me a what-was-I-suppose-to-do look.

'Steph, I'd very much like to hear about this new young man of yours,' says my dad.

Kayleigh smirks with satisfaction, knowing I'm going to have to engage this time. Dad has me over a barrel with this one because it's his birthday. If I try to fob him off or tell him it's none of his business, my mum and Kayleigh will be on me like a pack of wolves. I can already see they're poised to pounce.

'Right… um… OK.' I take a sip of wine and clear my throat, stalling for time so that I can formulate a response that satisfies their curiosity, while telling them absolutely nothing of any use. 'He's a guy… obviously… around my age…' I realise this is another key piece of information I don't know about Jamie and resolve to find this out. 'He's smart and funny… we've been out a few times now, and it's going well.'

'And what does he do?' My dad goes straight for the jugular.

'He's an entrepreneur.'

'Which means?'

'Anything from being a millennial Richard Branson to a Just-Eat delivery rider,' Mickey unhelpfully pitches in.

I see my parents and Kayleigh recoil at this possibility, and I feel myself start to seethe.

'What does it matter what he does?' I challenge them. 'Wouldn't you rather I end up with a great guy who treats me well, over a rich arsehole who cheats on me and knocks me around a bit?'

'Steph.' My mother scolds me, glancing around her once more.

'They're not mutually exclusive, Steph,' says my dad. 'You could just as easily end up being knocked around by someone on the bread line. In fact, it's perhaps more likely if financial stressors are an issue.'

'Oh yeah, because money and materialist crap solve everything in life, don't they?' I throw back.

'OK, that's enough,' snaps my mum. 'Your father was trying to show an interest. There's no need for this overly defensive behaviour.'

'*Whatever.*' I plonk my cutlery down on my plate with a loud clatter that does attract attention from our fellow diners, causing my mum to sink down in her seat.

'Hey, did you not say this guy's gonna be a billionaire?' Mikey tries to rescue the situation he has inadvertently stirred up.

'That's what his friend said,' I grumble. 'I don't know how true it is. Jamie seemed embarrassed by the comment.'

'If his friend said it and your man got uncomfortable, it's probably got some truth behind it.'

'Possibly. Look, can we move the conversation on? I'm not comfortable with either Jamie or I being under the microscope.'

'I like the name "Jamie". It sounds like a name that belongs to a strong and successful young man,' my mum philosophises, completely ignoring my request. 'How about you bring him home for a meal? That way, we can all stop imagining the worst and meet the boy in person.'

'That's a good idea, Marjory,' says my dad. 'We'll get a date scheduled in.'

And as usual, I have no say in the matter.

'I'm going to the loo.' I get up and grab my handbag. 'Back soon.'

The highly attentive waiter shows me the way to the ladies, where I take refuge from the friendly fire at our table. Being in a Michelin-star restaurant, the toilets are naturally very plush, and a nicer place to hang out in than some bars I've been in. There's a beautiful aroma that I can't quite put my finger on, but if I were to hazard a guess, I'd say jasmine, lime and… freshly cut grass? Is that a thing? The communal area has very modern and expensive-looking sinks with freshly laundered mini-handtowels perfectly arranged in gorgeous little baskets beside them. There's even a chaise longue to complete the luxurious ambience.

Checking the cubicles to make sure I'm alone, I take a seat on the chaise longue, lean back against the wall, and let out a long, exhausted sigh. It takes everything I've got to resist the urge to stretch out and have a catnap. After my late night with Jamie, the stress of this morning's 'conference call' with Anna, and the subsequent verbal beating I received for being late to lunch, I'm feeling quite done in. The Champagne is also making me a little sleepy. To keep myself from nodding off, I pull my phone out of my bag, and to my delight, I see that there's a message from Jamie on my home screen.

> Hi Steph. Really enjoyed our time together yesterday. Are you free for a coffee this afternoon? I'm just grabbing a sandwich for lunch from the supermarket, but could meet in half an hour X

It's another straight to the point message, but once again it does give some indication of where Jamie's head is at. Thank goodness. Because if he hadn't led with the fact that he enjoyed our date the day before, I'd be panicking that I'm about to be dumped.

While drafting a response to let him know that I'm unfortunately tied up at the most 'unfun' birthday party I've ever attended, I decide that I should just call him. Who knows what kind of text response I'll get by having to put him off? And I'm already dying to see him again – preferably this evening once this familial torture is over.

I put my phone to my ear and wait for him to answer.

'Steph, hi.' His voice comes clearly down the line after a few rings. 'How you doing?'

'I'm good thanks, you?'

'Can't complain. Or maybe I can. Since when does a BLT sandwich include cucumber? I hate the stuff and it's made the bread all soggy and… "cucumber-y".'

'Well, that is a travesty.' I chuckle. 'You should start an online campaign to end this outrage. "#cucumbergate".'

'Maybe I will. Or maybe I'll get a life and get over it. So… coffee?'

'I'd love to, but I'm at my dad's birthday lunch right now, and I can't even make an excuse to leave early because I was late.'

'That wasn't because I kept you up till three a.m., was it?'

I try to keep my focus as the memories of what we were doing until three a.m. dance into my mind in the style of a particularly sexy mental tango.

'Um… no, not at all.' I clear my throat awkwardly. 'It is the reason I'm considering having a snooze on the chaise longue in the restaurant toilets though.'

'There's a chaise longue in the toilets?' His voice climbs half an octave, making me giggle. 'Where are you having lunch? Holyrood Palace?'

'No, obviously. I'm in a restaurant, called Malkin's. It's just off the bottom of Dundas Street.'

Jamie gives an appreciative whistle. 'I know exactly where that is. Your family do like the finer things in life.'

'Well, yes.' I purse my lips. 'But do note the fact that we're having lunch here, not dinner. That's my parents' way of *pretending* they live like the other half. They'd never fork out for a Michelin-star dinner for all of us, unless they'd saved for months, and it was a *really* special event.'

'Still. There are worse places to be.'

'That is true. It's a bit pretentious for my liking, but I do have a foodie streak in me, much as I don't like to admit it. I'm loving that side of it.'

'Good. Make the most of it. Just think about how the kids you look out for in your job don't get opportunities like that. They'd probably give their right arm to have the experience you're having right now. Not literally, of course, but you know what I mean.'

'You know, I've never thought about it like that.' I shift my position, and in trying to get comfortable, end up lying out on the chaise longue, though I'm careful to keep my shoes off it. 'You do make me think, Jamie, you know that?'

'I'm glad. It's a shame you're stuck there, because I'm only about a three-minute walk from you right now.'

I sit up suddenly. 'I thought you said you're at the supermarket?'

'I am. In Broughton, not Leith,' he clarifies.

'Ah, right. Gosh that's annoying…' I pause as an idea flits through my mind. 'Actually… I've just thought of something. Can I call you back in two minutes?'

I hang up and dash back to our table, where Kayleigh raises a judgemental eyebrow — a clear indication that she thinks I've been in the toilets far too long.

'Where have *you* been?' says Mikey. 'You got the runs or something?'

'Michael, please.' My mum screws up her face in disgust.

'No, I haven't.' I cuff the back of his head affectionately. 'When I was in the toilets I saw that Jamie had messaged, so I called him back.'

'Oh, for goodness' sake.' Kayleigh looks like she's about to throw a fit. 'Steph, could you at least *try* to be present at this meal?'

'No, wait… you don't understand. Turns out he's just along the road. He wanted to meet me for a coffee and I told him I couldn't because I'm here. Then I wondered… given you're all so interested in him, would you all like to meet him now? He could join us for dessert and coffee if the restaurant is all right with it.'

'Steph, I'm not sure about that,' starts my mum. 'It's a little unorthodox for someone to "pull up a chair" at a restaurant like this.'

'I think it's a great idea.' Kayleigh's eyes light up like a python who has detected a particularly plump and juicy mouse; Mikey simply shrugs in a gesture that says he's fine with it.

We all look to my dad; given it's his birthday celebration, he should cast the deciding vote.

'Why not,' he says. 'The more the merrier, eh? The waiting staff will be fine. I'll tell them there will be a bit extra in their tip for the trouble. I'm keen to size up this young man you've been spending time with.'

Having secured my dad's blessing – though his motives for agreeing aren't quite what I was hoping for – my mum comes round to the idea pretty quickly. As I look around at my family's eager and somewhat unsettling faces, I wonder if maybe I've had too much Champagne, and this isn't such a good idea after all.

'Well, go on then,' my mum prompts me. 'Call him back.'

'OK… sure.' I hover uncertainly for a moment, then head back to the toilets, making sure to avoid the over-enthusiastic waiter as I go. He'll also think I've got stomach trouble – heading for the ladies again so soon.

'Hi, again.' Jamie answers on the second ring.

'Hi, sorry about that. How do you feel about having that coffee after all?'

'Great. Are you sure though? Will your dad not be a bit put out?'

'It would be coffee with my family. Here at the restaurant.' I wince in anticipation of his response. 'You'll get dessert too though.' I quickly add as a sweetener.

There's a short silence and in those few seconds my mind takes me to the worst-case scenario: Jamie thinks it's way too soon for this, then decides I'm too much of a desperado and dumps me.

'OK. Let's do it,' he says eventually. 'I'll be there in about five minutes. Provided it's OK that I'm wearing jeans and a casual shirt?'

'Really? Amazing.' My hand flies to my mouth in delighted surprise. 'Jeans and a casual shirt will be fine. I was worried you might think it was too fast and then ghost me. Anna's warned me about this kind of stuff.'

Why the hell did I say that? Well done on blabbing about your insecurities, Steph.

'Hey, *we* decide the rules on us, all right?' Jamie's voice is firm and reassuring.

'All right.' I smile down the phone. 'See you in a few minutes.'

Chapter 19

Five minutes later, I'm standing outside the restaurant waiting for Jamie to appear. As I see him come around the corner from the direction of the supermarket – his grin is so broad and genuine that I can make it out from several hundred feet away – I swear my heart doesn't just flutter, it jolts into a full-on percussion rendition of 'The Hills Are Alive'. It's like the world around us fades into the background and the slow-mo kicks in, and for a moment everything is movie-perfect.

'Hi, you.' He slips his arms around my waist as he reaches me, pulling me into one hell of a greeting, before I even have the chance to say hello back.

He smells of spring air (and a little of the supermarket) and his mouth tastes of something sweet like cola.

'Hi.' I bite my lip coyly as we make every effort to control ourselves.

Given that we're about to join the rest of my family – and it's Jamie's first encounter with them – arriving at the table hot and flustered is probably not advisable.

'Any last-minute tips on how to win them over?' he jokes, and I'm amazed by how chilled out he seems.

'You're surprisingly calm.' I eye him with admiration. 'I'd be a panicked mess if it were the other way around.'

'They're only humans, aren't they?'

'I guess.' I bob my head from side to side in a non-committal way. 'Though sometimes I wonder about Kayleigh.'

Jamie chuckles at this. 'Well, I like a challenge.'

'You're sure this is OK?' I take his hand in mine. 'I don't want you to feel obliged to do this, or for you to think I'm jumping the gun given it's only the fourth time we've met up.'

'Is that all it is?' Jamie seems to ponder this for a moment. 'It feels like more — like we've skipped a few steps or something.'

'I know, right? It's like that for me too.'

'There you go then.' He gives a confirmatory nod. 'I think we're definitely in "meet the parents" territory, don't you?'

'I do.' I'm unable to hide the delighted and sickeningly loved-up smile plastered across my face.

'Great. Then lead the way, beautiful.'

We enter the restaurant, where the staff member looking after front of house has clearly been primed for this moment.

'Ah, here you are. May I take you coat, sir?'

'Thank you.' Jamie slips his jacket off and hands it to him.

I feel a slight sense of relief when I see that the casual outfit Jamie described is quite smart, then feel annoyed at myself for such a thought. It shouldn't matter at all what he's wearing.

We make our way across to the table, where my family stop mid-conversation as they see us approaching. While I'd like to think this is out of politeness to give Jamie their undivided attention, I strongly suspect that it's really because they've been discussing his suitability ahead of even meeting the poor bloke.

'Jamie, this is my mum, dad, Kayleigh and Mikey... everyone, this is Jamie,' I announce as we reach the table.

The place settings on the side of the table where I'm sitting have been moved discreetly and an extra chair added so that Jamie's able to sit with us. I consider offering him the middle seat so he's not left on the end, but since that would leave him flanked on all sides, I decide that it's better to allow him the breathing space. Instead, I sit myself next to Mikey again. The only downside to this seating arrangement is that it means we're facing Mum, Dad and Kayleigh, which is a little bit like facing an MI5 interrogation.

'Hello, Jamie.' My dad gets to his feet and reaches across to shake Jamie's hand. 'I'm Ron. Good to meet you.'

'Good to meet you, too.' Jamie clasps his hand firmly and confidently, I notice. 'Happy birthday and thanks very much for allowing me to crash your party.'

'Not at all. It's a pleasure to have you join us.' My dad smiles broadly at him.

Well, that's a good start. One down, three to go.

My mum's next to get up.

'Jamie, it's lovely to meet you.' She holds out a hand and clasps his gently. 'I'm Marjory. We're pleased you could join us.'

'Thank you, Marjory. As am I.' Jamie bows his head a little then fixes my mum with such piercing eye contact, she actually blushes.

One hundred per cent success rate with two of the most difficult members of my family. I'm impressed.

Jamie then turns to Kayleigh with a genuine smile.

'Kayleigh, it's lovely to see you again. Did you get some good material from your visit to the market yesterday? I do hope it was a fruitful venture for you.'

My mouth hangs open as Kayleigh simpers like a shy five-year-old.

'It was, Jamie. Thanks for showing an interest. I broke my record for likes and comments with a rather spectacular shot that really captured the core essence of veganism.'

'Fantastic. You must show me that later.'

Wowsers. Jamie's like a magician. Or a wizard. I need to get him to teach me how to cast these spells on my family.

'Jamie, mate.' Mikey reaches around the back of me and shakes his hand in a very buddy-buddy way. 'Great to have you with us. This party's needing a bit of life in it. You a pint in the pub over a game of footie man, are you?'

'Definitely,' says Jamie.

'What's your team?'

'Partick.'

'I'm a Celtic man, but I'll let you off, given we've demolished Partick in almost every game since ninety-five.' Mikey gives Jamie a wheeler-dealer wink.

'Very gracious of you.' Jamie plays along perfectly. 'Celtic are my number two. I support them when I need a win.'

As I watch this exchange, it's clear by his expression that Mikey's smitten.

'Enough of the football chat,' my dad pipes up. 'Jamie, a more important question, are you a whisky man?'

'Never known to refuse a malt, Ron.' Jamie takes a sip from the glass of water that's been poured for him by the waiter.

'Splendid. Let's get the sommelier across for some recommendations with dessert then.'

Observing this scene as it unfolds around me, I couldn't be happier. With things going the way they are – that is very, *very* well – and my subconscious resuming the wedding daydreams, I want nothing more than Jamie to be accepted by my family, and it seems just that is happening. I can't believe my luck. With Connor it was like an endless losing battle, but this… this makes for a much easier time of things.

Once the sommelier has offered some guidance with the whisky and we've ordered our desserts – an incredibly difficult task given the delicious options on offer – my family turn their attention back to Jamie.

'So, Jamie, what is it that you do?' my dad asks. 'Steph tells us you're an entrepreneur, but we're a little unclear as to what that means.'

Oh great. This is where things have the potential to go south very quickly.

Jamie, however, doesn't miss a beat.

'It's pretty straightforward. I started my own business when I was twenty-five, after taking on a couple of different corporate roles and realising that world wasn't for me.'

'It's not really for anyone,' says Mikey. 'We all secretly dream of sticking two fingers up to it one day – preferably after a huge lottery win.'

'Mikey…' My mum shoots him a warning look.

'What?' He looks at her defiantly. 'I'd put money on it that's true. So many folk make out their careers are the be-all and end-all, but that's because it's the only thing that makes them feel worthwhile. It's all a game. Just a way for the most power-hungry people to get rich and satisfy their egos.'

'That's certainly a colourful description.' Jamie chuckles, as my mum continues to aim disapproving looks at Mikey. 'Though I have some understanding of your perspective on it, Mikey. I felt I was working hard to line someone else's pockets. Also, some of the senior people I reported to wouldn't listen to the great ideas of their more junior colleagues, which meant many opportunities were missed.'

'So you decided to take the initiative?' my dad prompts, to put Jamie back on track to answering his question.

'Exactly that. I started dabbling with projects in my free time to see what would stick and I got lucky.'

'What did you get lucky with?' My mum leans in, intrigued.

'That's the thing. I can't share specifically because I'm bound by a non-disclosure contract.'

My whole family seem to visibly deflate at this revelation. All other than Kayleigh, that is.

'That's very convenient.' Her eyes narrow slightly. 'Have you any other successes that you can share with us?'

'I understand your scepticism.' Jamie shrugs easily. 'It's difficult not being able to talk about my projects. I'm the equivalent of a "ghost writer" in the publishing industry. I produce the goods, but I have an arrangement in place to make sure that the credit goes elsewhere. Businesses come to me to have their proposals turned into reality.'

'So, you run a manufacturing company?' asks my dad.

'That would be the best description for it, yes. Although it's more than that. I do the R&D, add some creative flare and bring the ideas to life.'

'R&D?' My mum appears to search her memory for what this means.

'Sorry, research and development,' says Jamie. 'It's sort of a scientific process.'

'And are you even able to share what industry you do this work in?' asks Kayleigh, not letting Jamie off the hook.

'It's a mix really. Once you know a few basic elements, it's a broad field. I've delivered contracts for toiletries, skincare products, soft drinks, all sorts of stuff. If you think of big brands like Unilever, it's like that but on a much smaller and narrower scale – for more of an artisanal market.'

Kayleigh's ears prick up at this. 'Have you produced for any of the market traders at the Edinburgh markets?'

'I couldn't possibly confirm that,' Jamie grins, which immediately gives away that he has.

While my family share impressed nods, I almost burst with pride, while making a mental note to share this new information with Anna later. This'll finally get her off her quest to out Jamie as some sort of fraud.

Our desserts arrive along with the whisky, the two waiters who bring them offering a detailed description of what's on each of our plates.

'Oh, my word, that has to be the best thing I've ever tasted.' I take another mouthful of my caramelised pear souffle with salted caramel drizzle, dark chocolate dust and honeycomb pebbles, and sigh with pleasure.

'You are quite the foodie, aren't you,' says Jamie.

'It's my guilty pleasure.'

'I wouldn't call that something to feel bad about.'

'It is in my line of work. It's hard not to be reminded of those who go without when I'm indulging like this.'

'Fair enough.' He nods understanding.

'You know what you can do to address that unnecessary burden?' Kayleigh flicks her hair precociously. 'Get a better job in a better paying industry and stop playing rescuer to the down and outs.'

This comment riles me and I'm about to bite back and call Kayleigh out for being the heartless snob that she is, but I think better of it. I realise I'll get told off like a naughty child by my parents in front of Jamie, mortifying in itself, and I don't want him to see too much of this side of my life. Kayleigh brings out the worst in me – no question – behaviour I'm quite frankly ashamed of. I seem to lose control because she winds me up so much, and I don't want Jamie beginning to question if I am who he thinks I am.

Instead, I pretend my mouth's too full to answer, while counting to ten in my head to help the moment pass without incident.

'How's the Balvenie, Jamie?' my dad asks to fill the silence.

'Superb, Ron,' Jamie inspects his whisky while he says this. 'I've only had the twelve-year-old before. This twenty-one-year-old PortWood is in a league of its own – almost creamy but with a sort of sweetness and spiciness to it as well. It's got a long finish that stays with you.'

'I wouldn't describe it much differently myself. You certainly seem to understand your whiskies, young man. I'm impressed.'

'I took a tasting course once upon a time. Can remember a few things from it.'

'Aww… look at them,' Mikey whispers in my ear. 'Jamie's like the son Dad never had.'

I try to stifle the giggle that suddenly rises up.

'Everything OK?' Jamie looks at me curiously.

'Yeah, fine.' I squeeze his thigh under the table reassuringly and lower my voice. 'You're doing great.'

After dessert, we have coffee, which comes with homemade petit fours that none of us have any room for, but we force them down all the same. The conversation flows easily. Perhaps more easily than it normally does between us, and I can't help thinking that Jamie's the perfect addition to our dysfunctional set-up. He brings a calm that's not normally there, but also seems to be able to balance the stuffiness of my parents and Kayleigh with Mikey's and my need for some level of banter. If I didn't now know Jamie to be a successful businessman, I'd wonder if he were trained for undercover work. His ability to slot right in is almost uncanny.

By the time we're getting up to leave, I'm actually able to say that I enjoyed my afternoon with my family: a first in my adult life.

'Bye, Mum. Bye, Dad. Kayleigh… Mikey.'

I make my way around them one by one, my brother giving me a big hug, while Kayleigh offers her usual superficial one. I note however, that she lingers a bit, fluttering her eyelashes, when Jamie reaches in for a polite goodbye kiss on the cheek. Perhaps having Kayleigh approve of my new boyfriend isn't as good as I first thought. I may have to watch her around him.

'Marjory, Ron, thank you ever so much for allowing me to join you this afternoon,' says Jamie. 'It was extremely kind and generous of you.'

'You're very welcome, Jamie,' says my mum. 'It was a real pleasure to have your company. I hope we didn't scare you off.'

'Not at all. You'll be seeing me again for sure. And, Ron, I hope you'll enjoy the rest of your birthday.'

'Thank you. I'm sure I will,' says my dad. 'There's a log fire, an armchair and a whisky cabinet with my name on it. Tell me, Jamie. Do you play golf?'

'I don't.' Jamie shakes his head. 'But I'm always up for trying something new.'

'That's clear from your profession. How would you like to join me on the course sometime? I'm a member of Craiglockhart Golf Club.'

'I'd be happy to. Sounds great.'

'What did I tell you?' Mikey leans in and raises a comical eyebrow at me. 'He's never once asked me to go golfing with him.'

I chuckle by way of a response, but mentally add Dad to the same to-watch list as Kayleigh. I'm all for my family warming to Jamie, but I've a feeling I'll be fighting them off before long.

Chapter 20

The day after my dad's birthday lunch, I find myself with some rare space in my calendar at work, so I decide to take that opportunity to visit Mrs Carmichael and pick up the additional item she's offered for next month's fundraiser. With all the extra hours I've been doing, I haven't had a chance yet and I know she'll be wondering where I am.

Just as I'm heading out the door, Lizzie pops her head out of her office and calls after me.

'Steph, where are you off to? I was thinking we could take a look at the draft strategy again. I'd appreciate your eye on this new version.'

'Oh…' I hesitate. 'I'd love to, Lizzie, it's just that Mrs Carmichael's still waiting for me to pick up that extra item for the auction, and I'm working late all this week because of those two new cases that have been assigned to me.'

'Absolutely.' Lizzie waves her suggestion away. 'It was just a thought.'

'How about we do it over lunch?'

'Perfect. It's a date. I'll treat us to something nice.'

I give her a thumbs up and hurry out of the door with the thought that, right now, I'm not only shadowing Lizzie, I'm emulating her behaviours. She's always rushing around, thinking about ten things at once. It's not my usual style, but I find myself feeling energised, excited even. Busy may not always equal productive, but in this case, with everything I'm getting involved in, I really do feel like I'm starting to make more of a difference. Lizzie's certainly showing me a whole new way of thinking, and it's fuelling something in me that's like an itch I need to scratch.

Half an hour later, I pull up outside Mrs Carmichael's mansion and crunch my way across the gravel driveway to her enormous porch. I've barely rung the old-fashioned clanger of a doorbell when the door opens, and Mrs Carmichael's housekeeper greets me with a kind smile.

'Steph, how are you? Dorothy's in the drawing room waiting for you. Come on in.'

'Thanks Angelika.' I follow her across the high-ceilinged entrance hall, past the grand mahogany staircase (a feature I love of this old house) and into the drawing room.

'Steph, how lovely of you to stop by.' Mrs Carmichael gets up slowly from her embroidered armchair to greet me when I enter the room. 'I was delighted when you called. Was starting to wonder if you had received my message.'

I pull an apologetic face. 'Sorry, Mrs Carmichael, I did hope to come last week, or over the weekend, but I've had so much going on.'

'Well, why don't you sit down and relax, and Angelika will bring us some tea and cake.'

'That sounds lovely, thank you.'

I turn to thank Angelika as well, but it seems she has already left the room to prepare the refreshments without me noticing. Instead, I take a seat in the armchair opposite Mrs Carmichael in front of the huge cast-iron fireplace, which is belting out such a heat, I wonder if my eyebrows are at risk.

'I know we are in spring now,' she says. 'But I find I feel the cold so much more these days.'

'It is still a bit chilly. Best to keep yourself cosy.' I eye her frail frame, wondering if she's lost some weight since I last saw her.

'Mmm… quite. How are things at work?'

'They're good.' I bob my head enthusiastically as I say this. 'I'm working on our April fundraiser as you know, and I've been doing some work on the frontline again as a key worker. I get a lot out of that side of things. The people I'm working with are in very difficult situations, so I'm helping them get training, find work, that sort of thing, so that they can move into accommodation of their own.'

'It is so awful that youngsters find themselves in these situations.' Mrs Carmichael looks truly saddened by this. 'They should be nurtured and supported by their families at that age.'

'You're absolutely right. Unfortunately, though, that's not the case for various reasons. That's why we do what we do. Did I tell you that Lizzie, my boss, has been giving me experience in other areas of the organisation?'

'You did not. That sounds interesting.' Mrs Carmichael sits forward in her seat, prompting me to tell her more.

'It's very interesting. I obviously already had an understanding of the work management does, because Lizzie shares things at our team meetings, but this has given me some solid experience – and I'm pleased to find I'm picking things up quite quickly. Lizzie's a bit of a whirlwind, so she can sometimes be hard to keep up with, but she says I'm a natural. Especially with the relationship management and influencing side of things – you know, meeting with MPs and all – and I've got my head around the financials way faster than I would ever have expected.'

'That's wonderful, Steph. And what will you do with these newfound skills?'

I puff out my cheeks whilst I consider this question. 'I'm not sure. But the whole thing has got me energised and thinking about what's next for me. I'm obviously more capable that I've allowed myself to believe – probably as a result of the endless stream of criticism from my family – and maybe I need to find a way to put these capabilities to good use… in the charity sector, obviously.'

'Well perhaps you should do just that. Show that family of yours what you're made of.'

She gives me a knowing wink, which makes me smile. I sometimes feel like Mrs Carmichael is trying to live vicariously through me. Having grown up privileged, and never having worked or had the experiences some women now take for granted, I feel like she's not just lonely, but also bored, rattling around in this big house by herself.

'So, tell me, apart from work, what else is keeping you so busy?' she asks. 'Is there perhaps a young man on the scene? I remember you telling me during one of our telephone conversations that you were courting a few different men. How exciting. That would have been frowned upon in my day.'

I'm used to this kind of chat with Mrs Carmichael. She probably knows way more about me than I should share with her, given the 'professional' nature of our relationship. But as she's living alone and has very little company, except for Angelika and her gardener, I don't see any harm in being another source of companionship every now and then. Also, if I don't share when she asks, there are a lot of long silences and even longer conversations about the contents of the artisan shops of Edinburgh. I learned that lesson the hard way.

'Now when was that?' I make a show of trying to remember our last conversation. 'Oh yes, I think that was when I was doing the online dating thing and I'd been on a few first dates.'

'That's right. When we caught up about my dietary requirements for your fundraiser. This online dating thing sounds like oodles of fun.'

A mental montage of all the worst elements of my brief online dating experience races through my mind: innuendos, dick pics, inappropriately intrusive questions, borderline verbal abuse.

'It was... a learning experience.' There's no way I'm bursting Mrs Carmichael's romantic bubble with the bare-faced (or as one of the photos in my messages went – bare-arsed) truth.

'Did any of these young suitors turn into something more long term?'

I almost choke with laughter as I try to think about any of the blokes I interacted with as 'suitors'. Oh, how the world has changed.

'No, but I am dating someone now. Someone I met at New Year – at the street party.'

'How lovely.' Mrs Carmichael's face lights up with interest. 'Tell me all about it.'

I happily launch into the story of how Jamie and I met, and everything that's happened since. While I'm in full flow, Angelika appears with a tray of goodies – a huge pot of tea and a selection of homebaked cakes to rival even the best of coffee shops – and we dig in. I moan with satisfaction as I bite into a moist slice of date and walnut loaf with a slather of butter on it.

'Angelika, you are one mean baker,' I say to her when she pops back in to check we're all right.

'Thank you, Steph.' She backs off to leave us in peace once again, giving me a semi-bow in the process.

It's something that still feels surreal, despite the fact I've visited many times now: like I've been transported back through time to Downton Abbey.

'So, there you are...' I say to Mrs Carmichael once I've given her a slightly edited rundown of my budding relationship with Jamie, so not to make her blush. 'That's where things are at.'

'I am so pleased for you, Steph.' She sips from her china cup reflectively. 'This issue your friends have raised about Jamie not sharing information about himself, is it not a concern to you?'

Damn it. In trying to keep things clean, I've overshared in a different respect.

I take a moment to weigh up how to answer this. 'No. Well, maybe a bit. But only because Connor and Anna won't let it go. It probably is a bit odd that Jamie's not shared some of these details, but there have always been reasons why – like we've gotten distracted or whatever. And he has told me he's in a "complicated" situation. I figure it's just really sensitive and he'll share it when he's ready. Do you think I should be concerned?'

Mrs Carmichael ponders my question whilst staring into the flames of the fire. 'I would like to say to you, Steph, to follow your heart; that men have pride that gets in the way of many things. However, I am aware that my experience in this area is somewhat outdated. When I met my dearly departed husband, George, it was a much simpler affair. Our families knew each other, so we were introduced, and we were enraptured with each other right from the start.'

She smiles wistfully at this memory, while I gag a little at the thought of my family setting me up with some high-earning, narcissistic arsehole and acting like they'd given me the gift of life in the process.

'This world has become a complicated place,' Mrs Carmichael continues, drawing my attention back to her. 'With all that I see on the news, I feel compelled to urge you caution. To not get too involved emotionally until you have the facts…'

OK, it's way too late for that.

'…and protect yourself from any possible hurt that may come your way – whether that be to your heart or other-wise. You are a strong, independent young woman, Steph. You do not need a man to validate you, and any man who deserves your time should show you mutual honesty and respect. That is what got George and I through all those decades together.'

Mrs Carmichael looks at me expectantly and I can feel myself flapping inside. I thought it was pretty much guar-anteed that she'd go with the romance side of things and reinforce my point of view, particularly given her earlier (and somewhat naive) comment about online dating. Turns out she's more aware of the world around her than I thought. This is unsettling, because I can easily write my friends off for being irrationally overprotective, but I can't do the same in this situation.

'I… um… I think your words are very wise,' I manage eventually. 'I shall heed them.'

'Good girl.' Mrs Carmichael seems pleased with my response. 'Now have some more tea and cake. The chocolate gateau is simply divine.' She pops a large slice on a plate and hands it to me with a fork before I have the chance to decline.

We chat some more, but as time is ticking and I need to get back to work, I make my excuses sooner than I might ordinarily have. Crunching my way back across the driveway, with Mrs Carmichael's latest donation for the fundraiser tucked under my arm, I feel queasy from all the cake. But there's also another unpleasant feeling that I recognise as a seedling of doubt: because it's very hard to ignore so many voices of concern.

Chapter 21

For the next few weeks, things are quite blissful – provided I don't think too deeply about them. Because while I am now experiencing some doubt about Jamie, I'm not yet ready to face up to that. And I definitely don't want Anna and Connor to know about it.

Jamie and I spend most of each weekend together: mainly hanging out at mine, watching films, cooking nice meals or going for walks, which often culminate with us stopping off for a beer or a coffee at The Shore. Everything is perfect, apart from one thing: I still only see him at weekends.

'Yeah, why is that?' Anna locks her laser-beam stare on me over her computer screen, as I get up to make myself a coffee one Monday morning in late March.

'I… um… I don't know. I've never asked.' I attempt to slope off to the kitchen, but she's having none of it.

Unfortunately – and to my deep frustration – sharing the news about Jamie's job with Anna the day after my dad's birthday lunch didn't put her off her quest to 'find out what he's hiding' as I had expected. Instead, I was subjected to a number of interrogations over the weeks.

'So… he runs a business, but he can't tell you what it's called or anything about it,' she had said on one occasion. 'I assume you also still don't know where he lives or his surname either. All very handy for him: it means you can't look him up online.'

'Oh, he's not on social media,' I had replied. 'Apparently came off it a while back.'

'This gets better and better.' Anna's face had become incredulous. 'Steph, are you not even the slightest bit suspicious about these things? Is there not even an ounce of doubt in that lovely, but slightly naive head of yours?'

I had stood my ground. '*No*. I trust Jamie. These are all insignificant details. It's who he is when he's with me that counts. He's just met my family for goodness' sake, and he's going to play golf with my dad. I know he's looking for this to be long term, and I have no real reason to doubt him.'

That was then, and little has changed in our dialogue since.

'Seriously, Steph.' Anna absently twirls the pen she's holding in her hand. 'You need to ask him what's going on. You've been seeing each other for just over a month now, and if it's getting serious as you say, then you have a right to ask why things are the way they are. Why is he only available to you at weekends?'

Deep down, I know Anna's right. Since visiting Mrs Carmichael, it has been niggling at me why I still don't know some of the most basic information about Jamie, and I now feel like I can't ask, but why am I having to wait right through the working week to see him? I had assumed we would naturally progress to mid-week dates, even if it meant him staying over at my place more. Yet here we are at another Monday, and Jamie and I have only tentatively agreed our next meet up for next Saturday afternoon. Not even Friday night.

I've casually suggested going out for a nice meal a couple of times, but he's never bitten. Perhaps that's just not his thing and he prefers a more relaxed environment. That's what I want to believe anyway. The truth is I'm extremely reluctant to rock things with Jamie in case I push him too far, and on top of whatever 'complicated' situation he's dealing with, it all becomes too much, and he disappears again. This time forever.

'I'll bring it up when I see him this weekend,' I tell Anna with my fingers crossed behind my back, in case I wimp out.

'Good.' She nods with satisfaction at having finally gotten through to me. 'Cause if he's leading one of these double lives and he's actually got a wife – or husband – and three adorable children back in Glasgow or wherever, then it's better you know sooner rather than later.'

'Sure, whatever.' I walk away towards the kitchen, then stop and turn back to face Anna. 'You know, it was *you* who encouraged me at New Year. I was unsure, but you said you sensed he was one of the good ones. Does that mean you have a faulty radar?'

She shrugs. 'I'm able to accept that I'm not always right. The question is: are you?'

We're locked in a (friendly) standoff, when Lizzie bustles into the office in her usual 'busy' manner, her salt-and-pepper curls bouncing off her shoulders, her freckled face filled with intent.

'Anna, Steph, good, I'm glad you're both here. I want you to come to the venue for next week's fundraiser to meet the staff who'll be supporting the event. They're having a rehearsal of sorts, and I think it's important we're all acquainted, so that we gel on the night itself. As you know, this event needs to go seamlessly to meet our fundraising target and keep us on track with our annual budget.'

'Of course. When are we leaving?' I ask.

'Now. If that's OK with you?'

This is quite typical of Lizzie. She's a brilliant manager, so thoughtful and caring: interested in people and relationships, but keeps everything in her head and often doesn't share until the last minute.

'No probs.' I return to my desk, looking longingly at my coffee mug as I set it down and pack up my stuff.

'They'll have coffee there.' Lizzie smiles at me.

'That's a relief. I'm exhausted today.'

'Out late with that new man of yours?'

'No.' I avoid Anna's eyeline.

'Are you bringing him to the fundraiser as your plus one?' Lizzie asks. 'I know Anna's coming alone, but I'm bringing my husband.'

'Oh… I don't know… I'll see. Maybe best if I don't so that Anna doesn't feel like a spare part.'

'I won't feel like a spare part at all, Steph.' Anna's tone is deliberate. 'You should *definitely* invite Jamie. We'll be working as well as enjoying ourselves, so it'll be good for Lizzie's husband to have some extra company.'

'Exactly that.' Lizzie beams at Anna, completely unaware of what's bubbling away between us.

As we gather our stuff and head out the door to a waiting taxi, my mind ticks over: partly resenting Anna for putting me in this situation, as well as trying to come up with an excuse for Jamie that won't raise Anna's suspicions even further. The reality is that I'll probably chicken out of asking him both the questions I've committed to: *why do I only ever see him on a weekend, and if he'd like to be my plus one at the fundraiser, which — oh, by the way — happens to be on a Thursday night.*

The rest of the week passes relatively uneventfully, and my extra hours keep me occupied enough not to obsess over things. I suppose there is some benefit to me not seeing Jamie on a weeknight: once Anna's chewed my ear off about him on a Monday, there are no further updates for her to pick at for a week. By the time Saturday rolls around again, I'm almost climbing the walls with frustration. Not only because I don't get to *see* him during the week, but we also have minimal contact because of his curious messaging style. A couple of times, at the height of my frustration, I've called him, and we've had great chats, connecting just as well on the phone as we do in person. But the thing is, he never calls me. And sometimes when I call him, he doesn't answer, which makes me feel awkward trying him again later on.

Today Jamie and I are heading out to South Queensferry for a walk on the Dalmeny Estate. It's a favourite childhood spot of mine, with its tree-lined country lane that runs parallel to the light sandy beaches that slope into the Firth of Forth. I had many enjoyable walks there with my family when I was young, and not yet wise to their more questionable behaviour.

Jamie arrives at my apartment just after midday. I open the door to his dazzlingly sexy grin and gorgeous moss-green eyes, and he sweeps me into his arms the minute he's inside.

'I've missed you.' He kisses me tenderly as I melt into his strong body.

'I've missed you, too.'

So why can't we meet up during the week? If only I had the courage to voice this.

We pull apart after a long sensual kiss that nearly has us heading straight for the bedroom, rather than to the kitchen to finish making the picnic.

'This looks great.' Jamie surveys my work-in-progress on the kitchen countertop. 'Need some help?'

'You could do the sandwich fillings while I chop the carrots if you like?'

'Sure. I brought crisps, some dip and some chocolate mini rolls for after.' He pulls them out of the shopping bag he's holding to show me.

I glance at his offerings. 'Perfect. This looks like it would feed a family of six. Maybe we've gotten a little carried away.'

'Better to have too much than too little. We can always keep the leftovers for later or tomorrow.'

'That's true.'

We prep the last of the picnic and take it down to the car in two backpacks, having borrowed one from Connor. Jamie loads them into the boot while I get into the driver's seat.

'All set?' I ask as he jumps into the passenger side and puts on his seatbelt.

'Let's do it.'

We drive out of the underground car parking garage and slowly make our way across the north of the city – through the heavy traffic – until we join the A90, where I can finally get some proper speed up. There's less chat between us than usual and I can tell Jamie's trying to be respectful, allowing me to concentrate on the road.

'Look at the trees,' I say, as we whizz along the dual carriageway. 'Spring is finally here. I love it when the new leaves come out, that delicate, fresh green, and the smell of the blossoms.'

'It is good.' Jamie lets out a relaxed sigh. 'I'm just glad to be out of the city. Can't remember the last time I was in the countryside.'

'Really? Why's that?'

I don't get out of the city much myself either, but this feels like an opportunity to encourage Jamie to share.

'Just… life, I guess.' He shrugs. 'It gets in the way.'

'Right.'

While I do understand this simple explanation, I can't help feeling disappointed that it didn't lead to something more informative.

We arrive in South Queensferry and I navigate the car through the tight squeeze of the cobbled town centre, frequently having to stop to allow other cars to pass. Once we've successfully made it through, past the quaint old fishing village buildings, the road widens and our surroundings open up, treating us to a front row view of the Forth estuary and the iconic Forth bridges. The imposing red steel structure of the rail bridge towers above us like a giant Meccano model.

Jamie's face immediately lights up at the sight of it. '*Wow*. That's some view.'

'Impressive, isn't it?' I throw him a side-glance and a smile. 'I always feel like I'm in a miniature toy town when I come here because it's so huge.'

'I totally get what you mean. That's really something.'

'Have you never been here before?'

'No, never, but now I'm wondering why.' He continues to gaze up at the bridge in awe.

'It's more of a tourist trap. Locals are less likely to visit, I suppose. Do you see any spaces in the car park? I'm not sure I want to go into it if there aren't any. It always gets jammed up.'

He cranes his neck to check. 'Nah, not seeing anything, I'm afraid.'

'No surprise. It's always packed here. Especially on a Saturday.'

I continue along the road, which sweeps off to the right and up a steep gradient adjacent to where the rail bridge joins with the land above us. About halfway up, we get lucky and find a space, then walk back down the hill and along the short lane onto the Dalmeny Estate. It's a warm day – the mid-teens temperature being generous for a Scottish spring – so there are plenty of people around, making the most of it. We nod politely as we're passed by families and couples, all heading back from their own walks.

Following the narrow meandering country lane, we chat away easily, holding hands, flirting and stealing kisses like a pair of teenagers. After about twenty minutes, we reach an opening on the left that leads us onto a beach. It's what I'd describe as a wild beach – linked with the lane by a trampled path through the unmanicured grasses. Having been left to its own devices, the beach is more of a nature reserve than an intended tourist destination: one of the reasons I love it so much. The fine sand stretches for a few hundred metres in either direction, while the water feels almost as far away as it is low tide. The soothing crash of the breaking waves and the sound of the gentle wind adds to the sense of wilderness, while seabirds pick along the shore, foraging for marine life left exposed and vulnerable by the retreating water.

'*Ahh.* This is what I'm talking about.' Jamie seems completely invigorated by the experience. 'The fresh, salty air and the smell of the beach. It's great for the soul.'

'It sure is.' I agree. 'I try to get out here every now and again to get a break from the city. I may live right by the water, but it's not the same. Newhaven and The Shore are great for the practicalities of life – they have everything you need and great bus routes into the city centre, but they don't have enough greenery. Sometimes I feel like I'm living on a huge concrete block.'

'I get that.' Jamie nods his understanding. 'Growing up in a small town, I had easy access to woods and country walks, that kind of thing. Not that I appreciated them back then. Was desperate to move into Glasgow to be part of the big smoke and the nightlife. It's funny to think that it only takes ten years to start craving the reverse.'

'Ha, yeah, that's so true.' I steer Jamie in the direction of the water with a gentle tug of his hand. 'I might have grown up in the city, but Colinton is a lot greener. Sometimes I worry that I'm going to end up back there and turn into my parents.'

'I don't think there's any danger of that. You're quite different to them from what I can see.'

I look at him questioningly, and even though I can guess what he's getting at, I want to hear him say it.

'I mean you just seem less preoccupied with social status and whether you're keeping up with others,' he clarifies.

'What gave them away?'

'You mean apart from the fact that the first question your dad asked me was what I do for a living?'

'I guess, yes.' I feel myself redden at this. 'What else?'

'Let's see… maybe the expensive whisky, the mention of the golf membership and the way your mum would glance around nervously whenever your brother came out with some inappropriate remark. He's amusing. I'm guessing you get on best with him.'

'Very perceptive. Mikey's less about the meaningless BS than the rest of them. He sees the world a bit differently, thankfully, and he says it as it is. To my parents and sister, success is about how much money you make, how grand your job title is and who you know. They think I'm wasting my life in the career I'm in, and the annoying thing is that sometimes I let them get in my head about it. But the cause is important to me, you know?'

'I do,' says Jamie. 'You've got to live your life for you.'

'Exactly. But I'd definitely have an easier time if I packed my charity job in and worked my way up in some big corporation. Sacrifice my happiness for some peace and quiet from my family.' I gaze across the water to Fife, feeling the weight of that never-ending conflict in my life. 'You don't have to play golf with my dad, by the way. We can subtly put him off. I'm surprised he hasn't put a date in with you yet, but Mikey and him have been clearing out the garage the last few weekends, so he's probably trying to get that done first. He stills mentions your pending golf date at every opportunity on our family WhatsApp group.'

'No way.' Jamie shakes his head. 'I'm up for playing, provided he can supply the golf clubs and I'm not expected to be kitted out in designer golfing gear.'

'He definitely won't expect you to have any. He'll make you wear his.'

Jamie laughs and groans. 'Well, if that's what I have to do for love, then it's worth the sacrifice.'

I jolt with shock as he says this. Glancing up at him, I'm expecting him to have registered his own comment and either be looking at me meaningfully, or blushing for having let it slip out of his mouth. Instead, he's just gazing out across the water contentedly, as if nothing happened.

'Thank you for bringing me here.' He turns to me with an appreciative expression. 'I've been needing this.'

'You're so welcome.' I beam at him, and all of a sudden, the look I was anticipating just seconds before is there.

He steps forward, tucking a flyaway section of my hair behind my ear, his face only centimetres from mine. I feel my breath leave me in anticipation.

'I mean it, Steph. You've no idea how much this means to me, being here with you, as well as you sharing an important part of your life with me like this. I hope we'll be able to create memories of our own – and our own special places.'

'I think we're already starting that, right now,' I murmur, eyes locked on his. 'This place can have two different meanings for me.'

'Agreed.'

Jamie cups my face with his hands and reaches in to kiss me. It starts tenderly, expressing the feelings he communicated moments before, but then quickly changes to a hungry kiss, where he's pulling me into him and I'm mirroring him in response. It's clear that we want each other badly and the isolation of the beach fuels that longing. Just as things are getting a bit steamy, we hear a dog barking and we're reminded that we're still in a public place. Pulling apart somewhat breathlessly, we maintain eye contact, the warm spring breeze whipping around our faces.

'Picnic?' I suggest.

'Definitely.' Jamie grins at me cheekily, well aware that we both need something else to focus on before we get ourselves arrested for indecent public behaviour.

Chapter 22

We retrace our steps and find a partially sheltered spot on the sand by some low-lying dunes, giving enough protection from the wind for us not to have to chase our lunch around as we try to eat it. Jamie spreads out the tartan blanket we've brought with us, while I unpack the food and arrange it on the blanket. Once it's all sorted, I stand back and admire our feast.

'There's just one thing missing.' I look at him expectantly.

'A bottle of bubbly?'

'Correct. Pity I'm driving or we could have had one.'

We load our plastic plates with cheese and pickle and tuna mayonnaise sandwich triangles, mini sausage rolls, carrot sticks with hummus and the crisps Jamie brought. Then we happily munch our way through a decent amount of the food – while chatting about our favourite beaches and holiday destinations. It's far from a tropical experience: the chill breeze from the water making it feel cooler than when we set out, but it's perfect because we're together.

'Speaking of holidays...' I venture, feeling uncharacteristically brave. 'How do you fancy a weekend away together? We could visit another coastal area – and claim it as *our* spot.'

'Eh… yeah… sounds great.' Jamie tops up our plastic cups with sparkling spring water and loads his plate again.

'We could go after the schools are back from the Easter break so it's not so busy – or too expensive. Is there anywhere specific you'd like to go? I could start looking at hotels.'

'Um… nope. Nowhere I'm particularly itching to visit. Maybe we could leave it till the summer – like the second half of August? That would give us more time to plan and the weather will be warmer, too.'

'Oh, OK then.' My spirits are dampened by Jamie pushing the date out so far. I had hoped that a weekend away would be a stepping-stone towards a proper holiday together in the summer – maybe somewhere abroad.

'But it doesn't mean you can't start thinking about it now.' He seems to sense my disappointment. 'Maybe shortlist some options, then we can do a last-minute booking – make it kind of spontaneous and exciting, you know?'

'Sure. Yeah, I can do that.'

I dunk a crisp in the cheese-and-chive dip and pop it in my mouth as my brain kicks into gear. Am I being oversensitive or is Jamie trying to subtly kibosh our weekend away? He's indicated he's up for it, but if he is, why do we have to wait so long to go? It's like he's intentionally kicked it down the road so far that there's no point in thinking or talking about it for the foreseeable future. We don't need four and a half months to plan a mini-break.

I try to push this thought out of my mind, but the harder I try, the more it weighs on me: to the point that my niggle over only seeing Jamie on weekends decides to join the party. Before I know it, I'm battling a raft of insecurities about his behaviour, which, quite frankly, is bordering on elusiveness. Why do I only see Jamie on *his* terms? Why do I not even know his surname? And why have I never seen where he lives? I had convinced myself that these were insignificant details: for no reason other than I'm desperate to cling onto him. Anna's suspicions suddenly mushroom in my mind, and I feel like I'm mentally suffocating.

'Are you OK, Steph?' Jamie obviously tunes into this change of mood and places a concerned hand on my leg.

'I'm… yeah… I think I've eaten too much.'

I instinctively get to my feet, but then don't know what to do with myself, and hang there awkwardly with my arms folded. I desperately want to ask him all the questions that are crowding my mind, but I can't bring myself to articulate my concerns.

'You're not feeling sick, are you?' Jamie stands and joins me.

He strokes the pressure points on my wrists in bid to alleviate any nausea I'm experiencing, his face etched with concern, and I can't bear it any longer. He may have stuff to hide, but I'm straight up. I can't pretend to be anything else.

'No, I don't feel sick, Jamie. It's not actually the food.'

'What do you mean?' He stops delivering his 'first aid' and threads his fingers through mine.

Feeling the warmth and security – and at this moment, unwelcome desire – that his touch brings to me, the instinct to push my worries aside and melt into him is almost overwhelming. But I know I have to deal with this once and for all. No more holding back out of fear of losing him. If we can't have an honest and mutually respectful relationship – which Mrs Carmichael rightly highlighted being as being essential for a future together – then we don't have a relationship at all.

But do I have to do it in such a direct way? my brain pipes up. Maybe I can try another approach. He's put me off the weekend away, but what about the fundraiser? That's a minor commitment in comparison, and it's on a weekday. Bringing it up will tell me if there's any sign of real progress between us.

'What's on your mind, Steph?' Jamie prompts me, pulling me back from my torturous deliberations.

'Eh... sorry...' I clench my teeth, feeling stressed by the weight of this situation. 'Was just thinking about something. I have a work-do coming up: a fundraiser that Anna, my boss and I have been preparing for over the last few months. It's a black-tie event at a plush hotel and we have loads of potential donors coming.'

'Right... and are you concerned about it? Is there an issue at work? Because no problem is ever as big as it seems. You can tell me anything, you know that.'

Do I? From where I'm standing, it seems I can't bring up what's really on my mind.

'No.' I shake my head. 'It's nothing like that. We've been told we can bring a plus one, and, well... I was wondering if you'd like to come with me? It's this Thursday.'

Jamie's face immediately falls. 'Steph, I'm sorry, I'd love to be your plus one, but I'm afraid I can't. I have an appointment that evening that I have to keep.'

'I see.' Disappointment slices through me like a knife. 'Oh, well. I thought I'd ask.'

'And I love that you did. You have no idea how much I wish I could come.'

'It's fine, never mind. Maybe we can meet up on Tuesday or Wednesday instead then?' I ask automatically. 'Go out for a bite to eat together?'

'I… um…' Jamie falters, rubbing his forehead in what looks like a sign of unease. 'What about next Saturday night? Maybe get a takeaway at yours?'

As he says this, it's like something shatters in my mind. The tolerance that's been holding me back from making a big fuss becomes as fragile as a pane of glass. He's suggested another weekend date, which means another week of frustration, another week of wondering whether to call him or not, another week of Anna picking my relationship apart. I can't do it. It's all too one-sided. Jamie needs to open up, because this isn't working – and it's unfair to me.

'Jamie, what's going on?' I demand, a bit more aggressively than I'd intended.

'Sorry, what?' He seems caught off-guard by my sudden change of tone.

I look him straight in the eye. 'Why do I only get to see you on weekends? And why don't I know anything about your life, other than historical stuff? You're so closed and secretive. You talk of this "temporary" situation you're in. How temporary is it? On the one hand, you seem to let me in, but on the other, I'm like a stranger you keep at arm's length. It's messing with my head, Jamie. I don't know where I'm at with you.'

I stop talking and stare out across the water: the sole thought in my mind being that I don't want this unpleasant memory to take over from the good ones I've associated with this view for so long. Please let there be a simple explanation. Please let him share it with me right now so we can go back to happy. I so badly want this to work out.

Unfortunately, my instincts tell me that today I'm not going to get my wish. Jamie's clearly torn and distraught. It almost breaks me as I turn and look into those gorgeous eyes, knowing that he's not going to give me the answers I so desperately need. We've reached deal-breaker territory.

'Steph, I'm so sorry,' He looks away, unable to hold eye contact. 'I… can't share my situation with you. I just… can't. And I honestly can't give you a solid date for when things will change either.'

'What could be so awful that you can't tell me what's going on?' I feel my eyes start to sting.

I want shake him and tell him that relationships don't work like this. I want to keep pushing until he gives in and tells me what's going on. I want to get down on my knees and beg. But I do none of those things. Instead, I plead at him through glistening eyes not to ruin this.

'It's… complicated.' Jamie now looks as though he's ready to cry as well and I want to reach out and hug him, but I resist this urge. 'Do you trust me, Steph?'

I realise I don't know how to answer this question. I thought I did. I really want to.

'I don't know, Jamie.' I sigh heavily. 'How can I when you're clearly hiding something? You hear of stories like this all the time. People being duped by someone they fell for and trusted implicitly. I don't want to become one of those stories. Anna's been on my case—'

'*Bloody, Anna.*' Jamie looks pissed off.

'Hey, she's my good friend. Don't be like that about her.'

'Sorry. She's got in your head is all.'

'Jamie, this is not Anna's fault.' I dig the toe of my shoe in the sand frustratedly. 'Even without her and her conspiracy theories, I'd still have gotten to this place, though it might have taken a bit longer.'

'I know. I'm out of order. Forget I said anything.' Jamie this time looks me straight in the eye and I can almost feel his pain. 'I want to ask you to trust me, Steph, but I know that's asking too much. You deserve better. I was crazy thinking that we could go on indefinitely like this.'

As we continue this exchange, I can feel my heart breaking into tiny pieces, and I realise that despite all the gaps in my knowledge of Jamie, I've fallen hopelessly in love. Losing him all over again is going to be unbearable, but the alternative is worse. I can't continue with a man whom I don't really know and who won't share his full life with me. I'm learning that the bond of trust which existed between me and Connor all those years is not something to take for granted. It was rare.

'So what now?' I wipe away the fat tears that have finally spilled over, already knowing the answer, but unsure what else to say.

Jamie's demeanour has changed to one of resignation and sadness. He shrugs and nods as if coming to an agreement with himself.

'Let's take these things back to the car. You can drop me at the station.'

Chapter 23

Two hours later, I'm back at my apartment, bundled up under my duvet on the sofa with Connor on one side and Anna on the other. Tears relentlessly track their way down my cheeks as I stare absently through the window of the Juliet balcony door.

'I'm so sorry this is how things turned out,' says Connor. 'I had my concerns as you know, but I had hoped there was a simple explanation for it all.'

'Me too.' Anna hands me yet another tissue, which I take from her without even glancing in her direction. 'Though it's better you know he's not the guy you thought he was – sooner rather than later.'

'I suppose.' I blow my nose noisily and turn to her. 'But that's the thing, I still don't know that he's not. All I know is that he's hiding something and he can't... he won't share it.'

'And that in itself is strange. Steph, he played the trust card to guilt you into backing off.'

'Anna, I'm not sure that's—'

'OK, put it this way.' Anna cuts me off. 'If whatever's going on in his life isn't something dodgy or questionable, why can't he tell you what it is?'

'Anna...' Connor gives her a gentle warning that's she's overstepping.

'*What*, Connor?' She throws her hands up in semi-defiance. 'I'm right, aren't I?'

'I'm not sure the important thing right now is you being right. What's important is that Stephy gets through this experience in one piece.'

'You're right, sorry.' Anna pats my hand. 'I'm so disappointed that it didn't work out. But I'm more disappointed that he's a bastard and it was me who encouraged you to give him the time of day in the first place.'

I wince as she says this, not wanting to think of Jamie as a bad person, but equally having no justification to come out in his defence.

'Good for you for being brave and calling it though,' she continues. 'If there's one positive that will come from this, it's that you've learned early in your reintroduction to the world of dating that trust has to be earned. Putting your faith in someone unconditionally is a dangerous thing.'

'Anna...' Connor tries again.

'It's fine, Connor.' I reassure him. 'Anna's always been a bit blunt. She's right though. I was naive in thinking that my forever man would appear the moment you and I had split up, and that I wouldn't have to go through the same crappy dating experiences as everyone else. I'm guessing that includes falling for the charms of the unbelievably hot guys who are bad for me.' I give a weak smile, then screw my face up at the thought of Jamie being bad for me, and start to cry again.

'Hey... come here.' Connor pulls me into a hug.

I allow myself to snuggle into him and hold on tight, breathing in his familiar smell. For a moment, I wish that none of this had ever happened, and that Connor and I were still together – even though that's a ridiculous and completely irrational thought. I felt so safe with him. Now I feel lost and vulnerable.

'Why don't we watch some TV to take your mind off things?' suggests Anna.

'Sure.' I shrug. 'How about one of your gruesome crime thrillers? Think I'd like to watch something where someone's having a worse day than me.'

'That's the spirit.' Anna chuckles. 'I know exactly what we should watch.'

She turns on Netflix and finds the programme she's looking for using the search function, then hits play.

'You'll love this. It's about a serial killer whose modus operandi is killing through the postal service. People receive an anonymous parcel and then *bam*, they're dead.'

'Getting killed by your mail definitely qualifies as having a worse day than me,' I say. 'Let's watch it. Anything to take my mind off Jamie.'

I well up again as I mention his name, and Connor pulls me in for another hug, while Anna goes to the kitchen for reinforcements – a.k.a crisps and chocolate.

About fifteen minutes into the programme – which I have to admit already has me hooked and is the perfect distraction from my woes – my phone buzzes on the floor in front of me, alerting me to a new message. My immediate thought is that it might be Jamie messaging to say he's thought things over, and he's ready to tell me what's going on after all. Anna pauses the programme and nods towards my phone.

'Go on, hon. If you don't check it, you won't be able to focus on the programme.'

'Thanks.' I reach down and snatch my phone from the floor.

Unfortunately, it's not from Jamie, it's my dad.

> **Dad:**
> Steph, I've been looking at my diary and I can manage an afternoon on the course with Jamie next Sunday. Will you ask him if that date suits, please?

'Oh no,' I whimper.

'What's up?' Connor leans across and glances at my phone. 'Oh.'

'What is it?' Anna asks.

Connor looks at me and I nod permission.

'Steph's dad is asking about a date for playing golf with Jamie.'

'Ignore that for now.' Anna's picks up the remote to press play again.

'She can't,' says Connor.

'Why not?'

As if on cue, my phone buzzes again as the inevitable flurry of messages from my family starts to appear on my phone screen – following up my dad's message on the group chat. With a defeated sigh, I hand the phone to Connor, and he reads them out loud in real time as they stream in.

Mum:

Can you also invite Jamie to dinner at ours afterwards? I can roast a lamb shoulder for us all. You'll need to let me know quickly, because I'll have to put in the order with the butcher to make sure I get organic.

Dad:

Good idea, Marjory. A solid meal for us after a brisk few hours on the course will be just the ticket.

Mikey:

How do you know Jamie eats meat, Mum? He could be veggie, like Connor, or even vegan.

Mum:

Don't be silly, Mikey. A strapping young man like Jamie can't be vegetarian or vegan.

Mikey:

You really show your age, Mum.

Dad:

Mikey, behave yourself. You're not even part of this conversation.

'That's why Steph can't ignore it,' Connor adds by way of a conclusion. 'The longer she stays silent, the more she'll get harassed for an answer. Tell them now, Stephy. It'll be painful in the moment, but once it's done, they'll get on to the next thing fast enough.'

'Poor you.' Anna exhales heavily, then rubs my shoulder sympathetically. 'I think I'd go spare if my family were that annoying.'

'This is only a taster.' I grimace. 'OK, Connor, pass me the phone. It's the only way.'

He does as I ask, and I quickly craft a response and send it without thinking. There are only so many ways to say 'I got dumped'. I know technically speaking that's not what happened, but it certainly feels like that. My heart is broken and Jamie could have stopped this happening by being honest – provided said honesty didn't confirm one of Anna's many dark conspiracy theories.

'What did you say?' Anna interrupts my rambling thoughts.

'I said something along the lines of, you can all settle down, as Jamie and I have broken up, wasn't meant to be, etc.... Oh, here come the reactions.'

Connor clutches my free hand supportively as I read the replies.

> **Dad:**
> That's a shame. He seemed a charming young man. I could have gotten on well with him.

> **Mum:**
> Very disappointed to hear this, Steph. He was exactly the kind of boyfriend who would have helped you blossom. Is there no possibility of a reconciliation?

I shake my head at the intrusiveness of this question and the suggestion that somehow, I need improving. Within seconds, two further messages pop up on my screen, almost simultaneously.

> **Mikey:**
> Really sorry, wee sis. He seemed like a top guy. Hope you're OK.

Kayleigh:
What did you do, Steph? I hope you didn't bore him with your do-gooder stuff or try to bring home a stray cat from one of your dates!

Kayleigh:
By the way, how about you pass me his number? A hot, successful guy like that is probably more my thing than yours.

Mikey:
Kayleigh, shut your mouth or I'll come round and do it for you. You're seriously out of order.

Kayleigh:
I was only kidding. You know that, right, Steph?

Dad:
Mikey, don't talk to your sister like that. Kayleigh, show a little compassion, please.

'OK, it's official – I hate my family.' I burst into fresh tears, unable to muster any level of self-control.

'You don't mean that.' Connor gently takes my phone from me and sets it down on the sofa. 'They're lacking in some of the more "caring" life skills, which creates an issue between you, but you don't hate them. And you definitely don't hate Mikey. He looks out for you.'

'That is true.' My watery gaze is focused on the duvet. 'He's generally a good one. Just a bit overprotective at times.'

'Which is not such a bad thing. How about I switch your phone off? They know now. You don't need to respond until you're feeling stronger.'

'Sure.' I give a pathetic sigh and blow my nose.

Connor turns off my phone, then gets up and moves it across to the dining table.

'Just in case you're tempted to reach for it.' He gives me a little wink. 'Now, shall we get back to watching this middle-aged woman meet her untimely and somewhat embarrassing end?' He tilts his head a little and examines the unfortunate freeze-frame the TV character has been caught in.

He settles back down beside me and I snuggle into him, his armpit providing a very comfortable and reassuring cocoon. Anna pats my leg gently and hits play on the remote. The scene starts up again and the woman meets her brutal end. But I have no idea what happens after that, because within minutes, I'm overcome with drowsiness and I don't have an ounce of energy left to fight it.

When I finally waken, the blinds are down and the living room lamp is on. I'm also stretched right across the sofa, and there's no sign of Connor or Anna. I sit up groggily and reach down for my phone to check the time, then remember that Connor switched it off and put it on the table. Throwing back the duvet, I get up and wander across to retrieve it, and as I do, Connor walks into the room.

'Hey, sleepyhead.' He smiles at me. 'I wondered when you were going to come round. You've been out for ages.'

'What time is it?' I ask through an all-consuming yawn.

'Nearly nine p.m.'

'*What?* I've been asleep for over four hours? You should have woken me rather than being confined to your room all that time.'

'Don't worry, I wasn't. I made my dinner and ate it in here with subtitles on the TV. You didn't even stir.' He chuckles at this memory.

'Oh.'

I'm a bit embarrassed by the idea of Connor going about his life around me as I lie there unconscious, though I'm not sure why. We've lived together for years and seen all aspects of each other that we'd never want anyone else to know about.

'I made enough for two and put a plate in the fridge for you,' says Connor. 'Quorn spag bol. Want some?'

My stomach rumbles hungrily as he says this. Though I'm clearly heartbroken, my appetite is still fighting fit.

'Yes, please.' I pull out a chair at the table and sit down.

'So, how are you feeling now?' Connor potters around, re-heating my dinner and passing me cutlery and a glass of water.

'Um… I don't really know.' I glance at my phone. 'Think I'm still half-asleep. Sad, I guess – that it didn't work out.'

'That's to be expected. Even with my situation, when you and I split up, I felt gutted.'

'Because you thought we'd lost our friendship.' I say this as a confirmation rather than a question.

'No.' He shakes his head. 'Gutted that I couldn't love you in the way that I wanted to. It was weird. I guess there was still some confusion there, but I felt like I was throwing away the best thing that had ever happened to me. Doesn't make much sense.'

'Actually... I kind of get what you're saying. I had that same feeling earlier – like a feeling of regret that the two of us are not together, despite the fact that it makes zero sense. I think it's because you're the person I trust most in the world and I know you'd never hurt me. It's so inconvenient that we can't spend the rest of our lives together.'

Connor's mouth spreads into a grin. 'We're a bit messed up, aren't we?'

'Maybe.' I shrug. 'Or we're both scared of being out in this big bad world alone after years of facing everything together. Thanks for looking after me, Connor. I really do appreciate it.'

'I'll always be here for you. You know that.'

I eat my spaghetti while Connor chats away, filling me in on his romantic liaisons – which I've asked about. I'm pleased to hear that he's arranged a first date with Lukas. It's just for coffee, and Connor's decided to keep it short by making plans to meet his mum straight after, which makes sense. He's obviously still being cautious after New Year.

'I'm feeling positive about it,' he says. 'And I do think Anna's done a great job of weeding out the "hell nos".'

'That's good.' I'm amused by this description. 'Take things at a pace that works for you, and make sure you're totally comfortable with how things progress. I wish I'd done a bit of that rather than diving in headfirst and getting majorly burned.'

'You went in with an open heart. No one can blame you for that. It's a shame we have to be so on our guard when it comes to finding "the one".' Connor nods at my phone. 'I assume you still haven't heard from Jamie?'

'I haven't switched it back on yet.'

Reaching across, I press the power button. We both watch in anticipation as my phone searches for a signal then bursts to life with a backlog of messages that have built up. My heart quickens and I feel a momentary blaze of nervous anticipation that Jamie might have been in touch. But this is quickly doused when I all I find on my home screen is more WhatsApp chat between my family – picking at the carcass of my now dead relationship – and a couple of texts from Anna checking I'm OK.

'Nothing,' I confirm miserably to Connor.

'It's only been a few hours.' He puts a comforting hand on mine. 'I know Anna's already written Jamie off, but I haven't. Not yet. I know how complicated life can be, especially having been through something difficult myself so recently. Jamie needs to think things through. If he feels the way about you that he claims to, he may decide that sharing his secrets with you is worth the risk.'

'You think?' I feel a little surge of hope at Connor's words.

'All I'm saying is it's a possibility. And if he doesn't, he wasn't the one for you, Stephy.'

Chapter 24

The days following my breakup with Jamie feel long and empty – which is strange in a way, given I wouldn't ordinarily have seen him during the week anyway. I trudge to work and lose myself in the fundraiser preparations, and then trudge home again. Jamie doesn't contact me, and it becomes clear that he's not going to.

By Wednesday lunchtime, I can't take it any more. I feel like my heart's been ripped out and left to slowly waste away. A bit like one of the more gruesome scenes in another crime thriller series Anna's now got me watching. As I attempt to chat away to Mrs Carmichael, who's calling to double check her complex dietary requirements will be attended to at the fundraiser, I feel my mask slipping. Before I know it, I'm swiping away rogue tears, my voice quivering as I desperately try to keep my emotions under control.

'Steph, dear. Are you all right?' Mrs Carmichael asks. 'You sound like you're upset.'

'Oh… I'm… fine, really.' I continue to swipe at my face, but the tears are now coming thick and fast, so I reach down and pluck a tissue from the pack in my handbag to try to stem the flow.

'You are not fine at all. I think you need to take a break.'

'You know, you might be right. I'm sorry, Mrs Carmichael, this is very unprofessional of me.'

'Don't be silly, my love. We all have off days. I will let you go for now, but perhaps we can have a little chat tomorrow evening at the fundraiser, so I can see how you are.'

'That would be nice,' I say, and I realise I do mean it.

I hang up and blow my nose, thankful that I'm the only one in the office right now. The others are all out at meetings or on last-minute event-related errands. Slipping on my jacket, I lock up and hurry along Great Junction Street, keeping my head down to hide my tearful eyes and puffy red face.

Minutes later, I join the Water of Leith pathway at Coburg Street. With it now being well into spring, the ducks are trailed by clusters of adorable cheeping duck-lings, while the pair of swans in the vicinity are gliding protectively around their curious cygnets, hissing omin-ously at the passers-by when they come that bit too close to the water's edge. I wander up the path a bit in the opposite direction to The Shore, and take a seat on a bench overlooking the slow-moving river, which hasn't seen much rain in recent weeks. The combination of the aquatic noises and the feel of fresh cool air in my lungs immediately calms me, allowing me to think a bit more clearly.

I need to pull myself together. Bursting into tears on the phone to a donor is not like me. Yes, I fell for Jamie – big style – but he has let me down and I have to get over it. It's that simple. How can I be in love with someone I don't really know?

I ponder this for a while, trying to make sense of it all and trying to convince myself that what I'm feeling isn't genuine heartbreak, but it's a fruitless exercise. No matter which way I spin it, I know it's the real thing – that I'm completely in love with Jamie. And part of the reason I know that, is because it's so different to what I had with Connor in the latter years of our relationship. What I feel for Jamie doesn't come from a place of seeking comfort, fondness and belonging, nor is it an inane infatuation. It's an intense feeling of vulnerability and longing that I can't describe properly. It feels like a part of me is missing. It's a kind of sick feeling because it makes me feel so exposed, but at the same time it feels as though nothing has ever been right in my life before it. I *need* Jamie in my life. He's the one, I know it.

Suddenly, I'm filled with determination. I have to speak to him, I have to make this right. Whatever's going on with him, I can trust that he'll tell me when the time is right. He's a good person; all my instincts are screaming this at me. And I know Anna would put this down to my naivety – I have been naive in many respects – but ultimately, I think she's wrong about Jamie's motives. No. I *know* she's wrong. I made a bad judgement letting Jamie go and now I need to fix it.

Pulling my phone out of my bag, I look him up in my contacts. A text is not enough. I can't deal with an agonising wait for a response. I hit the call button and put my phone to my ear, my heart hammering in my chest, my whole body jittering with nerves. Then a recorded voice comes through the receiver.

'It has not been possible to connect your call. Please try again later.'

Confused, I disconnect and double check that I've dialled the right person. It's Jamie's number all right. I try again, but get the same message. Then again. And again.

'*What the hell?*' I glare at my phone accusingly.

On the fifth try, I feel myself starting to panic. Whenever I've phone Jamie in the past, it has always rung, and if he didn't answer, it would go to voicemail. This sounds like his phone is either temporarily switched off, or he's ditched it.

My gut tells me it's the latter and before I know what's happening, I let out an almighty sob and put my head in my hands as the enormity of the situation washes over me. He's moved on already. If he's ditched his phone or changed the SIM card, that means that we're over — for good. And worse, he doesn't want me to contact him.

As I lose myself in my heartbreak, my phone buzzes on my lap. Looking down hopefully through my tears, I see that it's Anna. For a moment, I consider letting it ring out, but then realise that's not a good idea. I'm on work time and she might need something from me.

'Hi, Anna.' I'm aware that I sound weak and pathetic as I greet her, so there's little chance I'm going to be able to cover this up.

'Steph? Where are you?' She doesn't appear to register my tone. 'I'm back at the office. Lizzie wants us to starting shifting the items for the auction across to the venue.'

'OK, sure. I'll be back… um… shortly. I'm out for a walk.'

'Hey, what's up, hon?' Her voice fills with concern.

'Nothing. I… um… I tried to call Jamie.'

'Aww no. What did he do? I'll rip his balls off if he was even slightly off with you.'

'No… no. It's nothing like that, I couldn't get through to his phone. I don't know what's going on. Think he might have changed his number or something.'

There's a short silence, then, 'Where are you, Steph? I'm coming to get you.'

I give her my location, then cut the call and resume my pathetic sobbing as I wait for her to come and rescue me from my misery.

'How you doing now?' Anna joins me by the table plan in the function room we're using for the fundraiser.

'I'm OK.' I put down the printed catering schedule on which I'm triple-checking everyone's dietary requirements, and turn to her. 'Thanks for earlier. I'm not sure I would have made it back to work if you hadn't come to get me.'

She reaches out and tucks some flyaway hair behind my ear. 'Of course, you would. Your integrity and your need to help others is far more powerful than any heartbreak, hon.'

'I guess you're right.'

'Lizzie's said we can call it a day. How do you fancy grabbing a drink in the bar before heading back? We could chat a bit more?'

'That would be great.' I smile at Anna appreciatively. 'But only a soft drink for me. Don't think I can trust myself with alcohol right now. I'll end up a blubbering mess again.'

We say our goodbyes to Lizzie and the hotel staff, and wander along the corridor from the huge function room situated in a modern annex back to the reception and then follow the signs for the bar.

The main hotel building is an enormous eighteenth-century edifice that's like a warren inside, with lots of hidden corridors and cubby holes. It looks like it used to be a castle or a mansion that was owned by a seriously wealthy family. The kind that would have had servants and a groundskeeper. On reaching the bar, I'm pleased to note that it has an outdoor seating area. I had almost suggested a walk through the hotel grounds instead of a drink, so this will give the best of both worlds.

'Can we sit outside?' I ask Anna. 'I know it's not that warm, but I could do with some fresh air.'

'Absolutely. I was thinking the same thing myself. Air con in a function room just isn't the same as the great outdoors, is it?' She eyes the rolling expanse of grass and the perfectly manicured bushes and plants, framed by majestic trees that must be decades, if not centuries old.

'Good afternoon, ladies,' a polite man with an Eastern European accent greets us from behind the bar. 'Would you like to take a seat and I'll come and take your order? The drinks menus are on the tables.'

'Perfect.' Anna flashes him a sparking smile, which is readily returned, and it's clear the barman is attracted to her, but is also too professional to act on it.

We head outside via the large conservatory and pick a table right at the edge of the stunning gardens. There's no one else outside, which is an additional bonus because it means we can speak freely.

'This is what I'm talking about.' Anna puts on her sunglasses and positions herself so she can make the most of the view and the omnipresent April sunshine that's been playing peek-a-boo all day with the white fluffy clouds chasing each other across the horizon.

'It's definitely good for the soul,' I agree, making myself comfortable as well, while scanning the drinks menu.

The barman comes out to take our order. I leave Anna to her master-flirt experience, and focus on breathing in big therapeutic doses of the fresh spring air and the scent of the beautiful bright flowers in the garden.

'He's cute,' says Anna, as soon as the barman is out of earshot.

'I thought you'd like him.' I tip my sunglasses down and give her an appraising look. 'I think he likes you, too.'

'Do you think? He's very polite. I couldn't get much out of him.'

'The good ones often are – especially when they're working. Maybe he's just different to your usual type.'

'Hmm…' She contemplates this. 'I guess that could be a challenge. Wonder what it would take to get him to have a snog in the toilets with me.'

'What are you like?' I shake my head at her. 'Do not corrupt that poor bloke, Anna.'

'OK, but only because you asked so nicely.' She shoots me a wicked grin.

We sit quietly for a few more minutes until our drinks arrive and the barman leaves looking disappointed that Anna's turned off the charm. I can't help feeling a little guilty as I watch him go, but it'll help him in the long run not to get tangled up in her web of seduction.

'So, Jamie…' Anna watches the effervescing bubbles in her Prosecco. 'Where's your head at now?'

I take a deep faltering breath, the mere mention of Jamie's name pulling me back to the brink again. The last couple of hours doing the final checks for the fundraiser have been a welcome distraction, making me realise that keeping my mind on other things is how I'm going to get through this. That said, I also want to talk things through – to understand this whole mystery. Problem is: it's like trying to play *Cluedo* with half the clues missing.

'I honestly don't know,' I say eventually. 'I want to hate him, but I don't even have enough information for that. It's like a season finale cliff-hanger, but the most painful one I've ever experienced – because I know there's nothing planned as a follow-up. I'm going to be left wondering what happened for the rest of my life.'

'So, hate him for that then! Hate him because he's left you in terminal limbo after breaking your heart. That's a solid love crime all right.'

'If only it were that simple.'

'How is it not?'

I exhale heavily. 'Because I just can't get my head to a place where he disappeared without a good reason. No matter how hard a try, I can't see him as a criminal mastermind, or a duplicitous bastard. He's Jamie. I might not properly know him, but I got enough of a flavour, and he was everything I could want him to be.'

'Because he made you *think* he was all that,' Anna almost cries out in frustration. 'If he duped you and he was good at it, you'd never know it was all false. That's what I've been trying to tell you.'

Anna's words sink in, and with no strength to resist them, I finally see the flaw in my unconditional trust in Jamie. 'You know, I couldn't help but wonder how he was still single. He just seemed too good to be true. And if he liked me as much as he claimed, why wouldn't he share his "situation" with me? Maybe he *was* manipulating me.'

Anna nods, clearly relieved that I'm starting to see things for what they really are. 'Maybe he was days away from asking you for "a loan" to sort out whatever "personal issue" he was dealing with. That would have left you heartbroken – and cleaned out.'

'Shit. You're right.' My mouth drops open at the enormity of that statement. 'Stuff like that happens all the time – people get completely sucked in. I've been such an idiot. I've fallen for the version of him that he wanted me to see. How did I not see that, given all his secrecy?'

Anna shrugs. 'Love blindfolds us and then kicks us up the arse.'

'How wise.' I chuckle with a wobbly lip, then start to cry again, but at least this time I know it's my one-for-the-road cry.

I've been taken for a ride and I need to pick myself up and get over it. I'll do that and count myself lucky that I've lost nothing more than my naivety – and perhaps some of my faith in men.

Chapter 25

By the next day, I'm feeling more positive and am looking forward to the fundraiser that evening. As it's going to be a very long day and we'll be semi-working at the event, Lizzie kindly gives us the afternoon off to recharge and get ourselves all glitzed up. So, after a short nap, which was greatly needed after the week I've had, I pack an overnight bag and take the bus to Anna's flat in Newington. As neither of us is taking a plus one, we've decided to get ready at hers and take a taxi together. I'm also staying overnight there because she lives closer to the hotel – which is just south of the city.

At 6:30 p.m., we step out of a taxi onto the tarmac outside the front entrance of the hotel. As it's still light, and this time we're not bustling around dealing with pre-event details and issues, we're able to take in the full grandness of the experience. We gaze up at the impressive entryway, flanked by two tall turrets stretching into the clear blue sky. They make me think of Rapunzel for some reason and I find myself wondering who looked out of those windows in the centuries before. Probably wealthy Scottish aristocracy rather than prisoners.

'How's about this then?' Anna's in her element. 'Sorry, Steph, I know you're not a selfie girl, but this is a definite Insta moment. Come on.'

'Oh no. Please, Anna. I'm not feeling—'

'*Rubbish*. This is for a good cause. Might get us some extra donations.' She yanks me into the frame she's already set up on her phone camera and does one of her signature poses, while I attempt a natural smile.

'How bad is it?' I wince in anticipation, not really relishing being plastered across her social media.

'Beautiful.' She shows me the picture, which I have to admit is quite attractive, with the combination of us being all glammed up and the way the evening sun makes the hotel façade even more majestic and alluring.

'I actually look all right in that.'

'You look gorgeous, hon. Don't let that man wreck your confidence.' She taps away at her phone finishing off her post, commentating as she goes, 'Two belles off to the ball. Raising money to give disadvantaged young people the future they deserve. #bignightout. #pleasedonate.'

'Ooh, I quite like that.' I clap my hands together excitedly. 'Imagine if some big celebrity saw it and made a massive pledge.'

'That's exactly what I'm hoping for. Shall we go in?'

'Sure.' I'm almost reluctant to leave the fresh air and the warmth of the evening sun, but duty calls.

We walk inside and wave to the receptionists whom we've gotten to know a little during our previous venue visits, then we take the long corridor into the modern extension where the function room is. As we enter, we gasp with delight. The clinical feel the place had while we were doing the preparations has been replaced by a magical atmosphere, with stunning decor and mood lighting that subtly switches through a spectrum of colours.

'*Wow*. This place looks incredible. The hotel staff have done a brilliant job.' I gaze around the room at the perfectly set white clothed tables with their modern centrepieces and the uniformly dressed chairs.

Unfortunately, the romance of this scene kicks my mind into an unhelpful gear and takes me off down the path of what a perfect wedding venue this would be – and unsurprisingly, all my previous daydreams about Jamie swiftly follow suit. Seems the part of my brain that deals with elaborate fantasies didn't get the memo that we've broken up. I do my best to banish these thoughts from my mind, but not quickly enough to stop them putting a dampener on the whole experience.

'Put him out of your mind.' Anna gives me a supportive nudge. 'This will be your venue for when you meet Mr Amazing. He'll come, Steph. And when he does, you'll wonder why you ever gave Jamie so much of your energy.'

'I know.' I give a melancholic smile. 'Just got caught off guard. I'll go and set up the auction table to distract myself.'

I trot across the huge room, weaving my way between the large tables at which our regular donors and other guests will be sitting in just under an hour's time. As I reach the front of the room where the AV system is set up, Lizzie bustles through a side door looking incredibly busy. It never ceases to amaze me how she never slows down, not even when everything is perfectly under control. There's little reason for us to be here this early, other than to set up the prize table and support her.

'Ah, Steph, you're here... oh, *look at you...*' She stops momentarily and clasps her hands together with delight. 'You're stunning.'

'Thank you. You look beautiful, too.' I eye her perfectly styled chignon, which has clearly been done in a salon, and her scarlet A-line dress. 'Shame we don't have more excuses to dress up like this, eh?'

'Perhaps we should manufacture a few more opportunities.' She gives me a little wink. 'Would you be a love and set up the auction table for me?'

'Sure. Was already on it.'

'Wonderful, thank you. Make sure the best items are most visible – especially the ones that offer something that you can't easily buy. I want our guests salivating over them.' She looks around the room anxiously, checking nothing is out of place. 'OK, I'll leave you to it and get back to checking the food.'

I smile at Lizzie. There's really no need to check on the food. That's the hotel's job. I imagine they're probably having a challenging time trying to keep her out of the kitchen.

'Oh, a couple of things before I go.' She turns back to me. 'I'm sorry to hear about your breakup. I know you're upset, but from what Anna tells me, that man sounded like trouble. Seems you've had a lucky escape.'

'Thanks.' I force an appreciative smile.

'Also, how would you feel about running the auction? That would free me up to work the room and give my time to our most important donors.'

'Um… OK, sure. I think I can manage that.'

I immediately feel a nervous swirling in my stomach at the idea of standing up and presenting in front of about two hundred people – two hundred rich and important people.

'You're an angel, Steph.' Lizzie places a grateful hand on my upper arm. 'Get that voice of yours warmed up and have a practice before the guests arrive. You might want to throw in a little humour while you're welcoming them.'

'Wait a minute… you said you wanted me to do the auction, not MC the whole event.'

'Did I?' A guilty look momentarily passes across her face. 'Sorry, I meant would you take over leading the event? It would be such a help to me.'

My stomach swirling quickly evolves into full-on nausea.

'Would Anna not be a better fit, Lizzie? She's way more confident doing that stuff than I am.'

'Which is precisely why you should do it. Steph, you're one of the most talented and dedicated people I've ever worked with, and what I've seen from you over recent weeks has made my decision much easier.'

'What decision?'

'That's another thing I wanted to speak to you about.' Lizzie's lips curl into a loaded smile. 'I had a health scare recently, Steph.' She waves away my reaction as my hand shoots to my mouth in concern. 'I'm fine, but it put some things into perspective for me. I can't keep going at this rate forever, so I need a successor. You told me you want to make a real difference to people's lives, right?'

'Um… yeah.' My eyes narrow as I wonder where this is leading.

'Then what better way to do that than leading the charity I built from the ground up?'

I blanch at this casually shared revelation. 'You want *me* to be the future director of Edinburgh Youth Kickstart?'

'Absolutely. It's my baby and I need to leave it in safe hands. I see no safer hands than yours.'

'You don't mean right now, do you? Because as much as I've learned a lot from you, I'm miles away from being ready for a role like that.'

'Don't be silly, of course not.' Lizzie chuckles. 'I'll need to train you up and share all my wisdom with you. And I'm not planning to step away altogether; I'll just be taking a backseat to let you to take the place to the next level.'

'Gosh, Lizzie, I'm honoured… and a little terrified.'

'You have no reason to be terrified, Steph. I wouldn't be saying any of this if I wasn't one hundred per cent confident in my decision. You know me.'

'I do. And I guess this is exactly what I'm looking for, but what about Anna?'

Lizzie fixes me with a look. 'Steph, for once, will you please stop thinking of everyone else and put a little focus on yourself?'

'Right, sure. Of course.'

'Great, that's sorted then.' Lizzie pats me on the back encouragingly, then sweeps back out the side door in the direction of the kitchen.

'What was that about?' Anna seems to appear out of nowhere as I'm recovering from the multiple bombshells that Lizzie has dropped on me.

'Oh… um… Lizzie has asked me to MC, and…' I wince in anticipation of Anna's reaction. 'She's also asked me to be her successor.'

I scrutinise Anna's face, waiting for the hurt, but all that I find is a big broad smile.

'Steph, that's amazeballs.' She launches herself on me with a huge hug.

'Really?' I gasp for breath as she crushes the air out of my lungs. 'I thought you might be upset. You have as much reason to want that role.'

'Are you kidding?'

'What do you mean?'

'You think I'm patient or politically minded enough to take on a job like that? Nah, I prefer the virtual world. I can be your right-hand woman... your social-media guru. Plus, what an opportunity to stick two fingers up to your family. You don't obsess over the meaningless materialistic shite. You fight the good fight and you're going be a director because of it. Suck on that, Mr and Mrs A!'

'How eloquently put. Maybe I should put you in charge of giving them the good news.' I chuckle and then hug her again. 'Seriously though, thank you. You've no idea how much your support means to me. I suppose I can't imagine you meeting with MPs and drinking tea with our most influential donors.'

'Yeah.' She smirks. 'Ten minutes of their narcissistic bullshit and we'd be hitting the headlines for the wrong reasons.'

I laugh at this colourful play on Anna's lack of suitability for the job and we start setting up the auction table.

'I'm not sure that's an entirely fair representation, Anna, but I accept your point. Your tolerance levels are a little lower than average.'

Once we're done, I decide to make a quick trip to the ladies before things get started, and as I do, I notice a group of people coming out of the function room next door, laughing and joking with each other. They seem to be part of some corporate event. I pay little attention to them as they walk ahead of me until my eyes zone in on a man at the front of the group. I can only see him from the back, but he's tall with brown man curls that look very much like Jamie's. And that walk seems familiar, too.

I stop with a jolt. *Surely not.* It would be too much of a coincidence. Shaking my head to bring myself back to reality, I turn down the corridor to the ladies, but my steps become slower as my brain continues to tick over what I might have seen. Could it have been Jamie?

Chapter 26

Before I realise what I'm doing, I've made a U-turn and I'm hurrying along the corridor in the direction the group went. I've no idea where they were headed, but I can make an educated guess: the hotel bar. Moments later, I'm entering the high-ceilinged room with its ornate decor, eyes scanning the space for the man I saw. It's pretty packed with people in corporate gear, so this isn't as easy a task as I might have expected. But within moments, I've located the group from the corridor in the far corner of the bar and I'm staring straight at the back of the man's head again. Willing him to turn so I can get a better look, I weave my way through the crowded room until I'm just feet away. He turns his head slightly, giving me a partial profile view of him, and my breath catches in my throat. It's him. I'm sure of it.

As I gather myself together, unsure how to approach him, a tall woman with long sleek dark hair walks past me, drink in hand, and joins the group, obstructing my view. Then to my horror, she slips her arm around Jamie's waist, and they kiss.

I'm frozen to the spot, heart hammering in my chest as I watch them nuzzle each other intimately. So, Anna was right after all. Jamie is a liar and a cheat. My overriding instinct is to bolt out of the bar, but there's another driving force within me that's keeping me rooted right where

I am. I don't want him to get away with it. Jamie has hurt me and now I want to hurt him back, and the only way to do that is to expose him for who he really is. The adrenaline kicks in and I march up to the two of them.

'You lying bastard.' I practically spit out, as the woman's face drains of colour and a bewildered Jamie turns to look at me.

Only it's not Jamie. The man before me, now I'm seeing him face on, bears a striking resemblance to Jamie, but he's not him. And he's looking at me as if I'm a complete lunatic – which to be fair, is exactly how I look.

'Who is she?' the woman demands of the man who is not Jamie.

'I've never seen her in my life. I swear.'

'I'm... oh man, I'm so sorry...' I stammer and start to back away. 'I thought you were someone else.'

My face blazing with mortification, I turn and leg it out of the bar, my super-sensitised hearing picking up the comments being murmured behind me of, '*crazy bitch*', '*wouldn't want to be her right now*' and '*what was that about?*' as I flee.

A short while later, after I've pulled myself together enough to return to the function suite, I'm standing in front of a sea of faces: some interested, some looking surprisingly bored by the affair, and some who appear to have gone to town on the welcome aperitifs – or they got tanked up ahead of arriving. Funny, I thought people grew out of that habit by their late twenties. This is a room mainly full of forty-plus, glamorously turned-out citizens of our fine city and beyond.

My heart thudding, I try to ignore the burning humiliation that reignites every time my mind involuntarily flits back to what just happened, I nervously tap the microphone and clear my throat. Then I kind of sway back and forth like a well-dressed scarecrow, until I can no longer put things off. Out of the corner of my eye, I can see Lizzie watching me intently, willing me to start the proceedings. *Here we go.* I have to hold myself together, because this moment will either make or destroy my career.

'Good evening, ladies and gentlemen.' My faltering voice booms through the cordless mic, making me cringe a little. 'Thank you so much for joining us at this evening's hugely important fundraiser. As many of you know, Edinburgh Youth Kickstart was set up back in 2009 by our wonderful Lizzie Chalmers.' I extend my arm – which is shaking slightly from my double whammy adrenaline rush – in Lizzie's direction, and all eyes follow: putting her very firmly in the limelight.

There's a swell of applause as she gives a little wave and blows kisses from her seat wedged between an older woman dripping in expensive-looking jewellery, and a red-faced man who looks like he was involved in the pre-event partying.

'Lizzie's passion for giving young, disadvantaged people a real chance at a future has been the lifeblood of this organisation,' I continue, finally getting into my flow; which thankfully sends my sense of humiliation into retreat for now. 'It's no secret that this passion comes from Lizzie's own experience of facing struggles no young person should have had to face. Tonight, our aim is to feed you, give you a good time – though I can see some of you have already achieved that...'

I pause as there's a ripple of laughter, and the tipsier of our guests assume slightly shame-faced, but thoroughly entertained expressions. So far so good.

'And our final aim, in the nicest possible way, is to take your money, of course…'

There's another peal of laughter and a lot of nodding.

'We have some fantastic items in our auction tonight, so please do take some time to look at the table and think about what you might like to bid for. The higher the better.' I add in a mock whisper. 'And remember, every penny goes towards to the great work we're doing to give our young people hope and prospects for the future. But, before you dig into the delicious food the hotel has donated to this event, I'd like to introduce you to Samira, who found herself facing destitution after having been forced to leave her home at the age of eighteen.'

I step aside as Samira takes centre stage and shares her story of how Edinburgh Youth Kickstart helped save her from a life of poverty and drugs, and quite probably, an early death. She handles herself with such positivity and decorum that there's barely a dry eye in the place – including mine.

Once she's done, I wish everyone an enjoyable evening, then make my way across to the table at which I've been placed. Taking my seat between Mrs Carmichael and a man in full Highland dress, I glance across at Lizzie, then Anna, both of whom are watching me and giving me clear signals that they think I did a great job. Thank goodness for that. Now all I need is to get through the next few hours without making an idiot of myself again and get my feet firmly back on dry land.

The relief that the person I had seen wasn't in fact Jamie came quickly after I was out of sight of the patronising eyes of the people in the bar. But it was short-lived, because it reminded me that Jamie could be anywhere with another woman – his girlfriend, fiancée, wife – and I had been just someone to con. I didn't mean anything to him.

'Steph, dear.' Mrs Carmichael brings me back to the moment. 'That was quite an opener. You are a natural.'

'Oh, thank you.' I force a smile. 'Between you and me, I was quite nervous.'

'Of course, you were. We all get anxious about things like that, but it did not show at all.'

'That's good to know.' I lean slightly to my right as my starter of smoked salmon and crab terrine is deposited in front of me.

'Tell me, my love...' Her voice lowers almost to a whisper. 'What was on your mind when we spoke yesterday? I felt very vexed for you.'

I hesitate, unsure after what's just happened at the bar, whether I should be opening Pandora's box right now. It's clear that I'm not coping very well. Mrs Carmichael reads my troubled expression and squeezes my hand gently. Although small, this gesture of support combined with the alcohol I've consumed creates a wave of emotion inside me.

'It's over with Jamie,' I tell her, keeping my own voice low. 'He... wasn't who I thought he was.'

'Oh, you poor love. I am terribly sorry that things did not work out between you.'

'Thanks. Me too.' I blink rapidly to stop the tears that are forming. 'You, my friends, Anna and Connor... you all told me not to get in too deep too soon and you were right. I only have myself to blame.'

Mrs Carmichael gives my hand another squeeze. 'You must not be so hard on yourself, Steph. This time it did not work out, but you opened your heart and that is a wonderful thing. Too many people go through life guarded and missing out because they fear rejection. Just make sure whoever he is, that he is the right man for you, then share everything with him. Create a lifetime of happy memories together like I did with my dear George.'

'That's a lovely way of looking at it. It certainly makes me feel better. You were right when you said that I don't need a man to define me, but that doesn't stop me hoping that one day I'll find my own George to share the good times with.'

'I have every confidence that you will. He may even be sitting right beside you.' She nods towards the man on my right and I turn to see what she's on about.

'Great speech,' he says to me as soon as I make eye contact.

He's younger than the majority of people here, and he looks like he's walked off a catwalk – one that's been showcasing this season's hottest Highland dress. How did I not notice him when I sat down? Taking in his incredible dark eyes, just-styled-enough dark brown hair and his formal Scottish ensemble, the more primal of my senses instinctively jolt to life.

'Thank you,' I reply after too long a pause, which he clearly notices.

'I'm Calum.' He extends his hand and I shake it.

'Steph.'

'Great to meet you, Steph.' His eyes linger on mine and I feel myself redden.

'Are you… um… here on behalf of an organisation or do you have a personal interest in the charity?'

'Bit of both. I'm Director of Social Responsibility for KR Finance Group. We've recently made Edinburgh Youth Kickstart one of our charity partners. I obviously can't use company budget for the auction, but I thought

I'd make a personal bid. I'm particularly interested in the boutique hotel stay.'

'Yeah, that's a great one. We were so pleased to get that donation. I'll cross my fingers that you win it, so you can treat somebody special in your life to a lovely experience.'

'That's the thing, Steph,' he says, almost regretfully. 'I hope the stay has a reasonably long expiry date, because I'll need to find someone to share it with.'

My flush deepens as he continues to watch me. It's all very light and flirty and not inappropriate at all. Perhaps it's the couple of glasses of Prosecco I sank to recover from the scene at the bar, as well as calm my nerves before my speech. I don't know. But I find myself thinking that if Jamie doesn't want me then maybe I need to move on and find someone who does. Maybe Calum is exactly the type of distraction I need tonight.

By nine p.m., we've had all three courses and the staff are serving coffee and petit fours – which means it's time for the auction. Having drunk more alcohol than is probably appropriate for a work event, the prospect of the auction now seems far less daunting. In fact, I'm almost relishing the idea of getting up there, which Anna immediately flags as a warning sign.

'Are you sure you're sober enough to do it?' She holds me square by the shoulders in the ladies and gives me a little shake. 'This is not our usual Steph I'm looking at. You hate being the centre of attention.'

'Yeah, well, maybe I don't like being that Steph any more.' I flick my hand flippantly. 'She doesn't seem to work for my family, and she didn't work for Jamie either.'

'Jamie's an idiot. No, Jamie was a danger to you. His motives and the way he behaved has nothing to do with who you are.'

'Oh, really? Because Connor said that if Jamie loved me, he'd risk telling me his secret... so that tells me that I'm not lovable.'

'He actually said that?' Anna looks sceptical.

'Yes.' I raise my eyes to the ceiling, trying to ponder this through the haze of my alcohol-soaked brain. 'At least I think that's what he said.'

'Well, Connor's the idiot – for filling your head with that nonsense.'

'Hey, you leave my lovely Connor alone.'

'I thought we agreed that Jamie was up to no good and that you were better off without him.' Anna's frustration with me is evident, but right now, I really don't care.

'We did.' I nod. 'But then he wasn't kissing that woman at the bar and I don't know where he is or if he's kissing anyone, but the point is... I've changed my mind.'

'OK, you're not making any sense and you've clearly changed it back over the course of too many wines, so do me a favour... forget Jamie for now, get this glass of water down you and sober the hell up before Lizzie sees you like this.'

'I'm fine.' I feel myself sway a little and I giggle like a schoolgirl. 'OK, I'm not *fine* fine... but yeah, gimme the water and I'll be off to do my duty.'

'Oh, Mr Man Upstairs, please let Steph get through this in one piece.' Anna pleads, while force-feeding me the glass of iced water she got from the bar.

'Ooh, did you see the guy I'm sitting next to? He's a hottie all right.' I waggle my eyebrows at her. 'Think he likes me too.'

'I did see him, and I saw how much attention he's been paying you.'

'Yeah, see. I'm not unlovable. No wait, that would be unlikeable. Does that mean I'm still unlovable?'

'You're becoming more unlovable by the minute,' Anna mutters through gritted teeth and I pet my lip in response to this, causing her to alter her tone. 'You know I don't mean it. You're just a bit… challenging at the moment. Come on, keep drinking.'

I allow Anna to make me drink, because somewhere in amongst the wine-marinated tissue in my brain, I'm aware that I do need to sober the hell up.

'OK, that's it. We need coffee.' She darts out of the toilets and returns a few minutes later with an espresso. 'Here, down this. The caffeine will sort you out.'

I do as I'm told, and within moments of the hot, bitter liquid hitting my stomach, I feel my mouth start to water, followed by a lurch in my oesophagus. I charge into one of the cubicles, throwing the door closed behind me, just as my undigested dinner makes a sudden and dramatic bid for freedom. I remain there, hovering over the toilet pan, retching and hurling until there's nothing left to come up.

'You OK?' Anna hollers through the door.

'I've been better,' I call back with a hoarse voice. 'But at least it's sobered me up a bit.'

Eventually, I feel safe enough to leave the cubicle and join Anna by the sinks. The amazing friend that she is, she's already been to reception to get an emergency tooth-brush and some toothpaste.

'Oh, you're a lifesaver.' I take them from her and freshen myself up. 'Honestly, thank you. There's no way I could have done the auction in that state.'

'You're welcome.' She pulls me into a side hug. 'That's what friends are for. I should have kept a closer eye on you tonight and intervened earlier.'

'Ah, well. No harm done.'

'And now you're fresh and sober enough for a snog with the kilted sex-god later on as well. He's exactly the kind of rebound fling you need after Jamie.'

My instinctive reaction to this statement, now I've sobered up a bit, is to reject it. Then a million thoughts of Jamie swoop into my mind, making me almost dizzy with the mix of emotions they fire up, and I swiftly change my mind.

'You know what, you're right. Maybe Calum's just what I need to get Jamie out of my system.'

When we eventually exit the toilets, I'm in better form, and as we head back towards the function suite, Lizzie marches towards us looking flustered.

Chapter 27

'There you both are.' Lizzie throws up her hands in relief. 'I've been looking all over for you. We need to get the auction started.'

Anna and I share a look that says, thank goodness 'looking all over' didn't include the ladies' toilets we were in. That might have led to me being the world's shortest ever role successor.

'Of course.' I flash Lizzie my brightest smile. 'Let's get this done.'

Returning to my earlier spot at the front of the room, I get mic'd up again. I then address our guests, whom, this time, it takes several tries to quieten down enough for me to get started. I'm clearly not the only one who's more well-oiled than usual.

'Ladies and gentlemen, I do hope you're enjoying your evening—'

'I've not had this good a night out since my divorce,' hollers a very large and merry man in a kilt.

I chuckle into the mic. 'Thank you for sharing that, sir. I do hope you're as loose with your wallet as you are with your tongue.'

The man hoots at my swift comeback and a collective guffaw rattles around the room.

'OK...' I continue. 'If I can have your attention once again, we're about to start the auction.'

I work my way through the items, managing the bids, while Anna operates the AV, displaying an image of each prize on the projector screen. It turns out to be a lot of fun and I'm amused by how competitive some of the guests become, trying to one-up each other with the highest bids. Lizzie looks positively gleeful, and I can see her mentally counting up the pledges.

'All right!' I call out. 'We have a bid of two-thousand three-hundred pounds for the one-year gin subscription with a private tour of the distillery and tasting event for up to ten people. Going once... going twice... *sold* – to the lady in the beautiful purple dress.'

I laugh as the woman who put in the winning bid gets to her feet and takes a series of bows in all directions, then shoots a triumphant look at the man she's just outbid. He simply shakes his head by way of a response, but I can tell that he's gutted that she's beaten him.

'You can come to the tour and tasting as one of my guests,' she calls across to him, and his face immediately brightens.

As the rest of the eyes in the room turn back to me, I see him mouth 'thank you' to the woman, who blushes and then they share a look. My heart swells as I realise I may have witnessed a tiny seedling of a blossoming romance, and suddenly I feel a deep longing for that myself.

Anna clears her throat loudly from a few feet away and I pull myself together.

'Right... last item of the night... this one's a cracker: a two-night stay in a suite at The Blenheim boutique hotel with dinner, an exclusive wine-tasting package and an afternoon in the kitchen with their pastry chef. This is something you can't buy, so if you fancy this experience for yourself and a special someone...'

As I say this, I involuntarily glance across at Calum, my table companion, feeling myself redden once again as a broad grin spreads across his face. A vision of him dressed in his kilt, throwing me onto a four-poster bed with *Braveheart*-style paint on his face flits through my mind and I almost get lost in the myriad of confused feelings (mostly about Jamie) that follow this.

'Steph. Where have you gone?' Anna hisses at me from nearby.

'So, yeah…' I recover as her words pierce my subconscious. 'This is the biggie. Get your gloves on because this is going to be a fight to…' I stumble as I realise I'm about to say something inappropriate. 'Well, to the winning bid.'

'Bring it on,' a man cat-calls from the back of the room.

'I'll see you in the car park if this doesn't go my way,' another bloke, who's big and burly, shouts back at him.

'Ahem… indeed.' I clear my throat and have a momentary word with myself about toning things down.

I'm obviously still tipsy and working a whole load of drunken people into a frenzy, which no matter how light-hearted it's intended to be, is probably not what Lizzie had in mind.

'We'll start the bidding at eight-hundred pounds.'

The bids come thick and fast, to the point I'm barely able to keep up with them. The two men, who I sincerely hope are not going to be taking it outside afterwards, bid furiously against each other, while others chime in with their own offers. Surprisingly, in the midst of all this, and after the big deal he made about wanting that item, there's not a single bid from Calum.

By the time the bids top three thousand pounds, most of the bidders have dropped out and it's the same two testosterone-fuelled blokes competing against each other.

It's clear though that they're running out of steam and the amount of money they'll need to part with if they win is starting to pinch. However, it also appears that neither is willing to swallow their pride and let the other win. As the bidding tops three-thousand five-hundred pounds, the man who was all for starting a car-park brawl wavers. Everyone in the room is watching with baited breath to see if he'll concede, when out of nowhere there's another bid.

'Four-thousand pounds.'

There's a collective gasp and everyone turns to see who has swooped in out of nowhere. It is, of course, Calum, looking super smug and giving me a look of 'didn't I say I wanted it?'.

'We have a new bidder.' I smile back at him. 'Four-thousand pounds. Is anyone going to top that?'

I look to the two existing bidders, who are both stunned at the idea of taking their pledges above four grand. They glance at each other and then shrug and wave it away – it seems, to my relief, that as long as neither of them lost to the other, then they're not that bothered after all.

'OK...' I give them one last glance and it's clear that they've both conceded. 'Four-thousand pounds going once... going twice... *sold* – to the hot man in the kilt.'

My eyes widen as I realise what I've just said and I feel my face turn beetroot. A wave of laughter flows through the room and my eyes immediately zone in on Lizzie, then Calum, who's looking immensely pleased with my comment.

I turn to share my mortification with Anna, but she's disappeared, and when I turn back to face the front, I notice that Lizzie's on her way across to me. Shit. Here's hoping I've not dented my chances of my future promotion – or keeping my current job.

'Steph, well done.' She hugs me the moment she reaches me. 'Between the ticket sales and the auction, we've done it. We're nearly fifteen grand over our target.'

'Fantastic.' I hug her back. 'Look, I'm sorry about that slip there. In fact, for all of it. I realise these are important donors whom we want to keep hold of and my style perhaps needs a little—'

'What are you talking about?' Lizzie looks confused. 'You were incredible. Nobody wants to go to a stuffy event and yawn their way through it. You're a natural.'

'Oh, OK, great. I did quite enjoy it.'

'Then it's win-win. Although next time, maybe try to drink a little less so you don't have to throw up in the toilets midway through. That's definitely not in the job description and the adrenaline will keep you going as you now know.'

'Um… OK. Thank you for… the developmental feedback.' I'm now hot with embarrassment once again. 'I didn't realise you'd seen me. I'm so sorry.'

'I didn't see you.' Lizzie chuckles. 'Anna inadvertently gave the game away when she asked reception for a toothbrush and toothpaste for you. We all had a good laugh about it.'

'Right. Well, I'll just go and—'

'No, you stay right where you are.' She plucks the microphone from my hand and addresses the room. 'Ladies and gentlemen, may I take a moment to extend my heartfelt thanks to you for helping us smash our fundraising target tonight.'

She stays quiet as the room erupts into delighted applause, and lets it peter out before continuing.

'When I set up Edinburgh Youth Kickstart, I couldn't have imagined it would grow into what it has become today, and I certainly couldn't have done it alone. I am eternally grateful for the hard work and dedication put in by our team: our key workers, many of whom are actually volunteers, and all those who keep things running behind the scenes.'

She glances at me and I beam back at her.

'Many of you I've gotten to know over the years and your loyalty as donors is more than appreciated. I do hope that you will continue to support us when I step down as director in the summer.'

Wait. *What?*

'I'll be passing over the reins to someone who is more than capable, and who has shown herself to be an all-rounder with a heart of gold.' She turns to me and I blink at her in shock. 'Steph here will be taking over from me at the end of July. I'm relieved to be leaving the charity in such safe hands, because, with the economic and social challenges of recent years, the need for our services is greater than ever. So, if you're willing, please can I ask you to show Steph that you're behind her.'

The room immediately bursts into another round of applause as I break into a sweat and try to regulate my breathing.

'Lizzie, I thought you were meaning a couple of years, not a couple of months,' I say in her ear while at the same time nodding my appreciation across the sea of smiling faces.

'Why on earth would you think that?' She looks at me quizzically. 'Oh, did I not mention the timings earlier?'

'*Eh, no.* And I don't know that I would have agreed to them. I'm nowhere near ready.'

'Sorry, give me a moment.' Lizzie wraps up her little speech with some closing words and wishes everyone an enjoyable evening to more applause, then guides me away to the side of the room.

'Ah, what am I like?' She pulls an apologetic face that tells me her forgetfulness is not down to her accidentally omitting something in haste. 'You'll be ready. I'll make sure of it. And anyway, I told you I'm only stepping back. I'll mentor you for as long as you need – but I don't expect that will be long.'

'You'd bloody better,' I eyeball her and then remember that I'm talking to my boss. 'But… um… thank you.'

'You're welcome. Off you go and see your "hot man" then.' She gives me a little wink. 'He's quite the looker.'

I give her one last mortified look and then shuffle across to my table, from which Calum is watching me a little too eagerly.

'Congratulations on your promotion. Shall we go for a drink at the bar?' He gets up from his seat before I even have a chance to sit down. 'I get the impression you could do with some time out of the limelight.'

'How did you guess?'

'Call it intuition.'

'Sounds good, but give me a moment to send a quick message first.'

Despite my disdain of my family and their attitudes towards my life choices, this revelation about my career is something I'm keen to share with them. I'm thinking it might even make them proud, because I am going to be a director after all. I send a short message to our WhatsApp group with my news then wait. Within seconds, the first response pops up on my screen.

> **Kayleigh:**
> Ooh, what kind of pay rise are you getting?
> Directors earn shedloads.

Shaking my head, I realise I should have expected that to be the first question. I quickly type a reply to shut that avenue down.

> **Steph:**
> I don't expect I'll be making megabucks, Kayleigh. I do work for a charity so it would be unethical for the salaries to be sky-high. Plus, not everything is about money. I want the job because of what I'll be able to do for the disadvantaged young people of Edinburgh.

I'm hoping that will get the message across and that some positive acknowledgement of my news will follow. At this stage, I'd even settle for lukewarm. Unfortunately, even that is too much to expect.

> **Kayleigh:**
> Sounds like you're being treated as cheap labour to me.

> **Mum:**
> This is good news, Steph. You can gain some experience at that level and then use it to get a senior role in a better paid sector.

Dad:

Just what I was thinking, Marjory. Steph, you are on the up! It's taken a while to get there, but ending your relationship with Connor seems to have been exactly what you needed to get you on the right track.

By the time I've read all three messages I'm seething: why is everything about money or status with them? They couldn't see this as a genuine success for me; all because it won't come with an obscene pay rise, and isn't in some highfalutin private sector company. I'm so hacked off, I don't even wait around to see what Mikey's reply will be. I snap the cover across my phone and stuff it into my handbag.

'So that drink?' Calum's clearly picked up on my mood.

'Absolutely,' I mutter and follow him out of the function room, trying to ignore the handful of eyes on us as we go.

'Well done on getting the hotel stay,' I say, once we're out in the corridor, heading for the bar. 'Was that your plan all along to swoop in like that?'

He shrugs. 'I didn't see the need to join the early bidding. I was always planning to make a sizable donation, so I thought I'd leave the others to provide the entertainment — which they certainly did.'

'Yes. I thought at one point I was going to have to referee their fight in the car park.'

'Now that I would have loved to see.'

'Thank you, by the way.' I give him a sideways glance. 'For making such a significant pledge. It means so much to us.'

269

'I'd give more if I could. It's a great cause. So important that all kids have a fair chance in life.'

We reach the bar and Calum insists on buying the drinks, which we then decide to take outside to the same area where Anna and I sat the day before. The darkness and the night air feel so good after the intensity of the evening so far.

'Can we walk a bit with our drinks?' I ask.

'Of course. Where would you like to go?'

'Into the garden.' I point across the rolling lawn, which is illuminated by a bright full moon so big and imposing, it feels like we could almost reach out and touch it.

We wander across the grass and I feel an urge to take off my shoes – not least because my heels keep sinking into the grass, making it difficult to walk. Calum reaches across and takes them by the straps, making me feel like a privileged young woman in a historical drama being courted by a wealthy man. It's also useful because it means that if I trip then I have a free hand to save myself with – and hopefully my drink.

'Tell me about yourself, Steph,' says Calum. 'Apart from working for a charity, what's your thing? What makes you tick?'

Jamie. Jamie makes me tick.

I push this invasive thought aside and take a slug from my G&T. 'I… um… gosh, I don't know. I like walking, reading…'

'Drinking…' Calum jokes.

'Ha ha… funny. I don't always overdo it the way I have tonight. I was nervous about leading the event and…' I trail off: the truth is that my breakup with Jamie and the fact that I thought I saw him earlier is also why I've drunk like a fish all evening.

'And what?'

'Oh… err… it's nothing. So, are you going to kiss me or what?'

Nothing like diving into the arms of another man to get Jamie off my mind.

Calum stops and looks at me. 'I'd like to, but you seem a bit… heartbroken. And well, your friend said to go gently with you. I get the impression I'm going to be nothing more than your rebound guy.'

I wince at how that makes me look. 'Sorry, Calum. I'm fresh out of a breakup and a feeling a little delicate.'

'I'm sorry to hear that.'

I shrug. 'It is what it is.'

As we stand there awkwardly, I feel angry at Jamie. He doesn't want me, so he shouldn't get to interfere in my life.

Suddenly, I hear a giggle and a murmur nearby, followed by a long moan. Calum obviously hears it, too, because he puts a finger to his lips and listens. It's difficult to make things out in the dark, but the noises appear to be coming from the other side of a tall hedge, several feet away from us.

'That sounds like two people having sex.' My hand goes to my mouth in astonishment, my voice almost a whisper.

'It does.' Calum chuckles and keeps his voice low, too. 'I wonder who it is.'

'Maybe we should allow that to remain unanswered.'

'How about we head back to the outdoor tables?' he suggests. 'They'll have to come out some time and we'll be ready to bust them when they do.'

'What are you? The alfresco sex police?'

'You're not even remotely curious?'

'I don't know. Kind of figure it's their business.'

'Ah, where's the fun in that?'

Calum lifts my shoes and we creep away, back in the direction of the bar. Once we reach the outdoor seating area, we grab a table and chat away as we enjoy our drinks. It's pleasant enough, but he's a bit too smug and nosey for my liking. He's nothing like Jamie, and I'm beginning to regret coming outside with him. Rather than providing a distraction, all he's doing is reminding me of everything I miss about Jamie.

About fifteen minutes later, the silhouettes of two figures appear beneath the moon, walking in our direction, chatting and giggling.

'Here we go.' Calum sits forward in his seat as if he's reached the long-anticipated reveal in a gritty whodunnit.

'You might want to be a little more subtle than that.' I suggest, but he doesn't seem to hear me.

The figures approach until they're within the reach of the outdoor lighting, and we can see them in their full glory. As recognition dawns, I facepalm and shake my head. I should have guessed. The mystery lovers are none other than Anna and the barman from the day before.

Calum looks delighted at having caught them out, and I kind of want to skelp him across the back of the head for being such a loser. At the same time, I want to do the same to Anna for corrupting that poor barman, who hopefully will still have a job at the end of all this. Because Calum, it seems, is not the kind of guy who's going to keep quiet.

'*Hoi hoi*,' he greets Anna and her 'conquest' as they approach. 'Glad to see someone's getting some action tonight.'

This ribbing doesn't faze Anna at all. She simply throws back a 'jealous, are you?' at Calum, but the barman looks mortified, and scared out of his wits that he's going to end up in trouble.

'I'll call you,' he says to Anna before he shoots back to the bar, smoothing out his shirt as he goes.

'I thought I told you not to corrupt that poor guy,' I say to her as she takes a seat at the table with us.

'I tried not to. He's just so damn cute. Think I might keep this one around.'

I laugh loudly and pin her with a look. 'Like I haven't heard that before. Shall we call it a night before we get ourselves — or anyone else — in any more trouble?'

Chapter 28

A week and a bit later, I'm doing better than I was. The opportunities presented by my upcoming promotion and Lizzie's vote of confidence in me have certainly given me a lift, but Jamie is still on my mind for much of every day. I must be making progress though, because mixed in with the sadness and feeling like someone's gouged a big bloody hole out of my heart, I'm experiencing intermittent pangs of resentment. Resentment because he bulldozed into my life on Hogmanay, let me fall for him, and then buggered off again. But he's clearly some kind of crook, and none of it was real in the first place. There are players, and then – it transpires – there's Jamie. A big fat schemer – who's not actually fat; he's totally gorgeous and, frustratingly, I still have ridiculous wedding fantasies about him. I'm so confused, I start to wonder if I'm suffering from the I've-been-screwed-over equivalent of Stockholm Syndrome.

'So, are you and Jamie still broken up?' Kayleigh asks as she plays with the foam on her skinny latte.

'Yup, we are.' I let out a deflated sigh and take a sip from my cappuccino.

It's Saturday afternoon and I'm engaging in a rare catch up with my sister. Not something I do often, but as we're unfortunately blood related, I have to make the occasional effort. Plus, she's been trying to organise it for weeks and there are only so many excuses I can deploy before she has a hissy fit and dobs me in to our parents for being a bad sister. That's happened before and I did not enjoy the fall out.

'Have you even heard from him since?'

'Nope.'

'Huh.' She assumes a thoughtful expression. 'It's weird, isn't it? That he's nowhere to be found on social media. I've tried a few times.'

'Can we talk about something else?' I fidget with the empty sugar packet in front of me. 'I'm trying to forget about Jamie and move on, and you're not really helping.'

'OK, fine. But I still reckon it's weird.'

'How's your Instagram following doing?'

This is a sure-fire way to get Kayleigh to move on. The only thing she loves more than gossiping about others is yapping on about herself.

'I'm nearing twenty-seven thousand followers.' She puffs her chest out proudly.

'Gosh, that's actually quite impressive.' Although I'm normally immune to Kayleigh's insufferable social media chat, I have to acknowledge that she's dedicated, and she appears to be building a genuine following.

'If you look at the definitions online – which change depending on what site you look at – I'm what you might call a micro-influencer.'

'Right, wow. And what does that mean?'

She makes a face. 'It means that I have a small amount of influence online – *obviously*.'

'*All right*, no need to be bitchy about it.' I hold my hands up in a gesture of self-defence. 'What I mean is, how does that influence work? What are your followers getting from you and what do *you* get from doing this?'

'Well, I've kind of claimed Edinburgh as my niche. I'm finding hidden gems across the city that people might not easily come across and then I'm sharing them.'

'So *that's* why we're in a cafe on Easter Road. Now it makes sense. Didn't think this was your kind of haunt.'

'It's not. But my followers are loving it. Look.' She thrusts her phone in my face. 'I've already had two hundred likes and a handful of comments on the post I published when we arrived.'

'I see. That's great.' I lean back so I can focus on the screen.

'And I love sharing this information with people to help them find great experiences. I enjoy improving their lives.'

'Now that I don't believe that for a second.' I smirk. 'What are you really getting out of it?'

'Why is it so hard to believe that I might want to help others, just like you do?' Kayleigh pouts and inspects her perfectly shellacked nails.

'Because you've never done anything for anyone else in your life, and you constantly pick on me for having a job that does exactly that.'

'*OK, fine.* I want to make a career out of it. If I can gain enough followers, I'll have local businesses paying me to share their stuff. Then I can take it national and then international—'

'And then you'll basically be paid to be on holiday permanently?' I raise a questioning eyebrow.

'You make it sound like I want a life of skiving off.' She sniffs.

'Don't you?'

'*No.* It'll be hard work.'

I let out a belly laugh, which attracts some attention from the customers around us.

'Yeah, right. Lying on a beach, eating amazing food and drinking cocktails at the best places all over the world will be such hard work.'

'Shut. Up. Steph.' Kayleigh glances around her uncomfortably. 'Someone might recognise me.'

'Sorry.' I suddenly feel guilty for mocking her. 'Well, I wish you all the best with that, Kayleigh. It certainly sounds like a nice life plan and something that will make you happy. Shall we get going?'

Kayleigh doesn't need to be asked twice. She gets up and scuttles out of the door with her head down.

We make our way up Easter Road towards London Road, where we can catch a bus to the city centre. The next part of our afternoon outing together is – going shopping. To say I'm dreading it is an understatement. It will inevitably play out with me sitting in changing rooms watching Kayleigh try on an endless stream of extortionately priced garments, probably buying none of them because she can't afford them either. She wants the experience and any valuable material she happens to uncover along the way for her Instagram account.

As we walk, I see a homeless man sitting on the street outside a grocery store not far beyond us. He has his hood up and his head down, and I wonder if it's the same guy I've given money to along at The Shore in the past.

'Hey.' I nudge Kayleigh. 'I'm trying to understand your world. Why don't you try to understand mine? Give the man some money to help him afford a hostel tonight – or whatever he needs it for.'

'*Ugh*. You are joking.' Kayleigh raises her eyes to the sky in disgust. 'Probably wants it for booze or drugs or something.'

'Don't be so judgemental. A lot of people who end up on the streets have no addiction issues. They're just unlucky – maybe lose their job or get sick. And need I remind you that addiction is an illness, not a choice? It's because of the inequalities of our society and often a lack of a support network that people end up sleeping rough. Go on. Try giving him something and see how it feels.'

Kayleigh gives me an exasperated look but doesn't argue. To my surprise, she reaches into her purse and pulls out a five-pound note rather than some pocket change, and stuffs it in the man's makeshift collection tin – a disposable coffee cup – as she passes.

The man obviously sees this and in his own surprise at her generosity, lifts his head to thank her. In that split second everything changes. At first, I think I've finally lost the plot and I've moved beyond fantasies to full-on hallucinations. Then Kayleigh squeals with horror and it's clear this is no apparition – the man we're both looking back at is a slightly dishevelled-looking Jamie.

'*OMG, Steph*. That's your ex!'

I stare mutely at Jamie as his own horrified eyes move from Kayleigh to me.

The moment is a blur and passes so quickly that it's over before I can register what's happening. Kayleigh starts yelping about Jamie being a fraud and possibly even a criminal, and stirs up one hell of a flap – attracting attention from all around. I just stand there with my mouth open, paralysed by the shock of it all. Jamie's face fills with mortification and shame as he jumps to his feet and takes off down the street as fast as he can.

'Oh, Steph.' Kayleigh steadies herself by leaning on the windowsill of a hair salon. 'I can't believe that happened.'

'Neither can I.' I finally find my voice, still staring in the direction in which Jamie ran off.

'I mean... *who does that?* Pretends they're some high-flying entrepreneur and weasels their way into the lives of people who actually work hard and have self-respect. He must have been trying to scam us. Steph, you were in real danger...'

She continues to bleat on as if we've had a near-death experience, while my mind rotates at warp speed. What the hell just happened? That really was Jamie... which makes no sense. Or does it? It would explain all the secrecy and why he talked of being in a temporary situation – no one wants to be on the streets indefinitely – but nothing else matches up. He was so well turned out, he was at the street party without a care in the world, he talked of being a successful entrepreneur and it was so convincing.

Suddenly the pieces fall into place. Why we never went out for a plush meal. Why our dates were always so cheap. Why I never saw his place. And why he only shared any information about what he did for a living when my family backed him into a corner – because it was probably what he used to do before... *what?* What happened that caused him to be homeless? I know the probable answer to this – I've just schooled my own sister on this matter. Bad luck and a shitty set of circumstances. No wonder Jamie didn't want to share this situation. He was ashamed; I saw that in his face. But instead of making him feel at ease and showing the understanding I show to the kids we support at the charity every day, I stared at him like he was an alien.

279

'I mean, it's going to take a while to recover from this.' Kayleigh's still making a huge drama out of the situation. 'You should probably change your locks, Steph, and maybe even inform the police—'

'*For what?*' I finally tune back in and lose my cool. 'Tell me, Kayleigh. What's Jamie done other than hide a situation that he clearly felt humiliated by?'

Kayleigh's startled into silence by my outburst.

'That poor man ran off because he was so ashamed that I'd learned the truth about him, and I didn't even try to stop him.'

'Probably for the best,' she says in a small voice. 'You don't know that he's a good guy.'

'I do.' I straighten my shoulders and take a deep, faltering breath. 'There's been all this doubt and suspicion, and I let myself be taken in by it. But that look on his face there, it told me *everything* I needed to know. And now, because I'm the one who's the real fraud – as it turns out – I've probably lost him forever.'

Chapter 29

Straight after the drama on Easter Road, I abandon my planned shopping trip with Kayleigh and call a crisis meeting with Anna and Connor. We meet in a hipster cafe over the road from the bustling Leith Market at The Shore.

'I can't believe he's homeless.' Anna shakes her head in disbelief, while stirring sugar into her coffee. 'I knew there was something dodgy going on, but *that* never crossed my radar.'

'There wasn't something "dodgy" going on.' I pin her with my best schoolteacher look.

'I just mean he *was* hiding something after all.'

'He was embarrassed and ashamed by the predicament he was in. Probably wanted a sense of normality in his life, where he wasn't treated like some down and out. And what did I do? I put extra pressure on him during what's probably the most difficult time in his life.'

'Hey... don't be so hard on yourself.' Connor puts a supportive hand on mine. 'You didn't know. You couldn't have known. Jamie chose to keep that from you, so you could only act on the information you had. You're not psychic.'

'I suppose.' I grimace, unconvinced by this argument. 'I'm so angry at myself for how I acted when I saw him. I live my life by a set of values that puts others first, with no judgement about the difficult situations they find themselves in. Then, the moment there's something a bit closer to home, I don't live up to them.'

'What do you mean?' Connor asks.

'Well… when he looked up, and Kayleigh started yelping and being all ridiculous, I should have gone straight to his defence. I should have shown empathy and understanding. Instead, I stood there, frozen to the spot, doing nothing to put him at ease or manage the situation.'

'So, you got a shock.' He shrugs. 'He was the last person you were expecting to see in that situation. That's hardly a crime.'

'I've not finished. I also…' I feel more tears prick at my eyes as my own shame washes over me. 'I… also… felt a bit embarrassed. It was only momentary, but the first thought that crossed my mind was, "I've been dating a homeless guy?". That's so judgemental and wrong on *every* level.'

'OK, I understand why you're horrified to have had that thought, but that doesn't mean you're a bad person, Stephy. Or that you look down on Jamie, or any other person for that matter. Look at the great work you do every day, helping people in need. Thoughts are just thoughts. You had an "in the moment" reaction – a kind of fight, flight or freeze response. That's all.'

'You think?'

'I do.' Connor nods earnestly and takes a bite from his scone.

'Steph…' Anna re-joins the conversation, having left Connor to counsel me through that moment of self-doubt. 'I know you're not going to want to hear this, but… are you absolutely certain there's nothing off about this situation? I know as well as you do that people generally end up on the streets because they've had a rough time of it, but – and this is completely unrelated to him being homeless – there *are* some bad eggs in the world.'

'I'm sure,' I say automatically, and clock Anna raising an eyebrow at Connor. 'OK, I can tell you think I'm being too impulsive on this. That all I'm going with is a gut instinct.'

'It certainly looks that way,' says Anna.

'Fine. Then let me think for a minute.'

I sit quietly, sipping at my cappuccino – decaf to avoid me getting too wired – and munching my granola bar. Pushing aside all my instincts to defend Jamie's honour, I try to weigh up the facts one at a time. Anna and Connor chat away between themselves to allow me some headspace.

'Right, I've properly thought about it,' I eventually announce.

'And?' Anna prompts me.

'And I stand by what I said before. It all makes perfect sense. Other than the fact that he's been so well turned out every time I've met him, and doesn't even remotely act like someone who's potentially been sleeping rough.'

'He could be staying in a hostel. That would give him access to showers and stuff.'

'That's true, he could be.'

'So, you're absolutely sure about this?' She looks me straight in the eye, perhaps to see if there's even the slightest hint of indecision.

'I am.' I nod resolutely.

'Then you need to find him.'

The moment she says this, I feel sick to my stomach.

'I can't, Anna. He's not going to want to speak to me after what happened today. Especially after Kayleigh was such a snotty cow and treated him like a lowlife criminal. I'm surprised she hasn't put something on the family WhatsApp group yet about her "real-life trauma" or some bullshit like that.'

'Or her Instagram account.' Connor chips in and I feel the colour drain from my face.

Snatching at my phone, I look up her page and breathe a sigh of relief. 'She hasn't. Thank goodness. Otherwise, I might just be going down for murder.'

'Maybe she's had a learning moment, too?' Anna suggests.

I snort into my drink, sending foam flying in all directions. 'You think Kayleigh's capable of developing some humanity? You must also think pigs can fly.'

As I say this, my mind transports me to the bar at The Shore where Jamie and I drank his favourite beer with flying animals on the can. *Serve Minus Pigs*. Such a strange name, but it tasted so good. Jamie tasted so good. I felt so safe and warm in his arms, despite it being freezing outside, because he had that effect on me. My super sexy, incredibly kind and funny security blanket. I felt that, with him by my side, I could conquer anything. And strange as it might sound, I know he felt the same about being with me.

I can't let that slip away. What if I never find it with anyone again? And my feelings aside, I want to help him get out of the awful situation he's in.

'You need to find him,' Anna repeats, reading my face.

'I do.' I instinctively get to my feet and start to pull on my jacket.

'I didn't mean right this second.'

'Yeah, Stephy, you need to think how to go about this,' says Connor. 'Let's sort a plan together.'

'You're right.' I sink back into my seat. 'I haven't a clue where to look. It's taking me back to the exact same position I was in when I did the beer-can thing. Actually worse. Needle and a billion haystacks.'

'Not necessarily.' Connor holds up a calming hand. 'He'll probably avoid anywhere you might easily find him, but he possibly won't go that much further from his regular haunts. Especially if he's staying in a hostel. Buses cost money, remember?'

'Of course.' I feel a twinge of hope that Connor's on to something.

'Also, we could check out the hostels. They're never going to tell us if he's staying there because of data protection, but—'

'We could do a stakeout.' Anna's eyes widen with excitement at the idea of putting one of her Netflix-inspired fantasies in action.

'Exactly that,' says Connor.

'Oh, my goodness, yes.' My own enthusiasm is now rising. 'We can map out an area to cover, and go from there. I just hope he'll be willing to listen to me if I do eventually find him.'

Making a plan is the easy part. Executing it successfully is the challenge. The lack of progress in achieving our goal is almost soul-destroying. We spend the rest of the day and the best part of the following one pounding the pavements and hanging around outside hostels, checking in with each other via a newly formed WhatsApp group named 'Operation Find Jamie' – which is similar to the email address I used for my beer can appeal. I even try bargaining with the staff on the reception desks to try and get them to tell me if he's staying there, but it's a fruitless exercise. With every hour that passes without results, my hope of finding him diminishes.

I resume trudging to work and trudging back home. It feels like Jamie and I have broken up all over again; a gnawing emptiness that nothing and no one but he can resolve. Anna tries her best to distract me while I'm in the office, but to no avail. He's on my mind almost every waking moment. As is my anger and frustration at myself for not giving him the benefit of the doubt when he asked me to trust him; then letting him down again in the moment he most needed my support and understanding.

As the evenings become longer following the recent change of the clocks, combined with my moping perhaps becoming unbearable, Anna decides that we should take another stab at 'Operation Find Jamie' on Thursday after work.

'I did a Google search and found a couple of smaller hostels,' she says as we walk along Great Junction Street to where we're meeting Connor. 'Thought we could maybe get some fish and chips for dinner while we do our stakeout.'

'Sure. Why not.' I sigh glumly, unconvinced that this escapade will be any more successful than the previous ones.

'Hey, we'll find him. I'm going to make sure of that. Have been feeling awful that I was the one who made you doubt Jamie in the first place. If I'd kept my big mouth shut, maybe things would have played out differently.'

'It's not your fault, Anna. You weren't the only who wasn't comfortable with it. Jamie chose to hide this from me, and while I understand now why he did, it gave the doubt in my own mind time to grow. I would have gotten to the same place. It might just have taken a little longer because I was in denial about the whole thing.'

'Thanks. I appreciate you saying that.' She links her arm through mine. 'I have a naturally sceptical mind, and I'm learning that my instincts aren't always right.'

'Don't beat yourself up about it. We all have blind spots.'

'We sure do. Actually, I've been wondering... if you'd known that Jamie was homeless when you first met him – before you had all these feelings for him – do you think you would have dated him?'

I grimace. 'I've been asking myself the same question, while deliberating over whether my moral compass is still intact. I'd like to say I would have – that it wouldn't have been a deal breaker. I know you and Connor would have been fine with it, provided he was a good guy who was trying to get back on his feet. The thing that would have got in the way, I'm ashamed to admit—'

'Would have been your family.' Anna finishes my sentence for me as we arrive at the meeting point at the Queen Victoria Statue, beside the Newkirkgate Shopping Centre.

'Exactly.' I give her a slightly shameful smile. 'They would never have been OK with that. I mean, look at how they were about Connor, and he has a job and a roof over his head. I would have found it difficult to hide Jamie's situation... Kayleigh would have been on me like a sniffer dog. And why should I have to lie anyway – all to please them?'

'It's complicated, eh?' She shoots me a sympathetic look.

'It sure is.'

'Everything OK here?' Connor appears seemingly from nowhere, scrutinising my face.

'She's having a moment.' Anna gives him a little nod to indicate that everything's all right but to tread gently.

'Aww… Stephy.' Connor puts his arm around me and gives me a squeeze. 'Come on, let's get this sting under way.'

I cosy into Connor gratefully as Anna fills him in on the plan and we set off along Duke Street in the direction of Leith Links. It's a cloudy, slightly breezy evening, but thankfully the wind is not the usual icy breeze that comes off the Forth Estuary, so it's warm enough to sit out.

We stop at a chip shop on the way and then park ourselves on a bench in Leith Links, not far from the entrance to the first hostel on Anna's list. In some ways, it's quite fun sitting there chatting and laughing together. Definitely the best distraction I've had all week. It also helps knowing that I'm doing something to try and find Jamie again.

Once we've eaten and discarded our packaging in a bin nearby, Anna reviews our plan for the evening.

'Right, how shall we play this?' she asks. 'As I said, I also found another place we should check out. It's only a few blocks from here.'

'How about you go there, and I'll stay here with Steph,' suggests Connor. 'I'm not sure she should be on her own at the moment.'

'I'm *fine*,' I protest. 'I don't need you to babysit me.'

'Still. Humour me, will you?' He gives me a brotherly dig in the ribs.

'OK, sure. Will be nice to have your company.'

'Perfect.' Anna gets to her feet and brushes herself down to get rid of any crumbs from her food. 'Keep me updated on the group chat.'

She heads back along the path through the park towards the main road and eventually disappears from sight.

'So, how are things going with Lukas?' I ask, suddenly recalling Connor's own love life. 'I'm sorry I haven't been very communicative recently.'

'No need to apologise.' His eyes don't leave the building we're watching. 'You've had a lot on your mind.'

'Yeah, but still. I could have asked.'

'It's all good. As you know, we're taking it slow, but we met for a third time the other night. He's a great guy. Did I mention he's German?'

'No, that's awesome.'

'It is. He's from the north, Hamburg. Has this cool accent, likes his beer and he's really smart. Works as an analyst for a finance company.'

'Does he give you tingles?' I prod Connor's leg theatrically.

'I'm not going to grace that with an answer.' He shakes his head at me and turns an interesting shade of crimson, telling me all I need to know.

We continue to watch the entrance to the hostel as we chat, and after a while, I find myself getting thirsty.

'Gosh, those chips were salty, weren't they? My mouth is like sandpaper.'

'Mine, too,' says Connor. 'You be OK here while I go find a shop?'

'I'll be fine.'

'Fair enough. Back soon.' He gets up and heads in the same direction that Anna previously took.

I sit back down and continue to watch the front entrance of the hostel. After a few minutes, my phone buzzes with a WhatsApp message to our group.

> **Anna:**
> Nothing to report here so far. You?

I quickly type a reply to the same effect, also letting her know that Connor's gone off in search of some drinks for us. She responds asking Connor to get her one for later, and I end up chatting to her online. After about five minutes, Connor pitches in.

> **Connor:**
> Remind me never to hire you two as private investigators. You can't be watching the entrance ways if you're yapping away on here.

'*Shit*, he's right,' I say out loud and stuff my phone in my bag.

Turning my attention back to the hostel, there's nothing out of the ordinary going on, but there is a man walking away from it in the direction of Duke Street. What if that's Jamie and I missed him because I've got attention span of a toddler?

Feeling a surge of panic, I'm suddenly certain that it's him and I'm about to miss my chance. I can only see the back of him and he's quite far away, but there's nothing to indicate it's not Jamie – the stranger has the same colour of hair, and from what I remember, is a comparative height and build. Fuelled by adrenaline, I take off across the park after him. My poor body doesn't know what's hit it as I attempt a speed I clearly can't manage.

Thankfully the man is walking at a leisurely pace and it doesn't take long to catch up with him. But even from even from several feet away, I still can't tell if it's him, so I call out to him.

'Excuse me?'

The man stops and turns to see what's going on. The moment I see his face my spirits drop. It's not Jamie. He's probably about five years younger and seems perplexed by my sudden approach.

'Sorry…' I bend over to catch my breath. 'I thought… you were someone else.'

Thoroughly disappointed by this red herring, and coming to the realisation that while I was chasing this guy, Jamie could have come out of the hostel and headed off in the other direction, I feel a wave of hopelessness once more. Maybe this is a complete waste of time. The chances of me, Connor or Anna being in the same place as Jamie at the exact moment, even with our carefully crafted plan in place, is highly unlikely as I learned from trying to find him the first time round. As this thought crystalises, my head droops and I despondently return in the direction of the bench.

As I walk – my head full of a million disappointed thoughts – I glance across at the hostel entrance and do a double take. Standing outside, talking to another guy is Jamie. I give my head a little shake and rub at my weary eyes to make sure I'm not seeing things, but it's definitely him. My heart starts to pound again as a second surge of adrenaline sets in. *I've found him.*

Glancing back in the direction of the bench where Connor's just reappeared, I see him furiously gesturing to me. I signal back that I've clocked Jamie and I'm on it. Then, with my heart hammering in my chest, I take a deep, courage-inducing breath and walk straight towards him.

Chapter 30

Jamie doesn't spot me at first. He chats away easily with his companion; his gorgeous smile as appealing as it always was, his sexy man curls bouncing lightly as he talks. But he's dressed differently to how he was on our dates. He's wearing jeans that look worn, scuffed trainers and an over-sized dark grey hoodie. If I'm remembering correctly, it's the same top he had on – and was using to hide his identity – the day I saw him on Easter Road. I feel conflicted as I take all this in: I'm jangling with excitement at the sight of the man I love, but I'm also hugely nervous about approaching him. There's also a tugging feeling of dismay that he's in this situation.

As I get nearer, he spots me and his expression quickly changes to one of surprise, then of appearing to have been caught out. He abruptly halts his conversation and his eyes dart around as if seeking an escape route.

'Jamie, please don't run,' I call to him. '*Please.*'

His companion turns and looks me up and down. He's dressed similarly to Jamie, and although I shouldn't assume, I'm guessing he's homeless as well.

'I'll see you later, mate,' Jamie says to him and the guy walks off, still checking me out as if I'm up to no good.

'Hi,' I wince as I greet him, unable to hide the shame that's been plaguing me since that unfortunate day.

'Steph, what are you doing here?'

His tone is colder and more clinical than I've known. It's nothing like my previous interactions with him, which totally throws me. He's also either unwilling or unable to make eye contact with me, keeping his eyes on the ground.

'I'm... eh...' I stammer. 'I've been looking for you... I wanted to see you.'

'Well, here I am.' He spreads his arms in a passive-aggressive manner. 'You've seen me. Take a good look. I'd have thought once would have been enough though.'

'What? *No.* It's not like that, Jamie. I'm not here on some kind of voyeuristic outing.'

'Then why *are* you here?'

'Jamie, please... don't be like that,' I plead with him, but he remains stony.

'Like what, Steph? What am I being like?'

'You're not yourself. You're behaving as if—'

'I'm homeless and humiliated by it? Good spot.'

'No, I mean, you're behaving as if... I've wronged you. And I suppose I have, but it wasn't me who made a scene last weekend. It was my sister.'

'Ah, yes...' He assumes a sarcastic expression, his gaze still fixed on the ground. 'Lovely Kayleigh who lives in her fantasy Instagram world and has probably never had to lift a finger – she's a right little princess.'

'Please don't.' I fiddle with the button on my jacket self-consciously. 'You know I hate her snobbish and self-indulgent ways, but she's still my sister.'

Jamie looks up and across the park, his mouth taut. It's clear he's trying to hold himself back from saying something even worse.

'Look, I know that was awful for you. I'm having a hard time forgiving Kayleigh for that outburst, and I hate her attitude to homeless people generally...' I wince again as Jamie momentarily looks like he might cry. 'But, Jamie, that was her. Not me. I didn't react that way.'

'You hardly came to my defence.'

'I know, and I'm sorry for that. I was in shock and I didn't cope well in the moment.'

'Shock, eh?' He clenches his jaw, and a bitter look passes across his face. 'Yeah, it was such a shock for you, finding out your ex is begging on the streets. That's *way* harder to deal with than actually going through it – sitting on dog-piss-stained, cold pavements, feeling like a piece of shit while people give you a wide berth and do their best to pretend you're invisible. *That's* the definition of hard, Steph.'

'I know. I know.' I wring my hands hopelessly.

This isn't at all going the way I'd hoped. I'd thought that Jamie would be understanding and willing to listen to my apology – that we'd be able to pick up where we left off, now this hulking great secret is out in the open. I look across to the bench where Connor's sitting. I can see him watching, but he's too far away for me to read his expression.

'Look, Jamie, I'm not trying to excuse my reaction.' I try and fail to make eye contact with him. 'I'm just trying to explain it. I've felt angry at myself and ashamed for not dealing with it better. If we could go back to last Saturday, I'd do things differently. I came to find you to apologise – to say how sorry I am for how I made you feel. I'm not judging you, Jamie. I want to understand and I want to support you.'

Jamie shifts uncomfortably on the spot. 'Fine, I accept your apology, but please don't do your charity-worker stuff with me. I don't want to be your project.'

'No, you misunderstand. I don't mean support you in that way. I mean support you as your girlfriend – as people in relationships support each other. I want us to be together.' I take a tentative step towards him to show that I'm serious.

Jamie looks me square in the face for the first time, and for a moment, I think maybe it's going to be OK.

'You're saying you want to be with me, even now you know the truth?'

'Yes.' I smile at him with loving eyes.

'You want to be with a guy who has no place to live, no job, no prospects?'

'I want to be with *you*.'

'Do you want to know what I think?'

'Uh-huh…' My smile falters as I sense a change of tone.

'I think you're a rocket, Steph. I think you don't know how to draw the line between work and personal. This…' He waves his index finger back and forth between us. 'This can't happen. Your family would *never* accept me.'

'It's none of their business.'

'But it is. Because as much as you see yourself as the black sheep, you're not that different from them. You've never known what it is to struggle and you probably never will. To lose your dignity to the level that other people are making decisions about your life. To resist begging on the streets until the realisation hits that it could be the difference between sleeping in a bed or under a bridge.'

'Jamie… I…' I have no idea how to respond to this.

'Steph. *No.* Think about it.' Jamie's tone is firm. 'I mean, *really* think about it for a minute. What we had was incredible, but it wasn't real. I can never be part of your world now, so let's just say our goodbyes and leave it at that.'

I feel choked with disbelief and emotion, my eyes stinging as I try to hold back the tears that are threatening to come. 'Jamie, please, no. We're so—'

'*Goodbye*, Steph.'

Allowing me no further opportunity to state my case, Jamie strides off into the hostel, leaving me shell-shocked and heartbroken all over again.

'I wish I'd been there. I'd have given him a right going over for speaking to you like that.' Anna lays my duvet over me and tucks me in mum-style.

We've arrived back at mine following Connor sending an SOS to Anna via the WhatsApp group and then us picking her up in a taxi. It's like déjà vu as Anna plonks herself at the end of the sofa where my feet are, and Connor settles down on the other side, inviting me to seek refuge in his armpit once again.

'He wasn't the Jamie I know at all.' I sniff and wipe away my tears, prompting Anna to hand me a fresh tissue from the box. 'He was so cold and unfriendly.'

'He's a bastard who doesn't deserve you,' says Anna.

'He's embarrassed and he's hurting,' Connor corrects her.

'Whose side are you on?' She pierces him with a glare.

'I'm not saying he's not treated Steph badly. I'm suggesting there's a reason why he has. You ladies seem to think we men are devoid of emotions.'

'That's what you let us think.'

'Because that's how society has set the rules.' Connor gives her an arch look. 'Well, guess what? We feel things just like you; but we don't know how to deal with those feelings, because we've grown up being told we have to be strong and solid – and that emotions are for wimps.'

'Connor, I'm not sure you're helping here,' says Anna.

'Anna, it's fine.' I gently prod her thigh with my foot from underneath the duvet. 'Connor makes a good point. In some ways, it even makes me feel a little better. I'd rather think that Jamie's rejecting me because he can't handle this situation, than that he hates me.'

'That's exactly what I mean.' Connor gives me a gentle squeeze of a hug. 'He doesn't hate you. He's just not in a place where he can have a successful relationship with you, because he feels humiliated and emasculated – whether that's a rational response or not.'

'It sucks though. I thought he was "the one".'

'He's not "the one",' says Anna. 'There is no "one". That's a false concept created by people who like to sell us books and movies.'

'Ah, Anna, you're such a romantic.' Connor chuckles.

'Yeah, she's more of a quickie in the hotel gardens kind of girl,' I quip feebly through my tears.

'I am not.' Anna feigns outrage. 'There was nothing quick about that hook up.'

'That is true,' I concede with a nod. 'You were with him for quite a while.'

'And we're dating now, so that'll shut you up.'

'You are?' My mouth drops open in surprise.

'Yup. Didn't want to say anything because you're having a crappy time of it.'

'Oh, forget me.' I wave my hand at her. 'I can handle others being happy while my own love life is down the pan. It actually gives me some hope if you've found someone you like – even if he's definitely not "the one".'

'It's not that he's not "the one".' She rolls her eyes at me. 'As I said, it's the concept that's flawed.'

'So... he could be "the one"?'

'Yes. I mean, no. I'm saying... *oh, shut up.*'

Anna looks flustered all of a sudden and it dawns on me that she must really like this guy. I've never seen her this way about anyone.

'Think Steph got you there, Anna,' says Connor.

'*Whatever.*' She makes a face at him. 'The important thing is that there are lots of great guys around. Steph will discover that once she gets back out there and allows me to manage her online dating.'

'I'm nowhere near ready for that.' I shake my head vigorously, repelled by the thought. 'But I have to admit, you seem to have done a good job for Connor.'

'Speaking of which, how's that working out?' asks Anna.

'It's going well.' Connor grins and the flush I saw earlier this evening returns. 'It's kind of cool, us working through things together. He's so thoughtful and he has these incredibly cute dimples that he hates me pointing out.'

'*Amazing.*' Anna clasps her hands together gleefully. 'There you are, Steph. Whenever you're ready, let's resurrect your dating profile and find you someone better than Jamie.'

'OK… sure, I guess.' I give a dejected shrug. 'But for now, can I just cry and watch people get brutally murdered?'

'Of course.' Anna pats my leg sympathetically and powers up Netflix. 'I'll make it a particularly gruesome one.'

As she searches for the programme and I continue to snuggle into Connor, my roving thoughts – which are heavy with the awful memories of earlier – are filled with a cavernous sense of loss. I may have agreed to let Anna manage my dating life in the future, but right now I can't imagine ever wanting to date anyone else, or accepting that there's no such thing as "the one" – because I'm pretty sure I've just lost him.

Chapter 31

Six months later

'I vote for a round of sambuca shots.' Anna's arm shoots in the air like she's in primary three.

'Definitely not.' I frown at her and cancel her vote by drawing an invisible cross in the air. 'And as it's my birthday, I get to choose the drink for my birthday toast.'

'That's not a rule.'

'It is since you tried to make me do shots.'

'I'm suggesting one shot. It's not like I lined them up on the bar and pulled out a timer.'

'You might if you thought you'd get away with it.'

'OK, ladies, break it up.' Connor laughs and shakes his head at the two of us. 'I'm sure Lukas and Mateusz have seen enough.'

'I am not sure…' Lukas flashes me one of his dazzling smiles, displaying the cute dimples Connor is so enchanted by. 'I like to see strong, powerful women standing up for what they are believing in.'

'Thank you, Lukas.' Anna high-fives him. 'And I know it turns Mateusz on – though he'll never admit that in public – so we're all good.'

Mateusz's cheeks sizzle with embarrassment and Anna reaches across, giving him a big smacker on the lips.

'So, what's your drink of choice then, Stephy?' Connor prompts me to check out the almost endless rows of alcohol bottles behind the trendy city centre bar we're in.

I deliberate for a moment. 'It has to be fizz.'

'OK, one bottle of Champagne coming right up. My treat.'

'*What?*' I gawp at him. 'No. That's too much, Connor.'

'Nonsense.'

'No, it is. You can't afford that.' I fix him with a look.

'I can. It's your special day and… well, I'm kind of celebrating, too.'

'Why? What's going on?' I glance between him and Lukas. 'You're not engaged, are you?'

Lukas bellows with laughter, while Connor pats my head soothingly.

'No, we're not engaged. Don't panic.'

'I wasn't panicking.'

'Yes, you were. Let me go grab a bottle, then I'll come back and reveal all.'

Connor hops off his stool and makes his way to the bar, returning several minutes later with five Champagne flutes. He's followed by one of the bar staff carrying our bottle of Champagne and an ice bucket. We fall silent and watch as the bar person expertly opens the bottle, teasing out the cork with a gentle pop and we all cheer.

'So, what are you celebrating?' Anna asks Connor, once we each have a glass of fizz sitting in front of us. 'Come on, spill.'

'OK, then… I've decided to go to college.'

'*What?* That's amazing news. When… how… *when*…?' I'm so excited I can't get the words out.

Everyone laughs at my inarticulate interrogation.

'Well, you know how I've been finding work a bit chal-lenging?' says Connor. 'With all the cuts they're making.'

'Uh–huh.' I wave my hand impatiently, prompting him to continue.

'It got me thinking about why I was there and what I wanted in the future. You see… I made decisions about my life when I didn't really know who I was. Now that I've figured that out, I've realised I want something different.'

'What do you want?' I'm riveted by this reveal.

'I'm not sure exactly, but I know I'm a good problem solver and I like technology, so I've decided to do a found-ation course in computer programming. I'm hoping if I do well in it, I can maybe go on to do a degree and eventually get a job in that area.'

'Connor that's *fantastic*.' I throw my arms around him and give him a huge, squeezy hug. 'I have no doubt you'll nail it.'

'Thanks.' He gives a satisfied smile. 'It's just a part-time course. I'll need to keep working to fund it and pay my bills, but my mum has offered to help me out. I can pay her back once I'm earning mega bucks as an IT consultant or whatever.'

'*Ooh, yeah*.' Anna's eyes light up. 'Or you could work for one of those cool tech companies in the city centre.'

'Hopefully something like that.' Connor grins at her.

'Congrats, man.' Mateusz reaches across the table and shakes his hand. 'I have a friend in IT if you want to make some connections. He will be happy to have a beer with you.'

'That would be great. Thanks, Mateusz.'

Anna beams proudly at her man as though he's just offered Connor his dream job, and while this news sinks in, I look around the table and feel an emotional tug inside me. I'm so pleased that my two friends have found love, and that Connor has found a new direction, but all of a sudden, I don't feel like celebrating.

'What's up, hon?' Anna spots this immediately.

'Oh… it's… nothing.' I force a smile to cover up my hurt.

'It's *so* not nothing.'

'I've not upset you, have I, Stephy?' Connor's eyebrows knit together in concern. 'That was why I didn't want—'

'You've not upset me at all.' I cut him off and involuntarily glance at Lukas and Mateusz.

'Would you like us to give you a moment?' Lukas asks.

'We can go to the bar,' says Mateusz.

'No, no. Sorry.' I shake my head. 'You're fine. I'm not having you leave the table for me.'

'It is no problem,' says Lukas.

'Steph?' Anna prompts me. 'These are good guys. You're safe with them, you know that.'

'Of course. I'm being silly, ignore me.' I try to play down the moment. 'It just that… having you all here like this… ten or so months ago, I would never have imagined that I'd be the single one.'

'You mean because Connor was in a "delicate place" and I was a man-eater?' says Anna.

I blanch at her comment, my wide eyes landing on Mateusz to gauge his reaction.

'Oh, don't worry about him.' She laughs. 'He knows exactly what I was like. The we've-just-met alfresco sex in the hotel gardens was a bit of a giveaway. Who would have thought it would be a shy boy who finally tamed me, eh?' She and Mateusz share a nuzzling kiss.

'*See*. This is exactly what I mean,' I practically wail. 'It was all so unlikely. I was the one who thought I'd found my dream guy – then everything turned upside down.'

'Your guy is out there.' Connor puts his arm around me.

'Really?' I look at him searchingly. 'Because in the last four months, I've been on about fifteen dates and not a single one of them had any potential.'

'Did they have no potential, or have you set an impossibly high benchmark for them?' Anna raises a sceptical eyebrow.

'Don't start this again.'

'*Anna…*' Connor warns her not to do this on my birthday.

'All I'm saying is that it's a classic mistake people make after a painful breakup,' she says. 'They look for the person they've lost in every single potential match after that. These poor blokes you've been meeting can never live up to your expectations, because they're not Jamie.'

I open and close my mouth wordlessly, unsure how to respond to this.

'Steph, you are wonderful.' Lukas reaches out and takes my hand. 'Wonderful people find other wonderful people. I have no doubt that you will soon find what you are looking for.'

'Thank you.' I give him a grateful smile. 'I hope you're right. Connor, have I mentioned that I think this one's a keeper?' I nod my head toward Lukas.

'Only at least once a week.' Connor grins and shares a gooey, emotionally charged look with Lukas.

'Right, well…' I lift my glass. 'We mustn't let this Champagne get warm and flat because I'm on the verge of a birthday meltdown.'

My companions seem relieved that my wobble has passed and pleased to be able to finally lift their glasses.

'Happy birthday, Stephy.' Connor clinks his glass against mine as I beam back at him. 'To the most kindhearted, wonderful woman I've ever known.'

I go in for a second clink. 'And to your exciting and courageous change of direction – in more ways than one.'

Connor and Lukas share another sickeningly gooey look, while Anna and Mateusz share a kiss as the glass clinking continues. I deep breathe my way through the moment, and sink half my drink in one go.

Thankfully, once it has passed, we settle into some light, humorous group chat and I begin to feel a little less like the 'single fifth wheel'. In fact, as the lights dim and the music is turned up – signalling that Saturday night has well and truly kicked off – I'm able to shake off the negative feelings that have been weighing me down, and make the most of my birthday night out.

While bantering away with Lukas over whether I could sink a stein of German lager without coming up for air (the answer being: I couldn't, I'd throw up), one of the staff doing table service approaches us with a tray of drinks and places a beer and a glass in front of me.

'Oh, excuse me…' I call after her. 'I didn't order this.'

She doubles back and checks the till receipts on the tray.

'I don't think it's a mistake,' she says. 'There's a note on here to say it's a birthday drink for the woman in the green dress at table nine. This is table nine and you're wearing a green dress.'

Although I don't need to check – I know what I'm wearing – I look down at my outfit in confusion.

'Did one of you order this?' I ask my friends.

They all shake their heads.

'OK, thanks… I guess,' I say to the server, who wishes me a happy birthday then walks away.

I reach out to pick up the can of beer, which is partly obscured by the glass, and Anna stops me.

'Steph, wait… what if that's roofied? You don't know who it's from.'

I frown. 'That's true. Although… it's obviously from someone who knows it's my birthday. Surely no one I know well would spike my drink.'

I crane my neck to see if there's anyone I recognise in the bar, but it's packed and I can't see much beyond the people standing around us.

'I suppose.' Anna still looks mildly concerned.

I pick up the can and I'm about to pour it, when I feel something odd – it's like there's something taped to it. Then I notice the distinctive pattern of flying animals, which in the low lighting, I had missed.

'*Wait a minute…*' I rotate the can and clock the brand name: *Serve Minus Pigs*. Then I turn it some more and see a handwritten label.

> *Steph, when you gave me your heart, I was too broken to share, but now I'm in a better place, and life without you is a 'mare. Please forgive me.*

'Oh, my goodness.' I stare at the label incredulously as my body breaks into tingly goosebumps.

'What is it?' Anna reaches across and snatches the can from me.

'Stephy, that isn't…' Connor's twigged, but he's wary about continuing in case he's wrong.

'It is.' My heart is in my throat as the realisation fully hits me.

Jamie's here. In this bar. And he wants me back.

'Oh *wow*.' Anna looks at me with wide eyes. 'This is real, right? Not some copycat?'

I let out an incredulous laugh. 'You and your bloody crime dramas. Of course, it's real. Who else would know about this? And know to write me a poem in such a similar style?'

I hop off my bar stool and look around me wildly, trying to spot where Jamie is.

'Steph, wait…' Connor gently takes me by the wrist. 'Take a moment to digest this before you charge across to see him.'

'Yeah,' says Anna. 'How do you actually feel about it? Jamie broke your heart – more than once. Do you really want to leap to attention the moment he snaps his fingers? And can you trust that he'll stick around this time?'

I look at my friends as if they're mad, then in that momentary pause, the rational part of my brain kicks into gear. They're right. I need – at the very least – to check in with myself on this. I close my eyes and take a deep breath, and when I open them again, Anna, Connor, Lukas and Mateusz are all watching me intently, waiting for my next move.

'OK, I've thought it through and provided there's a reasonable explanation for it all… and Jamie's willing to start afresh in a fully open and honest way… I want him back.'

'OK…' Anna nods slowly and smiles at me. 'But you'd better come back to this table knowing his surname and pretty much everything there is to know about him, or it's "no deal" from us, right, Connor?'

'I'm not sure I'd put it like that,' says Connor. 'But the argument stands up.'

'That seems fair.' I look at my two friends, and dance on the spot excitedly for a moment, then I grab the can of beer and make my way through the crowded bar.

At first, I can't find Jamie and quickly become frustrated, then I have an idea. I go to the bar and hover impatiently until I can get someone's attention.

'Do you have an outdoor seating area?' I ask the barman, who comes to take my non-existent order.

'Through to the next room, you'll see a door at the back.'

'Thank you.'

I hurriedly weave my way through the sea of people into the next room and outside to a small seating area with about eight tables. They're all occupied – for autumn, the weather is thankfully very mild – including the one right at the back of the terrace, where I see Jamie sitting by himself, looking back at me apprehensively.

Chapter 32

'Hi.' I reach the table and tentatively take a seat opposite Jamie.

'Hi, Steph.' He smiles at me nervously, his obvious concern that this interaction might not go well etched clearly across his face. 'Happy birthday. You look beautiful.'

'Thank you. How did you… what are you… I mean…' I trail off and take a swig from my can of beer. 'Thanks for the drink.'

'You're welcome. Shall I talk? Think I've got some explaining to do. It's not for you to lead this conversation.'

'OK, sure.'

I'm relieved that all I need to do is listen – and then try to judge things in a measured and balanced way. Jamie looks pained for a second, then starts to speak.

'Steph… the night we met… I felt a connection with you that I'd never felt with anyone else before. Didn't even realise it was possible to gel in that way so… instantly.'

'Me too.' I give an understanding nod. Some early reassurance can only be helpful, when Jamie's about to share something that's incredibly raw for him.

'I was spinning. I'd met this incredible woman. I already knew I wanted you to be part of my life, but…' He takes a faltering breath. 'I'd lost my home just a couple of weeks before that. I was broke and unemployed – and

310

I was couch surfing between the flats of two mates who knew about my situation. I only went to the street party to save face. My friend, Neil – the accordionist – didn't know anything about it, and I'd already paid for the tickets.'

'He really had no idea?'

'No. He does now. I've... learned a few lessons about pride over recent months.' Jamie swigs at his own beer then continues.

'After I had to leg it out of your apartment, I wanted to get back in contact. But as time passed and I didn't bump into you, I came to the conclusion that with my situation as it was, it would be too complicated anyway. So, I forced myself to put you out of my mind.'

I shrug. 'Makes sense. So what? Then I did the whole beer-can appeal and you changed your mind?'

'Yes. Well, no. I came across your message a while before I made contact, if I'm honest. Things had gotten even more challenging. My friends told me I was welcome to stay with them as long as I needed, but one of them had a son who stayed on the weekends – so it wasn't exactly appropriate me being there – and the other... well, I overheard his girlfriend giving him stick about it one night. I realised that, as much as they wanted to look out for me, I couldn't be that kind of burden on them. So, some of the time I would tell them I was staying with someone else—'

'When you were actually staying in a hostel.'

'Yes. And I needed money to pay for that. I was sitting on the street one day...' He hesitates, embarrassed at having to say something like this to my face. 'Two blokes walked past. They were drinking, and one of them chucked their empty beer can at me—'

'He did what? The absolute *shit*.' I feel a swell of outrage and protectiveness towards Jamie.

'That's nowhere near the worst of it, believe me. Anyway, I'm glad he did, because that's how I saw your message. I deliberated over it for a few weeks, talking myself in and out of contacting you. Then eventually I decided I had to do it. I needed to see your beautiful face, so I borrowed some money off one of those mates so I had enough to go on a date with you and made contact. I felt bad doing it at first, having no idea when I could pay him back, but I knew that you could potentially be the motivator I needed to get myself back on track, so I decided it wasn't so bad.'

'Of course, it wasn't.' My eyes start to well up at this revelation. 'That's why we would only meet at weekends and have dates that… were less costly, wasn't it? Because you didn't want to keep asking your friend for money. You needed to space out our dates and it certainly wouldn't have been appropriate or sensible to be asking for large sums.'

'Exactly that.' Jamie rotates his beer can absently. 'And meeting at weekends gave us more time together than an evening after work. Thankfully my friend was more than happy to help me out and kept insisting that I take some cash whenever he knew I was meeting you. It was also why I never called you. I couldn't afford the phone top-ups – and why I sometimes didn't answer. I didn't want to you to hear things in the background that might make you suspicious or concerned.'

'Wow… Jamie.' I shake my head in amazement at what I'm hearing. 'I can't believe you went to those lengths to keep seeing me. I kept asking myself, how did I miss this? But there were no signs at all. You hid it so well.'

'I had a gym membership nearby that I'd paid an upfront fee on – it had till mid-May left on it. When everything went south, rather than cancelling it for insolvency reasons, I kept it active. I'd gotten to know the staff there and was too ashamed to tell them anyway. It was somewhere I could escape to that wasn't someone else's place or a drab room in a hostel. And I kept the remaining decent clothes I still had in a locker there. They were pretty lax about people leaving their stuff.'

'Wait, you lived here in Edinburgh? I thought you lived on the west coast before this… situation arose.'

'That's where I grew up, as you know. I actually had an apartment up Bonnington way, but I went to the gym in Leith because it was near my business.'

'Your manufacturing business.'

'Uh… no.' A guilty look crosses Jamie's face. 'That was a previous venture. I sold that business and bought a brewery.'

'A brewery?' I try and fail to hide my confusion.

'Yes, with my friend… my now ex-friend. I didn't give you any details about my life that were current, because I didn't want to risk you finding out the truth before I was ready to share it.'

'Which is?'

Jamie pulls his phone out of his pocket, looks something up on the internet and hands it to me. My eyes scan the headline and text in front of me. I'm so baffled, I can't take it all in, but the key words dance in front of my eyes. *Local artisan brewery… accounting fraud… missing funds… questioned by police… facing prison time.* I look up at Jamie in dismay.

'You went into business with your friend and he screwed you over?'

'Yes.' The pain in Jamie's eyes is clear. 'He was a mate from uni. Convinced me to invest in the brewery with him as a start-up. I sold my business, re-mortgaged my flat, ploughed all I had into the project, and we also took out a business loan. It was a magical three years, creating a brand that I was so proud of and all these great products – then one of our tax returns flagged an anomaly. We were audited and I was convinced it was an error, but it turned out we were in dire straits financially speaking. The police were brought in to investigate and it turned out my so-called friend had been siphoning money out of the business for nearly two years.'

I inhale sharply from the astonishment that someone who was meant to be a friend could do something so awful. 'Jamie, that's unforgivable.'

'I know. I still struggle to believe it myself. Anyway, long story short: he's recently been handed a five-year prison sentence, and after losing my home as well as the business, I'm just getting back on my feet.'

Hearing all this, I'm consumed by a jumble of emotions. A deep rush of sympathy for Jamie, incensed anger at his uni friend for ruining Jamie's life, and a generous portion of guilt and self-loathing, knowing that I must have made an already impossible situation even harder for him.

'Jamie, I'm—'

'Don't, Steph.' Jamie puts a finger to his lips to stop me. 'You knew none of this. You are not to blame. I chose to keep it from you, and you drew the conclusions you drew, because I didn't give you the information to arrive at anything else.'

'But I could have at least—'

'No, you couldn't. Hindsight is a wonderful thing. I have no bad feeling towards you at all. You were incredible. You wanted to be with me even when you found out I was homeless. It was me that pushed you away, because I couldn't swallow my pride. I was ashamed and I struggled to deal with the humiliation. But I've dealt with that now and I realise that I should have put my faith in you from the start.'

'Oh, Jamie…'

Feeling a bubble of emotion in my throat, I leap out of my seat, rush to the other side of the table and on to his lap, kissing him with the strength of all the kisses I've missed out on these last months. As we lose ourselves in each other, I drink in his familiar scent, the feel of his close-cut beard tickling my face, the taste of the beer on his lips.

Wait a minute. The beer.

I pull apart from him and look at him questioningly, my brain flicking back to the news article I've just skimmed.

'Serve Minus Pigs. Is that your beer? From your old brewery?'

'Ten out of ten, Sherlock.' He grins at me. 'The place got sold on as part of the bank reclaiming the money it had loaned us, so at least the beer still exists.'

'It's your legacy.'

'Yes, I suppose it is.'

'So did you come up with that bonkers name, or was it your so-called mate?' I wrinkle my nose as I mention the evil bastard who screwed over my wonderful Jamie.

'It was my idea.'

'Were you on drugs? Or drunk on the beer?'

Jamie flashes his eyebrows at me, a twinkle in his eye. 'Neither. You remember me telling your brother that I'm a Partick Thistle supporter?'

'Uh–huh…?'

'Well, you know the whole what3words thing, where every three metres squared of the world have been given a unique combination of three words?'

My face lights up in recognition. 'Serve. Minus. Pigs. It's a square of the pitch at their stadium.'

'Spot on.'

'That's brilliant. I love it.'

'So, there you go…' He looks at me meaningfully. 'Now you know the full, ugly truth.'

My expression neutralises. 'Gosh, Jamie, you've been through so much. I wish I could have been there for you.'

'Don't think about that.' He reaches up and strokes my cheek lovingly. 'I had to do it myself. Only the two mates who I stayed with knew about it all. I didn't even tell my dad. He's not exactly loaded and he doesn't keep well – never really got over my mum's death. I couldn't have lived with myself if my news had made him worse. I have learned, though, that I need to let people in and to accept help.'

'Did nobody help you at the time, to try and save your home – like in an official capacity?'

'You mean the bank and stuff?'

'Yeah.'

'They did what they could. They were very good about it. I went through all the official channels, but the situation was dire. When I realised there was no saving the brewery, I tried to get a job to keep myself afloat, but it was basically impossible, because what does every prospective employer want?'

'Of course, references.' My heart sinks as I realise just how bad Jamie's situation was.

'Yup. My most recent employment had gone up in smoke and hit the local press in the process. I was vouching for myself because I'd been a business owner, and all it took was one Google search for those employers to find out why I was looking for a job – and that I'd been questioned in relation to fraud.'

'Oh, my goodness.' My hand flies to my mouth. 'But that's so unfair. You weren't involved.'

'Yeah, but the police didn't know that at the time. They were just doing their jobs. I was cleared of any wrongdoing obviously, but mud sure sticks. It didn't take long for me to realise that I wasn't going to get anywhere finding work, and I didn't even have a car or a bike to take up something such as takeaway food deliveries.'

'Oh, Jamie, I can't even imagine how awful it must have felt having no options. Or how demeaning it must have been being treated like a criminal.'

I shake my head, still unable to digest what I'm hearing. Then, to my horror, I feel myself welling up.

'Hey, no tears.' Jamie wipes a rogue one from the corner of my eye. 'This is a happy day. We're back together... aren't we?' He winces as he realises his presumption.

I nod eagerly and he pulls a relieved face.

'Great, so we're back together, I've got a flat and a steady job and I'm looking at business options again – though this time I'll be pursuing them *alone*...' He allows this pointed comment to hang in the air.

'Definitely after that experience,' I vigorously agree with him. 'If you don't mind me asking, how did you finally get back on your feet?'

'A charity helped me. Their volunteers would come by and give me food and check I had somewhere to sleep. They even arranged emergency accommodation on the nights I didn't have enough for a hostel. I resisted their help at first: my bloody pride getting in the way again. I thought I had to do it myself. But then I realised that I would be stuck in this cycle for ever if I didn't take some help. They told me they could help me get back on my feet, so I eventually put my trust in them. It's been a hard slog, but I'm getting there. They're amazing people.'

'Like angels.' I turn away and blink back the tears that are forming again so that Jamie doesn't see them.

'Anyway, that's enough of that talk,' Jamie announces. 'It's your birthday. Let's focus on that.'

'Oh yeah, I almost forgot. How did you know? Did I tell you and you remembered? And actually, how did you know we'd be here tonight?'

He looks a bit sheepish. 'It's all a bit of a fluke. I've been plucking up the courage to contact you – then you walk into this bar this evening while I'm out with some friends from my uni days. I couldn't believe it. I asked one of them to do a reccy to make sure none of the blokes at your table was your boyfriend. He reported back that it appeared to be safe territory, and he'd overheard that it's your birthday – so I had my in. They've moved on to another bar now and given me a pass for the night.'

'Ooh, you're a sneaky one.' I gently tap his nose like he's a naughty puppy.

'I'd have got you a present, obviously, but as it was all unplanned and I didn't know...'

I chuckle, then a thought occurs to me. 'I know what you can give me for my birthday.'

'What's that?'

'Anna says she's not approving "us" unless I return with your surname and other key info.'

'Ah, OK.' Jamie shrugs in easy acceptance of this. 'Well, you know my surname now.'

'Do I?'

'You didn't clock it from the newspaper article?'

'No. There was a lot of other stuff in there.'

'It's Morgan.'

'Jamie Morgan.' I test it out. 'I like that.'

'Regarding the rest… ask me you anything you want.'

'You're on.' I rub my hands together gleefully. 'Anna's gonna love this.'

Chapter 33

When I waken the next morning, I'm disorientated and for a moment I forget what went on the evening before. Rolling over, I blearily rub at my eyes and when I open them, I see Jamie propped up on his elbow beside me, grinning away.

'Morning, sleepy head.' He leans across and kisses me gently. 'How's the hangover?'

'Surprisingly, not too bad.' I reach up and ruffle his bedhead man curls. 'How did you sleep?'

'Far better than I have in a long time having you beside me.'

'Me too.' I gaze at him adoringly, then prop myself up on the pillows and look around me. 'I can't believe I'm in Jamie's flat.'

'I can't believe you just referred to me in the third person.' He chuckles.

'Well… it's exciting. To finally see something of yours.'

'I guess I can understand that, although this place is rented. It's not really mine.'

'I don't care. It has your Jamie things in it. That's enough for me.'

'Aww… look at you all cute.' He wraps his bare arms around me, which I notice are less muscular that when I first met him – probably because he no longer has a gym membership, and he's been through a hell of a lot.

'I am kind of cute.' I put on my most adorable look.

'Yes, you are. Cute and sexy and real. My favourite combo.'

'Ooh, I like that.'

'Want a coffee?'

'Definitely.'

We get out of bed and go through to Jamie's tiny kitchen, which, with it being a one-bedroom tenement flat, feels quite out of proportion. It's only about two metres by a metre and a half and just about fits a sink, fridge, cooker and a couple of cupboards, yet the ceiling is about three metres above us. Jamie puts the kettle on and preps our mugs, then turns to me and slips his arms around my waist.

'I've been wanting to ask you something...' He trails off uncertainly.

I reach up and kiss his nose. 'You can ask me anything. You know that.'

'OK... I guess I'm wondering, how are your family going to feel about this? About you being with a guy who was homeless?'

Irritation immediately stirs within me. Jamie should never have to worry about something like that, and it angers me that my family are the ones planting this insecurity in his head.

'You know what, Jamie? I'm past caring. After the scene Kayleigh made that day on Easter Road, and then seeing the impact of it on you when we spoke outside the hostel, I decided she wasn't worth a minute of my time.'

'You haven't spoken to her since?' Jamie looks surprised.

'No, I have. But only when it's absolutely necessary.'

'How did the rest of your family react when she announced my predicament on your WhatsApp group?' He tries to keep this question casual, but I know the answer means everything to him.

'She didn't announce it there.'

'She didn't?'

I shake my head. 'Nope. I was surprised. No one in my family has said a word to me about it, so I'm guessing she didn't tell them.'

'Because…?'

'I can only assume that she didn't want anyone to know about it – including my parents. She would have been thinking about herself, perhaps her reputation as a future influencer.'

'Right.' Jamie's expression turns thoughtful, and I can tell he's considering what this means for us. 'So… you're not going to say anything to your parents about it then?'

'I wasn't planning to. It's none of their business. Why, do you think I should tell them?'

'I think…' Jamie lets out a loaded sigh. 'I want a future with you, and I don't want to have to hide who I am any more. Look how complicated it got between us because of the secrecy. I'd rather face the pain now, than have it come out later down the line and your parents lose trust in me. I've already told them a pack of lies about my job.'

'For good reason.' I reach up and take his face in my hands. 'You were backed into a corner and what you told them wasn't a total fabrication. It just wasn't exactly current.'

'That's one way of putting it.'

'Jamie, I don't want what's happened to become a monster for you. So, let's deal with it now – right this second. They'll understand. How could they not? It's not like you're a criminal or anything. You were shafted by your supposed mate.'

I stride through to the bedroom and retrieve my phone, then tidy up my bedhead hair in the mirror and return to the kitchen.

'You're going to message them?' Jamie stirs our coffee and signals for me to take my mug.

'No, *we're* going to video call them.'

'What? All of them?'

'Yup, group call. We've done that once or twice before on birthdays and stuff.'

'Erm... OK. No, wait, I at least need to look present-able.' He dashes through to the bathroom and wets his hair, then returns and takes a slug from his coffee. 'OK, go.'

I set up the group call and hit the button to dial, keeping the camera only on me for now. Moments later, members of my family appear on the screen – Mikey first, then Kayleigh, then Mum and Dad, who are bickering over how to hold the screen.

'Hey, wee sis.' Mikey gives me a toothy grin. 'How was your birthday night out? You had your head down the pan all morning?'

'No, I haven't Mikey.' I chuckle. 'I know how to handle my booze – unlike you.'

'Ach... you haven't had a proper birthday night out until you're tasting your cake in reverse.'

'Ugh... Mikey, that's so disgusting.' Kayleigh complains, while using the call as an opportunity to check her appearance.

'Steph, good morning,' says my dad. 'To what do we owe this pleasure?'

He and my mum continue to jostle for space in the tiny window on my phone, which amuses me.

'I want to tell you all something – together,' I say.

'I see.' My dad looks understandably puzzled. 'And what is it that you want to tell us?'

'You'd better not be up the duff from some one-night stand,' Mikey jokes.

'Mikey, *enough*.' My mum is appalled, then her expression changes to one of mild panic. 'You're not, are you, Steph?'

I glance across at Jamie with a look of 'shoot me, now'. He nods his understanding, but gestures for me to continue.

'No, it's nothing like that.' I try to ignore the overexaggerated sighs of relief. 'There's someone here with me who'd like to say hello…' I angle the camera so Jamie can join the conversation.

'Hi, there.' He waves at them with a tentative smile.

'*Jamie*.' My mum's face immediately lights up. 'It's so wonderful to see you.'

'Indeed it is, son.' My dad is clearly also delighted by this turn of events. 'Does this mean the two of you are back together?'

I pause to assess Kayleigh's reaction before saying anything further, but her expression isn't giving anything away, so I plough on with my big reveal.

'Yes, we are. And this time we're not going to stuff it up, are we, Jamie?'

'We most certainly are not.' Jamie grins at me adoringly.

'Well, that's super news,' says my dad. 'Shall we get that game of golf in the diary then?'

'That would be great.'

'And dinner at ours after,' pitches in my mum.

'Absolutely.' Jamie seems chuffed by these invitations.

'Jamie, mate. Welcome back,' says Mikey. 'We'll need to get a pint in, too. You up for watching the old firm match in a couple of weeks?'

'Sure. Sounds good.'

With all members of my family other than Kayleigh having acknowledged Jamie's return, we naturally fall silent, waiting for her to say something. It takes her a moment to realise this, and when she does, she looks distinctly awkward.

'Hey, Jamie. Good to see you,' is all she can manage.

'Is it, Kayleigh?' I challenge her lightly and she becomes even more uneasy.

'Steph, why are you talking to your sister like that?' asks my dad.

'Here we go...' I mutter to Jamie under my breath before talking normally again. 'The reason is, Dad, that Kayleigh knows something about Jamie that the rest of you don't.'

'I'm sorry. I'm not following you.'

'Jamie doesn't run the business he told you he does. He used to, then he owned a brewery, which he lost because of circumstances beyond his control, and, well, that meant he ended up homeless and sometimes begging on the streets.'

The collection of horrified expressions I expected appears right on cue. The up side of this is that they're stunned into silence, so I continue.

'Jamie didn't tell me about his circumstances because he was too ashamed, and he thought you would all reject him if you knew the truth. We split up because I thought he was hiding something else – something far worse. He's now got a job and a flat and he's building his life again – with me in it.'

'So where does Kayleigh come into this, Steph?' Mikey's trying to stick with fact finding, but I can tell it's forced.

'Kayleigh knew because she was with me when I discovered the truth. We saw Jamie sitting on the street. I'm guessing she didn't tell you because she didn't want it to get out and impact her precious reputation.'

'Actually, that's not true,' Kayleigh pipes up. 'I didn't tell them because you were so mad at me, and I didn't want to cause a family blowout.'

'Wow.' I shake my head a little as I try to digest this. 'You're human after all?'

'Steph…' Jamie gives me a nudge to discourage me from scoring points for the sake of it.

'Right, yeah, so that's where things are at with us,' I say to my family with an air of finality. 'So, over to you.'

There's a stony silence. My heart pounds in my chest from the adrenaline as I wait for some kind of response. After what feels like an age, my mum finds her voice.

'Steph, I'm not sure what to make of this – and I'm wondering about your judgement in calling us like this with Jamie right there. How are we supposed to speak honestly when he's listening in? And for you to expect an honest response? How did it happen, Jamie – gambling? Drugs?'

'I'm more concerned by the fact that Jamie's had the balls to sit in a restaurant and lie to our faces,' Mikey pitches in. 'If dishonesty comes that easily to you, mate, then I've got to wonder about you being with my sister.'

'Exactly that,' says my dad. 'This lad has been on the streets. Who knows what he's picked up? The untruths rolled off his tongue a little too easily, how do we know you're safe with him? How would we know we're safe to have him in our house—'

'And what are we supposed to tell people if they ask?' My mum cuts my dad off. 'Some of us don't feel as comfortable lying—'

'Are you *kidding* me? What is wrong with you all?' I'm so outraged by these comments, I lose control of myself.

'Steph!' Kayleigh cries out in shock.

'Enough of that, young lady.' My dad's voice takes on the menacing tone he uses to pull me and my siblings back into line when we go too far, but this time I'm not having it.

'Or what?' I challenge him. 'What are you going to do, Dad? I thought you were a bit snobbish and judgemental. Now I think you're the pits. I'm embarrassed to be related to you, and any shred of respect I had for you has gone. Vanished.'

'Now wait a minute—' My mum attempts to wade in, but I cut her off.

'No, Mum. You don't get to make any demands of me any more. Jamie has been through hell and all you lot can do is ask – quite frankly – the most prejudiced and offensive questions I've ever heard. And it's so clear that while you're completely ignorant, you're also wondering how it will look if people find out the truth.

Four guilty faces blink back at me, which tells me I'm exactly right about that observation.

'Well, great,' I continue. 'Just great. I thought your reaction to my promotion was bad, but this… this takes you to a whole new low. Now I'm the one who's ashamed – ashamed to call you my family. You know what, I'm done.' My voice wavers on the last word and a lump suddenly appears in my throat, but I swallow it down. 'I'm never good enough, you never listen, and all you care about is money and appearances. I'm tired of trying to fit into your narrow, shallow lives when you won't even try to fit into mine. I'm done with the lot of you.'

Without saying anything further, I jab viciously at the screen to end the call and immediately leave our family WhatsApp group. Then, I turn to Jamie.

'I'm so, *so* sorry for that.' My eyes prink with tears, which quickly spill over, and throw my arms around him.

He holds me, but there's a limpness to his touch, so I pull away and look up at him. His face is ashen, his eyes glassy and it almost breaks me to see him like this.

'Jamie, I—'

'Don't...' He puts a finger to my lips and clears his throat. 'Steph, I can't be that kind of wedge between you and your family. This is exactly what I was concerned about.'

'What? You think I want them in my life now I've seen what they're capable of?'

'They're your family. Family's—'

'Don't say "important",' I interrupt him. '*That* is not important to me. I'm repulsed by those attitudes and behaviours, so don't even bother trying to talk me round. I'm sad that it has come to this, but I'm mature enough to realise it's probably been a long time coming. Even if you want to walk away — and who would blame you if you do — I still want nothing to do with them. It won't fix anything. So, it's up to you.' I look him straight in the face, silently begging him not to discard me because of the family I ended up with.

He says nothing at first and his expression remains troubled, leaving me wondering if this could be the final and uncrossable obstacle in our fledgling relationship. Then, his face softens and he gently takes my hands in his.

'I know who you are Steph and you're not one of them. It concerns me the idea of you cutting them out of your life, but I also respect that you know your own mind. But if for any reason your position changes, or it's too difficult for you, then I will understand that.'

'It's not going to change.' I throw my arms round Jamie's neck and kiss him deeply to emphasise my point. 'So, now the hard bit is out the way, what are we going to do today?' I ask him when we finally come up for air. 'I certainly don't want to spend it thinking about the car crash that is my family. And now I've found you again, there's no way I'm letting you out of my sight.'

'That may get tricky when Monday comes round and we both have to go to work,' Jamie quips and I'm pleased to see his mood lightening again.

'True. OK, then I'm not letting you out of my sight for the rest of the weekend.'

'Fine by me.' He kisses me tenderly and nuzzles his face against mine, sending a wave of wonderful tingles right to my toes. 'Although... I have an idea for today – a surprise – and it would involve leaving you for a short time to arrange it.'

I purse my lips and make a show of weighing this up.

'I suppose now I know where you live, I can allow that. I could probably do with a shower and a change of clothes anyway.'

'OK, great. I'll come get you at your apartment when everything's all sorted.'

'Sounds like a plan.' I'm about to go and gather my stuff when Jamie playfully pulls me back towards him.

'Where do you think you're going?'

'I thought we just agreed our plan for the day.'

'Doesn't mean we have to do it right this second.'

'Oh… well in that case…' I allow myself to be pulled against his torso and melt into a delicious kiss that makes it very clear what the plan is for the next half hour or so.

Chapter 34

At twelve p.m., the buzzer to my apartment goes and I grab the handset eagerly.

'Hello?'

'It's me.' Jamie's voice crackles through the receiver. 'You ready?'

'Am I ever.'

I put the receiver back in its cradle and lock up the empty apartment – Connor stayed at Lukas's place the previous night and has not yet returned home. As I make my way down in the lift, fluttery butterflies flap around in my stomach. I'm not sure I've ever been this excited about a date, especially with the added mystery of where we're going. Stepping outside into the unseasonably warm and sunny autumn day, I immediately feel warmth on my face and can see right across the calm, sparkling water to the coastal towns of Fife. Putting on my sunglasses, I look around for Jamie, but don't see him. Then a horn honks and I spot him sitting behind the wheel of a small red hatchback car parked in one of the spaces lining the breakwater.

'I didn't know you had a car now.' I slide into the passenger seat and close the door.

'I don't.' He leans over and greets me with a kiss. 'But I do know a place that does cheap car hire.'

'We could have used my car and saved you the money.'

'I know. But I wanted to do something for you today. Plus, I haven't driven in ages. I miss it.'

'Fair enough. So where are we off to?'

'You'll see.' Jamie gives me a secretive wink.

We drive through the north of the city onto the A90. At first, I'm convinced we're heading up to Fife, perhaps to St Andrews or one of the cute little coastal villages up that way. But as we near the Queensferry Crossing, Jamie leaves the dual carriageway and heads for South Queensferry.

'Are we going back to the Dalmeny Estate?' I ask.

'Correct. But that's all I'm saying until we park up.'

I do my best to sit on myself and not ask any further questions, while Jamie navigates the car through the narrow town centre and parks on the hill below the imposing rail bridge, same as last time. Once he's parked the car, he turns off the ignition and looks at me with a serious expression.

'Steph, when we broke up, one of things I felt most guilty about – apart from breaking your heart – was that I ruined this place for you. You had these great memories of a time when your relationship with your family was much happier and easier, and I felt that I had taken that from you.'

'Oh, Jamie, no, you didn't.'

'I did. We came here and you asked me perfectly reasonable questions and I shut down, leaving you with a new memory – a bad one – that would always taint this place for you. Be honest. Have you been back here since?'

I shrug reluctantly. 'Well, no.'

'And would you have normally had a couple of trips out this way, say… in the height of summer?'

'Yeah... normally.' I don't want to admit to this, but I can't lie.

'See, there you go. I ruined it for you.' Jamie takes my hand apologetically. 'So... today we replace that bad memory with a new one. The plan being that it, combined with your family memories – which are all the more important now things are so difficult in that space – will take centre stage and make you want to keep coming here in the future.'

'Jamie, I...' I shake my head in disbelief at the thoughtfulness of this gesture. 'Thank you so much for this.'

'It's the least I could do. And look, I know you said you don't want to talk about your family, but are you OK? I need to be able to check in with you on that.'

Out of respect for Jamie, I give his question some proper thought. 'I am. Perhaps it's not quite hit me yet, but I know I'll be OK.'

He gives me a sad smile. 'All right then. I'm here any time you want to talk about it.'

'I know that. Shall we?'

We get out of the car, and Jamie grabs a large backpack from the boot.

'I brought us a little picnic as well.' He grins as he swings it up and onto his back.

'Ooh, great.' I rub my palms together greedily. 'I have the hangover munchies.'

'Figured you would.'

We wander down the hill and onto the estate hand in hand, chatting away as we go. The single-track road is peppered with rusty coloured leaves that have dropped from the trees and the air has that slightly musty – but not unpleasant – autumnal smell about it. I'm so elated to be doing this with Jamie again – but this time with no secrets

333

between us – and that I can talk about anything that comes to mind. Which is exactly what I do.

'You mentioned last night that you're hoping your job will be temporary,' I say to him. 'Do you have a plan in mind?'

'I do.' He nods. 'I'm not very good at being an employee. Never have been. The call-centre role I'm doing at the moment is limited and restrictive, but it does give me the gift of time. I don't have to work a minute more than I'm contracted to, so I can use my evenings and weekends to work on business ideas. I've got something at an early stage in the pipeline.'

'That's great news. Do you mind if I ask what it is?'

'Of course not. Ultimately, I'd love to own a brewery again in the future. That's the dream, so I thought if I could play around with some flavours and start making beer again, I could try and grow it from there.'

'That's a great idea.'

'I think so. I can do it from my flat if I can set myself up with the right equipment. It'll be a squeeze with me living in a one-bedroom place, but it's doable.'

'You know, Jamie, I think you can do anything you put your mind to.' I drop his hand and slip my arm round his waist, pulling him towards me. 'You're resilient and likeable and clearly very entrepreneurial.'

He stops and looks at me meaningfully. 'Thanks, Steph. You have no idea how good it is to hear you say that right now. When it all happened, I was angry at myself for missing the signs and for trusting my mate. It knocked my confidence – that and losing everything, of course. I would never have admitted this to myself before, but I need someone in my life cheering me on.'

'Well, I'm your biggest cheerleader. You can bet on that.'

'I know I can. That's more than I could wish for. An amazing and seriously beautiful woman, who's the director of a charity, and acing that role from what Anna told me last night.'

'Oh, I not sure I'm acing it.' I wrinkle my nose. 'I am really enjoying it though, and I do feel like it's within my gift to do great things to support our disadvantaged young people. I'm going to do my best to make Lizzie proud.'

'Modest, too.' Jamie grins at me adoringly. 'I couldn't have struck it luckier.'

He pulls me into a long, dreamy kiss that's even dreamier with the leaves falling around us; then we continue until we reach the same spot of beach we were at last time. Making our way through the low dunes and onto the sand, I can see that the tide is higher than last time. The sound of the seabirds and the gentle crashing of the waves, as well as the briny air soothes my slightly hungover mind.

'Shall we set up here?' Jamie points to a partially sheltered area that might or might not be the same place we sat in last time.

He pulls a blanket from his rucksack and lays it on the ground, then unpacks the food: a couple of prepacked supermarket sandwiches, a large bag of crisps, a tub of mango chunks and a couple of small bottles of mineral water.

'This OK?' he asks. 'Not quite the spread we had last time.'

'It's wonderful.' I beam at him.

Being honest, he could have unpacked a tin of dog food and a mouldy cabbage and I'd still be smiling – because

335

all I care about is the fact that we're here. We're back together. And this time, I'll be leaving this beach with happy memories.

'Good.' Jamie seems pleased with my reaction. 'I also remember that last time you said there was one more thing that would have made it perfect.'

I rack my brains, but I can't make the connection with this reference. He chuckles at my intense deliberation, then pulls a half bottle of Prosecco and a small wine glass from the bag.

'Oh, wow.' My face breaks into a delighted smile. 'You have some memory.'

'I decided on a half-bottle because I obviously can't join you as I'm driving.' He searches my face for my reaction to this. 'Assumed you wouldn't want to sink a whole one, unless... was I wrong?'

'No, you're exactly right. This is perfect. Hair of the dog and all.' I reach out and touch the bottle. 'And chilled, too. The boy's done well.'

'Who drinks warm Prosecco?'

'Well...' My voice ascends half an octave and I bob my head from side to side. 'There have been occasions where it's been a necessity. I wish you could share it with me.'

'Me too. We can do that next weekend when I take you out for a belated birthday meal.'

My heart soars as he says this. A meal out together. It sounds so trivial, but to me, it's almost as if Jamie has proposed.

'Aww, Jamie, that sounds awesome. I can't wait. Although, are sure you—'

'Can afford it?' He finishes my question for me. 'Yes, I can. I expected that thought would cross your mind. It won't be a Michelin-star restaurant or anything, but we'll go somewhere nice. Maybe a rustic Italian.'

'That sounds perfect.'

I watch delightedly as Jamie expertly pops the cork on the bottle, pours me a glass and hands it to me. Then he twists the cap off one of the bottles of mineral water and clunks it against my glass.

'To new beginnings?'

I let out a little snort of laughter and Jamie cocks his head quizzically.

'You realise this is the third time we'll have used that exact toast.' I raise my eyebrows at him.

'Ah.'

'Kind of feel like it's a bit cursed.'

'OK, let's find a new toast.' He thinks for a moment. 'To… the power of beer cans?'

'Love it.' I giggle, and then look deeply into Jamie's eyes. 'And one more… to us – like, properly this time.'

'Yes, to us.' He returns my gaze, and I instinctively know that this will be third time lucky.

Epilogue

The following year

'Jamie, watch that picture frame!'

There's a thud and a tinkle of broken glass.

'Sorry.' He peeps out from behind the huge moving box he's carrying and I start to laugh.

'It's fine. I wasn't fond of that print anyway.'

He puts down the box and sweeps me up into his arms instead. I pretend to struggle, my legs waggling inelegantly, but only because it's part of our little game.

'What about this?' He nods at me. 'Where does this go?'

'I'm very fragile, and also priceless, so you have to be careful with me.'

'That you are.' He pulls me towards him and kisses me on the nose. 'So, are you ready to say goodbye?'

I look around the empty apartment. 'I'm ready. This place has loads of great memories, and I'll really miss living with Connor, but I'm so excited about us living together.'

'Me too.' Jamie sets me back down as Connor and Anna walk through the open door of the apartment.

'That the last of it?' Connor asks Jamie.

'Sure is.'

They carry the remaining items to the lift, while Anna and I do one final check round the place.

As I'm locking up, Anna pulls out her phone and gasps. 'What is it?' I ask.

'It's your story.' She looks up at me with eyes like saucers. 'It's gone viral.'

'What do you mean?' I grab the phone from her and I gasp in astonishment. 'More than three thousand likes on Twitter... and counting.'

I watch, mesmerised, as the number of likes and retweets continues to grow in front of my eyes.

'I told you this would get the charity noticed.' Anna plucks her phone out of my hand delightedly. 'The comments are mostly all supportive as well. Usual arse-holes pitching in, but we ignore them.'

We take the lift down the ground floor and head out to the car park, which is cold and blustery from the bitter wind blowing in off the river estuary in front of us.

'Jamie, look.' Anna thrusts the phone at him the moment we reach the guys.

'Wowsers.' Jamie rubs the back of his head in wonder. 'I believed you when you said you thought the story was worth sharing, but this is phenomenal.'

'What is it?' Connor's clearly feeling left out of the excitement.

'Anna persuaded me to share the story of how Jamie and I met on the charity blog,' I explain. 'She thought it was a strong human-interest piece. It's also perfect timing now that Jamie's had that offer of investment to start up a new brewery. The fact that he wants to run it as a social enterprise with a mentoring programme for disadvantaged young people linked in really well.'

'Fantastic. Congratulations, both of you! That's great coverage for your respective causes.'

'Thanks,' Jamie and I reply in unison while gazing at each other adoringly.

'Aww… look at you two. Edinburgh's third-sector power couple.' Anna holds up her phone and snaps a picture of us.

'Do *not* put that on social media,' I immediately warn her and she gives me a sly look.

'Sure, whatever, Steph. You ready, Connor?'

'Bye, roomie.' I pout at Connor.

'We'll see each other loads.' He steps forward and hugs me tightly. 'Lukas and I will only be five minutes away from you.'

'I guess. And I suppose we *are* all having dinner together tonight.'

'There you go. You'll end up sick of the sight of me.'

Connor gives me a final squeeze and lets me go. Then he and Anna get into his car, which is crammed with his remaining things.

We wave them off, then put the last of my stuff into the back of the van we've hired. Jamie slams the doors shut and turns to me.

'Ready to go to our new home?'

'Am I ever.' I bounce lightly on my toes with excitement.

'You're so damn cute.' He pulls me into him and kisses me tenderly. 'I almost can't believe we're doing this. It wasn't so long ago that I wondered if I even had a future, and now I feel so lucky: having you, my investment offer… it's a bit of a head-wrecker.'

'Just enjoy it. You've worked hard to get back on track.'

'That's true. It was hard graft getting you to fall in love with me.' He gives me a cheeky wink and kisses me again. 'Shall we head off then?'

We get into the van and as I'm putting my seatbelt on, I feel my phone vibrate in my pocket. Pulling it out, I frown at the screen.

'What the hell...'

'What is it?' Jamie asks. 'That tweet about your story trending now or something?'

'No. Kayleigh just added me to a WhatsApp group called "Please join this".'

'Huh. What do you think that's all about?'

'I guess I'll soon find out.'

Rather than starting the van, Jamie sits patiently, waiting to see what will happen next. At first, there's no more activity on my phone, and we have little else to do but stare out across the ominous-looking choppy water to the Fife coast. The sun, having spent most of the morning behind rolling dark clouds, makes a sudden appearance, lifting the seascape into a more appealing aspect.

I'm about to tell Jamie just to head off, when a message appears on my home screen, shortly followed by others. I open up the group chat and read them one by one.

> **Kayleigh:**
> Hi Steph, I saw your story on Twitter this morning. Congratulations, you've gone viral! Anyway, we've all been missing you and we've realised a few things since you cut us off. We hope you'll let us explain and apologise in person.

> **Mum:**
> Hi, darling. We hope you'll be willing to get together for a chat. Jamie included, of course.

> **Dad:**
> Hello, Steph. That was quite a story you shared. We didn't know most of that. We have learned a few things, as Kayleigh says, and would appreciate the chance to make things right with you both.

'You didn't know most of it because you were so quick to judge,' I mutter.

'Everything OK?' Jamie asks, and I angle the screen so he can read the messages, too.

> **Mikey:**
> Hey, wee sis. We're all good, because I got to this place way sooner than these numbnuts – and they're way worse than I am (!) – but I wanted to pitch in and say, please. give them a chance. I do think they've learned a lesson.

> **Dad:**
> Mikey, do you really think this is the time to be points scoring?

Mikey:

Absolutely. And, I'd pipe down unless you
want Steph to tell you to get lost.

I wait for my dad to tell Mikey off good and proper, or
for my mum to do it for him, but instead there's a pause,
and my dad simply replies with, 'That seems fair'.

'Wow.' I look at Jamie in astonishment. 'I don't think
I've ever seen this level of humility from my parents or
Kayleigh.'

He shrugs. 'Maybe they have "learned a few things".'

'Normally my reaction to that comment would be to
scoff and tell you there's more chance of me winning the
Nobel Peace Prize. But I've never seen anything like this
from them.'

'So, do you think you'll give them a chance then?'

I give a tentative nod. 'Perhaps. But they have to
prove that they've changed. If it's only about them missing
me then that's not enough. They have to accept you
completely – as well as my life choices. They have to take a
genuinely more empathetic tone towards social issues, and
try to understand them, rather than just judging. And stop
acting like money and position are all that's important—'

'So not much then.' Jamie grins at me and I come to a
halt.

'*Ha*, OK. Maybe I shouldn't expect too much too
soon. But what I mean is that I need to see something
in them that I can respect and connect with.'

'That sounds a bit more realistic. You can teach them
the rest now you have an open door. Shall we go?'

'Let's do it.'

As Jamie starts the ignition and we drive out of the
development, my excitement for setting up our new home

together returns – alongside a flicker of optimism that I may be able to rekindle my relationship with my family.

Acknowledgments

One Night in Edinburgh is a story about two people finding love. It also continues a theme from my other published novels: everyone deserves to have love in their lives. When I was writing, one thing on my mind was the Covid-19 pandemic. I was creating a story about a world that had dramatically altered from the way I was portraying it. Like many authors, I reflected on this and kept going: reasoning that, unless I was writing a story with the pandemic central to the plot, it was likely my readers would prefer the escapism of a fictional world. I was also holding on to the hope that by the time the book was published, we would be in a better place.

One Night in Edinburgh is my third novel to be published and my second to be set in Scotland's capital. I loved using my home city as a canvas again, with the story largely set in its northern areas (Newhaven, Leith and The Shore), places I know well and of which I have many fond memories. I have applied some creative licence, but in the main, I've kept the setting and the local events featured as true to life as possible.

I have a string of people to acknowledge who have offered me ideas, guidance, support and a critical eye. Starting with my family, thank you to my incredible husband, James, for his unconditional support and his help when I'm struggling to find the right way to say something, or I need to flesh out my ideas further. A big thank you goes to my dad, who voluntarily acts as an informal early-stage editor of my work, and also, to my mum and my sister-in-law, Geraldine, who read my first drafts and offer useful feedback.

Then there are the wonderful publishing professionals whose backing I am lucky to have: my agent, Kate Nash, and my editor at Canelo, Emily Bedford, both of whom keep me right and provide me with invaluable support and guidance. Thank you also to the whole team at Canelo for everything you do to get my books out into the world.

A special thank you goes to Dr Evvie Smith (PhD, BA Hons), who kindly agreed to do a sensitivity read of One Night in Edinburgh and offered valuable feedback and reassurance that I had represented Connor's sub-plotline appropriately.

Next is my wonderful author friendship group: Sandy Barker, Fiona Leitch and Andie Newton. Your companionship and guidance mean the world to me. You make a potentially lonely process so much easier, sharing the highs and the lows, as well as a lot of crap (and highly entertaining!) chat – I really can't wait for the day we finally meet in person.

Finally, a big thank you to all my amazing friends and colleagues for continuing to cheer me on. And also, to my readers: nothing is more warming and motivating than hearing that you've enjoyed my stories. I hope to be able to bring you many more uplifting reads in years to come.